China Mountain Zhang

China Mountain

A Tom Doherty Associates Book New York

Zhang

Maureen F. McHugh

This is a work of fiction. Jellybean the goat is based on an actual existing goat. However, all the events and all the other characters portrayed in this book are fictitious, and any resemblance to real people or events is purely coincidental.

This book has been printed on acid-free paper.

A Tor Book
Published by Tom Doherty Associates, Inc.
175 Fifth Avenue
New York, N.Y. 10010

Library of Congress Cataloging-in-Publication Data

McHugh, Maureen F.
    China Mountain Zhang / Maureen F. McHugh.
        p.   cm.
    "A Tom Doherty Associates book."
    ISBN 0-312-85271-1
    I. Title.
PS3563.C3687C48   1992
813'.54—dc20

                                                    91-38139
                                                    CIP

First edition: March 1992

Printed in the United States of America

0 9 8 7 6 5 4 3 2 1

A simple way to get to know about a town is to see how the people work, how they love and how they die.

—ALBERT CAMUS, *The Plague*

China Mountain

Zhang

The foreman chatters in Meihua, the beautiful tongue, Singapore English. "Get he over here. All this trash here! Got little time." He is a stocky little Chinese man who has suffered disappointments. "Someone work that cutter, *xing buxing?*"

Someone is me, the tech on the job. *"Xing,"* I say, "Okay." Good equipment can't be trusted to stupid New York natives. I heft the cutter, balance it against my thigh. My goggles darken, shutting out the buildings, even the lot we are clearing to build.

"Okay," he says, backing away, glad to have an ABC engineer. ABC—American Born Chinese, or like the *waiguoren*, the non-Chink say, Another Bastard Chink. With my goggles dark I can't see anything but the glow at the end of the cutter as it goes through rusted, twisted steel, girders in tangles and lying there like string dropped in a pile. Where the cutter touches it goes through like butter, and where the steel is cut it will shine clean and rust-free. Steel drops spatter like quicksilver, glowing metal white. The air smells like a thunderstorm coming.

I swear softly at the foreman in Spanish, but he is too far away

1

to hear anything, which is good. He does not know I speak Spanish. ABC; he knows I speak Mandarin—*Poutonghua*—and American Standard and the Singapore English Asians call *Meihua* and *waiguoren* call Chinglish. (*Waiguoren* don't get the joke. *Meihua*, beautiful language, because this is *Meiguo*—America. In Mandarin, Meiguo means "beautiful country" because "Meiguo" approximated the sound in A-mer-i-ca to Chinese ears.)

The foreman is all right, for someone born inside. He speaks English as if he learned it in school in Shanghai, which he did, but at least he speaks it unaugmented. He likes me; I work hard and I speak Mandarin better than most ABC. I am almost like a real Chinese person. My manners are good. An example of how breeding will out, even in a second rate country like this. He can talk to me, and there are probably very few people Foreman Qian sees each day who he can talk to. "You here what for?" he asks me. "You smart. You go Shanghai?" Everyone inside thinks that all the rest of us are dying to go to China.

If I went to China to study I'd be doing a great deal better than working as a tech engineer on a construction crew. Maybe the rest of us are dying to go to China, maybe even me. But maybe Spanish is the first language I ever learned because my mother's birth name was Teresa Luis and it's just because my parents paid to adjust the genetic make-up of their son that I look like a slope-head like my father. So Qian doesn't know; my last name is Zhang and I speak Mandarin and when he asks me why I don't go to Shanghai or Guangzhou to study I just shrug.

It infuriates him, that shrug. He thinks it is a native characteristic, that it indicates indifference and a kind of self-defeating fatalism. But just looking Chinese is not enough to get someone to China. My parents weren't rich and tinkering with genes is expensive. Maybe I would map close enough to Chinese standard to pass; then again, maybe something in them would prove me Hidalgo. I don't apply so I don't ever have to take the medical.

Pretty soon the steel is lying in pieces that can be carried away.

I shut off the cutter, my goggles lighten and I'm back in the real world. "Give it fifteen minutes to cool," I say, "then get it out of here." The crew has been watching me cut, they'll stop to watch anything. The foreman stands there with his hands on his hips. *Waiguoren* think that Chinese never show any expression, so of course he's not showing any and neither am I. So the crew thinks we are angry because they're not doing anything and drifts back to work. They're a good crew except when Foreman Qian is here, then I can't get them to do a damn thing.

"Zhang," the foreman says and so I follow him into the office. Inside, over the door it says "The Revolution lives in the people's hearts" but the paint is wearing thin. It was probably painted during the Great Cleansing Winds campaign. I don't think Foreman Qian is very pure ideologically, he has too much interest in the bottom line. It is like the crucifix in the hall of the apartment where I grew up, something everyone passes every day. I have no religion, neither Christ nor Mao Zedong.

"I often ask you, what you do with your life, you pretty good boy," Foreman Qian says. "We each and each respect, *dui budui?*"

"*Dui,*" I say. Right.

"Here, you tech engineer, job so-so."

"*Bu-cuo,*" I answer, Not bad.

"I have daughter," Foreman Qian says. "Request you to my home come, meet her, *hao buhao?*"

I have the momentary sense that this conversation, which Foreman Qian and I have had before, has just gone way out of my depth. "Foreman Qian," I say, stuttering, "I—I cannot . . . I am only tech engineer. . . ."

"Not be fool," he says and drops into Mandarin. "How old are you, twenty-five?"

"Twenty-six, sir."

"My wife and I, together we have one daughter. There is no one here for her, I would like her to meet a nice young man."

"Foreman Qian." I do not know what to say.

"I have no son, and I will not get to go back to China—" He is a Chinese citizen and if the best he can do is a job as a construction foreman, he's in disgrace. I wonder what Foreman Qian did during the Great Cleansing Wind to get in trouble. "I have a cousin at Shanghai University. I would sponsor a son-in-law there."

This is unexpected. This is disaster. Whatever has old Qian thinking that I would make a good son-in-law? It looks great from the outside, offer a twenty-six-year-old a chance at Shanghai University and citizenship-by-marriage which is almost as good as born-inside-citizenship. Maybe I would get a chance to stay inside, then his daughter would have a home there. Foreman Qian and his wife would retire to China and live with their daughter and son-in-law.

"I understand that you have not even met my daughter," Foreman Qian says. "I mean nothing except that you should meet."

"I cannot, Elder Qian." I am quaintly formal in my attempt to say something, falling back on school book Mandarin, ludicrous phrases. "I am unworthy." *Mea culpa.* I am violently flushed, for the first time in years I am so embarrassed that I actually feel hot. "I, I am a foreigner."

He waves that away. "Accident of birth place."

I open my mouth to say no, but I cannot say it. Not only is it rude, but I can't say it. I am impure, a mongrel. I am an imposter. And there is more that he doesn't know. When I tell him what I am, he will look foolish because he has mistaken me for Chinese, he will lose face. We will pretend that nothing was ever said. Then when this job is finished he will inform me that the company can no longer use me. It is not easy to find jobs.

"You think about it, meet her. Maybe you will not get along, maybe you will. No harm in meeting."

I should finish this now, explain, but I flee.

*   *   *

I meet my mother for lunch every six months or so. Filial duty.
Teresa Luis lives in Pennsylvania and commutes to work here in
Manhattan. She has another family, a husband and two sons. She
and my father were divorced during the Great Cleansing Winds.
Elder Zhang lives out on the West Coast where he is an office
manager for a company that builds robots to do precision robotics.
I have not seen him for fifteen years.

I meet her in the market, getting off the subway at Times
Square.

I don't know why she likes to eat in the market; I think it is
a tacky place with all the close streets and the booths and sidewalk
sellers. She says it has charm. My mother works at Citinet in
International Banking. She is a clerk. She always wears those
suits that are almost like uniforms—drab colors with tails to the
backs of her knees. Never short tails, never the long ones. She
is very religious and she believes in Marx and Mao Zedong. Do
not make the mistake of thinking her stupid; she has to juggle a
lot of Kierkegaard and Heiler to explain but she manages a full
wipe.

"Hello," she says and takes my arm. I am never sure I am her
son, although I don't rationally doubt it. It's just that the connection between us is very tenuous. Perhaps I have so few of her
genes that we are more like cousins.

"Zhong Shan, what's wrong?" Zhong Shan is my Chinese
name, Rafael is my Spanish name. There isn't any similarity. I
am named for a Chinese revolutionary, and for her Spanish great-
great-grandfather, who was a union organizer before the great
collapse. He was a party member in the secret days of the Second
Depression, and later, during the American Liberation War, a
martyr.

"I am in trouble," I say, and tell her about Foreman Qian.
While I am talking I watch the copper marks under the skin of

her wrist. Then I watch the copper marks on my wrist, almost like bruises. She ties into her terminal every day, I use my jacks only when I'm working with machinery. With those jacks, Foreman Qian can access my records. But only my surface records, not my deep records, he doesn't have clearance. There is nothing personal in my surface records, and my mother's name is listed as Li Taiming, her name from when she was active in the party.

When I am finished she says, "The Chinese are the worst racists in the world." This is not surprising, nor is it helpful. Nor is it a good political thing to say but everybody knows it. "What are you going to do?" she asks.

"Turn him down. I don't even know the girl. Even if it worked out, when I apply they'll do a medical. They'll do a background check. If I pass a medical I'll still fail the background check." Legally everyone is equal, but even here at the other end of the world in the Socialist Union of American States we all know better than that. Be it Rome or Beijing, we bring tribute but we are not admitted. Unfortunate day I was born.

"You can go to dinner," she says. "Maybe the daughter won't like you. Maybe you'll forget your upbringing and sneeze at the table."

"It's a lie," I say, "and you always told me that a lie always creates complications." But my face is a lie as well, and she condoned that. I am sure she hears the accusation, but we never talk about my mother's contradictions.

She does not touch me, although for a moment I think she is going to cover my hand with hers and I am afraid.

"It is not the revolution that is at fault," she says, "it is the people who are implementing it."

I don't believe in socialism but I don't believe in capitalism either. We are small, governments are large, we survive in the cracks. Cold comfort.

*   *   *

There is a game I play when I am out by myself among people. I play it on my way home, descending into the bowels of the city, taking a three-hundred-year-old train to the bottom of the island and under the choked harbor to Brooklyn. The subway sways and like idiots we all nod together. My game is this: I become other people.

A man reading a cheatsheet flimsie, picking the horses. An office clerk in his boxy suit. This evening I am a power tech, a young woman sitting under a subway sign listing the number to call for info on resettlement on Mars. She's wearing Edison Fission Authority green, her sturdy calves outlined by the tight legs of her coveralls. All day she sells and channels power and I imagine the city's energy pouring through her hands, the hair on her head rising with the build-up of static charge. Of course that's not true, she sits at a terminal and feeds information, watches the lines, drains the power reservoirs when they're needed and fills them when demand falls.

The train stops at Lawrence and the doors open. My power tech gets off and I'm just Zhang: 1.80 meters (almost), sixty-four kilos, leaning against the door with my feet spread to brace myself, right under the sign that says in English, Spanish and Chinese, "Do not lean against doors." I could go cruising, stay on the train and head for Coney Island and see what I could pick up. But that's just to avoid thinking about Foreman Qian and anyway, I'm too tired from work.

Still, I don't get off at my stop, I ride the train all the way to the end. Coney Island used to be a nice neighborhood, condos on the water and all, until the smell in the water drove everybody away. The smell is better now, what with the project to filter all the water that comes into the bay, but Coney Island is still the end of the line. The young couples are starting to move in and brave the crime to get permits to cheap condos and establish communes where everybody knows everybody else in the building. Pretty soon everybody will be begging permits to move out here and the little free-market greengrocers will open up, but right now Coney Island is gray in the transition and the hawks like me ride the train there to spread our wings.

Gray is a good word; when I come up on the street it's twilight, the buildings are gray, the wind off the water smells gray and ashy. It's quiet. A quiet neighborhood is a bad sign out here. My jacket isn't very warm but I walk down to the water. I wonder if part of the harbor has been burning again, but the ash at the water's edge could be old.

I walk the cracked concrete walk beside the water, my shoes crunching in the sand blown across it. A young man leans against a bench and my heart quickens. He looks twenty, younger than me. He is wearing coveralls, utility blue, and they hug his legs and pelvis. He is dark though, and I have blond Peter on my mind. Our eyes meet and he is arrogant, dangerous-looking, but his gaze lingers with the possibility of invitation. I think about slowing down, asking him what he's doing, I just keep walking. I didn't really come out here for a coney. When I glance back he is prowling stiff-legged in the other direction.

So I find a public call box. The chain on the bracelet is short, to reduce the chances that someone will yank it out, so once I get the bracelet on I have to fumble one-handed for my number book. I read Peter's number, the call clicks through. Waiting for him to answer, the only part of me that's warm is my wrist where the contact's made, and that's just an illusion anyway, just excited nerves at the periphery of contact.

"It's Zhang," I say.

"Hey," Peter says, looking preoccupied, by which I mean he is looking at something on his lap rather than me.

"Hey. I'm out on the beach."

That perks him up, blue-gray eyes on me and he sounds interested. "Yeah? Come up."

Peter lives in a wretched commune, Lenin knows how they ever got a permit. Just goes to prove that five years ago anyone could get permission to live in Coney Island. The slogan over the door says, "The force at the core of the people is the Revolution" from the *Xiao Hongshu,* the Little Red Book. I press my wrist against the contact and Peter has told the building to expect me because the street door opens.

I climb the stairs because I have a theory that Peter's building dislikes me and I won't get in the elevator. Peter only lives two flights up. I knock on the door and he opens it and kisses me there in the hall. He swears nobody cares but I still hate when he does it; if anyone suspected I'm bent it could cost me my job. Not that Lisa and Aruba, who live next door, are in any position to complain about our morals.

"China Mountain," he says, "where the hell have you been?" China Mountain is a possible translation of my name, Peter likes it.

"I work," I say. "Got any *pijiu?*"

He hands me a beer. Peter and I lived together for three months, we're still friends. Better friends than lovers. "Want to go to the kite races?" he asks. Peter works in an office but sleep deprivation has never seemed to bother him.

No, I don't want to go to the kite races. "Foreman Qian wants to sponsor me to Shanghai University." I sit in one of his big cushions, sink into it like it was a hug and it thrums gently and starts to warm me up.

"Isn't that kind of surprising?" Peter frowns. Three little lines appear in the middle of his forehead. His eyebrows arch like gull wings. They are lighter than his summer tan, just beginning to fade.

"He wants me to marry his daughter. Then I'll go to the university, get a job in China, and he can retire back inside."

For a moment Peter looks as if he is going to laugh but he takes a long pull on his beer instead. "He's kidding, isn't he? I mean, arranged marriages are pretty feudal, you know."

"He's a pretty feudal kind of guy."

He thinks a moment. "Can you tell him you already have a fiancé?"

"No, he's asked before."

Peter shakes his head. "You have such a complicated personal life."

No kidding.

"Hey, China Mountain, don't sit there all stony. You're all in your skull again. Come on, Rafael, don't go all Chink."

"Maybe I shouldn't have come," I say, sulking.

"Guilt, guilt, guilt, I feel horrible. Now get off your ass and let's go to the kite races. I'll introduce you to a flier and he's skinny and blond and you can polish your obsession for yellow hairs. He doesn't have a brain in his perfect little cranium but he's still *hao kan.*"

"If I go I'll be up all night and I'll be a wreck at work tomorrow." But I go, and we watch the silk gliders race all night above Washington Square; red and yellow sails swooping and skimming in the searchlights. Peter never does find his flier.

Next day, Friday. I get back to my flat, shower, change and catch the train back to Manhattan. How does Peter do it? I am at work at six-forty-five, pouring coffee in the vain hope that if I drink enough I won't accidentally cut my foot off with the cutter. Foreman Qian is there at seven-thirty. I do not know what I will say to him. I will tell him that there is really a girl. I will tell him that I am involved in the sale and transfer of illegal goods and not a suitable choice. I will tell him I am against feudal arrangements like this. I will tell him I have an incurable disease and only have six months to live.

I follow him into his office and he sits down. I notice his jowls hang a little, like a tired bulldog's. Then I stare at the wall in back of him.

"Engineer Zhang," he says in Mandarin, "Please you come to dinner on Sunday."

The wall is white and needs painting. "Thank you, Foreman Qian," I say, "I would be honored." And then slink out onto the site.

Long terrible day, with Foreman Qian smiling at me as prospective son-in-law. The crew knows something is up, and with Foreman Qian lurking around the site, nothing gets done. I do not ever reprimand them directly, it is not the way to get them to work, instead I find small ways to express my displeasure. But my heart is not in it. At noon I lie in the sun on a sack of cement—it's not comfortable but I only mean to sit a minute. I put my forearm over my eyes and fall asleep, jerk awake and drink more coffee. We finally finish at four. As I pass out pay chits I look at each one, "Your hard-earned pay," I say.

I hear Kevin from Queens mutter, "Qian been bustin' the bastard's ass again."

Little do you know.

Friday evening I sleep for about five hours and then meet Peter at eleven to drop in on a friend's party. I fully intend to be home by two o'clock, three o'clock at the latest. When I get home it's eight in the morning and I sleep the day away. Saturday I promise myself I will stay home that evening, but I end up meeting a couple of guys for a vid. Sunday morning finds me, as always, tired, broke and with a flat that desperately needs cleaning. It's not a big flat, it doesn't take any time to straighten up, I just don't get around to it for weeks on end.

At six I present myself at apartment sixteen, in a complex on Bay Shore. I am carrying a carefully wrapped copy of Sun-zi's classic on strategy. Not that I think Foreman Qian is such a fan of military strategy but because I think he will be flattered by the insinuation he reads the classics.

Foreman Qian's daughter answers the door, "You are Engineer Zhang?" she says. "I am Qian San-xiang."

She is astonishingly ugly. More than ugly, there is something wrong with the bones of her face.

She is a flat-faced southern-looking Chinese girl of twenty or twenty-two. She has a little square face like a monkey and small eyes even by Chinese standards. Her little wizened face is so unexpected I blink. I think instantly of some sort of bone defect that would create that almost nonexistent chin. She looks at me expressionlessly and then drops her eyes and glances sideways at her mother. Her mother is a matronly-looking woman clasping her hands together and smiling at me; Foreman Qian comes into the doorway to the little foyer and says hello and there we all are, four of us crowded into this little space. San-xiang slides between her mother and father and disappears into the next room.

"Let me take your jacket," her mother says. "I am Liu Su-ping." Chinese women do not take their husband's names, and it is evident that I have left the West in the hall.

I shrug out of my jacket and casually leave my package on the little table by the door. As a polite person I do not call attention to the gift; as polite people the Qians pretend not to have noticed it. We go into the living room, full of heavy wooden furniture clearly brought over from China. The elaborately paned window faces the harbor. The apartment is pretty but extraordinarily cramped. I sit and am offered something to drink, which I decline.

"No, please have something," Liu Su-ping insists. She has small soft-looking hands which she keeps clasped tightly together. I decline respectfully. Am I certain I would not like some tea? "San-xiang," she calls, "bring Engineer Zhang some tea."

"No, do not bother yourself," I say. I am not an engineer, I'm an engineering *tech*. A technician. Two-year degree, not four. I hate when people call me an engineer.

"It is sent by my sister, Dragon Well tea, from Huangzhou," she says.

Having politely declined three times I can now say yes, I would be pleased to have some tea. It is always easier to let people give you something than to convince them that you are not being polite, that you really just don't want it.

Now, however, while San-xiang makes tea, silence falls.

"So," I say in Mandarin, "I have always meant to ask you, Foreman Qian, where is your family from?" There is a little burst of conversation. His family is from Chengde, in the west. Her family is from Wenzhou, in the south. They met when he was on a two-year assignment in her province. Where is my family from?

I can only say I don't know. Elder Zhang was born and raised in the States. I have a grandfather on the West Coast but I haven't seen him in twenty years. And there is no need to discuss my mother so I don't mention her.

"You speak Mandarin very well," Liu Su-ping says. "Where did you learn it?"

"I went to the Brooklyn Middle School of Theory and History and all of our classes were in Mandarin," I say, "but I am afraid I was not so quick as my classmates. My Mandarin is very poor."

Oh no, oh no, they say, it is very good, very smooth. Oh no, I say, they flatter me.

We lapse into silence. My only consolation is that I must not be making a good impression.

San-xiang brings in tea on a tray. The tea is served out of a pretty porcelain tea pot. It is nice tea, smoky and strong. I say so.

San-xiang serves tea and sits down, eyes on her lap. She is dressed nicely but more casually than I expected. Foreman Qian is in tailored coveralls, he is dressed exactly as he is every day at work. But San-xiang and her mother are dressed in tunics with mandarin collars over tights, very casual. The clothes might even be from China. I am overdressed and conservative, wearing a long black shirt to mid-thigh, but I thought this would be more formal. It is too late to worry. I wish I was brave enough to do something truly rude.

After a moment San-xiang gets up and goes back into the kitchen and returns with a plate full of peanuts, candied walnuts and ersatz quail eggs. I hate ersatz quail eggs, but I carefully taste everything.

I am relieved that I have to get up early tomorrow, it will provide me with an excuse to leave early.

Dinner progresses pretty much as the rest of the evening has, that is to say, laboriously. The food is good; pork stuffed with hard-cooked eggs, dumplings, a fresh salad, and lastly, soup. Foreman Qian and I talk business and in the course of the evening San-xiang says hardly anything to me. I keep waiting to hear her speak. Her voice, when she does speak, is high and soft, a little girl's voice. I know she is in her early twenties. A very sheltered girl, I think.

At nine I apologize and say I must be at work early the next day, I have a strict boss. Foreman Qian laughs. "It has been good to have you, we don't have guests often."

I am not surprised, considering that they seem to have little social grace. "I have had a wonderful evening," I lie.

"I realize that you two have not had much chance to get to know each other," Foreman Qian says. "Next you must spend some time together."

San-xiang glances sideways at her mother. I feel the color start to rise in my face. Why does his suggestion sound somehow illicit? Not sexual, but I feel compromised. "Yes," I agree. "Perhaps next time we will have more chance to talk."

"Perhaps on Saturday, you two might take the time to get to know each other."

Lenin and Mao Zedong. But I beam like an idiot. "That would be very nice," I say. "Saturday."

"Fine," Foreman Qian says, "you decide what you should do. And I will see you tomorrow."

The door closes and I am standing in the hall. I stare at the closed door.

Oh shit.

* * *

"Perhaps," I suggest to Foreman Qian, "your daughter would like to go to a vid with me." This is a nasty comedy we play, one of Shakespeare's problem comedies, like *Measure for Measure.* A tragedy that has lost its nerve and is trying desperately to pair principals who have no business with each other.

He nods, he is doing accounts. After he has finished whatever he is writing he looks up at me. "I think you with her to kite race go. Often you tell me you to kite race go. *Hao buhao?*"

"I don't know. Maybe kite race have no interest," I say, falling into Chinglish.

"This time, first time my daughter to kite race go. She tell me it have interest."

"Ah, good," I say. "We to kite race will go."

I don't want to take her to the kite races, they don't start until nine-thirty and if I took her to a vid I could take her at seven-thirty and have her home by eleven-thirty, midnight at the latest. If she's as charming as she was at dinner it's going to be a night that will feel like six months anyway.

So Saturday I again present myself at flat sixteen at the building on Bay Shore. The door is opened by Liu Su-ping, San-xiang's mother, and I am forced to make small talk while San-xiang finishes getting ready. She finally appears in tights and a long red jacket. She has nice taste in clothes but the night already has the same out-of-synch quality as all those times in middle school when I took a girl out. At least now I am not hoping that something will arouse some sort of latent heterosexuality.

We are told to have a good time and then we leave. She watches the floor, and then the numbers in the elevator. I resist the impulse to say, "Nice weather."

We walk towards the subway and suddenly she says in English, "I want to tell you I'm very sorry about this."

"Nothing to be sorry about," I say brightly.

She glances up at me, that same sidelong glance she gives her mother. "I know you didn't plan to spend your Saturday night dragging me to the kite races. I know you are doing this because of my dad. You probably have a girlfriend." The last with such bitterness I am taken aback, even as I find myself thinking her English is good.

"No," I answer honestly, "I don't have a girlfriend."

"Look, we'll go to the kite races for awhile, then I'll take a cab home and you can do whatever you want to do."

The world is unnaturally cruel to ugly girls. "Why don't we just go to the kite races and not worry about it," I say. "Have you ever been?"

"No, I've only seen them on the vid."

"Well, they're better when you're there."

I pay her way into the subway and we head for Manhattan and get off at Union Square. We don't talk on the subway but then the subway is loud. At Union Square we head for the Huang Tunnel pedestrian walkway and come up in Washington Square Park, where the race begins and ends. Washington Square is packed on Saturday night. I buy us a ticket for the stands because I'd much prefer to jack in. "Would you like something to drink? A beer?" I ask.

She shakes her head.

"Don't be polite," I say, smiling, "I'm a New Yorker. I'm going to have a beer. Did you eat dinner?" She lets me buy her a beer and I get a bag of finger dumplings and find our seats. I even buy two programs, although usually I just use the board.

We sit down, she holding her beer carefully. I watch for awhile but she doesn't drink. Maybe she doesn't like beer.

"How old were you when you came to New York?" I ask.

"Nine," she says.

"Do you like it?"

"I hated it at first, but I guess it's all right." She shrugs. "Places are pretty much the same, underneath."

"Do you think?" I ask. "I've never been anywhere but New York, except once when I was six and we went to San Diego to see my grandparents. It seemed different."

"Things are different from place to place," she says. "New York is really very different from China, not as—" She pauses, diplomatically searching for the word.

"We're backward," I supply, grinning.

"Not backward," she says. "Things are less advanced, maybe. I used to think I was unhappy because my father was in trouble and we had to come here, but now I don't think it makes any difference. If you're a certain kind of person, you'll be unhappy wherever you are."

I have no doubt she considers herself that certain kind of person.

"Are you happy?" she asks.

"Do you mean at this moment, or with my life?"

"With your life. Answer the first thing you think."

"No," I say.

"Do you think you would be happy in China?"

"I don't know," I say, "I've never been to China."

"Do you want to go?"

I wonder if she is playing a game. Does she know that her father has dangled China in front of me as her dowry? "Sure," I make it sound as nonchalant as I can, "I wouldn't mind going to China. I'd like to see China."

"Would you like to live there?"

"Go to school there? Live there forever?" In China deviance is a capital offence, I don't know about living in a country where my natural tendencies could see me end up with the traditional remedy of a bullet in the back of the head.

"It doesn't make any difference if you did or you didn't," she says, "because you would still be you. And if you were unhappy here, you'd be unhappy there."

"But much of our unhappiness is caused by social conditions,"
I say.

"That's naive socialism," with some disgust.

Actually it's evasive on my part. What started us on this conversation? Perhaps my expression gives away my unease.

"I'm sorry," she says. "I was just trying to explain."

She is fascinating to look at. Her teeth are straight, her hair
nice, her clothes lovely. But she has no delicacy of feature. Her
nose is too broad, her lips are narrow, her forehead too low. And
she has no chin. It is an amazingly simian face. I find myself
drawn back again and again to studying her. Where did that face
come from? Foreman Qian is not handsome, but his face is
rounder. And her mother, Liu Su-ping, is no beauty, but she
doesn't seem to possess any of the features I find in her daughter's
face.

"Why do you keep looking at me?" San-xiang says suddenly.

Caught out, I look away. "I am out with you," I say. "If you
don't like beer, I'll drink yours. Would you like a soda?"

"I like beer," she says, and sips hers.

She doesn't like beer. I make some sort of small talk about kite
racers, and every time I glance at her she sips her beer. Lipstick
bleeds at the lip of the cup. The fliers spiral lazily up, bright silks
in red and blue. I show her how to place a bet, jack her into the
system. "You have to bet on someone to be jacked in with them,"
I explain. "But once you've jacked in, you can bet any additional
way you want. Even against your flier if you want. I usually jack
into rookies because they're less accustomed to racing and it's
more exciting."

She bites her lower lip in concentration. Above us the kites
swing in a huge arc over the square and head into the darkness
towards Union Square. The system cuts in and suddenly I'm in
synch with a rookie flier named Iceberg. I can feel his/my muscles
pumping, I can see the kites ahead of me when we come into the
lights over Union Square. The kites swing over Union Square and

come back towards Washington Square, gearing up to begin the race when they cross Washington Square. My flier is tense with anticipation. It's not the same as really experiencing it yourself, everything is flattened, at a distance. I know he feels the cold, but I'm not cold. I open my eyes and see the silks above us.

I glance at San-xiang. She is gazing up into the darkness and when the kites flash brilliant into the lights above Washington Square she shivers and takes a drink of her beer.

I don't know why it is so much more exciting to see the race live. Everybody jacks in at home, too. And at home the race is clearer than it is out here. But it is wonderful to see them up there and at the same time be able to close your eyes and see some sense of what they see.

The race is quick—at two laps they always are—and Iceberg doesn't finish in the money. "Ready for another beer?" I ask San-xiang.

"Yes, please," she says. She has color in her cheeks, whether from the race, the chill, or the beer, I can't tell.

When I come back she smiles up at me. "Thank you," she accepts the beer. "This is fun. You do this a lot?"

"Pretty much," I say.

"Would you like to be a kite racer?"

"I'm too big," I say, laughing. Kite racers are small, usually around forty, forty-five kilos.

"Yes, but wouldn't you like to be? If you could?"

"If I won a lot," I say.

She laughs and sips her beer, watching me over the rim of the glass. Flirting. We pour over the program, I haven't heard of any of the fliers in this race but I recognize a lot of the racers in the last three races, the big ones. San-xiang decides not to bet on a rookie, she wants to win.

She doesn't win the second race, nor the third, but her flier comes in second for the fourth race and pays 3:1. The credit light flashes and I take her up to pick up her chit. When she stands up she is a little unsteady on her feet from the beer. She refuses my arm but she's delighted when they pay her off. She turns that monkey-face up at me and smiles.

"I'm having a wonderful time," she says, "one of the best times in my life!"

We walk a bit rather than go back to our seats and the chill clears her head.

"We won't miss the next race, will we?" she asks.

I shake my head. "There's a break between the first four races and the last four. The first four are the minor card and the last four are the major card. The best fliers race the major card."

Peter and a guy from Bed-Stuy are standing where we always stand by the Arch. I hadn't intended to walk that way, just habit. I think about pretending not to see them but decide what the hell and wave. Peter grins and waves back.

"Who's that?" San-xiang whispers.

"A good friend of mine," I say.

We stop for a moment and talk to Peter and Bed-Stuy, whose name I can't at this moment remember. "Peter, this is Qian San-xiang. My friend Peter and"—I make those motions one makes when one can't remember a name.

"Kai," Bed-Stuy says.

"Is that an American name?" San-xiang asks.

"Scandinavian," Bed-Stuy says, "but I'm American." Peter and Bed-Stuy are both fair, both anglo-handsome. Neither one of them is very attractive by Chinese standards—big-nosed for one thing and Kai in particular has the kind of angled face that Chinese don't like. Chinese always think westerners' eyes are set too deep in their heads, that they look a bit Neanderthal. This is not a prejudice I share. But Peter and Kai are dressed well, both in sweaters with leather ties and shimmering reflective strips dangling off the shoulders and shaded glasses sitting on top of their hair. Bed-Stuy has his hair in a tail, like me. They look so bent I wonder if she will guess.

We are carefully low key, talk a little about who is expected to win the seventh and eighth races, and then I say that San-xiang and I have to get back to our seats.

"We're going out to Commemorative afterwards," Peter says. "Drop by if it's not too late."

"Okay," I say and head us back to the stands.

"What is Commemorative?" San-xiang asks.

"It's a flier bar that Peter likes," I say. "Do you want another beer?"

I buy two more beers and we make our way back to our seats. We pour over the program and talk about who to bet on. I'm tired and want to go home, but San-xiang is clearly enjoying the evening so I feign interest. She sips her beer and looks coyly at me out of the corners of her eyes and not knowing how to respond I pretend not to notice. Clearly she does not think I am gay and that is a relief but the night is beginning to depress me.

"Your friends are handsome," she says.

"Do you think so?" I ask. *"You da bizi,"* I say. They have big noses. The Chinese slang for westerner is "big nose."

She giggles and looks down at the program.

Finally the last four races start. It's a so-so card, the seventh race looks good. I pick a flier at random in the fifth race, San-xiang deliberates before picking the odds-on favorite. I find myself watching for Peter and Bed-Stuy between races. San-xiang is disappointed when her flier doesn't come in. She wins the sixth race and is so excited she spills her beer. With some trepidation I buy her another, she has had two and a half and it is obvious that she's not accustomed to them. But I am hoping that if she has another she will be drunk and sleepy enough to want to go home after the races.

I finally pick a flier who places in the eighth race. San-xiang is giggly and unsteady.

"Are you hungry?" I ask.

"What about that place your friends are going, Commemorative, do they have food?"

"Not this late," I say. "I know a little Thai place on West 4th Street, it's not far from here."

"I am having such a good time, I want to stay out all night!" she says. "Are you having a good time?"

"Of course," I say. "When you go with someone who's never seen the kite races it reminds you of your first time."

"It's so exciting. It's so much better than watching it on the vid."

This is a night she will remember all her life, the night when she went to the kite races. How many nights do I remember? How many special nights have I had in my life? Is it so much to give up a night?

"Let's get something to eat and then see how late it is, maybe stop in for a drink," I say. She smiles up at me. Oh, the dangers of pity.

The restaurant is crowded and we pick up our orders of curry and noodles and eat standing on the street. The streets are full of students in outrageous clothes. San-xiang watches a girl in a lavender tunic with no sides, belted in the middle. Underneath she wears a pale green transparent body suit. She is arguing with a boy, shaking her copper hair to make her points. The boy—as drab as she is vivid—is in one of those gray diaper things like they wear in India. He has long, impossibly skinny black-clad legs sticking out of his dhoti. I wonder what he would look like if he didn't rat his hair. "Leave her," I urge him silently. He is angry and sullen, regarding her out of hot bruised eyes. He crosses his arms and shifts his weight from one leg to the other. He is so thin that there is nothing under his skin but long, striated muscle, and the muscles are clear as diagrams over his face bones. Suddenly he turns and walks off.

The girl flips him the finger and stands, rigid with anger, before whirling and walking up the street.

"Dog," San-xiang whispers in Chinese. She looks up at me for collaboration and I nod, although I know she means the boy. San-xiang takes my arm and I tense, startled, but she doesn't notice.

Commemorative is crowded and loud. Hot and noisy. I try to see Peter and Bed-Stuy but can't, so I take her hand and force my way through the crowd. I finally find them near the back, at the end of the bar. They're talking with a flier, he only comes to Peter's shoulder, and he's dark and ugly. Not many fliers are pretty, like most of them he looks as if his head is too big for his body.

"Zhang!" Peter shouts, "This is—!"

I miss the name in the noise but nod and smile anyway. I don't share Peter's preoccupation with fliers. He says they're athletes, good in bed. I signal the bartender "two beers" and she puts them up on the bar. Peter hands them to me, we can't get close. Peter is happy and animated, trying to converse with his flier. Bed-Stuy has the patient look of a man who has stood at a lot of bars and is willing to wait to see if his luck changes. San-xiang seems a little overwhelmed.

I smile at her and shrug to show my apology. She smiles and drinks some of her beer.

I watch her drink her beer, and she watches me. Then she turns pink and looks down at her glass. How fascinating she is. I can't help looking at her, trying to define just what went wrong. What would she need to become beautiful? Larger eyes? More bone in the jawline? And why hasn't she done it?

We don't stay long, it's too loud. She is a bit unsteady when we leave.

"Are you all right?" I ask her.

She leans against me and whispers conspiratorially, "I'm a little drunk." Her body language, her gestures, are all the actions of a girl being cute, of a flirt, and yet looking up at me is that square monkey-face, those tiny porcine eyes. She wrinkles her nose and her eyes almost disappear, and I gaze, entranced by the grotesque.

It feels lewd. All my life I have been careful not to stare. I don't stare at war veterans, I don't stare at street people. I guess, unconsciously, I don't stare at people who are ugly, either. But I can stare at San-xiang. I have the sudden urge to kiss her on the forehead, I don't know why.

We take the subway to Brooklyn and walk to her parents' apartment. In the hall we stop and I think of being in middle school and bringing the girl to her door and trying to decide if I was supposed to kiss her or not. I kiss San-xiang, a nice brotherly kiss.

"I had a wonderful time," she says and gives me a trembling smile. "You are very nice."

"So are you," I say.

"Why don't you have a girlfriend? You're very handsome."

I like to be told I'm handsome as much as anyone does but coming from San-xiang it is a bit disconcerting. I make the *Nali-nali*, the don't-talk-about-it motion with my hand, looking away embarrassed. "No reason," I say. "I just don't really want a girlfriend right now, I guess." The walls in the hallway are China red.

She rubs the back of her hand across her eyes and her voice is full of tears when she says, "I have to go, good-night."

She unlocks the door and closes it behind her and I am left standing in the hall, wondering, what did I do?

I do not expect her voice when I answer the call. It is Tuesday evening and I've only been home from work for a few minutes.

"Zhong Shan?" she says, "It's San-xiang." We make inconsequential small talk, how is work? I ask her how her work is and realize that I don't even know what she does.

"Some friends of mine and I," she says, "on Thursday nights, we have, well, it's kind of a political study meeting but it's really not, we sit around and talk, mostly. I was wondering if you would like to come? It won't be late, I mean, I know you work on Friday, we all do, so it . . . it won't be late. But if you're busy, I'll understand. I mean, this is short notice and I know you probably have plans, or, really that you might have plans. That's what I meant, that you're probably a fairly busy person, and it might not be convenient."

She is so nervous, I want to save her. "No," I say, "I don't have plans. I'm not very political though. I'm pretty dumb about politics."

"But you went to the Middle School for Political Theory, didn't you?"

"Yeah, but that was ten years ago, and we didn't learn too much about politics. Mostly we studied Mandarin."

"Oh," she says in her high voice. "It doesn't really matter, we just mostly talk, anyway."

"Sure. What time?"

"About six-thirty," she says and tells me where to come. I usually start at seven A.M. and get off about four-thirty in the afternoon so that gives me time to get home and change. But Thursday comes and the project we are working on includes a side wall that will eventually have an artificial water-wall and a court-yard for the public. The wall is to be done in a continuous pour and for all the usual reasons we are late beginning the pour. Of course a special crew does the pour but I have to be there until it's finished to secure the site.

At six I head for Brooklyn, still in coveralls and workboots. The proletariat. Well, that ought to go over big in San-xiang's political study group.

I am late, it is quarter of seven when I get to the address San-xiang has given me. I need a shower and a beer, not necessarily in that order. The door opens and I say, "Excuse me, I am a friend of San-xiang?"

The face in the doorway is Chinese. A man, about my age.
"Come in," he says, "we were afraid you got lost."

"I'm sorry," I say, "I had to work late."

There are five people in the little main room of this apartment,
including San-xiang, whose eyes almost disappear in her delight.

"So you are the man with the incredible name," drawls a tall
woman, not Chinese.

I smile and nod. "One cannot choose one's parents," I say. Oh
my foolish mother. Zhong Shan is the name of a famous Chinese
revolutionary, the first president of the Republic; it is the Mandarin version of the Cantonese name Sun Yat-sen. To be named
Zhang Zhong Shan is like being named George Washington
Jones. I sit down next to San-xiang and she introduces me around.
I catch only two names, the woman is Ginny and the ABC who
met me at the door is Gu Zhongyan. There is also a couple, clearly
married, in their forties, I think.

I apologize again for coming late, and for coming straight from
work without a chance to clean up.

"We hope to eventually establish a neighborhood association
or a commune," Gu Zhongyan explains, "but we are none of us
financially able yet. So for now we have a study group."

The male half of the couple passes out flimsies of an article out
of a magazine. It's political theory. I read through the first couple
of paragraphs and don't much understand, it's something about
optimum community size. San-xiang studies hers carefully for a
moment, then puts it in a folder and pulls out another stack of
flimsies carefully underlined and highlighted. She has made notes
to herself in Chinese along the margins. Her characters are tiny
swift swirls of line.

They talk for awhile about the article. Ginny and Gu appear not
to have read it as carefully. The male half of the couple is clearly
the most committed. I gather in the course of the conversation that
he and his wife lived in a commune before but there was some
trouble and they left.

The only commune I am familiar with is Peter's, which has no ideology and exists merely as a tenants' association to keep his building running. And doesn't seem to do that too terribly well. I'm tired, it's been a long day, and they talk carefully about the relationship between competition and productivity.

I feel inadequate. I know that politics is important, I just don't like to think about it. I don't know what my opinions are, I just know that very little I hear ever seems to have much to do with me, or with my life.

This apartment is the apartment of a serious person. Disordered, but in a serious way—a large system on the wall, equipped for information and music, but no vid. There are flimsies in a stack on the floor, obviously down-loaded. The wall at the back has home-made bookshelves filled with books and stacks of flimsies in binders. The books look like non-fiction. I used to read a lot during my alienated adolescence. Fiction. There is a book lying on the floor near Gu's chair, *The Social Matrix: Religious Communities in Capitalist America.*

San-xiang talks. She is serious and involved. "A community doesn't have to be autonomous to be a community," she says. "People can work outside the community."

"Then what makes it a community?" Gu Zhongyan asks, sounding irritated.

"A community is a group of people united by shared interests," San-xiang says. "It can be work, or family, or even something like a theater. That's why a community should do something, have a product that everybody works with, because the profit and loss unites people."

"But there you have competition," says the husband, "and whenever you have competition you're going to have inequality. Some members are going to be less able to contribute."

"So the community adapts," San-xiang says. "It adjusts. We're adults, we can recognize that someone taking care of a new baby has less time, or that someone else isn't going to be able to handle bookkeeping."

"But if you have competition," says the wife, "people's judgments become clouded. You get resentment. You can't expect people to recognize and adjust, somebody is going to feel put out." She sounds wistful, as if she speaks from experience.

"Sometimes a community doesn't adjust," San-xiang says, "and sometimes it doesn't work. But that doesn't mean we shouldn't try."

After the discussion we have green tea and cookies and then San-xiang and I walk to the subway.

"What did you think?" San-xiang asks.

"I think you are very smart," I answer.

She frowns. "No, I mean are you interested?"

"In joining your commune? I don't know."

"We don't even have a commune yet," she says. "You didn't say very much, I guess it isn't as exciting as kite races."

"I'm not a very political person," I say by way of apology.

She looks at me sharply but doesn't say anything.

"It's true," I say, "I don't even like to watch the news. I'm not the kind of person who gets involved in political things."

"Everybody is involved in politics," she says.

"Not me," I say. "Not because I think they're bad, I think I should be involved, I'm just lazy."

"No, listen to me. Everyone is political. You can't help it. You make political decisions all the time, just as you make moral ones."

I shrug.

"Zhong Shan," she says gently, "get this through that handsome empty skull of yours, okay? No one can escape politics. You're ABC, are you a party member?"

"No," I say, expecting her to be disappointed. A lot of ABC are party members. "Like I told you, I'm not interested. I think the party is mostly a means of advancing one's career anyway."

"Exactly, and your decision not to join is a political decision."

"Well, then my political decision is to not be political."

"Exactly, that's a political statement. You are expressing your opinion about current politics. Except you are political, everything we do is political," she says, doggedly explaining to the unenlightened. "You do things. You rent a private apartment, right?"

"Because if I took housing I'd have to live in some complex in Virginia or northern Pennsylvania," I say, irritated.

"But by doing so you condone landlords."

"I don't condone or not condone landlords," I say. "It's a practical decision, not a political one. The Great Cleansing Winds campaign is over, San-xiang. We don't have to analyze everyone's lives for motives."

"I wasn't saying it's wrong," she says mildly, "I was just pointing out that your life says something about your politics whether you think about them or not. You can either just let that happen or you can think about the kind of choices you want to make."

"I'd like to continue to make my choices because they fit my life rather than out of some sense of ideology," I say. "In my experience ideology is a lot like religion; it's a belief system and most people cling to it long after it becomes clear that their ideology doesn't describe the real world."

She smiles up at me. "That's as pure a description of an applied political theory as any I've ever heard."

I look at that little monkey face and say coldly, "Pretty good for a dumb construction tech, right?"

"*Bu cuo,*" she says airily. Not bad.

Ugly girls have to have something, I think. Sports or ideas.

Lenin and Mao Zedong. I am sitting in front of the vid, leaned over unlacing my work boots, when I get a call. I assume that it's Peter and I think to myself, this time I won't let him talk me into

going anywhere. It's Tuesday night, I'm tired. I pick up my beer
and wander into the kitchen to take the call, trailing boot-laces.

"Zhang here," I say, not bothering with the visual.

"Zhong Shan?" San-xiang says.

"*Wei,*" I answer, surprised and a little disappointed.

"My parents threw me out," she says in her high, soft little-girl
voice.

"What?" I say. "What for?"

"We had an argument."

"About what?" I say foolishly.

"Oh, everything. Can I come to your flat?"

"Oh, sure." I say. I give her directions and then lace my boots
and run down to the little Thai place (The Ruby Kitchen) and get
takeout noodles and fried chicken. I stop and pick up more beer,
too. Then back to my flat, where I take the shirts I brought back
from the cleaners off the chair and throw them in my room. The
place looks okay. It needs to be cleaned but I'm not going to worry
about that right now.

And then I wait, sitting on the edge of the chair, watching the
vid. If I sit back in the chair, I'll probably fall asleep. I fall asleep
a lot of evenings in this chair, sitting in front of the vid.

The building system says someone's at the outside door, I check
the console and there she stands with a slouch bag over her
shoulder. Until I see the bag it doesn't occur to me that she might
want to stay here the night. Hell, doesn't she have friends? I let
her in, tell the building to recognize her and let her in whenever
she comes, and leave the door off the latch.

San-xiang stops at the door. I am in the kitchen, but I hear her
heels and then I imagine her stopping, her chinless little face
upturned. "I'm in the kitchen," I call.

When she comes in the kitchen she doesn't have her bag.

"*Yao pijiu ma?*" I ask and hand her a beer without waiting for
her to answer.

"Hi," she says, looking at the beer as if she doesn't know

whether she wants it or not. She takes a sip. She stands, uncertain of her reception.

"This is my decadent flat," I say, gesturing. It is two real rooms and a kitchen and bathroom roughly the size of closets. Compared to her parents' apartment it's little bigger than a drawer. And it's a rathole. The flooring is that synthetic stuff and doesn't go quite to the corners and the wall covering needs to be replaced. The apartment is brown except where the gray concrete shows in the corners. I could fix it up, I think about it once in awhile, but I never know how long I'm going to live here. And I'm rarely here except to eat and sleep.

She looks around, looks back at me. "I'm sorry to just show up this way."

"Sit down," I say, "have something to eat. Tell me what happened."

She sits down and I stick chopsticks in the noodles. I hand her a plate and a pair of chopsticks, sit down and pick up a piece of chicken.

She sits for a moment, looking at the noodles but clearly not seeing them. Her attitude reminds me of someone saying grace. I put a piece of chicken on her plate. "Thank you," she says.

I eat and watch her eat. Finally she says, "I had an argument with my parents."

"What about?" I ask.

She shrugs. "Nothing. Money. Everything."

I wait.

"It was just a little argument, and things kept coming in. Like why I didn't study hard enough to go to the University and how my father spent the money that was supposed to be for me, for," her voice drops to a whisper, "my face."

For just a second I think she means "face" in the Chinese sense, as in "not lose face." Then I realize she means her physical face.

"My father thinks I should save my money for that, not for a commune."

I don't know what to say, everything I say may be wrong, so I say the innocuous. "What do you think?"

"I think I am an adult and it is my decision," she says. "He says that as long as I live in his house it is his decision. But I can't get assigned housing unless I get married and I want to save my money so I don't want to pay rent. But maybe it's an excuse to stay at home?"

"It sounds very sensible to me," I say.

"Do you think I am immature?" she asks.

Yes, but I cannot say that. "I think you are very sensible," I say.

"You don't live with your family," she says.

"I don't have a family," I say. Which is not true, strictly speaking, but my father has been gone for years, and my mother has a new family. I couldn't live with either of them. And wouldn't want to.

"This is a nice apartment," she says.

I laugh and she is startled. "It's a dump," I say. "But it is what I can afford."

So we eat.

"I have to get up early," I say, "let's get you settled."

She nods, all tension.

I go into my bedroom and dig a sheet out of my closet. I have two pillows on my bed, so I skin one out of the case and put a clean case on it. San-xiang stands in the doorway and watches me. I feel as if something is wrong, but I don't know what it is. My bedroom is a mess, I wonder if she is upset. Did she have some idea that I lived this elegant life? If so, the actual squalor of coffee cups in the bedroom could be a little distressing.

I have a quilt and use the pillow, sheet and quilt to create a makeshift bed on the couch. It's not going to adjust to body temperature but it should be comfortable enough. I probably should put her on my bed and sleep out here, but damn it, I didn't ask her to come over, and besides, all the rest of my sheets are dirty and I'm not going to bring dirty sheets out here to sleep and put her in my bed.

"I have to be at work at seven tomorrow," I explain, "so I'll be leaving a little after six. What time do you have to be at work?"

"Nine," she says.

"What time do you need to wake up?"

"About seven-thirty?" she says.

"Okay, I'll tell the system. There's coffee and tea in the kitchen. Feel free to watch the vid, make yourself at home."

She sits down on the couch, her hands folded in her lap. Again I have the feeling that she is upset. It is probably strange to her.

"Have you ever been away from home before?"

"Oh yeah," she says. "Every year I go somewhere for a couple of weeks and Cuo sent me to Arkansas for training two years ago. I was there for eighteen weeks." She looks up at me, straight at me instead of her usual sidelong glance. "Why are you always looking at me?"

Flustered I say, "What do you mean?"

"You are always studying me. Is it because I am ugly?"

"No," I say too quickly, "of course not."

"It's okay," she says, "I know I'm ugly. Someday, when I have enough money, I will have my face fixed. It's a bone problem, it only happens to one in twenty thousand children. It's not so expensive if they do something right at adolescence, but my father was in trouble, so we had to come here."

"What happened to your father?"

"He managed a branch of Huang-Kamakai in Guangzhou and his branch lost a lot of money, hundreds of thousands of yuan. So they transferred him to the United States and sent him to work at Hong Fangzhen Construction. They used to own it. Then during the Cleansing Winds it lost so much money they sold it to an ABC so now we can never be transferred back."

Well, I have to get up, so I go to bed. After a few minutes I hear the vid on very low. I go to sleep with my back to the crack of light showing under my door.

The system gets me up and I creep through the front room to the bathroom, clean up and dress. When I come out of the bathroom, the hills and valleys on the couch shift and San-xiang sits up.

"Go back to sleep," I whisper, "it's only quarter of six."

"I'm awake," she says and turns on the light. She blinks in the glare. "I can make you coffee," she says.

"I always get it at the site," I say, "go to sleep."

But she gets up, wearing a loose shift and barefoot, her hair tangled, and takes her bag into the bathroom. I'm ready early, I usually sit around, watch the vid a bit, sometimes make coffee. Or I sleep too late and rush out at six-thirty.

This morning I make coffee and sit down with a cup. I wonder how long she'll stay. I don't have the ambition to bring it up in the morning. She comes out dressed.

"Coffee?" I ask.

She pours a cup.

"Sugar is by the sink, I don't have milk," I say.

She gets sugar and brings it back to the couch but sits with the cup untasted.

"Did you sleep well?" I ask.

"Fine," she says brightly.

We make small talk. I ask her about her work, she works for Cuo, one of the big Chinese conglomerates, she's a clerk in the international transport department. She routes orders.

She doesn't like coffee, but I pretend not to notice. And in a few minutes, I leave for work.

When I get home that evening—we are on rush work which means we work long hours and I don't get home until nearly seven-thirty—she is already there. I hear her in the kitchen when I open the door. The living room is neat, the sheet and quilt neatly folded on the end of the couch. She is chopping in the kitchen, I wait until I hear the cleaver stop before calling hello.

"Zhong Shan?" she calls.

I am tired to the bone. Foreman Qian was not on the site today, a small blessing, but there were too many things to do. I worked for twelve hours, the hard physical work of pounding excess off forms and pulling the forms, polishing the face of the building. Painstaking hand work with a crew that wants to get it done and go home. I have shouted myself nearly hoarse. The crew is mutinous. But the job will be done by Friday if we don't get disastrous weather.

I don't really want company. If Peter called I would tell him to go pound sand. "San-xiang," I say. I smell rice cooking.

"Are you always so late?" she says. She is chopping scallions.

"No," I say, "usually I am home around five." I find a beer and collapse in a chair.

"Did you see my father?"

"He wasn't on site today. He might be tomorrow."

"Will you tell him where I am?"

"If he asks," I say.

She frowns at the wok, tosses chicken in sesame oil. It is a smell that reminds me of growing up. "Don't tell him, okay? Tell him you don't know where I am. I don't want him to know."

I don't like this. I shrug.

She stirs the chicken, tosses in green scallions and Chinese chilis and adds a glob of sesame paste. Then she spills it onto plates. "Are you hungry?"

"Yeah," I say. "This is very nice of you."

"It's nice of you to let me stay," she says.

I hadn't planned on her staying this long. "How long will you be here?" I ask.

"Whenever you want me to go," she says, "you tell me. I'll understand."

I don't exactly know what to say. Tonight. I want you to leave tonight. Go stay with one of your friends from the political study group. I don't say anything, just shovel food into my mouth while I think about this.

I decide that tomorrow I'll tell her to leave. "This is very good."

"Thank you."

I should tell her to be out by the weekend. I should tell her right now. But it seems terrible to sit eating her food telling her not to stay. Tomorrow I'll eat before I get home. She doesn't think about the position she's put me in because she doesn't have any friends, she's not accustomed to being around people. I am furious. But as always, I hesitate to reject her. I look into that monkey face and think, she's been rejected and hurt enough, and I put it off. I am a coward.

We sit and watch the vid for awhile. "Do you want to see kite races?" she asks.

"I don't really care," I say. Actually I don't watch the kites on vid much, but since I took her she thinks it's the most important thing in my life. We watch a serial. We make small talk. I fall asleep in my chair and wake up with a jerk. Where can she go? She can't get housing, not unless her parents will file a separation. Surely she has friends. Surely it is not my problem.

I go to bed and sleep badly. I dream of middle school.

In the morning San-xiang doesn't get up when I do, so I leave early without coffee. I am on the site by six-forty-five and sit in the gray morning waiting for coffee and for the day to begin. The crew greets the sight of their tech engineer perched on the back of a concrete bench with dismay—"Jesus, Zhang, you goin' to be bustin' balls all day today?" And the tone of the day is set.

We are under deadline and I am mean, I do not want to be here Friday night under the lights, working. I want to be here Saturday even less. If we work on Saturday, the men will expect big bonus and I will get chewed out.

Foreman Qian shows up at a little before nine and disappears into the trailer. If he stays in the trailer, maybe I will get some work out of the crew. But he doesn't. He comes back out, coffee cup in hand, and surveys the crew work.

"Zhang!" he snaps.

"Foreman Qian," I say, trotting over, dutiful dog.

"You think Friday already you finish?"

I drop into Chinese. "If the weather is good, yes. If the weather is bad, or we have problems, no."

Foreman Qian nods. Sips his morning tea.

"Engineer Zhang," he says, "Have you talked to my daughter?"

"Lately?" I ask. "Not since Thursday."

He looks unhappy and tired. "She gives you a call, you call me, okay?"

"Something is wrong?" I ask.

"A misunderstanding," he says. "She is staying with one of her friends."

I nod, we stand looking at the crew for a moment in apparent camaraderie. Then I trot back and Foreman Qian goes into the trailer. I don't like being in the middle of this, tonight I'll tell her to call him. That will take care of my problems.

In the afternoon we have a box playing—we always have a box playing, sounds of Brooklyn—and I catch a weather report. Rain tomorrow. The crew watches me, obviously they already know. I rest a polisher on the edge of the granite planter I am working on.

"Okay," I say, "I hear it. Work starts at noon tomorrow. Tell your mothers to put your dinners on the counter, we'll be working under the lights."

"Shit," someone says. But I turn the polisher back on and go back to work. I pretend not to notice them bitching. They knew what I was going to say, but hell, bitching is one of the few satisfactions they have.

*   *   *

It is seven-thirty when I leave work. I get my dinner on the way home, stopping for a hamburger on the way to the subway. The subway isn't crowded. Above me a paper sign says *"Una luz brillara en tu camina/Ven a la iglesia. Descubre lo que has perdido."* I think whatever I have lost was gone before I was born. I fall asleep on the subway and nearly miss my stop.

The apartment is dark, for a moment I think she has left, but then the lights come up and I see her bag sitting by the door. I check through the whole apartment. No sign, no note.

Perhaps she, like me, is working late? Maybe she went to dinner with someone from work?

So I sit in my chair and go to sleep with the vid on.

The door wakes me and I sit up. The system has shut the vid off, which means I've been asleep for more than twenty minutes, I am confused and feel as if it is later than that.

"San-xiang?" I say.

"Hello," she sings out, "I thought you'd be asleep."

I was. "I was watching the vid. Did you work late?"

"Tonight is my political study meeting."

Oh yes, the optimum size of a community. Now what? Tell her she has to go. "Your father is very worried about you," I say.

"Did you talk to him today? What did he say?"

"He asked me to call him if I saw you. I think you should talk to him. And I think you should decide what you are going to do." Well put, I think to myself.

She sits down on the couch. "If I call him, he'll make me come home."

"But he threw you out," I say.

She makes a gesture with her hand, waving that away. "He didn't really mean it."

"What are you going to do?" I ask.

"I don't know." She looks down at her feet, "Call him, I guess. Do you mean tonight?"

Shit. Grow up. All right, if you want me to be the parent. "Yeah, tonight."

She sits there for a moment, then gets up and goes into the kitchen. There is a long silence, longer than it takes to jack in and connect. Finally I hear her say, *"Baba? Shi wo."* Papa, it's me.

A pause. *"Zai Zhang gongchengshide jiali."* At Engineer Zhang's place.

A long pause. *Dui,* she breathes. *"Wo dengideng."* I'll wait.

I hear the snap when she takes off the contact. "He's coming to get me," she says. She is about to cry and escapes into the bathroom. I think about getting a beer but decide I am too tired. At least I can sleep late tomorrow and there won't be anyone here.

I try not to listen to San-xiang crying in the bathroom.

She comes back out and sits down on the couch. It is not my fault she is ugly, I have no reason to feel guilty. I have always had tremendous trouble defining the limits of responsibility.

"My father is very upset," she says, and has to regain her self-control.

I nod.

"I am in big trouble," she says.

"You're an adult," I point out.

"Sometimes my father makes that hard to remember. He is pretty good at making people do what he wants."

"You can just tell him 'no'."

"Like you did when he told you to take me out?" she asks.

"That's different," I say, "taking you out is enjoyable."

She nods and looks at the vid. She is crying again, without allowing any sound to escape. I feel trapped. A few minutes and her father will be here. She takes a shuddery breath. "It's okay," she says, "you don't have to ask me out anymore. I mean, you're very nice but I know you really don't want to."

"That's not true," I lie. "I enjoy our evenings together." It's not altogether a lie.

She shrugs.

"I consider you a friend, San-xiang," I say as gently as I can.

"Well maybe I'm not looking for friendship," she snaps and then covers her face with her hands.

I don't know how to respond but she doesn't say anything else. After a moment she goes back into the bathroom. I hear water running. My water bill is going to be terrible this month, last month it was pretty good, but this month will be bad. If I took public housing I wouldn't have to pay anything for the first 800 liters of water I used.

She comes out with her make-up repaired and her eyes red and we watch the vid until my system tells me that her father is outside. I check, and sure enough, there he is in his coveralls. I let him in, and while I am at it I take San-xiang out of the system so she can't get in unless I let her.

I open the door and say, unnecessarily I'm sure, "Your father is here."

I hear the lift open and then Foreman Qian walking down the hallway. I open the door, and he glances at me once and brushes past me. "San-xiang," he says.

"Baba," she says poised on the couch, holding her back very straight but keeping her eyes down. Perfect posture for a Chinese girl.

In Chinese he demands, "How do you explain this?"

"I am not explaining," she says.

"This is terrible, what you have done to your mother! You could have at least called and told us where you were. Where have you been!"

"Here," she says so softly I can barely understand.

"Here? With Zhang Zhong Shan?"

"Here."

He looks at me, his face very red. "You told me you hadn't seen her!"

"She asked me to."

He looks back at her. "You stayed here alone?" He is trembling with fury, I have never seen him like this. His face is so red I am afraid he will make himself ill.

"Foreman Qian," I say, "perhaps you would sit down. I have tea, beer."

"What have you been doing for two days! What is your mother going to do when she hears about this! And you," he turns to me, "how could you do this! I have had you to my home and now you are taking advantage of my daughter!"

"Foreman Qian," I say, the words sounding as ludicrous in Chinese as they do in English, "I have not taken advantage of your daughter, I did not even ask her to come here."

"I cannot believe this!" he says to her, ignoring me. "You want us to treat you as if you are an adult, but you do this?" I am embarrassed. Foreman Qian sounds like the cliché of the Chinese father, protecting his daughter from bad influence. Like a vid. People do not act like this in real life. But then, people don't try to marry their daughters to bent foremen they barely know, either. "What if they found out at your job! Do you think you would ever be transferred to China if they thought you were an immoral girl?"

"The Great Cleansing Winds campaign is over," San-xiang says, "No one talks that way anymore."

"Well why don't you just tell them at work that you are staying with an Engineering Technician without citizenship and see how they talk."

San-xiang flushes.

Foreman Qian rounds on me, "I would have been happy to treat you like a son, I had no idea you were so stupid."

"I have been entirely respectful with your daughter," I say. "She called me Tuesday and asked if she could come here, she told me she had an argument with you and her mother."

"A man alone with a girl, you expect me to believe this?"

"It's true," San-xiang says coldly, "Engineer Zhang is not interested in me, *baba,* I am too ugly for a man."

He takes that like a body blow. For the first time I see his position, a father with an ugly daughter, trying to make up to her for spending her face money. But he rolls right on, not even acknowledging her comment. "I don't believe this foolishness. You have been here two nights. The neighbors know you are here."

If this were a Chinese building, the auntie watching the hall would report what we are doing to the building committee, but this is not a Chinese building, I'm the only ABC living here and there are no Chinese. "Here," I say, "no one cares."

"I can believe that," he says, looking at my apartment. "What about your mother?" he says to San-xiang.

"I will tell her I'm sorry," San-xiang says.

"Do you think that will erase what you've done?"

"What do you want me to do?" she cries.

"Do you expect to continue on after this?" Foreman Qian asks.

"No," she says, "we have already decided to stop."

I expect that to mollify him but instead he turns back to me. "So! You have had her here! Now you are finished with her? Is that it! She is trash and you discard her?"

"No—" I say, astonished and angry.

"You are a stupid bit of dogshit!" he says.

"Enough!" I shout back, this is a real Chinese argument now, conducted like any good Chinese argument, at full volume. "I didn't ask your daughter to come here! I treated her well! I told her to call you and now all you do is shout at me! Don't shout at me because you can't control your daughter!"

"What do you expect me to believe! I find my daughter in this dirty little apartment where there is barely room to turn around and you tell me you have been living like sisters? And then you say you do not want to see my daughter again? How can you tell me you are not interested in a Chinese girl! In citizenship! Maybe this was just to get my daughter in trouble so she would have to marry you!"

"You wanted your daughter to marry me!" I say. "You tried to bribe me with your talk of Guangzhou University!" My face is flushed, I feel it. "Well Foreman Qian, something you did not know, my mother is not Chinese. I am not really Chinese. My mother's name is Teresa Luis and she is Hispanic!" *Wode mama jiao* Teresa Luis *ye ta shi Hai-si-ba-na!*

Foreman Qian is shocked into silence. The Spanish name stands out from the Chinese.

After a moment Foreman Qian stutters, "Your mother; her surname is Li. I read your records."

"Li is her party name. Only my father is Chinese. Now, please leave," I say, "I have to work tomorrow."

I see a different anger building in his face, a colder anger. Finally Foreman Qian says, "Ah, now you remember that you work for me."

"I have told the crew to be on the site at noon, hopefully the rain will be over," I say. His face frightens me, the red is gone and now the anger is white.

"We will talk," Foreman Qian says and it is clearly a threat. "San-xiang, let's go."

She collects her bag silently. "I'm sorry," she says in English.

"San-xiang!" her father snaps.

And I close the door behind them. I stand there for a minute, and then I go to the kitchen and get a beer. There are only five beers, I suspect that isn't enough.

Before I go to the site the next day I go to the employment office and check the jobs on the board. I cannot look for a job until I no longer have one, so I don't stay long for fear someone will ask to look at my work card. I do not see any jobs.

I do not know what I will do when I am unemployed. I may have to give up my flat if I am unemployed for very long and accept approved housing. Living in Virginia or northern Pennsylvania and taking the train to the city. I will be able to take the train but only during non-peak hours. Maybe I can live with Peter for awhile.

I have a skill, so I will be able to wait until a job comes that matches my skill, rather than being assigned to menial labor.

If I had enough money and could keep paying my rent, I could keep my flat. I cannot ask my mother for money. There are jobs, free market jobs in Times Square. Maybe I can sell something. I get back on the train to go back downtown to the job site. In the subway there is a torn advertisement, the same I saw the night before, *"Una luz brillara en tu camina/Ven a la iglesia. Descubre lo que te has perdido."* Discover what I have lost? Not by going to church. *Una luz brillara en tu camina.* A brilliant light in your path. There is a brilliant light inside of me. It is not Christ, it is not Mao Zedong. I do not know what it is. I am Zhang, alone with my light, and in that light I think for a moment that I am free.

But I am only free in small places. Government is big, we are small. We are only free when we slip through the cracks.

⚓

Kites

Angel

The door is flanked by two curtained windows with big flower arrangements in them, it makes the place look more like a discreet and expensive restaurant than a funeral parlor. The first person I see is Orchid—long white hair and black satin quilted jacket with, of course, a huge white silk orchid appliqued across the back. Then Cinnabar, who isn't wearing red. Cinnabar is really Cinnabar Chavez' first name, so I guess he doesn't have to prove anything, he only wears red when he flies.

Some fliers take on their flying name, like Orchid. Everybody calls her Orchid. I don't even know what her name is. But nobody calls Eleni "Jacinth" except the marks. Nobody calls me Gargoyle, they just call me Angel. But everybody calls Johnny B "Johnny B," even though we all know his name is Gregory.

Cinnabar sees me, waves me over. He's a good flier for a guy, a little tall, he's 1.55 meters but so skinny he doesn't mass over forty-eight kilos. Flying runs in his family, his brother was Random Chavez—bet you didn't know he even had a last name. Of course, he was killed in that big smash, Jesus, five years ago? I'm

45

getting old. That was the year I started flying the big kites. I was there, I finished that race.

"Pijiu?" Cinnabar says. We give each other a hug. There's a spread, a funeral banquet, but I can't eat at funerals. Just as well, since I have to keep my weight at about thirty-nine kilos, and beer has too many calories. Orchid preens, looking strange and graceful as a macaw. I check, no cameras and of course she's not synched. She must do it by instinct.

We don't have anything to say to each other. So we stand around the viewing room feeling guilty. The dead can feel virtuous I suppose. Dead dead dead. That's for all you people who say "passed away."

People die for different reasons; the young ones—the ones with good reflexes die because they take risks, the older ones die because their reflexes or synapses let them down. Not that we don't all cut up and take risks, it's just that the older you get, the less often you get in positions where you have to, or maybe you know that there's another race.

"Kirin was a nice girl," Cinnabar says.

I didn't really know the deceased all that well. I mean, she'd flown and all but she'd only been riding in the big kites a year or so, and I was out for three months because I tore a ligament in my shoulder. Besides, she was ABC, American Born Chinese, she even had citizenship in China. Opens a lot of doors. ABC don't have to associate with *waiguoren* from Brooklyn. Especially *waiguoren* having a bad year. Funny, when I was growing up I didn't know that *waiguoren* meant foreigner, because the ABC were the foreigners to me. I always thought it meant not-Chinese.

"Are you flying tonight?" I ask.

"I'm going down to Florida this afternoon," Orchid says. She goes down there a lot to fly.

"You be out at Washington Square?" Cinnabar asks me.

"If Georgia can get the Siyue off the ground." Georgia's my tech.

"You're still flying a Siyue?" Orchid asks, white eyebrows arching all disdainful.

Cinnabar looks away as if he hasn't heard, to save me face. Last year Citinet dropped me and I've been flying independent. Orchid knows that. *Meiqian*, I'm a poor woman, last year's kite. Bitch. But Orchid isn't going to be dropped, no. Even if she isn't having a good year, she makes a good cover story. Pretty girl, a popular synch.

"Angel," Cinnabar says, "jailai tonight on Guatemala Avenue, want to go back to the old neighborhood?"

"Let's see how the race goes."

Cinnabar is such a sweetheart. He comes from Brooklyn, like me. Orchid looks bored, pampered little Virginia girl.

"If you come in money," Cinnabar says, "You pay."

I laugh.

At Washington Square, Georgia and I have got the Siyue working and I lift the kite over my head, holding it so I can feel the wind in the silk. It hums, a huge insect. I'm wired into the half-awake kite and moving in sensory overlap—I have arms and wings both feeding through parallel synapses and if I think about which I am trying to move it's like trying to pat my head and rub my stomach at the same time. But I'm lit and my mind is chemical clear. My black silk wings are taut and light above me. I am called *Angel*, with the soft "h" sound of Brooklyn for the "g," and I am burning, waiting for the race. I stand 1.47 meters tall and weigh thirty-nine kilos but I'm strong, probably stronger than you. My joints are like cables, the ligaments and tendons in my shoulders are all synthetic after the last surgery, strong as spider web, far stronger than steel.

If my kite holds together, there is no one who can beat me. I feel it.

I jog a few meters, and then start to run lightly. There is the faint vibration of power as the sensors signal that I've reached the threshold between drag and lift and the system trips into active, and when the power feeds through the kite the full system comes on, and I swing my legs up into the harness by habit because I don't even have a body anymore. My body is the kite. I feel the air on my silk, I balance on the air. The kite is more than a glider, because it needs a power source which is fueled by my own metabolism, but the original kites—hang gliders—were true gliders; a kite *does* fly. I mean, I'm not a rock. I won't just fall.

I climb in lazy circles, there's two fliers spiraling up above me, one below me. *Loushang* is Medicine, her kite patterned like a Navajo sand painting even from where I see it underneath. *Louxia* I can't see, they are between me and the groundlight, so all I can see is the silhouette of a Liuyue kite. I test the kite, my left shoulder aches like rheumatism. It's an old kite, it has aches and pains.

Then they are starting to form up; eighteen kites, two abreast, I am six back, on the outside. I drop into place, and we do a slow circle of the course. Eighteen triangles of bright silk. The course goes from Washington Square Park to Union Square and back, following The Swath. Over the Square the ground is a maze of lights, then suddenly the groundlights end and there's nothing below us but the undergrowth and debris of the 2059 riots. Off to my right I see the bracelet of lights where Broadway goes under The Swath—I never remember to call it Huang Tunnel, it's still Morrissey to me—and then there's nothing but the floaters lighting us until we're over Union Square. Long sweeping turn over Union Square and just as we straighten up, like a long strung-out New Year's dragon made of kites, we're back over The Swath. Off to my right and slightly behind me now is midtown. I count floaters, there are five and then we are over Washington Square Park. I catch a glimpse of the betting board but it's too small to read from up here.

I wonder briefly how many people are synched with me. I used to be self-conscious about the people who are tied in, experiencing what I experience as I fly. Now I don't think of them as separate people much—a teenage boy somewhere in Queens, maybe an old man in the Bronx. If the numbers get high enough, Citinet will sponsor me again. But why sponsor someone with last year's kite? Someone who probably won't win? When they dropped me at Citinet, they told me I was too precise a flier. I made all the rational choices, took no chances. I am too cold, no fun.

I told them no one was going to follow me down into The Swath, fighting to regain control of my kite, until the automatic cutoff kills the synch just nanoseconds before impact. One of them muttered at least then I'd be doing something interesting.

We come back over Washington Square Park for the second time and the kites begin to pick up speed. We glide past the floater marking the start and already I'm climbing, trying to get altitude. Ten kites are in front of me and I sideslip slightly inside, cutting off Medicine, flying to my left. She's forced to go underneath me, ends up flying *xialou*, my shadow underneath except that my kite is black silk and hers is a Navajo pattern in red, black, white and blue. I see Cinnabar ahead, flying third—a scarlet kite with edges that bleed into cinnamon.

And we are over The Swath. I dive. Not hard, just enough to gain speed. A black kite disappears over The Swath, there is only the silver of the lights reflecting like water on my silk. I hang there underneath Kim (whose work name is Polaris but who I have always called Kim). The dive has put merely the lightest of strain on my frame and the ache in my shoulder is no worse. Still, I wait, to see where everyone is when we flash out over Union Square. I settle in, working steadily. I'm not winded, I feel good. I drink air out of my facemask.

Out over the lights of Union Square.

I am somewhere around fifth, we aren't in neat rows anymore. I feel strong, I've got my pace. I look for Cinnabar. He has dropped back, but he is high, high above me, *shanglou*. When my kite was new, I rode up there, *shanglou*. We are a spume of color, a momentary iridescence over Union Square, and then we are back over The Swath. I am climbing, forcing myself up. I feel rather than see someone swoop underneath me. Not Cinnabar, he's waiting. I push a bit, counting under my breath as I pass floaters. One, two, three, four, five, and we are out in the lights again. I have held on to fifth, and am even with most of the pack, but Cinnabar is above me, and Riptide has taken low lead. She was the swoop I felt. Kim is slightly in front of me, and in the light, she dives a bit and then rises like a sailfish, sprinting forward. She arcs up and starts to fall into acceleration, but a blue kite flown by some rookie whose name I don't remember neatly sideslips across her trajectory, and she must spill air to avoid. And then we are over the darkness for the second and final circuit. Again I climb. One, two, three, four, five, and we are over Union Square. I am higher than Kim and Riptide, but Cinnabar is somewhere higher above me, so I continue to climb. Something, some sense, tells me just as we are going into the dark that he is diving, and I dive, too. A kite has to come in at least two hundred meters above the ground, that's for safety. I am ahead of Cinnabar, I don't know how far. Everyone is diving through the dark, ahead of me I sense the rookie, she is in my arc. I let my wings catch lift just for a second, feeling the strain, coming just over the top of her, and for a moment I'm afraid I've cut it too close.

But I'm over her, and I feel her lose it for a second, brake, spill air, startled and trying to avoid a collision that would have happened before she had time to react. The wind is so cold across my wings. I'm taking great gulps of air. My shoulder is aching.

Something moves faster, over me, Cinnabar, and I dive deeper, but the frame of my kite begins to shudder and I'm afraid to trust it. I ease up on the dive, trying to power-sprint forward, but my shoulder twinges and the kite shudders and is suddenly clumsy. Something has given in the left side of the kite. Frantic I spill air, lose speed and altitude as wings flash around me, over me, under me, but the kite is under control. I come into the light, crippled, losing altitude. The others flash across the finish. By the time I get to the finish, I'm at 150 meters, too low. Cinnabar Chavez is taking his victory lap as I touch down, running, feeling the strain in my knees of trying to slow the broken kite, then walking.

Georgia, tall and heavy-hipped, my tech, takes the kite, lifts it off my shoulders. She doesn't say anything. I don't say anything. What's to say?

I feel heavy, dirt solid. I take off my facemask and gulp air. God, I'm tired.

Cinnabar is flushed with winning, he's been having a so-so year, he's been hungry for a win. But everybody is always hungry for a win. He comes and finds me where Georgia and I are packing up my broken kite. It's nice of him to think of me. He's a little embarrassed to be standing there while we finish crating it, it takes a long time because part of the frame is bent and it won't fit.

I compliment him on his win and he says *"Nali-nali,"* making a don't-talk-about-it motion with his hand, looking away across the park. But he's wound up. "Come meet me, by my crew," he says, too tense to wait, and why should he when there are people waiting for him?

So I go to find him, and a bunch of us go out to a place on La Guardia where we can drink and make a lot of noise. It's called Commemorative, and fliers hang out there. Cinnabar's picked up two guys; a blond and an ABC, both clearly bent. So's Cinnabar. They aren't fliers, of course. Cinnabar has the hots for the blond, whose name is Peter. He isn't tall, not for, you know, a non-flier, I'm not good at heights, maybe one-seven? And not heavy. But next to him Cinnabar looks like nothing but bone and hair. He's pretty, too. And scrawny Cinnabar is not pretty.

They're talking about going to see some jailai, but I figure they don't need me along, so I say I'm tired and have to get up tomorrow to look at the kite. The ABC says he's tired, too, which surprises me.

"How are you getting home?" he asks me. It's the first time he's spoken to me all night, but then Cinnabar and the blond have been doing all the talking.

What's he think, I'm going home by limo? "Subway," I say.

"I'll walk with you," he offers.

There are the usual protestations, the don't gos and if you musts. Then I find myself going down the stairs and out onto the street with this gay ABC in his mirrors and his sharkskin jacket. ABC all act like their faces are made out of ice. We walk west. I'm not sure of his name, sounded like the blond kept calling him Rafe or something, so I ask and he says, "Zhang," real flat.

Fuck it, I think, I didn't ask you to take a walk.

We cross Sixth Avenue, and then all the sudden he says, "I'm sorry I wasn't synched with you tonight."

I'm a little caught off, so I say, "Were you synched with Cinnabar?"

He shakes his head. "Israel."

Israel? Who the hell is Israel? It must be the rookie. "She's okay," I say, "once she has some experience." The kind of stuff one says.

"She was okay until you dusted her," he says.

Neither of us says anything more until we're in the lighted subway. Then to be polite I ask, "What do you do?"

"I'm a construction tech," he says, which is hard to imagine because he doesn't look or talk like the kind of person who spends his days on construction sites, if you know what I mean. He takes off his shades and rubs his eyes, adding, "But I'm unemployed," then puts them on.

I mumble something about being sorry to hear it. He's chilly and distant but he keeps talking to me. I can't imagine him wanting me to invite him home, and I sure as hell don't want to anyway. So I look at the track.

Down the track I see the lights of the train.

"When the kite went," he says, "did you think about that *zhongguo ren*, Kirin?"

The flier that just died. That's why he wanted to be synched to me. "No," I say, "I didn't think about anything but getting it under control. You don't have much time to think. Did you ever fly a kite?" As if I had to ask.

"No," he says.

"It's not a cerebral activity," I say.

The train comes in fast and then cushions to a stop. We get on. He doesn't say anything else except "bye," when he transfers for Brooklyn.

I always forget that half of the people who watch us fly are waiting to see us die.

I *was* thinking, or rather, I had something in the back of my head when the kite shuddered. I was thinking of my first year flying the big kites. I was flying in the New York City Flight, it was only my third or fourth big race and it was the biggest race I had ever been in. I was a rookie, the field was huge—twenty-six fliers. I didn't have a chance. And I had a crush on Random Chavez. Five fliers were killed in that race.

That was the first time I ever felt afraid to die. When the kite shuddered, whenever something goes wrong and there's that instant of having no control, I'm always back at that race.

I ride the subway home to Brooklyn. It's not far from the subway to my building, but I'm glad to get to the door. Safe in the entry, safer in the elevator. I've been living here for two years, and the building knows me. I have an affinity for machines, call me superstitious but I think it comes of spending some of my waking hours as a kind of cyborg. I think my building likes me.

I get in the apartment and the lights come on dim, I get myself
something icy and bitter to drink and throw on my rec of that race.
The chair hugs me, and I prop my feet up and the apartment
darkens. I don't synch in with anyone, so it's like watching it from
a floater keeping pace with the race. Like being God. Or maybe
God is synched in to everyone. Same thing, though, total objectiv-
ity. I'm back in the thick of the pack, flying about ninth. Jacinth
has just snapped a connection, and her kite falls behind, then
clear, then disappears off the screen. She dropped out just before
anything happened.

Fox is in seventh, Random Chavez is in fifteenth, Fox dolphins
to rise over Watchmaker and just as she begins the swoop over
him she slips it—looks away, loses her concentration, who knows.
Anyway, she clips Watchmaker and he waffles, would have pulled
out of it maybe but he loses too much speed, and Malachite, in
front of me, tries to pull his kite over and they collide, I hear the
rip of silk, even though flying is really too noisy to hear anything.
I don't remember anything after that, but in the tape I slip
sideways, inside, and shoot past them. The pack parts around
them but Random is boxed, so he drops nose first into a steep
vertical dive deep into a crack between fliers and is gone underneath all of us, streaking, until he tries to pull up. If his kite had
been braced the way they are now he'd have made it, but that's
five years ago, and the silk sheers under the stress, and he tum-
bles. And he was dead. And Fox, Malachite, Hot Rocks and
Saffron were dead, and Watchmaker never flew again. And Angel
finished seventh.

I run it through a second time, in synch with Random Chavez.
I just want to feel the plunge when he saw no way through ahead
of him, but being in synch is really not the same as being there.
I don't see the space he knew was there, feel only the amusement
park sensation of drop, the shoot and cut out when the kite starts
to tumble.

The lights start to come up, but I want it dim. I think about my kite, and where I'm going to get money to fix it. Mr. Melman of Melman-Guoxin Pipe is one of my sponsors, I'll go to him, sign a note. Oh damn, I'm so deep in debt already. But it's just a frame and silk, everything else would be all right. And I have silk.

In Chinese, silk is *si*, first tone. Four is *si*, second tone—as in Siyue, April (fourth month). Death is *si*, third tone. Four is a bad luck number for Chinese. But I'm from Brooklyn.

My synch numbers pick up for the next race, but it's always like that after a crack-up. People like that ABC in Commemorative. I fly a careful race, come in fourth, just out of money. Afterwards I think that if I'd flown a more spectacular race—worried less about winning and more about how it synched—I could have picked up my numbers. But how can I go out and fly without planning to win?

It's two weeks before I hit money, and that's only second. Pays rent for Georgia and me. Nights I'm out with Cinnabar. He's been hitting, and his synch numbers are way up, with the requisite loss of privacy. He needs somebody to go places with, he surely can't pick up some bent groupie if a synch crew is likely to come out of the walls and snatch a shot or an impression.

Cinnabar and I share a fondness for kites and a reverence for his dead brother. Late at night, clear out to the vacuum, we talk about how wonderful a flier he was with that combination of seriousness and hyperbole the sober can't abide.

We go out dancing the night before the New Haven Flight, Cinnabar in his brother's red sharkskin jacket—so what if it's five years out of date—and me in a black dress cut so low in back you can see the copper bruise of the synapse junction in the base of my spine. We go to someplace way downtown in the area they're reclaiming, you know the place, where you have to fit the mix to get in. The building likes us, I told you I have an affinity for buildings, because we just saunter past all the people it won't let in and whoosh, the doors open. Dancing with Cinnabar is nice, on the sultry numbers I don't find myself regarding the middle of his chest and on the fast numbers he isn't as stiff as most straights. Or maybe it's because he's a flier.

We dance a lot, and then get synched, I see the crew from the vid. Some woman from the vid drags us in back for an interview with Cinnabar, and we sit in the kitchen. Cinnabar's soaked with sweat with his hair all stuck to his face and I can feel it trickling down my back. She asks all the silly questions about racing and if he expects his streak to continue. He just shrugs. It always amazes me that they ask that, what do they expect people to do, say yes?

She asks how he got from Brooklyn to flying kites, and he tells her Random was his older brother. I tell her that the jacket is Random's, I figure it will make good media. The kitchen is environmented, and it's *cold*. Cinnabar puts the jacket around my shoulders and sits with his arm around my waist. I can feel his fingers on my ribs tapping nervously. She asks us if we're ready for the New Haven tomorrow and says she notices we aren't drinking. I tell her it's too many calories. I don't tell her we're iced to the gills (no calories in chemicals.) But we're iced enough that we aren't really watching what we're doing.

She asks Cinnabar if he feels he has a good chance for the New Haven, and he makes like to spit over his shoulder, just like they do at home to ward off bad luck, then he says, "Gargoyle's going to beat me."

We all laugh.

Citinet calls me after the synch is on vid next evening, but I'm already out at the park, patching my old Siyue. I'm hoping the vid exposure will raise my synch numbers, but I'm thinking about my kite, not my publicity. I don't even see the vid until later, and in it we look like a couple of seventeen-year-olds cuddling, which hooks all the romantics, and there's that red jacket going from owner to owner to catch all the disaster addicts. Just shows nobody cares about how you race so much as what they think about your life.

There are bunches of people around my pit watching Georgia and me work, and another synch crew shows up. They want to know what it feels like to be racing against my boyfriend and how serious Cinnabar and I are. I say a race is a race and shrug.

"Do you think Cinnabar is right when he says you're going to beat him?"

I stand up and face the synch crew, put my hands on my hips. "Well, I'm going to try," I say, "but I'm flying a Siyue, and he's flying a Liuyue."

"What's the difference?"

"His is a newer kite," I say. "Now I gotta get ready for a race, si?"

They don't stop asking me questions but I stop answering. The pick-up chirps, and I leave Georgia testing systems.

"Angel," Cinnabar says, *"Esta loco aqui."*

"Aqui tambien amigo. I don't know how I can get anything done." It's so noisy I have to plug one ear with my finger. "We did good, huh?"

"No shit." He laughs. "Synch numbers are going to be great. Got an idea, going to send you the jacket, okay? Make a big fuss. Then, when you fly in that crate tonight, you make it look good, okay? Maybe somebody will pick you up and you can fly a real kite."

"Go to hell, my Siyue is a real kite."

"You like antiques."

"You're doing me a great favor," I say to him.

"Favor hell, the bigger this is, the higher my numbers, *comprende?"*

"Okay," I say.

Fifteen minutes later, as I'm putting on my facemask and getting ready to take the kite out, one of Cinnabar's crew arrives carrying the red sharkskin jacket. I make a big show of staring at it, then put it on slowly. Then I jog the Siyue out.

I'm out early, I need the time to remember I'm flying a race. It's cold up there, it feels good. It's empty, I take a lonely lap out across The Swath and Union Square. For the first time since I got out to the Park I get to think about the race.

I fall into line when I get back out over Washington Square, take one lazy lap with everyone. I'm back at eighth, Cinnabar is second. He'll go *shanglou* and so will Orchid. I haven't a chance against them if I fly their race, not in a Siyue. We flash over Washington Square Park. I climb a bit, but when we go over The Swath I put my kite into a long flat drive, pumping forward. It's not an all-out sprint, but I'm pushing faster than my usual pace. I ride far out, all the way down till I'm close to the two hundred meter altitude limit and when we flash over Union Square I'm low and way out in front. Everybody is still jockeying for *shanglou* which is ridiculous, because Cinnabar is going to be the best power diver, at forty-eight kilos he's got mass on his side. I'm using my light weight—damn few fliers lighter than thirty-nine kilos—and sprinting. I don't expect anyone to dive until we're over The Swath, but Israel breaks and is diving after me. As we go into darkness, the pack breaks above me.

Is that ABC synched with me tonight?

In the darkness. I climb a bit, maybe twenty-five meters. Kites are diving in the dark, and when we flash over Washington Square the second time, I'm third, and the field is a disaster. People are strung out *shanglou* to *xialou* and Orchid is first. Her kite is pearlized silver. She's in trouble because I know I can out-power her. I'm above her, she's down around bottoming out.

We go back into the dark. I'm pushing, I don't know how much longer I can keep this up. But I've made this goddamn race my way. I'm still third when we come out over Union Square, but three people dive in front of me including Cinnabar. I dive into the middle, still not as low as Orchid. She tries to dolphin up and rises into Medicine. We go into darkness.

It's the worst point of the race under the best of circumstances because one is half blind and acclimating, and the next floater is too far to see and I don't know what the hell is going on, but I know things are a mess. I feel someone over me, and Medicine and Orchid have to be tangled in front of me. The disaster lights go on and I have just time to see Orchid's kite waffle into Cinnabar and see the silk shred away from the left front strut. Polaris is above me coming down outside. Israel is coming fast inside me. I take the space in front of me, nose first and start a screaming, too-deep dive.

I know I'm below two hundred meters, but I'm more worried about pulling the kite out. My bones/frame are screaming with strain and the cross strut breaks away. I drop out of the harness to provide drag, and come into Washington Square too low, too fast. At twenty meters I try to throw the nose up, no longer trying to save the frame and the silk, and the frame distorts as easily as an umbrella turned inside-out by a high wind. *But the silk holds* like a slack sail taking up air. I try to land on my feet, the ground makes my foot skip off it, I can't get far enough in front of the kite, the balls of my feet keep skipping off the pavement as I try to run, I tumble and the ground comes up hard. . . .

I come to when they're cutting the harness off. They cut off the sharkskin jacket, too, because I've dislocated my left shoulder. "What happened," I keep saying, "what happened?"

"An accident," Georgia says, "you're okay, honey."

They've given me something, because I'm way out to the vacuum, and I can't think of the questions I want to ask, so I keep saying, "What happened?"

"Orchid got in. Almost everybody's in," Georgia says.

"Who's not in?"

"Cinnabar," she says, "he went down in The Swath."

*   *   *

Well, of course, you probably remember everything else since it was all over the media. How Cinnabar Chavez broke his spine. That they did surgery, and that it was awhile before they were sure he would live.

He was in bad shape for a long time but he's okay now. He lives in Brooklyn with his lover, I still see him a lot. He doesn't fly anymore. Surgery is wonderful, so is therapy, and he's still a sweet dancer, but he couldn't trust his reflexes in a race. He has a job as a consultant for Cuo, the company that makes the big kites, and he does commentary for one of the big vid organizations. His income is steady these days.

Mine is pretty good these days, too. I fly a big black and red kite for Citinet; a Chiyue, the new one. My synch numbers are in the 50's, and my picture's on the front of *Passion* next month. I'm wearing the red sharkskin jacket—I had it fixed—and the article is titled "Gargoyle's an Angel!" which is kind of cute.

I fly better these days. Cinnabar bitches about it, he says I'm too far out in front of myself. Sometimes when he says that I think of bringing that Siyue in and trying to get in front of it to stop it. But that's what the people want, right?

Besides, I can't say it to him, but I'd rather be dead than not able to fly.

Baffin Island

Zhang

I am unemployed.

The man who hands me the application says, "Filled out one before." It's supposed to be a question. He doesn't look up to see my answer so I don't say anything. I hope my interviewer will be *waiguoren*—not Chinese. Or if Chinese, at least *huaqiao,* like me. Perhaps an overseas person will be more sympathetic to another overseas person, unless perhaps they have to prove that they're as tough as a Chinese with citizenship. You can never tell, but I always feel Chinese are the worst.

I sit at the carrell. Surname: Zhang. Given name: Zhong Shan. China Mountain Zhang. My foolish mother. It's so clearly a *huaqiao* name, like naming someone Vladimir Lenin Smith or Karl Marx Johnson. Zhong Shan, better known in the West as Sun Yat-sen, one of the early leaders of the great revolution in China, back in the first days, the days of virtue. The man who held up the sky, like a mountain. Irony.

But better that than Rafael Luis.

I give my address, really Peter's address out in Coney Island as I'm Without Residence. When one has no job one cannot afford the decadent luxury of paying one's landlord, and one must accept government housing or stay with friends or family. I have been staying with Peter for almost six months. Soon I'll have to apply for government housing, I can't keep living with Peter. Living in Virginia won't be so bad, it is only ninety minutes to Journal Square Station in New Jersey, lots of people do it every day. If one is unemployed, the train is free at off-peak hours.

IDEX: 415-64-4557-zs816. Trade Designation: Construction Tech. Job Index: Comex Constr., 65997. Comex Constr. wants administrative experience I don't have, but I have three years experience in construction. In school, I wanted to be an Engineering Tech and my math scores were good, but there were no openings that year. I have an Assoc. Certificate instead of the full Bach. Sci.

I should study on the side, teach myself, take the exam. I should. Maybe when I get a job, have a place of my own again, I'll study in the evening after I get home from work, spend less time going out, waste less time and money. I've said it before, every time I was without a job.

I hand my application to the man at the desk, he glances up at me, his lips move while he keys into the network and puts my application on file, then he peels the contact off his wrist. "Have a seat," he says. I sit and read my paper. The waiting room is large, large enough to be a cafeteria or something. There are a lot of people, twenty or thirty, but that's not enough for the size of the room. While I'm reading more people hand in applications, people waiting are called for interviews. I want to check the time, but why? Time doesn't matter to me, I'm unemployed.

Still, I notice it is almost an hour before I'm called. My interviewer is a woman, a *huaqiao* I am sure. She looks too New York to be from China itself.

"Zhang," she says in English, "you have insufficient administrative experience for the job you are applying for." Her hair is

pulled smoothly back from her face, shining as if lacquered. It is
caught with a red cord, and the short ponytail curves under like
a "c."

I nod.

She looks at the screen in front of her. "You have turned down
two alternative offerings."

"I had hoped to stay in New York," I say. One job was in
Maryland, the other was in Arizona. If I turn down another
alternative it will go on my record. Perhaps she won't have an
alternative.

She says to me in Mandarin, "You are from New York?" She
is clearly *huaqiao,* she has a New York accent.

"I'm from Brooklyn," I say.

"I'm from Brooklyn, too," she says. "You like Coney Island?"

"I am staying with a friend, but I like it much better than I
expected," I say. "When I get a job I expect to get a place there."

"I am thinking of joining a co-op group," she says.

So nice! An interviewer has never talked to me so personally.
No doubt it is because of the address, but maybe she'll give me
the job. I study her. Watch her bite her bottom lip in concentration. She has lines at the corners of her eyes, but the way she
frowns makes her look very young.

Finally she sighs. *"Bukeqi, tongzhi,"* she says. I am sorry
citizen. "I cannot give this to someone with so little admin experience." The polite address softens the blow.

I nod. I understand. I thank her.

"Let me check new listings," she says, "Sometimes things do
not get posted." She feels bad, she wants to offer me something.

It is a kindness, I should not expect anything but I cannot help
hoping. She is relieved she can do something. I watch her flick
through entries. She stops and I become more hopeful. She reads
quickly then flicks expressionlessly forward. At each flick she
shakes her head slightly. Her lips are the perfect rose of a doll's
mouth. They shine like satin. She begins to flush, she is not so

happy now. Something is wrong. An alternative, not a good one, I am sure. Do not offer it, I think, pretend you didn't see it.

She straightens her shoulders. "Zhang, I have a job available for someone of your experience," she says, in English. She names a salary which is three times my present salary. She doesn't look at me. "It is working at a research center, the salary is high because you will have to live at the facility, but it is a six-month contract with the option to extend or renew."

"Where is it?" I ask.

"Baffin Island."

Baffin Island? Where the hell is Baffin Island?

"It is in the Arctic Circle," she says primly, handing me a card with the specs, but not looking at me. "You have forty-eight hours to decide on the job, should you want me to hold it for you, otherwise you risk someone taking it from you while you make up your mind."

"Don't hold it," I say.

The Arctic Circle, Arctic Circle, Arctic Circle, the train to Brooklyn rumbles. We stop at Arctic Avenue, and then I realize it is Atlantic and I get out to transfer. It is my third alternative. If no one takes it in forty-eight hours, I will have turned it down. That means I will be dropped from the category of prime candidates, I will only be offered jobs that have been available to prime applicants for fourteen days. No New York job will be available after fourteen days.

Why did she offer it? Maybe there is some rule that she had to. But who would ever know? It wasn't even posted. She knew I wanted to stay in New York. She was angry at something. She is a bitch. She has ruined my life. If only she didn't try to do me a favor. I would never have applied for so risky a position as the Comex Constr. job if they had had the Arctic Circle posted, for fear it would be my alternative.

I go back to Peter's. Peter is at work, he works in an office, doing paper sorting and filing for a dental clinic. I find beer in the box and sit down. Peter is supposed to get off work at four-thirty, but I'm not surprised when he doesn't get home by six. At nine-thirty he comes home. "Rafael?" he calls as he comes in, and the lights come up. I have been sitting in the dark.

"Hello, Peter," I say.

"What are you doing sitting in the dark?" He goes into the kitchen to put away groceries. I hear a low whistle. "Drink our dinner, did we. Good day at the employment office, no doubt."

"Celebration," I call, a little thick. "I think I have a job."

"Congratulations," he says, "In that case I don't care if you drank most of the beer." He sings something quietly as he puts things away, I hear him open a beer and he comes in to sit down. Blond Peter with his Eastern-European heritage and his easy, sleepy way. He is a good friend, bright yang to my dark yin. "Tell me the particulars," he says.

"It is a six-month contract," I say, "with option to renew or extend." I name the salary. His pale eyebrows arch, he is waiting for the punchline, but I draw it out, saying it is my third alternative.

"What's the kick," he says.

I smile. "It is on Baffin Island, somewhere up around the North Pole."

"Oh shit," he says. "You didn't take it, did you?"

"Not yet," I say. "There is a chance that during"—I check my watch—"the next forty-two hours, someone will snatch this wonderful opportunity away from me."

"You think maybe the salary will tempt someone?"

"No, do you?"

"It can't be that bad," Peter says gamely, "lots of people would be willing to do it for six months. Turn it down, you can stay here."

Good of him, the apartment is really too small for two room-

mates who aren't in love with each other. It is not that I don't love
Peter, I love Peter more than anyone in the world, but I'm not in
love with him. I was once, and he with me, but that was years ago.

"It's only six months," I say. "I'll use the extra time to study
for my engineering license."

"Six months in Siberia," he says. "Six months for you to brood
yourself into catatonia."

"But then I will have three alternatives when I get back. I can
get a job in New York." I am being very practical. "Besides,
catatonia is a symptom of bourgeois or maladaptive thinking,
something swept away by the revolution."

Peter is looking at me in a way that says he is exasperated with
me, that he doesn't trust me. Normally he would laugh, since we
are clearly maladapted by virtue of our preference. Angry, he
says, "Don't drink any more beer tonight."

"It's your beer," I say.

"That's right," he says.

And now we are both hurt and angry. He makes himself some
dinner, I am too drunk to be hungry. There is not much to say.
He goes into his room where he probably watches a vid, and I
make my bed on the couch and go to sleep.

I don't see much of Peter the next day, which is my fault. The
day after that I go back to the employment office. The Baffin Island
job is still posted. I take it.

Two weeks later, the first week in October, and I am sitting in
a copter. Five hours ago I was in Montreal, changing flights. Now,
since I only had a fifteen-minute transfer in Montreal and barely
made my plane, I am torturing myself about whether my luggage
was transferred. We will land in Hebron, Labrador. I have discovered that Labrador is part of the province of Newfoundland. I
have already heard my first Newfie joke. In Hebron they still have
the old-fashioned manhole covers that can be pried up with a

crowbar, big round metal things. A Newfie is jumping up and down on the manhole cover saying, "Sixty-seven! Sixty-seven!" every time he jumps. A man visiting on business stops to stare and the Newfie beckons him over, explains that what he is doing is a way of relieving stress. (This is told with a Newfie accent, every sentence ends with, "ay?") He tells the businessman to try. The businessman is not sure that he wants to, but slowly he is convinced to step on the manhole cover. He jumps into the air and says "Sixty-seven."

The Newfie says that he's got to put more into it (ay), really shout it out. So the businessman jumps and shouts "Sixty-seven!" He finds it is kind of fun, so he jumps higher, shouting "Sixty-seven!" louder and louder, until he's red in the face and his long coattails are flying. He jumps really high, shouts "Sixty-seven!" and the Newfie whisks the manhole cover off and the businessman disappears into the manhole. Then the Newfie puts the cover back on and starts jumping up and down shouting, "Sixty-eight!"

I wonder what Baffies do to American Born Chinese.

The field at Hebron, Newfoundland is small, most of the traffic seems to be freight. It doesn't have the usual amenities of public fields, there's no arcade of shops, and no vendors wandering around hawking things. It just slowly stops being an airfield and becomes a town. The town is all ancient pre-fabricated housing (the kind shipped on trucks and fitted together) but the units have been painted and added onto, sometimes fantastically ornamented in vividly tinted aqua and red aluminum and plastics. It is terribly tacky and antique-looking, but very very real. I think I like it. There is one little restaurant. Once I have convinced myself that my luggage has transferred, I go into the little restaurant. It is run by Thais, which surprises me, although I guess there are Thai restaurants everywhere. I order Thai-Moo Shu, and it comes, pork and cabbage in a spicy coconut sauce, wrapped up in a pancake. The restaurant has a screen door that leads to what looks like a mechanic's yard where a gray and white dog with pale eyes is tied to a doghouse made out of blue tinted chrome/aluminum, but the Thai food tastes exactly like it would at any little Thai hole-in-the-wall back in New York. The restaurant is filled with men and women in coveralls. I feel a little conspicuous, everybody knows everybody else, but the beer and the food are reassuring.

Maybe there will be a Thai restaurant on Baffin Island, too. If so, I will probably go every day for the whole six months.

My last flight is a copter, smaller than the one I came in on. There is no one on it except for myself and the pilot and co-pilot. I imagine Baffin Island will be like Hebron. I left New York at eight A.M., at 7:22 P.M. we land at Borden Station, Baffin Island.

The cold hits as soon as the door is opened, blown in by a shockingly cold wind that smells like water. It is minus three Celsius, and already it is black as midnight. There is nobody there but the crew that ties down the copter; the bright, white outside lights illuminate the copter, it casts long insect shadows in three directions. The only building I see is the research complex, I glance around quickly, looking for the town, but it's too cold to look much. I walk across the tarmac and into the research complex with the pilot and co-pilot. "It gets dark early," I say.

The pilot says, "Sunset was at fifteen-ten this afternoon." Five P.M. I think, then realize I'm wrong. Three o'clock. Sunset was at three, because we are north of the frigging Arctic Circle.

Inside the station is all smooth, clean white walls and blue carpet, very institutional and not shabby at all. There are big windows looking out at the tundra on one side, and over the bluff at Lancaster Sound on the other. The shore ice is whiter than the finest of sand beaches and the open water is shining like black glass.

For a moment I think that the woman who has met me is Chinese. "Hi, you're Zhang Zhong Shan?" she says. "I'm Maggie Smallwood, come on, I'll show you your room."

"Just Zhang," I say. She is Native American, Eskimo I sup-

pose. Her face is round and her eyes are slanted. She chatters as
we walk, she is the one that tells me the water is Lancaster Sound.
She uses words I have never heard, polayna, belukha, bowhead.
I finally figure out that belukha and bowhead are kinds of whales.

"You're studying whales," I say.

She laughs. "I'm sorry, we're studying belukha migration patterns and their mating rituals." She keeps talking as she opens
the door to my room. It is actually two small rooms, the front room
has a desk and two chairs, the back a closet and bed. The bathroom is off the back. There's no kitchen. I was expecting an
apartment, this is more like a dormitory.

"I'll bet you're hungry," she says. "I'll show you where the caf
is."

The cafeteria is full of people talking, playing cards, watching
vids. Very few of them seem to be eating. There is food to flash
heat, but Maggie tells me that during breakfast and dinner hours
the food is made fresh. The cost of my dinner is debited against
my wages, but it's cheap food. We sit down with a group of people,
all natural behaviorists: Jim Rodriguez, bearded, with straight,
pale-brown hair; Eric Munk, blond, but not so blond as Peter, also
bearded; Janna Morissey and Karin Webster (one has brown curly
hair, and one has straight short hair, but I cannot remember which
is which even though I can remember that the one with curly hair
has a narrow face and a tough way of talking and the straight-
haired one likes to dress pretty. I'm very bad with names).

"Your English is very good," Eric says, "Aren't you hired out
of New York? How long did you live in New York?"

"All my life," I say. "I'm ABC," I explain.

They don't understand.

"ABC," I say, "American Born Chinese. I'm from Brooklyn."

They laugh, they have never heard the phrase. I shake my head
in wonder.

They're all Canadians. They are naive in a nice way. There are
not many Chinese in Canada because Canada has not had a

socialist revolution, it's still a constitutional monarchy. This is probably a little like the U.S. used to be before the revolution. They ask me if I can speak Chinese, and how I came to be born in New York. I almost tell them only my father is Chinese, my mother is Hispanic, but I don't. I've put my Chinese name on my application; I'm not going to loose the advantage of being Chinese, not even here.

They are all very nice, tell me about the complex. I tell my Newfie joke, and everyone tells Newfie jokes.

"How far away is the town," I ask, remembering Hebron.

"What do you mean?" Janna or Karin asks (the one with straight hair).

"The town, Borden Station, how far is it?"

Jim says, "This is it. There's nothing here but the station."

They laugh at my expression.

When I wake up it is still dark. Of course, it is seven A.M., not so late, but it is as dark outside my window as if it were much earlier. I stand and look out the window, there is nothing but the Lancaster Sound, far below me. I would really like a cup of coffee, I'm not accustomed to having to face other people before my first cup in the morning.

The room is warm, difficult to believe how cold it is outside. I keep standing there, half asleep, looking out at the landscape. There are so many stars! The sky is thick with stars, from glittering points to tiny scatterings. No moon. But the snow is bright, it must be bright enough to read a paper by. Right outside my window is tough, dried grass, then the steep fall to the water. There is a band of shore ice, like a long smooth desert from here.

Looking at the shore ice, I see it is not perfectly smooth. There are shadows. I can see very far to the water. I don't know if the shadows are indentations, cracks, or frozen waves. I have no sense of proportion, how far away is the ice?

How far away is the next nearest person? How far is Hebron? Montreal? New York? If there was an emergency here that we couldn't deal with, how long until someone could get here, how long until we could get to a hospital?

There are no edges to the landscape, no tourist lodges, no sidewalks, no ships, no aerials, no wires, no planes, nothing but gradations of white and blue to black. It has nothing to do with me. It is perfect, sterile, dead. I think I love this landscape. I know I am afraid of it.

I dress in pants and sweater and go to the cafeteria to get coffee. I will be working with Jim.

Jim is already there. He is wearing a pullover that looks like the top part of an atmosphere suit, which it is, complete with couplings. He has the hood pushed back. It makes him look like some sort of sea miner, or satellite tech, not like a scientist. He's big, with an open face and a kind of easy, aw-shucks way with people that emphasizes the dumb-tech look.

"Morning Zhang," he says. "You prefer Zhang?"

"Everybody calls me Zhang," I say.

He nods, slurping coffee. I sit down. He is eyeing me over his mug. "Nice sweater," he says, in that funny way people compliment you when they are really saying, "I don't know what to make of what you are wearing."

"Wrong, huh?" I say. It's just a sweater. It's woven in a sharkskin pattern, black, white and gray. It's good enough to wear out drinking or something, but it's still just a sweater.

"No, I mean, I just never saw one like that. It's not really sharkskin, is it?"

Of course it looks like sharkskin. "No," I say. "Wool and synthetic." Sweaters are big at home right now. What will he say when he sees the wine sharkskin sweater with the leather ties and mirrors? Obviously he will say nothing because obviously I will never wear it here. Maybe I'll send it back to Peter and he can get some wear out of it.

The woman with the tough face and the curly hair walks in and Jim says, "Hi Janna." I think, remember, *Janna* is the one with the curly hair, *Karin* is the feminine one.

Janna says, "Morning Jim, Zhang, I love your sweater! Is that what they're wearing in New York?"

Ah hah. Overdressed. "Well," I say, "It was when I bought it last winter."

"Karin will want one as soon as she sees it. But you're going to freeze." Janna stops and puts her hands on her hips. "Don't you have any winter gear?"

For the first time I think I jack Janna. Janna is tough, practical, no nonsense. That's her mechanism. Maybe Janna and Karin are a couple? "This *is* winter gear in New York."

"Well it's not winter gear here. You're supposed to be issued an ARC."

ARC. Artificial climate suit. What the rest of us call atmosphere suits. "I just got here," I say. "Maggie showed me my room and then the caf."

Janna looks at Jim, Jim shrugs. "He can't go out like that," Janna says.

"We'll have to find him something." Jim frowns. "He couldn't wear mine, it'd be too big, and I've got to wear it. Maybe Eric's. Is Eric going out?"

Nothing to do but ask Eric. We tromp to Eric's room, carrying our coffee mugs. Eric is asleep, after all it is only seven-forty-five. And dark enough to be midnight. Sunrise isn't until almost ten A.M. I have that disoriented sense of being up at the wrong time.

Eric says I can use his ARC if it fits. He hands it to me and I shuck my sweater. The air inside the station is cool but not cold. I work out a little, haul tools around all day, I can be casual about being bare-chested, especially next to Jim who looks big but undefined. If he worked out I could never compare with the width of his shoulders. Under his ARC what does he look like? Forget all that for six months, Zhang. It's a small place, people are in each other's laps. I am a monk in the service of research, and Jim is not my type anyway. I tug the ARC over my head, pull the hood off my hair. It is not a good fit, but it will do. It's too warm.

Jim nods. "Better."

Janna nods too.

Eric says, "Wear it in good health." He hands me the leggings and shuffles back to bed.

I look at Janna and Jim. "I think I'd prefer to put these on in my room."

Jim grins. "Yeah, probably."

I dress, feeling like I'm play-acting, and meet Jim at the caf. We walk down to the pool. Not a water pool, a vehicle pool. There's a cutter unit that looks like it's barely been used, it's not even dirty. I check it to make sure the seals have been broken, but actually it has been used before, so I load it in the back of the yellow floater. Then we load a couple of crates of pre-fab and I climb in the floater with Jim.

"Have you ever been under the ice?" he says.

Sure, I think to myself, I spend all my time under ice, usually up around Macy's. What the hell does he think? New York is a glacier? I don't know what he means "under the ice." I don't understand these people when they talk. "I just got here," I say.

"It's not so bad," he says.

Something never to believe, right up there with "It tastes just like chicken," is "It's not so bad." If it wasn't bad, they wouldn't have to tell me it wasn't bad.

We rumble out into the darkness and I can feel the force of the wind hit me and the floater; when Jim sets the hover he has to head the nose into the wind, but in my suit I'm not cold. If anything I'm a little warm. It's pretty. The sky is black, the land is white. It's so big and empty that it's scary. I wonder if I'm agoraphobic. Of course, I'm a city boy. It's not the space that makes me nervous, it's the absence of human reference. We head off, the nose of the floater about forty-five degrees left of the direction in which we are actually heading, so we are kind of skidding sideways. I glance back at the station, expecting reassurance, but we scoot over the lip of the big hill down to Lancaster Sound and the station looks smaller and smaller. So I look forward again, which is slightly less unnerving than watching safety recede.

Jim tells me about where we are going. We're heading for Halsey Station, which, when it is finished will be the first of a series of stations that will monitor belukha whales. It's under water in the summer, under the ice in the winter. "Why did you take this job, the chance to study in China?" he says.

"Nobody said anything to me about studying in China," I say.

"That's what the guy before you was out here for," he says. "He said your government wrote it into a hazardous contract, if you renew your contract you get some kind of chance to study in China."

I didn't really read the contract. All right, so you should always read a contract. "I'll have to look," I say. I don't believe it. They wouldn't give somebody a chance to study in China just for spending six months here.

"So why did you come? You don't seem very interested in the great outdoors."

I wonder what I seem like to him. He's a scientist, here because he wants to be, he must get pretty tired of techies who want to do their six months and go home. "It was my third alternative," I say. "I had to take it."

"You mean your government made you come here?"

"Not exactly." I explain about alternatives.

"Were you at all, you know, interested?" he asks. "I mean I know it's not New York, but like you said, it's only for six months and it's a change, you know."

"Yeah," I lie, "I thought it would be interesting. And I thought it would make me study for the engineering exam." He doesn't want to hear how horrible I think this place is, he chose to come here. And I should study for the engineering exam. There isn't much social life here.

"You should check out that education thing," he says. "Dennis only had to work a year and now he's in Guangzhou."

Stay here a year? It would be worth it if I could study in China. But I'm sure that it's more complicated than that, or that the regulations have changed. *Madre de Dios,* stay here a year?

"There's the station," Jim says. We coast out onto the ice and he points to something that looks like an old-fashioned lighthouse. The ice is run with cracks, long spiderwebs. And as we get closer to the station I can see how the ice has piled up around it. "Shit," he says, "we ought to clear that ice."

The ice has ground against the west side, mounting the side of the tower. We'd need a light-hammer. I mention that.

"There's one in the station," he says, "we have to clear ice every couple of weeks."

We park the floater on the ice and walk across to the station. Without the blow of the floater I can hear the ice groaning all around me. It groans like metal under stress, but there's *hectares* of it. Wind moan and ice groan, black sky and white-blue ice in the dark. We climb slabs of ice to metal rungs set in the side of the tower, and I follow Jim up to the top where he opens a hatch and we see the lit stairs curling down at our feet. He gestures for me to go first and closes the top after us. The wind stops and I realize I've been holding my shoulders tense. They ache. The stairs are a circular metal staircase in a reinforced concrete tower with a ribbon light down the wall, but ugly as it is in here it's better than out there.

Our steps echo as we go down. Underneath is a large space, maybe twenty meters across, with windows for the outer walls. It's bare unfinished concrete floor and ceiling except where someone has started finishing one of the walls in porcelain white. "The actual shell is raconite," Jim says. "We've got this level wired so the lights come on whenever anyone enters but then there are two more levels below us. The middle one isn't as finished as this one, the bottom is labs. I need some help setting up some stuff for a lab, then there's a building protocol you can use to do some work on the place while I run some tests. Ah, the hammer is under stairs, there's only one." He's embarrassed that there's only one, he doesn't want to tell me to do the ice myself.

"Well," I say, "that's what they're paying my inflated salary for."

He grins, relieved. He's a nice guy, big and wooly as a bear. "It won't take you too long," he says. "Just break up the top stuff and be careful not to cut too deep, remember there's water underneath. I'll be on the first level."

"*Meishi,*" I say.

"What?"

"*Meishi,* you know, 'no problem,' " I say.

"Is that Chinese?"

I guess it is, I never thought about it. Everybody says *meishi.* Except Canadians.

I hoist the hammer, brand-new, just like the cutter, but a little more used, and climb back up the steps with it. When I open the hatch the wind is still going and the ice is still groaning and creaking and my shoulders bunch up again. I close the hatch behind me and wonder if people get accustomed to this. Man is an adaptable animal, I tell myself, you'll get accustomed to this. I sling the hammer across my back with the shoulder strap and climb down. How am I supposed to use a hammer on a substance I have difficulty standing on? Cleats would help. Remember when back at the base to ask someone about ordering some kind of mountain-climbing boots. I wrap the contact round my wrist and jack into the hammer. Ice is freaky stuff, it's not like concrete because it's got a weird surface and the density is different. It's hard to judge how much headway I'm making, first I think I've done a lot and then when I look I haven't done anything. Then

I really whale and suddenly I've cut the surface too deep and the hammer is skipping all over the place.

Someone who knows what they're doing would finish a lot faster than I do, but in an hour I've cut away a lot of ice. I don't know how close I am to water and that makes me nervous, there are all these cracks on the ice and I'm not sure it's safe, don't people get killed out here? I walk away from the tower out on the groaning ice—I almost think I can feel it move—to the floater and pull the cutter out of the back. I walk farther out, about thirty meters away from the tower and jack into the cutter. I focus the beam as tight as it will go and aim straight down and in no time I've cut a hole straight through the ice to water. One meter before I register a change in density. The ice is about a meter thick. Well, a meter of ice isn't likely to dump me into Lancaster Sound. But if it stress fractures it would shatter spectacularly and I'd hate to be there when it happened.

When we get back to the base I'm going to do some reading about ice.

In the evenings I study engineering, and a letter to the Bureau of Education brings back the information that workers under thirty-five years of age who take hardship jobs for one or more years get preferential treatment when applying for school in China and qualify for loans to help with their education, if needed.

To go to school in China. Chinese citizens can take the entrance exams, and ten percent of the seats are open to overseas Chinese and foreigners by competitive exam. If I could get a B.A. Engineering in China I'd be set. I'd be able to get good work anywhere, in New York, maybe even in China. I could probably get a job and stay in it, I'd be assigned good housing, maybe after a couple of years I could live in Manhattan. Talk about luck, like winning the numbers. I begin to request math texts from the library so I can prep for the entrance exam.

Most days I spend at Halsey Station doing construction while everyone else checks recordings and makes observations. Maggie Smallwood tells me everything is going to happen in the spring, when the belukha and the bowhead mate. She says the Sound is just constant activity then. Even now the lights attract plankton and the plankton attract all sorts of fish. Everyone is nice, everyone is friendly, but distant. They're scientists, they have a mission. I'm a six-month techie, and although no one would say it, working class. Muscle rather than brain.

Still I hang around sometimes with a cup of coffee and listen to them talk about what they are doing. When Janna needs someone to label bottles I'm happy to oblige. When Jim's atmosphere suit—excuse me, his ARC—seems to have mike problems, I find the fault in the receiver and use one of the lab's microtools to repair it. Eric can never keep all of the tools he needs at hand, so I hang a toolholder over his lab table, like chefs use to hang pots and pans in a kitchen where they'll always be in reach. I hang a rack over Karin's and rig it so she can raise and lower it so her samples will be out of her way when she needs the workspace. Soon they're asking me to do little things for them and I'm busy all the time.

Then we go back to the base in the dark, and the evening is dark, and we wake up in the morning and it's dark, and since we spend most days under the ice at Halsey the only sunlight I see is the blue glow filtered through a meter of ice. Every couple of weeks I have to hammer the ice free of the tower and usually replace ladder rungs where it's torn them away—I never do get my mountain boots—and although I can't get used to the groan of the ice I look forward to it because I do it at noon, when the sun is above the horizon and the ice is blinding white and I feel surrounded by light. If it's after ten and someone mentions they left something on the floater I'm the first to volunteer to get it.

"Do you miss the sun?" I ask Maggie Smallwood. Maggie looks Chinese to me, but she doesn't act Chinese. She acts Canadian.

She thinks a moment, looking at the black windows. "Yeah, some. But after summer it's nice to have some darkness."

Summer. In July the sun never sets. "Is it warm in the summer?" I ask.

"Sure," she says. "There's grass and flowers and baby caribou. You'll see it. Wait, you won't, will you, you'll be gone in April."

"I don't know," I say, "I have to find out about this school thing in China."

"Great," she says abstractedly, then, "look at that seal!"

Outside the window a seal is coasting past, gray and sleek with a neat head like a cat's, looking in at the lights with its great almond eyes. Maggie turns to me, beaming from her round Eskimo face. "Isn't he wonderful?"

I've never seen a live seal before. "Yeah," I say, and then without thinking, "do they all look so sad?"

She looks at me oddly but doesn't answer.

Early in November we stand on the ice at 11:54 and watch the sunrise with the rest of Borden Station. The edge of the sun's disk flashes above the horizon for less than a minute and then sets. I watch the red sky darken. Tomorrow the sky will redden as if the sun will rise but then darken. This is the evening of a long night. Dawn is in February. The Arctic landscape is beautiful at night.

It just isn't meant for human beings.

Maggie's people have lived here for generations. She says I shouldn't worry about the darkness, but suggests full spectrum light therapy, so once a week I go to the clinic and get thirty minutes of full spectrum light. I feel foolish lying underneath the lights like a sunbather but the doctor explains to me how some people are more sensitive to light changes than others. "Do you experience bouts of depression in January?" she asks.

According to Peter I experience bouts of depression if I miss a subway connection. "Not that I noticed," I say, "but my friends say I'm moody." I smile apologetically.

She smiles back and says, "Why did you come here?" It occurs to me that in less than two months a lot of people have asked me that question.

I study engineering texts under full spectrum lights wearing only my underwear.

I work on construction on the first level and they work in the labs on the third.

So I cope, and people are nice to me, if distant, and it's only a year. It's a great experience, back in New York I'll be able to say, "When I was in the Arctic Circle . . ." One day Jim says to me, "I've got to go out on the ice, want to come? I could use some help."

I don't particularly want to go, I don't want to stay at Halsey all day. It will be an experience. It will make the time go faster. So we load gear into the floater and take off across the ice. We'll plant some pick-ups either in open water or drive them through the ice and then we'll come back. It will only take the morning.

Morning. It's not going to be morning until February. I keep thinking of it as "dark in the morning." I find myself waiting for it to get light. The doctor prattles on about the need for something to focus on, a goal. It seems that the reason the scientists are less likely to have problems with depression is because they have an obsession and that orders their *Umwelt,* their self-world. We live in the same physical space but our feelings about it make us order it differently. Maggie Smallwood tells me that her ancestors used to be able to draw marvelous maps from memory but that their hunting-grounds were always drawn disproportionately large. That's because in their *Umwelt,* those were the places where their lives were lived, and everything else was thought of in relationship to them. I think if Maggie had to draw a map, the largest place on it would be the open water of the Sound where her beloved whales live. Her whole life is organized around whales. Her lab is where she organizes her data on whales, so in a way that's where the whales are. If she goes someplace else, she's away from her whales, out of her normal world. She would probably be homesick.

When I look outside the window, I don't see whales, I see dark. This place isn't even in my *Umwelt*. Skimming across the ice with Jim I look out across the empty land. It has been a full moon for six straight days. It never sets, never rises. Sometimes it's east, sometimes it's north, sometimes west. It's hard to believe we are on earth.

We go farther away from Borden Station than I have ever been. I tell myself it doesn't matter, Jim has done this before, we'll get back. I could walk back across the ice if I had to. I realize that this morning I don't care. I'm too tired of it all to care. I am along for the ride.

As we go Jim explains that the ice we are on is called "fast ice" because it is shorefast, meaning it's attached to the shore. We'll cross the lead (that's a strip of open water) and then we'll be in "pack ice" which is ice that's floating. Ahead of us the ice changes abruptly from white to black. We come closer, the ice beneath us shading from blue-white under the moon to gray. Behind us a long streak of darker gray marks where the floater has crossed, and then we cross to the black ice. Jim shouts, "The lead!" over the sound of the floater. We're over open water. Across the open water I see more ice, rough and tumbled, not like the ice we just came over. Floating free. As we cross I see that between us and those mounds is a flat skirt of ice. Big flat gray plates that have ridden up over the edges of other big flat plates so they overlap. "Nillis ice," Jim explains, "when it does that it's called 'finger-rafting.' "

Why?

Jim turns the floater west and we run along the lead for about twenty minutes. He's watching his location on the board and when it satisfies him he cuts the motors and together we manhandle one of the pick-ups—with their pointed noses and tail-fins they look like old-fashioned missiles—and heave it over the side. It disappears into the water, heading straight down to anchor in the

bottom and monitor the area for animal life. Jim jams the floater
back into forward and makes a wide turn that kicks up the black
water and we head back the other way, east. With the full moon
hanging above us we can see quite clearly, but it's hard to tell how
near or how far things are. I know we came over a kilometer across
open water, but the ice shore could be just twenty meters away.

Jim cuts north towards the pack ice, but we run for over twenty
minutes before we reach it, then we're on the flat sheets. The
floater skims. There's no snow, this far north is a desert, it rarely
snows. We ride over a lip of bluish-white ice and then it's like
riding rough seas as the floater bounces over the terrain. Jim runs
fast but steers carefully, the floater could ram a spire of ice. We
rise over a lip—

A stomach-lurching drop of about a meter and a half and we
are in a lead. I yelp and grab and Jim looks surprised. He turns
us sideways in the lead and slows down. After a moment he sees
a gap in the pack and we're headed north again. This time we go
a little more cautiously.

I do not say anything. Jim does not say anything.

We are on the pack ice when Jim says, "This is close enough.
Cut fast, the pack is running east."

I climb out and he hands me the cutter. There's no sensation
of movement, the pack feels like solid land. "How fast are we
running?" I ask.

"I don't know," he says, "pack ice runs irregularly. Don't
worry, the floater will keep us oriented."

I wasn't worrying, but when someone tells me not to worry,
then I wonder. I want to cut a well of about a third of a meter,
it will take a few minutes. I set the cutter and start working while
Jim hauls the pick-up out onto the ice.

I cut through three-and-a-half meters of ice before I reach
water, that's pretty far for a cutter because I can't go down with
it. My arms are tired from suspending the cutter above the hole.

Jim heaves the pick-up into the hole and lets go, we hear it splash below.

"One more," he says, "let's go."

I climb in after him. "Is it in open water?" I ask.

"I don't know," he says.

I can only hope.

Off across pack ice, but slowly because the leads we find close up in front of us. The wind is high and as we watch the narrow leads become gray. I have never seen water freeze as I watch. I am not cold, not in my suit, but I can feel the wind hit me.

Jim is careful, we mount ridges of ice slowly. He calls this "close pack," and watches the location on his board. It feels to me as if we are going diagonally and I ask if we are going south. He says no, that the pack veers about thirty degrees off the wind. He skips us over narrow leads, running us fast enough that we don't have time to sink before we hit the other side. Finally, near a lead, he stops.

"Not open water," I say. I don't like cutting through this.

He shakes his head. "Make it quick, we're drifting.

"Could we heave it into the lead?" I ask.

He squints, looks back down at his location on the board. "Yeah," he says, "we could."

I climb out and he passes the pick-up to me, then while I hold the nose and he holds the fins, we set out under the night sky. We have to go slowly, the footing is uneven and we have to climb over boulder-sized chunks of ice. The edge of the lead is not even like the bank of a river. The lead is almost a meter below us and the "edge" is an irregular slope about a meter wide. The lead is gray, nillis ice that gently rises and falls. The ice looks like grease. Because I suggested using the lead rather than cutting, I go down the slope, gingerly, supporting the nose of the pick-up. I wedge my feet against pieces of ice and say, "I've got it." I take the weight of the pick-up, bent awkwardly towards Jim.

I feel as if I have over-balanced, my feet go out from under me,

I hit the ice hard enough to knock the wind out of me. Then I am under water. There's no air in my mask, which has shut off to keep the water out, and the suit is not made to insulate against ice water, so I feel the cold. I surface and flail for the edge, Jim is holding on to the ice, and I keep failing to reach far enough to grab the edge.

Get out, my mind is screaming. The slush is thick and gray and it sticks in clumps to my faceplate. I am not thinking that I will get out. Always before, when something happened, I have been afraid I would be injured, that it would be a long time before things would be okay again.

I am thinking, this is serious. I am thinking, I am not going to be okay. I realize, I don't care. Startling thought, that, I don't care. The worst that can happen is dying. The cold makes it hard to move, to swim, and I have half a notion to give in, but I am not sure how. If I give in, if I stop fighting, what do I do, tread water and look at Jim? Stop treading water? I flail and fight and watch myself as if from a great distance. I am trying to get out because it is too embarrassing not to. The truth is, I am not sure how to drown.

"Zhang!" Jim keeps shouting. I finally grab something. I can't get out, can't do more than hold on. For a moment Jim doesn't move, then he scrambles down and grabs my arm. I can't get leverage to get out, he can't find enough purchase to pull me out, but he keeps pulling and sliding, and I keep reaching for something to hold on to, and finally manage to get halfway out. My body is suddenly heavy, the way it feels after being in the water, and Jim helps me get the rest of the way up.

"The lead shifted!" Jim yells, although my mike is working fine and I can hear him clearly. "Are you okay?"

"Fine," I say, still feeling as if I am watching myself. "Where's the pick-up?"

"It's in! Are you wet?"

I'm cold, and I feel coldest around the waist. "No," I say.

"Are you okay?" He says again.

"Yeah," I say, "just cold."

"We better get back to Borden," he says. We make better time going back across the ice than we did carrying the pick-up and climb into the floater. I am curious about this not caring. I am aware that it is not a good thing, but it is a lot better than worrying.

"Damn," Jim says, "that was freaky! The lead shifted, I mean they do that, you read about it happening to Eskimo hunters, but I've never seen it happen. It just moved farther apart, like a goddamn earthquake. I saw you thrown in, just thrown in, wasn't a damn thing you could do about it, and if I hadn't grabbed that chunk of ice, I'd have gone right after you, and we'd never have gotten out!"

Jim talks except when he has to concentrate on the floater. I say, "Yeah," when I need to. I have nothing to say. The lead got wider, that's how I fell in. The lead opened up. It occurs to me it could have as easily closed.

Now that I am out of the water the suit is beginning to keep me warm again. My strange mood lifts suddenly, I am not the watcher anymore, I am Zhang, sitting in a cold ARC suit, wondering what it would have been like to have tried to come up for air and found only ice. My teeth start chattering. I realize I can't go home. I want very badly to go home.

By early December I have stopped studying. I always do. I do not like to study, I always tell myself I should, but then after a few weeks, I stop. Always before, I have slowly gone from studying five nights and going out two, to studying three nights and going out four, to not studying. Always before I have said that if I didn't have any distractions, I would study. Now there is no place to go, but I don't study. I sit at the window and look out at Lancaster Sound. Sometimes I watch the Arctic foxes, trotting along with their short legs nearly a blur of motion, and often after I see the foxes I go to the cafeteria and get a cup of coffee, sit and talk with Janna, or Karin, or Jim. But mostly the landscape is empty except for the slowly unfurling cliffs of the aurora borealis, glowing lavender and pink and pale green above the blue ice and snow. I see my own reflection in the window, so I turn off my lights and sit in the dark. I lose track of time. I discover that it's possible to listen to outside noises, and then the outside comes into my room. The wind is so constant that after awhile I don't hear it anymore, and then there is nothing to hear.

I am not adapting well, I know.

Once in awhile Maggie Smallwood comes to ask me to come watch a rec or a vid. "Corin is showing the rec he's put together on polar bears," she says, or, "It's a vid from the States."

So I go, and sit. If I can sit on the end I say I am tired and leave early. When Maggie traps me in the middle, then I have to stay to the end.

I am tired. All day when I am working, I want to sleep. I think about going to sleep. But as soon as I get back to my room, I am tired but not sleepy. The clinic sends me notes to come lie under the lights, but when I lie under the lights, there is nothing to do but study, and I cannot bear to think of my engineering text, so I stop going.

In my room I think about what I am trying to do. I am twenty-seven. I am thinking of trying to pass an examination to go to a university, so I may go to China and study engineering. Okay. Say I work very hard this winter, I study all the time, I pass the examination. Then I would go to China, where everyone wants to go. Old Mother China, where there is *possibility*. I would study for a couple of years in China, away from New York, in a foreign place—granted I am Chinese, well I look Chinese, and I speak the language, but I have never been to China. But I do this for two years. Then I have a choice, either try to stay in China, where I can get a good job, maybe become well-off. Or come back to New York, where I will be able to get a good job.

All of that work to make a little more money. But I will still be Zhang. I carry myself wherever I go, and it is myself I want to escape from. I hate myself. I hate this place. And I find it is very tiring to carry hate all the time. So I sit and listen to the night on the Arctic tundra, defeated before I start. And sick to death of all of it.

I remember reading about the first crew at Canalli Base on Mars, how they suffered from depression. I tell myself it's only dealing with an unfamiliar environment. But mostly I sit in my room surrounded by a wind I can't even feel.

Five of us go out to Halsey in the big floater, Jim, Maggie, Janna, Eric and me. I am almost finished with the construction on the first level, but all I can think of is the immense amount of work needed on the second level. I'll be gone before the second level is ever completed.

"Look at that ice," Eric remarks, referring to the ice piling up on the west side of Halsey Station. It is a lot of ice, but I cut Halsey free not too long ago (how long ago was it? Maybe sunset? A month?) I feel the implied criticism. "I'll take care of it," I say, and get out of the floater before anyone else. I go straight for the cutter, and wait for everyone to go downstairs, then back out of the warm light into the night. I start to work on the ice, which will come back again. And next winter, another tech will cut away the ice, and it will grow back. Each year they will cut away the ice, each year it will grow back, and eventually, when they no longer use Halsey Station, they will stop cutting away the ice, and it will erode the station away, and then there will be nothing here but the flat plane of ice, moaning with the cold.

And I am here, and it makes no difference. I have built part of this place, and someday it will be gone, so why am I here? I turn my back on Halsey Station and score wide shallow cuts in the ice. I cut Chinese characters, *"Wo zai jar,"* I am here. And then I use the cutter to smooth them over until it is smooth as glass, polishing away the traces.

"Zhang?"

Maggie is standing on the tower, lit from underneath by the light. She is faceless behind her face mask, hidden in her ARC, but I know her size and shape, her voice. It infuriates me to see another faceless person in an ARC suit. The Arctic makes people things. I do not answer her, but make abrupt, choppy cuts in the ice.

"What are you doing?"

I think the wind and the stressed ice sounds are answer enough. Then I think, damn it, I want to be in the wind. So putting down the cutter I take off my mask, pull back my hood. The wind is so cold it makes my eyes tear, the air is so cold it hurts to breathe, much colder even than going into the water. I open the seals, pull the top off. I don't care if I'm cold. The pain of the cold seems like the right feeling, seems real. I pick up the cutter and make a cut.

Part of me cannot believe what I am doing, but I have had enough, I want them to know I have had enough. "It's all shit!" I shout at Maggie. "This base, the polar bears and whales! None of it matters! We don't frigging well belong here! We are nothing! *Nada!*" Maybe I am posturing, but here in the wind I do not feel that. I cut through the ice, to the water underneath, a smooth shhhiffffzzz, as the laser hits water and vaporizes it. I start to cut a trench, burning along, but I cannot concentrate, so I throw down the cutter. I am talking, talking, talking, talking, but what I am saying does not seem important. Some of it is English, some of it is Spanish, my mother's language. I am talking to Maggie. I am talking to myself.

I am talking to the ice, and I am saying over and over, "I have lost my frigging mind, do you understand? I have *lost* my frigging mind. I have lost my *frigging* mind."

Maggie comes over and takes my arm and says, "Come inside. Come inside."

At first I think, no. But then I realize I am cold, and that I really want to, so I let her pick up my pull-over and the cutter and we go inside. Now she talks and I am quiet. "It's nothing," she says, "it happens in the winter. Come inside, have something hot, have some tea. The Eskimo call it *perlerorneq*, winter depression, it happens when it gets dark and you're unhappy, but now it's over, you're okay, you'll be okay. I'll make you a cup of tea, very sweet, here put this back on and get warm." To Jim and Janna, "Zhang is tired, I'll take him back, he's not going to work today. Don't worry, he's okay now."

Words wash over me, I don't care. I don't care, except I am so tired that I could weep. I wonder if I am going crazy, but I think that if I am, at least I will go home.

Maggie takes me back, and takes me to my room. She sits with me on my bed and tells me, "Right now, you are just sick of life, *perlerorneq*, but you'll feel better."

"I'm sorry," I mumble. But I have a feeling now, not anger. Underneath my tiredness I feel grateful. "Thank you," I say.

"Go to sleep," she says.

I sleep for sixteen hours, through the day and the next night. And when I meet everyone the next morning for breakfast, I am embarrassed, and they are all kind. I cannot look at Maggie Smallwood, so I don't.

Janna says, "It's hard for all of us, but for you, well, you didn't even want to be here."

"I don't know what happened to me," I say, penitent and confused. I go to work, and they keep me working on the third level, close to them, and they talk to me often.

Maggie talks to me, matter-of-fact. "When they had trouble with depression in space, they asked the Inuit Eskimo and the

Greenland Eskimo about *perlerorneq*. It's like a circuit-breaker. Now the Eskimo train research crews in space ways to deal with it. I learned about it in school, in my Native Studies course."

My unhappiness is still there, but it is gray, not black. I go back to the full spectrum lights, I study a little. Janna begins to teach me calculus on Monday and Wednesday nights, to keep me studying. I have taken calculus, and she is good at explaining, so it is easy. I do not talk much to Maggie, except to say hello. I am ashamed of my behavior towards her, but what is there to say?

So December passes. Christmas, a package from Peter, sweaters in the most outrageous styles, with little capes; all the rage, he writes. I give one to Karin. We exchange gifts, sing songs. It's not so bad.

We are expecting sunrise at 12:14 P.M. on February second. In January I study and wait through the days. I have the feeling that I have felt the worst and now it will be all right. I decide to renew my contract.

"Don't worry," Janna tells me, "You'll love the summer, a sun worshiper like you. Explorers used to wear felt blindfolds so they could escape the sunlight to sleep."

On January twenty-nine we are studying in the late morning. Eric is running an experiment at Halsey from eight P.M. until almost three A.M. and he needs a tech, so I won't go out to Halsey until later. Each day now there is a false dawn. The sky gets rosy and the sun threatens to rise, the stars paling in the south, but it doesn't quite come up. Still, I watch. Only four more days.

Janna is checking my figures, I am watching the horizon. Dawn seems so close, so possible. The sky is the pearlescent white of dawn, shading to pink, lavender, indigo, and then somewhere above, to black. The ice is the color of the sky.

And then, four days early, I see the edge of the sun, blinding, above the horizon. "Janna!"

She looks up and her eyes widen and then crinkle with delight. "Oh, Zhang, wonderful."

CHINA MOUNTAIN ZHANG   91

It's morning. I smile and smile.

"It's not a real sunrise," Janna explains, "it's refraction. The earth's atmosphere bending light rays. The sun is still five degrees below the horizon."

We sit in silence and watch the sun rise and then dip. In minutes it is over.

I expect to feel the weight of the night again, but no, the sunrise is enough. I can wait. I can study, I can pass the exam. And the second night is not so bad, never as bad as the first.

I have survived. And I think, finally, I am adapting.

Jerusalem Ridge

Martine

The little girl looks at me and asks, "What's that?"

"What?" I ask. The myth that all middle-aged women like children is just that, a myth.

"That," she points.

"It's a candle," the man working on the skid says. "Come over here, Theresa, I need you to hold something for me, okay?"

Clearly her father. They both have the same pale, washed-out look, like faded cotton. Newcomers. Maybe whatever life they'd been living before they got here washed them out that way. The little girl looks up at me, not sure what to make of me, then obeys.

I'm walking the perimeter, checking for an air leak. I know it's here, I just don't know where it is. We use a very old-fashioned way to locate leaks, whenever we get a flag that the air mixture is off somewhere in Jerusalem Ridge, I come out here and prowl around with a candle, using the flicker of the flame to find the leak.

Don't go looking for Jerusalem Ridge on your map, it's called New Changsha, or Sector 56/C-JRU, depending on whether your map is dated during or after the Cleansing Winds campaign. It's on the northern edge of the Argyre Basin in the southern hemisphere. JRU is actually the initials of the surveyor. Aron Fahey says the name comes from the initials, but I really couldn't say. Most of the people who were here thirty years ago and would remember have been relocated. Aron would have been nine then so I'm not sure he really knows. I came when they reopened the sector seven years ago and walked into a viper's nest of backstabbing and leftover animosities. Even now the Commune tends to break into two parts, the old people left who remember everything anybody ever did to anyone else during the campaign, and the new ones who left our mistakes on earth. The people who were kids during the campaign tend to stick with the new people.

These two are real new, transports. If I didn't already know, I certainly figure it out when the father carefully jacks the little girl into his troubleshooter. Kids don't get implants that young here; I don't think she's more than six. She looks younger than that, dressed in a red top that's been stretched out too much in the neck and is too small for her and pants too big. Cast-offs. He's wearing coveralls, regular issue. I find my leak and repair it. It doesn't take much to repair a leak; smear sealer on it, mark it for a structural check, although this one looks like someone slammed something into the wall—a common enough occurrence in the godown. While I'm waiting for the sealer to set, I watch the father and daughter. He's blond and sharp-featured, she has thin, limp hair that's no-color brown. She stands next to him without fidgeting, careful on her task. She seems to be concentrating more on him than the job; she watches him raptly, mouth open a little, the way kids do.

I leave before they finish their repair job.

When I get home, my separator is on the fritz again and I completely forget about them.

*   *   *

When I was a little girl I once walked two miles in my sleep. I'm just the walking sort. That was when there were still communes in West Virginia. I guess that's what I miss most, walking in West Virginia. After they put the train in, it wasn't the same. Then suddenly the place was crawling with New Yorkers, all looking for a clean place to live where their families could grow up in the country while they went to their good-paying jobs in the city. It was all cadres at first, and maybe a couple of green men. Officers, of course, common soldiers don't live that well.

I guess I became a soldier because when I was a girl that was the way to insure getting the best. That was right after the beginning of the Cleansing Winds campaign, when we were all trying to get back to the days when socialism meant something to the people. That was going terribly wrong and everywhere you looked people were getting in trouble for things that ten years earlier had been fine, like growing your own silicon chips and all the little backyard technologies. The Army looked like a pretty safe deal. I had a string—my uncle was a bird colonel and he got me in. I went in at fifteen. You could do that then. At thirty-five I had my twenty years, a failed marriage and about all I could take of the army. I went looking for West Virginia but while I had been gone it had somehow transformed itself into a copy of New Jersey, and I hadn't gone back looking for New Jersey. That's how I ended up on the settlement project on Mars. Patriotic Volunteers Turn Red Desert Into Productive Land.

But I was back to walking; besides minding my plot, my goats and my bees I walked the perimeter watching for leaks. Lenin knows it was hard. I thought I'd start a new life on Jerusalem Ridge, but I hadn't counted on the fact that wherever I went I'd still be there. And I hadn't changed just by getting on a shuttle and coming to Mars. I wasn't happy. I can't say it was a mistake, I wasn't happy on earth, either. But on earth at least I was comfortable. For a long time I wasn't comfortable on Mars. Six months after I got here I about made up my mind to go home, but

I kept putting off doing anything about it and now it's gotten to the point where it's easier to stay than to go.

I schedule my day based on what happens, sometimes I'm working at three in the morning, livestock makes its own times and doesn't really respect yours, but by four-thirty in the afternoon I'm often in the house. It is about four-thirty, a week or so after I first saw them, when they stop for a drink of water. I'm a bit off the tube, so they have had to walk, but I'm one of the last empty domes before the long stretch to New Arizona and it's not unusual for people to stop. We still don't have a surplus of drinking water. I always give, I never know when I'll be asking.

I wouldn't know him if it wasn't for the little girl. If he remembers me as the lady with the candle he doesn't say anything. Theresa, the little girl, stands half behind her father, shy in an unfamiliar place. He takes the glass, crouches a bit stiffly and offers it to her. She watches him as she drinks, as if this were something he has produced out of thin air. She hands him back half a glass, which he finishes, using her glass in that unselfconscious way parents do.

"Thank the lady," he says softly.

"Thank you," she says, and reaches for his hand.

"Going to New Arizona?" I ask.

"No," he says, "just in."

New Arizona is about nineteen hours away. Why did he take the child?

We don't know what to say to each other, and he starts to make the motions of someone getting ready to leave.

"Maybe you and the little girl would like something to eat?" It occurs to me that they're living in the dorms. What a shame to make that long trip and go back there to sleep.

He glances down at the top of her brown head, tempted I think, but shakes his head. "No, thank you."

"It's no trouble," I say, "I make soup to keep and flash and I just made a great, fresh pot. It's got to be better than dinner at the complex."

It's the little girl that decides him. She waits, neither hoping nor hopeless, just tired. "If it's no trouble then," he says softly.

The house is concrete, smooth rounded walls, like a hill. Inside it's all green and blues, probably because on Mars everything is red, a color I associate with politics. And I have plants, oxygenators. They take the strain off the recyc system. I've been here seven years, and done pretty well with my own side-business. I've nothing to do with the credit but spend it on the house. "I'm Martine Jansch," I say and stick out my hand.

"Alexi Dormov," he says. "This is my daughter, Theresa."

"Hello," she says, watching her feet.

"Hello Theresa," pleasant old-fashioned name, "are you hungry?"

"Yes," she says.

"Do you like soup?"

"What kind?" she looks up at me. Well, it was a stupid question on my part and a perfectly reasonable question on hers.

Her father doesn't know whether to be amused or embarrassed, and I like him for that. I don't like people who feel that strangers must be amused by everything that their child does.

"Bean," I say.

"I don't know," she answers honestly.

My kitchen is white and beige and blue with a wall full of plants. I pour Theresa a glass full of fruit juice and offer her father a beer, which he accepts with surprise and pleasure. I'm not showing off, I can afford fruit juice and beer.

"You live here alone?" he asks.

"Yes," I say, "but the telecom is set to open by voice and someone is always stopping by." For a moment he looms in my mind as this mentally deranged man who wanders around exposing his daughter to brutal acts of violence. Martine, I think, you have spent too much time alone. Not to mention that he's still clumsy in martian gravity.

He looks around, admiring the cool white walls with their strip of blue tile, the beige tile floor. Aron's wife makes ceramics and she made the tiles for me, then I installed them myself. "It's a big place for someone to live alone," he says.

"It's not so big. Two bedrooms, a front room and the kitchen. Although I imagine you're accustomed to more crowded conditions." I'm thinking of the dorms, of course.

"Yes, we are, aren't we, Little Heart." He ruffles his daughter's hair. "We've been living in Yorimitsu."

Yorimitsu, Yorimitsu. I've heard something about Yorimitsu. I don't pay much attention to news from home, it's always bad. "Something to do with Arizona, Colorado, Nevada, the corridor, Yorimitsu, isn't that . . ." I can't dredge it up.

"A resettlement camp," he says in the same soft voice he says everything.

People sent to develop the corridor near the end of the Cleansing Winds campaign. There weren't enough resources, they had to be resettled again, some of them spent years in resettlement camps waiting to be put somewhere. And Alexi Dormov and his daughter were put on Mars. Where is her mother? "This would seem big to you," I say.

"How did you come here?"

"Voluntarily. I retired from the Army," I explain. "I wanted something unstructured."

"You were in the Army?"

"Twenty years."

"I was in South Africa," he says.

Peace Keeping Force, volunteer. "Infantry?" I ask.

He shakes his head. "Atmosphere skippers."

Pilot. Well, he's short enough. I have the infantry's distrust for pilots; they tend to be hot-heads out to prove their righteousness by flying. I flash the soup and ladle it into blue and beige bowls.

Aron's wife, Chen, makes them as well. I think they're pretty, but
they probably don't look like much to someone fresh from earth.

I put tabasco on the table and when I put a few drops into my
soup they carefully copy me. Not everybody likes tabasco in their
bean soup but I don't say anything, I've no intention of embarrassing them. Alexi tastes carefully and then nods. "This is good. This
is really good, huh Theresa?"

She nods. The spoon looks too big in her hand.

"It has so much *taste,*" he says, "I thought the food in the
complex was pretty good, but this is really *good.*"

"Thank you," I say, embarrassed. It's just bean soup with a bit
of pork in it for flavor. Not even nine-bean soup like we used to
have when I was young. The food in the complex is filling; mess
hall food. But not what I would describe as good. Alexi has three
bowls, a bit embarrassed by his own greed. He so obviously enjoys
it that it's a pleasure to serve him. And Theresa eats almost all
her bowl and has a biscuit with honey on it. My business is bees,
the Commune sells Jerusalem Honey all over the quadrant. It's
how I can afford my fruit juice and beer.

Their presence wears me out. I'm not accustomed to company
and I got up at a little after four this morning. The conversation
wears dangerously thin, I'm not holding up my end. I take them
out to see my bees. Alexi carries Theresa who is stricken motionless with fascination and terror when I pull a panel out of a hive
and explain how I take out the honey. The bees, buttons of tiger
fur with glass wings, crawl in glittering, ceaseless motion.

Then we go to see my fourteen goats and I tell their names;
Einstein, Jellybean, Eskimo, Constantina, Miss Shapiro, Lucy,
Kate-the-Shrew, Lilith (who has the heart of a whore, although I
don't mention that), Hai-hong, Machina Jones, Amelia, Angela,
Carmin and Cleopatra. They jostle for attention, gently butting us
and trying to get into my pockets to see if I have anything. I feed
them for the night, and Theresa flings handfuls of sweetfeed into
their buckets, and she and they squeal with delight as they shove

and rear to get their noses in first, leaping over each other. Einstein does his trick, leaping high over Carmin and pushing off the wall to vault into the middle of the pack. Goats do well in light gravity, unlike cows, poor stupid things.

When Alexi carries Theresa back through the tunnel to the house she's heavy as a sack of grain, her pale sleepy face against his shoulder. I am drunk with the pleasure of showing them my little well-organized farm and the words pop out of my mouth, "Stay the night."

"Oh now we couldn't, we've put you out enough."

I regret the offer immediately and think to myself, why'd you make it if you didn't want to? Contrary as I am I insist more. He doesn't want to bed her down in the dorm, she's so tired she needs a quiet place to sleep and he has to be tired as well. The transport will be fine parked on my pull-off. I've a sofa that opens out to make a bed and an extra bedroom. Again it's the little girl that decides him. I expect that he'll put her on the couch, but he says they can sleep together in the bedroom. I'm relieved—once he says that, I realize that my offer could have been misconstrued.

He has to go out to the transport and get their little bag of things, then he sits her on the edge of the bed and pulls the shirt over her head. She is passive and limp, her head seems too heavy to support. He is matter-of-fact, helping her hands find the sleeves with an air of practice. Then he pulls the blankets over and sets the bed to keep her warm.

We go back out to the front room and have two more beers. I tell him a little about Jerusalem Ridge, find myself unexpectedly talking about what it was like when I first came here and so many people had been relocated that we had a severe labor shortage. He asks intelligent questions. He has been promised his own plot in three years, but I warn him that the way things get done around here it could be five.

He's thirty-four. I'm forty-two. Theresa is six-and-a-half.

We go to bed early. I lie awake, over-stimulated I suppose. I can't hear anything, but I feel as if I can hear them breathing. The house seems full. After a while the breathing turns into the ocean, and at four-thirty the bed wakes me and I have been dreaming of the Pacific. In my dream, the sky was full of crows.

My separator is on the fritz again. It is because it is built and programmed to handle five to ten cows and I have twelve nannies. It has the capacity to handle the amount of milk but I jury-rigged it to handle the nannies and it just breaks down all the time. I manage to get them milked myself and to start the damn thing manually but that means that a chore that should take twenty minutes takes over an hour. I get back in at six-thirty. My company isn't up yet, so I stir up biscuit batter. By seven the biscuits are baking, the second batch of coffee is ready. Alexi appears dressed at a little before seven-thirty, followed by Theresa rubbing her eyes. I serve biscuits covered with cheese and raisins, rice stir-porridge with milk, and fruit juice. I can't pretend I eat this way every morning, usually I eat a bowl of porridge and wash it down with coffee.

"Did you sleep well?" I ask, cruelly bright-eyed.

"Terrific. I can't believe you have made all this, what time did you get up?"

"Before five," I say.

"For us?" Alexi asks, conscience-stricken.

"Of course not, I have a farm to run. I hoped to get some honey ready to ship, but I'll have to call Caleb and tell him it won't be ready until tomorrow."

He asks why and I tell him about my troubles with my separator-milker manager system. While I talk I watch Theresa who has apparently never had biscuits with cheese and raisins. She eats her porridge for a while before working up the nerve to try it. Then she puts it down and I think she doesn't like it but after a bit she tackles it again and eventually eats half.

Alexi asks me questions about the system, eats a bowl of porridge and three biscuits, then polishes off what his daughter didn't finish. "Maybe I can fix it," he says, "I'm good at fixing things."

Fine with me. Theresa is excited about going to see the goats. I send him down to the goats while I call Caleb and explain that the honey will be late. When I get down to the goats Alexi is jacked into the system and Theresa is gingerly petting Cleopatra, who is pregnant. Five of the nannies are pregnant, which is going to cut down on my income for awhile, but I've decided to go ahead and have more space added to the farm so I'll be able to expand. Alexi has the absorbed look of someone jacked in, and Theresa seems happy so I decide to do bee work.

After an hour or so Alexi comes to find me. "I can fix your program quickly and it should be all right, but have you thought about when you have the new goats?"

I have but I don't like to. "I suppose I'll have to get a new system," I say.

He shakes his head. "I can modify the system, but it would take me awhile and today I have to get back to the complex with the transport. But if you'd like I could come back and do it, maybe on Sunday. I have Sunday free."

"I could pay you," I say. "That would be great."

"No need to pay, I owe you for all your hospitality."

We argue about payment, and finally I agree, stipulating that he and Theresa come for lunch and dinner on Sunday.

Then we all go back to the house and I walk them to the pull-off. He boosts her into the cab of the transport, swings in himself and closes the door. I stand politely and watch them off. Then, freed, I wander back to the house now given back to me. I strip the sheets off the guest bed and remake it, then I clean my kitchen, singing to myself. I work the rest of the day, checking my little bit of vegetables, cleaning the goat pen, and spend the bulk of the afternoon straining and cooking honey. It's good to be by myself.

I listen to music I haven't listened to in years, some things I always think of as West Virginia music.

In the afternoon I find myself planning what to cook for Theresa and Alexi. I have a fancy rice and bean dish, but if I'm going to make it there are a few things I want to buy. It's a bit of work. And maybe a cake. Theresa would like that.

Sunday they come at about eleven, Theresa first, skating down the corridor the way children and martian-born do, the way those of us who came to maturity on Earth never learn. Alexi comes after her, smiling. "Martine!" he says, "hello!" The cake is iced, there's a big pitcher of lemonade sitting on the table. Theresa is standing in the kitchen looking at the cake with white icing and strawberries sliced to make flowers on the top. Alexi whisks her up and says, "Look at that, Little Heart."

"What are the red things?"

"Strawberries. Fresh strawberries. We used to have strawberries when I was a little boy. They're wonderful."

Theresa has never had strawberries? What were things like in a resettlement camp?

We have rice and beans and then big slices of cake. Theresa wants a flower so I cut her a piece she can never eat but she makes a pretty good-sized dent. Then her father finishes it. For a little guy, Alexi Dormov can put away the food. He eats like he never knows when he'll eat again. Then he goes to work on the separator and I take Theresa out to the garden and teach her to pick beans. The dome is opened and the summer sun pours through the polarized glass. I bring Cleopatra in and ask Theresa to keep her from eating and the two of them run up and down between the rows. If Cleo drops a nannie-kid I'll name her Theresa.

I'm nervous with her; she likes me but I don't know how to act around a little girl. And I don't want to have to entertain her. But I don't have to, she's busy with Cleopatra.

After awhile I go to check on Alexi and bring him a fresh glass of lemonade. He's still jacked in, sitting mesmerized. He has a pad on his lap and he's scribbled some symbols down on it but he's not looking at it. I know reprogramming is complicated so I just wait until he notices me and jacks out. He grins and pushes his hair off his face.

"How's it going?" I ask.

"Okay," he says, "It's going to take me awhile. Is Theresa driving you crazy?"

"No, she's playing with one of the goats."

"Just my luck, my kid's best friend is a goat."

A world of regret in that comment, although he says it lightly enough. When his smile disappears and his face is still for a moment I assume he's thinking of Yorimitsu. I almost say, "Kids are resilient," even though it's one of those fallacies like middle-aged women liking children. But that's not what he's thinking at all. "Martine," he says, "they're going to transfer us again, and I don't know what to do."

"What?" I say.

"They're going to transfer me again. Isn't it enough to send us to Mars?" He never raises his voice, it is easy to miss the despair in what he says.

"They're shipping you off Mars?" I ask. I can't imagine where else they would send him. Or why.

"No," he says, "not off Mars. They're talking about the water reclamation project down at the pole."

"What about Theresa?" I ask. Life down at the pole is primitive and dangerous.

"I don't know," he says. "They haven't really said we're going yet."

"What makes you think they're going to send you," I say, and realize as I say it that it sounds as if he's some sort of paranoid.

"I *know*. I've been through this now four times. I know when they're going to ship us off." He balls his fists and puts them together as it all boils out of him. "First Geri and I volunteered for resettlement in Nevada because they were going to send us anyway, then the water dried up and Geri got dysentery while they were shipping us to Yorimitsu and I gave her all my water and even some of the baby's but she still dehydrated and died. I volunteered for South Africa because I thought that a veteran would be treated a little better and because they were criticizing me for my attitude after Geri died—I thought I didn't want Theresa to grow up with a counter-revolutionary father and now it doesn't matter at all because everybody's just embarrassed about the whole Cleansing Winds nonsense. When I came back they put us in Buffalo. Then when we were in Buffalo they started all this nonsense about Mars. I thought, I'm a vet, Theresa's six, they won't uproot us again. But they did. And now they're talking about the water reclamation project at the pole."

"They won't send you, they couldn't send a man with a six-year-old daughter," I say, thinking that the Commune couldn't possibly.

"You don't understand," he says, "we've no *guanxi,* no connection, no string. Everybody just wants to get rid of us. We're human trash. Disposable. Less useful than goatshit, because you can dump that back in the soil."

The Commune won't send them, I think. How would you feel if your wife died of dehydration, I also think, and what kind of society allows that? The Commune must be better than that, must be better than earth if that's what earth is reduced to.

I hear the sniff and look around. Theresa is standing there holding on to Cleopatra. Cleopatra looks at us with golden eyes expressionless as agates. Theresa rubs her nose with her arm and rubs her eye with her fist, crying and trying to be quiet and trapped between backing away and coming towards us. Did she hear? Or did she just fall or something?

"Baby?" Alexi says, "what's wrong?"

"Are we going to move again?"

"Oh, baby," Alexi says helplessly.

Theresa is easily consoled, but that afternoon she pesters her father. She tries to pick up Cleopatra—possible because the gravity is weak but not probable because Cleo isn't interested. I don't think Cleo is likely to get hurt, even if dropped, but a flailing hoof could hurt Theresa so I finally have to put the nannie up. Theresa plays awhile but is clearly bored and pesters her father some more. At dinner she doesn't want soup, just cake, and bursts into angry tears when told that they can't stay the night.

"We're a little monster tonight, aren't we," Alexi says.

He carries her out to the scooter and puts her in front of him on the seat. I walk down with them, mostly because I am so eager to see them go and don't want them to know. I send them home with soup and cake.

The program on the separator isn't finished and Monday morning I milk by hand and manually start the separator. Then I check my bees. I'm creating queens to sell, feeding larvae royal jelly. I have to keep them separate, of course, no queen is going to let my royal larvae live in her hive. The little unit that controls environment has gone on the fritz. It's a cheap little unit, it wouldn't cost anything to replace on earth but we're moving away from opposition, when earth is closest to Mars, to conjunction when Mars is on one side of the sun and the earth is on the other side. I'll order by transmitter but it will probably be about eighteen months until we start getting regular shipments. It's a twenty-six-month cycle from opposition to opposition and the shipping window is about eight months, we've got another month and a half, but many of those ships already left earth. And right now I'm going to lose some of my royal larvae.

I wonder if Alexi could fix it and decide to have him look at it when he comes in the evening to finish the separator.

*   *   *

He comes alone this evening. Forgive me, but I am relieved. "Where's Theresa?" I ask.

"At the creche," he says, "sometimes I need a little time off."

I realize that I'm alone with Alexi for the first time and I'm nervous. My hand smooths my hair. I'm eight years older than Alexi and not interested. I don't want him to think I'm interested, I want to be friends. I'm sure he's not interested either, so why am I nervous? "Have a beer," I say.

"Let me get to that separator," he says.

When he is finished he says he has to get back, has to get up early the next day and all, but he does stay for the beer, sitting in my living room with the little environment unit. "I can't fix it," he says, "it's all fused inside."

"Have you heard anything more?" I ask.

"About being reassigned? No." His voice is soft and curiously flat. "But I've talked to some of the other guys and they think that the Commune probably wouldn't send Theresa to the pole."

I am relieved, I wanted to deny that anything could go so wrong, and now I learn that I was probably right. "I think that's true," I say.

"So I'd probably go on a two-year assignment and she'd stay with the creche. That's not so bad, I haven't been much of a father. It's just that the separation is bad for her, she's already withdrawn and immature—at least that's what all the counselors say. She's shy, but so was her mother and after all the moving around. . . ."

"They wouldn't send you and leave her here," I blurt out.

He shrugs. "They'll say it's temporary and that some sacrifices have to be made to open up Mars. I hate to leave her, when I came back from Africa she didn't know who I was and then she had tremendous separation anxiety." His soft voice goes on and on and I discover that the flatness is really bitterness.

I didn't ask you to come here, I am thinking. I didn't ask you and your daughter to stop for a drink of water. And at the same time I am understanding why he takes her with him when he goes to New Arizona. He talks about temper tantrums in the creche when he leaves. I think of her behavior yesterday, when she was upset, the tantrums and tears.

Finally he doesn't say anything more. The silence is thick, but I can't think of anything to say into it. He finishes his beer and says, "I'm sorry, I didn't mean to dump my troubles on you like that." But he's only apologizing because he's supposed to, when he leaves he looks around my house, and then he looks at me as if he hates me. It's not fair, I am thinking, I worked for this. My life wasn't easy either. I don't walk him down to the pull-off where the motor scooter is parked.

When I go to bed and set the alarm for five, I realize that I forgot to thank him for reprogramming my separator.

McKenzie comes Monday, Wednesday, Friday and Saturday to pick up milk. She gossips a bit, I look forward to her coming. She helped me impregnate my nannies. (My billies are just company for my nannies, I get seed from earth.) I tell her about Alexi reprogramming my separator.

"Would he do it for someone else?"

"Sure, he doesn't have a business. It would help him generate credit for when he's assigned a plot." Actually I have no idea if Alexi would do it.

McKenzie has wild curly hair and a stub of a nose. She brushes her hair back. "Nearly everyone who has goats has a separator programmed for cows," she says. "I bet a lot of them would love to have their systems converted."

"I'll ask him and let you know," I say. Then, because the subject of the Dormovs makes me uncomfortable I ask her about the last council meeting.

"Boring. I'm stepping down, I'm sick of it. I don't know where they're going to find a landholding newcomer to take my place." She starts the pump and my milk is drawn into her tank as we talk. "It's nothing but a headache," she says. I've told her this for years.

The council is twelve people; by common consent, six are people from before the shutdown, those who went through the Cleansing Winds (including Aron Fahey who is sort of unofficial head) and six are from after. I'm one of the oldest newcomers, they used to ask me to be on.

"Maybe I should serve a term," I say.

McKenzie laughs, and then looks at me quizzically when I'm not laughing. "Martine," she says, "you're not serious?"

"Well, if it's not me it'll be that horse's ass Waters." Lilith butts me and I reach down and fondle her long, leaf-shaped ears. She spreads her legs to brace and lowers her head a bit in pleasure. Maybe I should get a cat, I've got a family of mice in my garden. Some things come from earth whether you want them or not. "Do you know anyone whose cat is going to have kittens?"

"Sure, I'll bring you a cat. Are you really going to run for council?"

"Maybe," I say. "Bring me a calico, if you can." Calicos are usually female. McKenzie asks me why I'd serve and I tell her I guess that I can't keep letting other people do all of the dirty work. Which isn't true, I could go the rest of my life and let them worry about who gets how much land and air and water. When she leaves I go back to the garden and check the CO_2 levels in the air. I open the dome and the normally blue sky is red with the violence of a dust storm. The sand shushes softly against the dome.

Alexi Dormov, I'm doing something. That will wipe out the anger that was in your face when you left last night. I'll deny that I'm joining council to help you and Theresa, but you'll know. You'll be grateful, aware that you misjudged me. I feel a surge of self-righteous anger, how dare you look at me and think that I have it soft.

At the same time I know that I'm being the perfect martyr. "You're pathetic," I say out loud. Who is this Alexi Dormov that his opinion matters so much? I'm angry all morning, and I make the mistake of working with the bees. Sure enough, I get stung.

I don't see Alexi and Theresa for awhile. I talk to him by transmitter and thank him for fixing my separator, but it's a hectic week. Two air leaks, and that means the next council meeting they'll have to decide if the problem warrants an investigation. Three of my larvae hatch into queens and I box them and send them north to Calhoun to a woman named Jessup who does a little bee-keeping. Calhoun is out of the sector so she won't compete with my honey sales. My nannies start dropping kids and that means a lot of interrupted sleep. Cleo drops a nannie-kid. So do Hai-hong and Machina Jones. Angela and Lilith drop billies. I'll get rid of the billies as soon as they're weaned; someone else can raise them for slaughter, I'm a dairy operation. McKenzie brings me a tiger-striped female kitten, and it cries all night for the first four nights. It sounds like a baby and I grit my teeth and stumble around half-awake all day while it sleeps curled up in the strawberries.

And there is the council meeting. I haven't been to a council meeting in years. They hold them in the Commune cafeteria at the long hour on Thursday nights. I don't know who decided that since the martian day is thirty-seven minutes and twenty-three seconds longer than the earth day we should have the hour from eight to nine P.M. last one hour thirty-seven minutes and twenty-three seconds. If we're going to have a long hour I'd rather have it in the morning. But it's a bureaucrat's dream, an hour and thirty-seven minutes to have an hour meeting.

The cafeteria is red and gold. Across the back wall are the

words "The force at the core of the People is the Revolution" in English and Chinese characters. At least I suppose that's what it says in Chinese but it could say "Western Barbarians Have No Revolutionary Spine" for all I know. It's been there since the days of the Cleansing Winds campaign and nobody really likes it but nobody really has the nerve to suggest we take it out.

The meeting is opened and they discuss the problem of Aron Fahey's eldest girl who is twenty and has applied for a plot of her own. It seems to me that she should just go on the list like any newcomer but there is some question about whether the work she has done with Chen, her mother, qualifies her for any work credit or if that work goes to Aron and Chen's household. After twenty-five minutes of discussion they decide she should go on the list like any newcomer. It's almost eight-thirty. I usually go to bed around eight-sixty.

The meeting drags on, trivializing anything it touches. They talk about the two air leaks and decide not to investigate, but to put a note on the next calendar to see if there has been an unusual number between this month and next. That takes fifteen minutes.

Philippa makes a report stating that the Commune has been asked to come up with five people to send to the water reclamation project at the pole for two years. I sit up. Aron asks that a committee be formed to look into the matter and report back with a list of names for next month. He asks for volunteers. I stand.

"Martine," he says, "you wish to be recognized?"

"No, Aron," I say, "I wish to volunteer."

Aron Fahey looks perplexed and strokes his brown beard. "All right. Anyone else?"

No one else volunteers. Finally Philippa says she'll be on the committee, and Aron browbeats Cord into saying he'll join.

Then he nods at McKenzie who has been frowning at me. She stands and announces that she'll be stepping down next meeting and that the seat is open. I stand again.

"Martine?" Aron says, sounding anxious.

"I would like to announce that I am interested in taking McKenzie's seat." I sit down. Then it occurs to me that this sounds peremptory so I stand, "Unless the Commune finds someone who would be better suited, of course." I sit back down. My face is calm, my knees are shaking.

"Okay, it's on the record. If there's no further business?" Aron dismisses the meeting. It's eight-seventy-five.

McKenzie makes her way over to me. "Martine," she says, "Martine." And when she has my elbow, "Why this sudden interest in politics?"

"Maybe I'm tired of having no one to talk to but goats," I say.

"And whose fault is that?" she says.

"Obviously I'm not going to disagree with you."

It is four-thirty in the afternoon and I'm in the kitchen weighing the kids on my kitchen scale when my transmitter clicks open and Alexi says, "Hello, anybody home?"

"Yeah," I say, "what's up?"

"Theresa and I are on our way to New Arizona on a run and we thought we'd stop and say hello."

"You're at the pull-off?"

"Right."

"Just come on in, I'm in the kitchen."

"What's that noise?"

The noise is the clatter of Theresa-the-goat and one of the billies' hooves tapping against the tiles on my kitchen floor. "Come in and see," I say.

I stay in the kitchen, but I am bursting with things to say; about the chance to start his own business adapting the programs on other people's separators, about the council meeting.

"Hello," Alexi says from the doorway, "the door was open— oh, my, Little Heart, look at this."

Theresa pokes past his legs and sees the kids. I am weighing one, two are standing in the middle of the floor. They stand and the little billy waggles his head. Theresa kneels down, amazed. Then the kids bleat and wheel and bolt under the kitchen table. I take the one I have out of the bag I put them in to weigh them and put her on the floor. She scrabbles as I put her down and jets directly towards Theresa then realizes her mistake. She tries to veer, slides into the wall with a thump and bleats. The two under the table answer back and she scrambles to her feet and joins them.

"What's this?" I say, "new clothes?"

Theresa is wearing a yellow shirt and a pair of pale blue coveralls. She has barrettes shaped like rabbits. The difference is amazing.

"They let me have my first draw," Alexi says, over the sound of goats.

"I didn't know you were earning credit," I say.

"Newcomers earn a luxury allowance," he says. "I finally earned enough to get something. I got them a little big, so she can grow a bit." His voice is a little questioning, looking for approval.

"That's good," I say. I've never bought clothes for a little girl in my life—ask me about goats, I know a lot about goats.

"Well, we can't stay long, we're supposed to be on the way to New Arizona. He shifts from one foot to the other. He's still in the utility coveralls the Commune issues and since he's small, they're too big.

"I'm glad you came by," I say. "Listen, I was talking to McKenzie, she picks up the milk delivery, and she thinks that a lot of people would be interested in having you adapt their separator programs. It would help you earn some credit, you could use credit when you get your own place."

"Okay," he says, " 'Resa, we've got to be going."

She is halfway under the table and doesn't pay much attention. I am surprised at how blasé he is about my suggestion.

"I'm sure that there's more than separators that need to be

adapted, you could probably get quite a little business started."

He nods pleasantly. I bite off the impulse to add that my honey business has made all the difference, paid for all the little extras in this house.

"Have you heard anymore about reassignment?" I ask.

"No, just that they've got some sort of committee to handle it. Theresa, come out of there, we have to go."

"I'm on the committee," I say, sharply.

"What? *You* are?" he says, and I feel as if I really have his attention for the first time since he walked in. "Why?"

"I volunteered."

Goats run across the kitchen floor and Theresa backs out from under the table, blue bottom appearing first.

Alexi and I are looking at each other and my heart is pounding. He is looking at me and what is he thinking; what right does she have? Is he wondering if this is some sort of declaration I am making? Is he angry at me? I want to look down and I can feel heat in my face.

"You didn't have to do that," he says.

"I'm running for a position on council," I say, "it will help to look as if I am involved."

He looks away first, perplexed. "Oh. I didn't know you wanted to be on council."

"There's a lot you may not know, Alexi," I say sharply. Only afterwards do I realize that he might mistake that to mean something about my feelings for him. Which is not what I mean at all. And then suddenly I am tired of them. I want to be finished with this conversation, I want them out of my house. Theresa has gotten one of the nanny-kids to stay still and she is petting it.

"What's its name?" she asks.

"Theresa-the-goat," I answer. "It's Cleopatra's baby." I meant that to be a surprise, a big deal, but it comes out matter-of-fact.

"That's my name!" Theresa says.

"How many people are they sending?" he asks.

"The request is for five, but the committee hasn't met yet."

"Is it two years? Really?"

"I don't know," I answer, "Philippa is going to send me the notice, but I haven't seen anything."

"Come on, Theresa," Alexi says, "we have to head on to New Arizona." But the peremptory note is gone from his voice. He's off balance.

"Can Theresa-the-goat come with us?"

"No," he says, "she has to stay with Martine and Cleopatra, she's only a baby."

"Can she come to the transport with us?" Theresa begs.

"No," I say, "but she'll be here when you get back." Theresa skips and bounces in the martian gravity. Alexi alone seems strained. He opens the hatch on the transport and lifts Theresa in and I see a big duffel bag behind the seats. I'm surprised only because I remember how little he had the first time they came; a little bag with a nightgown and a change of clothes for Theresa, a change of coveralls for himself.

He is looking at me oddly, and I think he is going to say something. But apparently he changes his mind and says, " 'Bye Martine, thanks for everything." Then he grabs the handle by the door and swings himself into the cab.

Theresa waves energetically and blows me a kiss, but I see only Alexi's profile as he starts the transport and shifts into forward.

Another air leak, this one comes in at about ten-thirty at night and it's after one when I find it. When I first started it took me six, seven hours to find an airleak, but by now I know where to look. Still, I'm worn out when I finally get to bed. I wake up from a dream of forests and squirrels; the red fox squirrels from where I grew up, big-eyed and leaping from tree branch to tree branch. I am standing in the passageway that leads from the house to the goat yard, standing barefoot in my nightgown. I haven't been sleepwalking in years and it scares me a great deal.

The committee on the allocation of people for the water reclamation project finally meets. Cord has been unable to make time until a week before the next council meeting. He doesn't bother to hide his irritation at being on the committee. He's middle height and stocky, an old-timer. During the height of Cleansing Winds he was publicly accused and convicted of anti-revolutionary behavior in one of the infamous "People's Trials," a polite euphemism for trial by unruly mob. He was badly beaten, I'm told. It explains his attitude toward the Commune.

We don't like each other. Cord doesn't really care for anyone, he and his wife are still married but the gossip is that their eldest son sleeps in the front room so his father can have a room away from his mother. I don't care for Cord because when the Army moved against the W.P.B. (Winds of the People Brigades) we arrested people who'd run those trials and I'd seen the Army allow them to be tried by the same mob. That eye for an eye justice doesn't seem right to me. As an officer I allowed it because it served as a kind of catharsis for the people, but Cord reminded me of decisions I'd never been proud of.

Philippa is a teacher, a newcomer; she's been here six years. She's married to an old-timer, a man twenty-five years older than she is. She's in her early thirties but her hair is graying and she wears it pulled back. It's a matronly look. I don't know her very well, our paths don't often cross. We were in the dormitory together or I wouldn't know her at all.

First we discuss the requirements, or at least Philippa and I do. Five people to be sent to the reclamation project at the pole. It's understood that landholders don't go. What would happen to my goats, or Philippa's corn if we were gone for two years?

"So it'll have to be five from the dorms," Philippa says. "And it probably should be newcomers who've been here a year or less since the others are eligible for a holding after three years."

"But we never have a holding ready," I point out.

Philippa shrugged. "We might."

We have a list of all the newcomers who've been here a year or less. There are four. Alexi's name is first on the list.

"Well, that's four," Philippa says. "What happens if we can only come up with four?"

"This man, this Dormov fellow, I know him," I say. "He's been relocated four times, he's a widower and he's got a six-year-old daughter. The counselors on earth said that all this dislocation was bad for her."

"But we've only got four," Philippa says. "Besides, he'll earn credit. They get hazard credit. That'll help him get started when he gets back, and we'll keep the daughter at the creche. What I'm really worried about is that there's only four. New Arizona will give us hell if we don't come up with five."

"So much for equality," Cord mutters.

"What?" Philippa says.

"Send the newcomers. It's like a draft. The people like Aron Fahey never go."

"Aron Fahey is a landholder," Philippa says.

"So who's to say he's any better than this comrade with the daughter?"

Cord is an unexpected and not altogether wanted ally.

"So you think landholders should be considered, too?" Philippa says dryly.

Cord sits up, "Yes, I do." He looks straight at her, malice glinting. "I think you, Martine, and I should be considered. And the Fahey clan and the Mannheims and everybody else."

"I suspect that would be thrown right out of council," Philippa says.

"Perhaps it should be brought up, anyway," Cord says.

"Well then, why don't you make the report," Philippa suggests.

"I'll do that," Cord says.

And that is the committee meeting. I don't know what to do.

Cord's idea is ridiculous. He'll raise it, everybody will be made uncomfortable. Aron or someone will quote "The good of the many outweighs the good of the few." And the four newcomers will go. We'll discuss what to do about the fifth person and what will happen if we only send four.

I go home. I'm tired and I keep thinking about the look on Alexi's face the night he came alone to fix the separator. How different he turned out to be than the way I thought of him when I first met him—the hidden bitterness, and the awkwardness the last time I saw him.

The bitterness doesn't surprise me, scratch the surface and it seems a lot of people are bitter.

And why not?

I go down and feed my goats. I spend some time down there just fussing so as to be near them. I like goats. People have the wrong idea about goats, about how stubborn they are and all. Goats are just smart, that's all. My goats are mostly even-tempered and they aren't hard to deal with. God knows, a person who can't outsmart a goat is in pretty sad shape. I am cleaning up, shoveling manure to be used to make alcohol for fuel and as fertilizer when I think again of Alexi swinging up into the cab of his truck, the easy strength in martian gravity. And I think of the duffel bag. He could probably get nearly everything they own in that duffel bag.

What if he has? What if he doesn't plan to come back?

Martine, use your head, this is Mars. Where could he go? New Arizona where my beer comes from? Then west to Wallace which would put him on the big north-south artery. Sure, he could run, but where would he get fuel? (He's a clever man with machines, but a thief?) And even if he could get fuel, there's just no place to run. There aren't more than seventeen, eighteen million people on the whole planet. He's not stupid, he wouldn't try it. When they caught him they'd take Theresa away from him, execute him if he wasn't lucky, sentence him to reform through labor if he was.

That would mean mining, or the real hazardous duty on the water reclamation project for the rest of his short life.

It's foolishness to think he would run. I think about Alexi too much, I have middle-aged fancies. He's young and attractive and friendly and yes, I'm lonely and goats aren't enough.

Nonetheless, I fret.

Tuesday he should be back from his run. Surely they'll stop on their way in. At least say hello. Tuesday comes, slides past. In the evening I call the dorms. Dormov isn't in, he's running late. Do I want to leave a message? No, I don't want to draw attention to his absence.

He could have had transport trouble. They could have stayed an extra day because he has a little money in his pocket. She has a cold, maybe, or ate something that disagreed with her. Or he did. Although the thought of him sick and them alone bothers me. I imagine him sick in a dorm and Theresa in a creche in a commune in New Arizona.

He wouldn't run, I tell myself. He knows they'd put a bullet in the back of his head. Theft of a transport, he *knows.*

It's hard enough to protect myself from my own stupidity, how can I be expected to protect myself from someone else's?

Wednesday evening, watching the kitten chase across the floor, batting a plastic spool across the tiles. The transmitter says, "Martine?"

"Alexi?" I say.

"Yeah."

"You came back." The words are out of my mouth.

I expect him to laugh and say something about it took them long enough, but instead he just says, "Yeah." It's like a sigh. It's full of regret, it doesn't pretend that we don't both know.

"Are you at the pull-off?" My voice is so matter-of-fact, I'm astounded. None of my relief is in it.

"About twenty minutes out."

"Come by, you can sleep here tonight."

"Okay," he says. "Theresa's asleep."

"Okay."

And then I'm in the kitchen, digging out tofu, bread, running down to the garden for a tomato and parsley and a handful of strawberries. I cook onions, slice in the tofu, the tomato and the parsley. Basil from my kitchen plants. I slice cheese onto brown bread, slice strawberries to put under the cheese, put it on a plate to flash when they get in. And coffee; decaf, or I'll be awake all night. I scrub the cutting board, the sink, the counter, water the plants, clip off the dead leaves, fill twenty, then twenty-five, then thirty minutes with activity. Finally, thirty-five minutes later I hear him call, "Martine?"

"In the kitchen," I answer.

He comes to the kitchen door. Good thing it's martian gravity because he is carrying Theresa and he looks done in.

"Sit down," I say.

Theresa has her head on his shoulder and opens her eyes only when he shifts her to put her down. I put the bread in to flash, wait for the timer and then pull it out. "Theresa," I say, "have a little bread and cheese and then you can go to sleep. Careful, it's hot."

I pour him coffee and heap food on his plate, pour coffee for me and take some bread and cheese. At first he picks at it, then he eats. Theresa eats half of her bread and cheese and then I take her in to the guest bedroom and take off her shoes and socks, her coveralls and top. Tonight she can sleep in her underwear. I turn the bed up warm and tuck her in and she falls asleep as I am sitting on the bed.

When I come back, Alexi is sitting at the table, the plate pushed away from him, his hands wrapped around an empty coffee cup.

"Thank you," he says. "I don't know how to say thank you."

"What made you come back?" I ask.

"I realized I couldn't do it. I thought, maybe in New Arizona, or in Wallace, I could slip into the free market or something. But it's not like earth, there's nowhere to go. I don't know what to do. And I kept thinking, you're on the committee, I know I've asked so much of you, but I thought maybe you could help."

I'm full of anger. Anger is boiling up inside me. Just looking at this man, sitting at my kitchen table, full of my food, asking me for help. I know that my anger is irrational, I know that it's the flip side of fear, but that doesn't stop me from feeling it.

"The Commune is supposed to send five people to the water reclamation project. We won't send landholders, because landholders are what make the Commune work." Anger makes my words come out crisp and clear. "We'll have to send newcomers and if they've been here for more than a year and we send them, then we're making them wait longer to get their holding."

Alexi is looking at me, vulnerable in the kitchen light.

"Including you, there are four newcomers who have been here for a year. I brought up the fact that you've been relocated so many times and that it's not good for Theresa, but the committee feels that sending you will give you a chance to accumulate a good chunk of credit for when you come back and do get a holding."

He opens his mouth as if to say something, and then changes his mind.

"Right now, the committee is more interested in trying to figure out how to select the fifth person than it is in listening to why you shouldn't go, and I can't think of anything to say that will change that."

He nods. "Okay," he says.

There is a little silence.

"Okay," he says, "so that's that."

"There's still some things to try," I say. "I have an idea, but I don't think it will go. Just don't do anything until I try my idea."

"What is it?" he asks.

"There are some other people who might go," I say vaguely.

He nods tiredly. "And if that doesn't work, it's only two years." He is defeated. He says "it is only two years" the way I imagine someone might say, "Everybody has to die sometime."

But if it doesn't work, I have one more idea. But I'm not ready to talk about that, because I'm not really sure I'm ready myself.

Goats, leaks, bees. Bees, leaks, goats. My life goes back to its expected rounds. Alexi and Theresa come the following weekend. Theresa is hyper and unhappy on Saturday, but Sunday she is fine until it is time to leave. Alexi and I are pleasant to each other. We don't talk much about his reassignment but once he says, "After I come back from the pole . . ."

They go back to the dorm, Theresa fussing and crying. Monday is goats and bees. Tuesday is bees and goats. Wednesday I get stung twice. Well, I'll never get arthritis. I sleep badly, dream and dream but I can't remember what I dream about when I wake up. At least I don't sleepwalk. And then it is Thursday, time for the council meeting.

There is an empty chair at the front, McKenzie sits in the audience. Aron opens the meeting and says, "We can't have a meeting until we have a full council. We have one person willing to sit on council, Martine Jansch. Any other nominations or volunteers?"

Kepet Waters stands up, "I'm willing," and sits down.

McKenzie looks at her lap and frowns. She agrees that Waters is a horse's ass.

I look around the hall, I have no illusions about my own popularity. Alexi, I am surprised to see, is standing next to the door.

Aron says to me, "Martine, would you like to say anything?"

I think for a moment. I can't imagine getting up and addressing all these people, even though I know most of them. "I guess everybody pretty well knows me, Aron."

"Anybody want to say anything about Martine?"

McKenzie pops up, "I think Martine would do a fine job and she's the person I'd like to follow me." She pops back down, shoves her hands in her pockets and frowns.

Aron waits to see if anyone else wants to say anything.

"Kepet?" he says.

The only thing I have going for me is that I don't think I've made many enemies. Not that Kepet has real, honest enemies, but, well, he stands up and says, "I'd like to say a little, Aron," and proceeds to talk for twenty minutes about what this Commune could be.

Most of us had our fill of speeches during the days of the Cleansing Winds; particularly speeches about how wonderful things are going to be. People are polite while Kepet talks, and a few clap politely when he is done, but I think most of us tend to distrust a man who talks that much.

Still, I'm nervous when everybody votes. Kepet and I don't vote. I glance back in time to see someone hand a piece of paper to Alexi, who doesn't know what to do for a moment, then takes it. Back on earth you don't vote unless you're a party member, but here everybody on the Commune votes on Commune business if they're old enough to receive credit for their work. You have to be a party member to vote on anything out of New Arizona, but even many of the party members, like me, don't bother with most of that. Who cares who our representatives are at the Martian Congress, all the major decisions are made on earth anyway.

They count the votes, it's eight-forty-five by the time they're finished but for once I'm not sleepy.

I'm astounded when they read off the totals. "Martine has one hundred and eleven, Kepet has thirty-four." I had convinced myself I wouldn't win, that I'm too sour a woman. Kepet's speech has been more of a drawback than expected. I'm even more surprised that almost a hundred and fifty people showed up for a council meeting. There are over a thousand people in the Commune, over two hundred landholding families, but council meetings are late, they're boring, and most of us have better things to do with our time.

Aron says, "Okay. When Martine decides to come up here and sit down we can start the meeting."

I stand up, embarrassed, and take my seat at the front. I don't hear much for a few minutes, it's been a long time since I had to stand in front of people, or even sit in front of them, and that was when I was Captain Jansch and had a uniform to hide behind. I can't look up for awhile, but finally, while Aron is talking about reducing our water use—a topic of council meetings for as long as I can remember—I glance up to see a little group of four or five people leaving. In fact it doesn't look like anywhere near a hundred and fifty people are at the meeting.

"Okay," Aron says—it's a verbal tic of his, every sentence begins with 'okay'—"now can we have a report from the committee on the water reclamation volunteers?"

An unfortunate choice of words, that. Volunteers.

Cord stands up, "We are required to provide five people to work for at least two years on the water reclamation project. We thought that we should look first at the newcomers who have been here for less than a year, since newcomers who have been here for more than a year are less than two years from possibly having their own holding." Cord pauses for a moment. "At least officially."

There is a titter, everybody knows that it takes closer to five years to get everything together, approved and built.

"So, the problem is there are only four newcomers who have been here for less than a year. This means that we are still one person short."

I wait for the proverbial other shoe. Cord sits down and doesn't say any more and I realize he has decided not to go through with it. And that puts the burden squarely on me. There are some people who are more than two years away from having a plot of their own, who are not newcomers. I don't know how many there are, but I'm thinking of people like Aron's daughter. But Aron isn't going to want to think about offering Lucille Fahey a chance to earn hazard credit at the water reclamation project. So I have to be careful how to introduce it. In fact, I don't have any idea how to introduce it. I must wait for that magic moment.

Leo Mannheim says, "Perhaps the fifth person should be whoever has the least time here among the people who've been here for more than a year."

Philippa says, "Everybody who has been here for more than six months has been here for thirty-two months at least." Of course, because we always get newcomers at the beginning of the shipping cycle from earth. We used to get twenty, thirty people at a time, but now they go to communes which aren't well established.

Cord stands up again.

Aron recognizes him.

"Aron," Cord says, "Is it true that we consider everybody in the Commune equal?"

Aron nods. I look at Philippa. Her mouth is set.

"Well, has anyone talked to the newcomers about whether or not they particularly want to go?"

Aron says as if talking to a child. "No one wants to go, Cord."

"So we send the newcomers? Can we consider them equal?"

Aron looks pained. After a moment Leo says, "The Council has to look at the good of the Commune. Newcomers are least likely to be irreplaceable."

Cord says, "Well, Leo, I'm intrigued to find out that you consider yourself irreplaceable."

"I don't consider myself irreplaceable," Leo says, stuttering a bit. "I mispoke, but everyone knows what I meant, that landholders are unable to leave their holdings. Not like a newcomer, who doesn't have a side-business and isn't trying to keep something going. And it would give a newcomer a chance to accumulate a good chunk of credit before getting their holding. And that would be helpful. It's actually a good opportunity, better than just living in the dorms, trying to get established."

Cord nodded. "So, then landholders can't go because our pottery kilns will be empty and the rest of us won't have breakfast bowls. No one can contest the logic of that. But I've thought of another group which has more than two years until they get their holdings. Young people, like Lucille Fahey."

I see Aron's face tighten and I close my eyes. Cord has effectively ruined my chance of introducing the concept diplomatically. And when Cord says it I see Aron's face tighten and I know he'll stop this.

"Cord," he says, "the water reclamation project is hazardous duty. This Commune will not send children."

I look back at the door in time to see Alexi leave.

The meeting ends fifteen minutes later with the question of who is going to the water reclamation project still unanswered. The feeling at the end of the meeting is ugly.

I leave the cafeteria and turn left towards the dorms instead of right towards home.

I haven't been in the dorms in six years, and I've forgotten how sparse they were; two bunk beds, a couple of dressers and a closet. Bathrooms down the hall. They're mostly empty, when I first came they were full. The Commune had just started giving out private holdings—during the Cleansing Winds campaign the desire for a private holding had been seen as a desire to own more than other people, to have for oneself. Now they hold mostly newcomers and a few single men who for one reason or another live there. Most people live one or two to a room that used to hold four or more.

"Alexi Dormov?" I say a couple of times, and people point. I finally knock on a door. There's no answer. I knock again and say, "Alexi?"

After a moment I hear a rustle, a foot hitting the floor. Then the door opens and Alexi is standing there.

"Martine?" he says.

"I saw you at the meeting."

He nods, "Yeah. Congratulations. You look nice."

I'm a little dressed up, a cotton blouse and slacks. I look past him into the room.

"Come in," he says.

It's painfully bare. He lives alone, there's nothing on the walls. The bottom bunk of one of the bunkbeds has sheets and a blanket on it, but it's unmade. Everything else is neat as a pin.

I sit down on the bare mattress. He sits down on the bed. "I don't have coffee or anything to offer," he says.

"I didn't expect anything," I say. "Alexi—"

"Don't worry about it," he says, "I appreciate what you've done already. I was there, I saw what it was like. They're not likely to be interested in my problems, not when the alternative is sending their own children. And I'd be the same way, if it were Theresa who was involved."

"There might be—"

"It's all right," he insists, "it's only two years. It's not going to be as bad as the Army, at least they won't be shooting at me."

"There's another way," I say.

"There is no other way," Alexi says.

"We could get married," I say. I mean to present it as a business proposition, but instead my voice comes out small, a bit pleading.

"What?" he says mildly.

"We could get married. If we were married, you'd be a land-holder."

"I can't ask you to do that," he says.

"It wouldn't be a real marriage, of course," I say. "There are two bedrooms, we can add a third for Theresa. And if you wanted to end it, after a couple of years, of course, that would be fine."

He shakes his head.

"Why not?" I say, in that little pleading voice I find so absurd.

"I can't," he says, "I can't. Martine, your beautiful house, all you've worked for. You're so, so self-sufficient. I'm nothing, just some refugee. Lenin and Mao Zedong, I can't believe this."

"It's getting to be a bit much for one person," I say. "And you could establish a side-business, we don't have much in the way of technicians here, you'd have more work than you knew what to do with."

"This wasn't what I had in mind," he says. "Not at all."

I shrug. "Things happen. Think about it. Don't make up your mind, we'll talk about it tomorrow. But remember, we should have decided before next council meeting."

"That's only a month," he says.

I know.

"Marriage is a big thing," he adds.

"I've been married before," I say.

"I know. I asked everybody everything about you." I must look nonplussed because he explains, "I know you were a captain. I know you're from West Virginia, I know you hated the Commune when you were first here, I know you're almost never sick, you never had any children and that your ex-husband is still in the Army and that he's stationed in California. People respect you, a lot of people came to the meeting tonight just to vote for you."

"How did you know Evan's in California?" I ask.

"Claire, one of the newcomers from two years ago, she works in transmissions. She told me you got mail forwarded from an E. Jansch from some base in Southern California."

I occasionally get stuff from Evan, not much, not often, and I usually pitch it.

"I admire you a lot," he says. "I don't want your charity, I want, well, to start, I want your respect."

"It wouldn't be charity, Dormov," I say. "I get up some mornings at three-thirty, four A.M., and I'd expect you to do the same."

He doesn't say anything.

"You checked up on me?" I'm not sure if I like this or not.

"Well, not exactly, I just remembered what people said about you, and then because people knew we were friends, it's a small place, people like to talk."

I find this all a little unnerving, and I find the way Alexi is looking at me, well, I'm not sure what it means.

"Think about it," I say briskly, "I'd like to have you and Theresa." I find as I say it, I mean it. Oh, I know that the moment Theresa throws a tantrum I'm going to wonder how I ever got into this, but for right now, I really feel it. I need not to be alone, and Alexi is someone I could live with.

"We could try it," I add, "at least for Theresa's sake. If it doesn't work out, I throw you out. It's not an irrevocable decision."

He nods slowly.

I know well enough when to leave, I stand up and he stands up, too.

He opens the door and then says, "Well, how about"—shyly—"I mean if we're thinking about getting married, if you wouldn't mind, a good-night kiss?"

And after that he says, "How about if I walk you home?"

Ghost

Zhang

"Ni hao ma?" the nurse says, smiling at me. Mandarin "How are you," literally translates as "You good, huh?"

"Hao," I answer, good. Actually I feel dreadful. I have finally decided that it's not adjustment to a different time zone, I have been sick the entire week since I got here. I am running a fever and I have the backache to end all backaches and if I throw up one more time I will hang myself in despair.

I catalogue my complaints for the nurse who frowns and tells me that I am not in the system. *"Ni gang lai-le ma?"*

I went to a special secondary school where we spoke nothing but Mandarin, I can dream in Mandarin, so how come my fever be-fogged brain has to translate laboriously to recognize, "You just got here?"

"Dui," I manage. Right.

"Huaqiao ma?" Are you overseas Chinese?

"Dui." I think for a moment before I add, "Can I sit down?"

He checks me with a monitor and informs me brightly that I have a fever, apparently an infection, and slaps a tab on my arm.

129

I'm not sure how long he says to leave it on, I'm not really paying much attention. I have decided it would be altogether too impolite to put my head down on the table. He comes back, peels the tab off and tells me to come back in three days.

Then I'm out on the street again. So much for the most advanced medical system in the world. I want to be home in New York. Instead I wait for a bus. I have to ask three times about where to sit. I keep getting up and down confused in Mandarin. I walk to the back muttering *loushang, houbiar,* upstairs back, like it is my mantra. It doesn't really bother me when the front separates from the back of the bus, but when the top separates and we cut up into the overcity there's this moment where the thing rises as if cresting a hill and my stomach rises with it. I am not violently ill, but it is purely a matter of will.

I manage to get off at Nanjing University, where I am a special student but where I have yet to attend a class. I go to the correct tower, take the elevator up and find the suite I share with Xiao Chen.

"What did the doctor say?" he asks in English, either for practice or out of deference to my condition.

"That I'm sick," I say, and go to bed.

I sleep for twelve hours and wake up feeling human. Whatever they gave me has worked wonders. I emerge wan but without fever, my mind burned clear. Everything feels new, amazing. Colors are wonderful, not feeling as if I am going to throw up is wonderful, people do not know how lucky they are. Xiao Chen and I go downstairs to get something for breakfast. I don't know him yet, we have only been roommates for a week and I've been sick all that time. I know he's from Singapore and he speaks Mandarin, Singapore and Singapore-English (augmented) and is learning to speak English (augmented). He seems nice enough, moon-faced and dark. I keep telling him he should learn Japanese but he is studying scientific history and all of the important stuff from the 20th and 21st centuries is in English.

He convinces me that I should have hot rice cereal for breakfast, that it's bland. I'm not really hungry but it smells nice.
Standing in line I drop my spoon and bend over for it, when I
stand up I see stars and things go black for a moment because all
the blood has rushed to my head, except that my ears start roaring
and my vision won't clear. I grab for the counter in front of me,
for Xiao Chen's arm, although I'm not sure where he is, the world
is turning or I am falling.

And that's the last thing I remember for three days.

I wake in a perfect little room, very clean. I am jacked in, the
unit on my left wrist is heavy. I'm comfortable, it is just difficult
to work up the energy to do more than turn my head. On the
windowsill is a bright yellow spray of forsythia. I have vague
memories of dreams.

The doctor comes in, crisp and businesslike in her dark red
tails. She sits and jacks in. "I am Dr. Cui. We'll speak English,
I think you have quite enough to worry about without trying to
speak Mandarin." Her English is dictionary perfect in the style
of someone who is augmented but either her system is very good
or her English isn't bad on its own because she doesn't hesitate
for translation time.

"When you came in on Friday the practitioner saw that you had
an infection and gave you standard treatment." She glances over
a flimsie, obviously my medical print-out. "We gave you a virus
to combat the infection."

"Pardon me?" I say.

"You don't do that in the West?" she asks, perfect eyebrows
rising. She is a very polished woman. "The virus we gave you
carries RNA which uses your body's own immune system to tell
it what cells are infection cells." She gestures with manicured
hands. "Your cells learn to identify a disease by the pattern of its

outer layer and then creates antibodies that are templates for that
outer layer, that fit the offending cell. Do you understand?"

I nod, although I am not really sure.

"All right, the virus we gave you 'learns,' so to speak, to
identify a bad cell from reading the cells of your own body and
then alters itself to attack those cells."

Okay. So why am I in a tiny clean room?

"Unfortunately, once in a while something goes wrong. In your
case most of the virus did what it was supposed to do, but a small
portion of the virus mis-identified. That is why you became so ill
on Saturday, and Saturday and Sunday you were a very ill man.
This is Tuesday, you have been here for three days."

"Am I okay now?" I ask.

She smiles benignly. "You are recovering nicely, *tongzhi*. However I am afraid you will be here for a few weeks until your new
kidneys are mature."

"You have to give me new kidneys?" I ask.

"Oh no," she says, "you already have them, we just have to
wait for them to come on-line, so to speak." She smiles, dimples
a little. "That is all right to say, isn't it? 'On-line?' In a sense,
what we have done is infect you with new kidneys, we have
implanted naive kidney cells, cells like fetal cells, to piggyback
on your old kidneys. The naive cells are also anonymous, which
means that they have no identification at all and your body doesn't
recognize them and so attack them. The unit on your wrist is
monitoring your condition and stimulating your new kidneys to
grow. Is that clear?"

"I think," I say, and smile back.

"All right," she says, "lie still a moment, I want to check you
out."

I have no desire to do anything else. She concentrates for a
moment, frowning at the air. She sees a display but I don't, I'm
not jacked into her system.

"Everything looks fine," she says after a moment. "Go to sleep."

It's as if she has tripped a relay, because I do.

Occasionally I am half awake, when Dr. Cui comes to see me I am fully awake, but mostly I am not. Dr. Cui explains that since my left kidney has ceased functioning and my right is badly damaged, they are keeping me as nearly suspended as possible. There is a fine line, she explains, between too much activity which would overwhelm my system and too little which would mean that the new kidneys would not grow. I take all of this placidly.

"Dr. Cui," I say, "you are controlling my moods, aren't you."

She pats my hand, the first time she has touched me that I remember. "Of course, you are new here, alone, ill. If we didn't you would be frightened and depressed. The unit"—she indicates my weighted left wrist—"is feeding back into your nervous system. In a sense, you are not jacked into it, it is jacked into you. That's how we control your moments of consciousness, as well as your moods, and stimulate the growth of your new kidneys. They are vascularized nicely, by the way. In a few days they will begin to take over. Your old kidneys will shut down and eventually will atrophy and be absorbed by your body."

How exciting. I find it hard to maintain interest in what she is saying, or in anything. Back to nothing.

After three weeks I am released. I have lost seven kilos and my pants don't fit. My kidneys, my new kidneys that is, are functioning well, but I have been instructed to avoid things like beer and spices and to watch my salt intake. October, only a few days after October first, National Day, the day the People's Republic of China was founded and here in the city the windows of some of the shops are still decorated in red and gold. I am assaulted by noise. Nanjing dialect, Mandarin, I am washed in Chinese. The people on the street are all well-dressed and healthy-looking.

Everywhere, elegant men in black and red business tails, or casually dressed in coveralls. Women with sprays of light in their hair. Light displays hang suspended in front of windows, light sticks refract into images whenever I turn my head, characters flash across the backs of my eyes.

I stand waiting for the bus. I feel dizzy again, but it's not physical. I put my hand against the signpole. The bus coasts to a stop in front of me.

Xiao Chen is at the suite, and he has friends over.

"Zhang!" he says, then beaming to the others, "See? I told you he existed." I collapse into a chair, worn out from the effort of getting to the dorm. His friends begin the obligatory, "You must be tired," and I shake my head, no, no, please do not leave.

"Beer?" Xiao Chen asks in English, proud of himself.

"No," I say politely in Mandarin, "I cannot, new kidneys."

They ask me how I am and Xiao Chen describes my spectacular collapse in the dining hall. He describes things I do not remember, says that when I came to I talked to him, but that my back hurt very badly and that I was very brave. He tells about medical coming and putting me out.

"I don't remember," I say.

"I to hospital go, see you," he says in clipped Singapore English, "They say you sleep. I send to you flowers, they come not come?"

"Yellow ones?" I ask, I don't know the word for forsythia in Mandarin.

He beams. Introduces his friends. A couple are from Singapore, *huaqiao*, overseas Chinese, like Chen and me. Two are from Chengdu, *Zhongguo ren*, Chinese citizens. They sit and chatter and I stop trying to follow the conversation, just letting the sound wash over me, drinking tea. It is nice to be with people.

Oh, I am lonely. And it is all so strange. I miss Peter.

*   *   *

I am three weeks behind in my classes. For my lab on tool-handling this is no problem, I have more experience than most of the class. The cutters and sealers we use are often different makes than I am accustomed to, and the steps we learn in class a bit more formal than the way I am used to handling them, but I've used so many different makes it really doesn't bother me. We stand, fifteen of us in the lab, jacked in, and the teacher tells us to turn on the cutter. The tip of my cutter glows ready.

The class has been practicing controlling the width of the beam. The teacher says he wants the beam the width of a pencil, we are supposed to burn a hole through a piece of plastic. I heave three feet of cutter into position, rest the tip where I want the hole and fire a quick burst (plastic keeps melting a bit after the cutter shuts off so it's always good to do a bit too little). Then I wait for fifteen minutes while everybody else practices and learns the texture and density of the plastic. I help the people on the left and right of me. The girl on the right keeps pulsing the cutter and has little keyhole shapes all over her piece of practice plastic.

For me the only real problem with the class is that I'm out of shape and the cutters are bulky.

The teacher suggests that I test out of the class, but it will probably be one of my two high marks so I respectfully decline. As a non-native speaker I also take Mandarin, *poutonghua*. Since many of the other non-natives are still augmented in our classes and we are not allowed to be augmented in this class, I do well. The teacher gives me books to read to improve my character vocabulary, my reading is not as good as my speaking.

It is the other classes, the math and engineering courses, that worry me. I have five courses, including an engineering lecture and an engineering lab. I'm going to be thirty in five months, I'm too old to be in school.

I am assigned a tutor for engineering, to help me make up the time I have lost. I am embarrassed. It is clearly my incompetence, they feel I am not quick enough to make it up on my own. It is

low self-esteem, I am aware. I am alone, Chen has his circle of
friends, it seems to me that in the four weeks I have lost, everyone
else has adjusted.

I am unable to fathom engineering, so I go to my tutor, taking
the lift to the bottom of the *Dong-ta,* the East Tower, where I live,
crossing the arcade of shops that connects the overcity complex
above the University to the *Bei-ta,* the North Tower, and taking
the lift back up to the address I have been given. I knock on the
door, and Yang Haitao opens it.

His eyes flicker down and up, very swiftly, and he smiles. He
is smooth-faced with a stiff brush of hair. "Hello," he says in
Poutonghua, "you are the man with the incredible name?"

"Zhang," I answer. Lenin and Mao Zedong, my *huaqiao* name!
"I suffer for the sins of my parents," I add, a glib response, a play
on Marxist-Leninist-Mao Zedong thought which says the child is
formed by the parents and the son of the landlord is also a
landlord, even if he owns no land. Only after I have said it do I
think, I am in China and I don't know this man and I watch to
see if he is offended.

Not at all. He grins. "Come in," he says.

His dormitory. How can I say what it is like to walk into
Haitao's dormitory? His name means "Sea-wave" although a better translation is tidal wave. The room is blue and lightfish swim
lazily near the ceiling, skeletons aglow. His room faces out, looking at the city—Chen's and my room faces into the inner well—
and the city is going to smoky twilight, so it seems as if the blue
goes on and on. Furniture is soft, dusky shapes.

He waves his hand and the room programming picks up. Lightfish flicker into shadows and are gone and the light comes up, the
window dims, and suddenly the room is bright. The furniture
revealed shifts chameleon-like to rose and the pale yellow walls
seem to be textured, like cotton.

"Nice room," I say.

"Thanks," he says. "Can I get you a beer? Nanjing beer."

Nanjing beer is supposed to be very good. "Thank you, but I can't. New kidneys."

"That's right, you've been sick," he says.

I tell it briefly, tired already of explaining and not wanting to bore him. He makes me nervous. He is polished, his clothes casual and, to my eye, expensive. I think to myself I will remember that open shirt, the brushed gray tights, the calf-high boots. Look for something like that. I wonder what he thinks of me in my American clothes, looking *huaqiao* and appearing with the outlandish name of Zhang Zhong Shan.

"How tiresome for you," he says, with sympathy. "How do you like China?"

I am ready to march out the platitudes but I don't. "I don't know, I've spent most of the time here in bed."

He laughs. My foolish heart, I am in love with him. This polished young man with his perfect clothes. He cannot be bent, I cannot be so lucky, and yet, and yet.

Does he dance? That's the way to tell. When a straight man meets a straight woman, they dance. When I meet someone bent, we dance. It is so subtle. I only know when I meet a straight man, he doesn't dance. It seems to me that Haitao and I are dancing, watching each other's faces a little longer, responding by looking away or with swift nervous smiles. But this is China, maybe I'm crossing cultural signals. I'm lonely and I want this young man, this polished tidal wave, to be like me. To like me.

We start at the beginning and he grounds me in engineering. He's a pretty good teacher, he understands my need to know what something means. I arrange to come back on Thursday.

That evening I stop in the arcade and buy a copy of a magazine called *Xiansheng*, a men's magazine I've picked up once in awhile in New York. It's as expensive here as it is in New York. Beautiful men in shirts that shimmer like lacquer and silk jackets brocaded with cranes and dragons. The sweaters have hoods. Everyone is wearing those calf-high boots that Haitao had on.

Thursday I have class from eight to ten (a math class) and then I am free until three. I go shopping.

I head north up Daqing Lu, the street is lined with stores. I stop and look in windows, the prices are ghastly. I have some of my Baffin Island salary on credit plus a stipend from the University. Because I study technology, my only cost was getting here, the rest is scholarship. Getting here was expensive enough. Clothes are five times what they would cost at home. And strange. The refinements of fashion look awkward to my untutored eyes. First I buy a pair of those skintight calf-high boots. I feel confident about those.

Then a pair of rust-colored coveralls. I've seen people in these and I have good shoulders. I think the coveralls will flatter me. I finger a brocade jacket, all yellow with circles of long life worked in it and stylized blue waves across the bottom. So expensive, three weeks of my inflated Baffin Island salary for a jacket. And I don't know what it means. What kind of person would wear this jacket, what does it say about the wearer?

If I don't know then it would undoubtedly call out, *"Huaqiao* with more money than sense."

So I buy conservatively, spending money to blend in, not to impress. How painful. But when I think of my sweaters with the leather ties and the mirrors and look out at Daqing Lu, filled with shoppers and scooters and segmented buses, I can only wince. If Haitao ever saw the way I dressed at home . . . At least I will not embarrass myself.

That night I study engineering and think of questions to ask Haitao. I want to catch on quickly, be brilliant. After an hour and a half of study I'm drawn back to *Xiansheng.* I study the clothes, but more closely I study the ads. The regular features show some sort of fashionable ideal, but the ads, they show something that has to pass for everyday life. A different ideal.

I wish I had someone to talk to, someone to compare notes with. Not Xiao Chen, who dresses like a tech; coveralls that he could have worn twenty years ago, and will probably be wearing twenty years from now, all in grays and navy blues. Peter. But Peter is in Brooklyn and I am in China.

I write him a letter that begins, "I'm in love again." It's ten here in Nanjing, so it's morning in Brooklyn and he's at work. Well, the letter will be waiting for him when he gets home. "Love from the Middle Kingdom, Zhang." And then I hit transmit.

Does he take in my new clothes when his eyes flicker over me? It is hard to tell. Maybe the rust coveralls are wrong? "Hello," he says. His room is all the color of a sunset until he rather absently waves his hand and then the only sunset is outside his window. And himself, dressed in a thigh-length tunic that shifts from red at the neck to indigo at the hem. The same brushed gray tights and calf-high boots.

He is distant and preoccupied this evening. I don't know how to act, so I open my book and feign diligence.

"You teach well," I say after awhile.

"Thank you," he says. "I was a teacher."

"Of engineering?" I say, surprised. I thought he was a student.

"No, I taught physics in middle school."

I had thought him younger than me. "What made you quit?" I ask, wondering, are those wrinkles at the corners of his eyes? Is he older than I am? He is an engineering marvel, full of suggested cables and supports, tense under his easiness.

He shrugs. "No money in teaching. No *guanxi*, either. Fifteen year olds aren't very good people to make connections with."

"How did you get reassigned?" I ask without thinking.

"A friend," he says vaguely. "How did you get to school?"

"I was a construction tech on an island in the Arctic Circle for a year. I got special placement." I shouldn't have asked him how he got to school. Teaching is an assigned job, a work unit job, cradle to grave security but the drawback is that it's hard to change. Like the Army. Not like my job, which is a free market job, but has no health care, no security, almost no protection. I get a housing allowance, but except for the Baffin Island job I've never had assigned housing until Nanjing. But I can quit any time I want to, go to employment and get on the job assignment list.

How did he get permission to leave his work unit to come to school? Maybe he has a lover with connections?

I smile to myself. I don't even know if he's gay and already I think he's got a lover in the Army or something.

"That's a secret smile," he remarks.

"Thinking about how different it is here," I say.

"What's the biggest difference?" he asks.

I think for a moment. Everything is different. In New York I ride a subway system built sometime in the 1900's, here buses segment and flow off in different directions. There's a city above the city, a lacework super-structure that supports thousands of four-tower living units and work complexes like the University complex we live in; what they call the *xin gongshe,* new communes. And there's the constant assault of Chinese, I get hungry for someone to speak English with. The food. I ate Chinese and Thai food at home, but not all the time. And there's food here I've never seen or heard of, from Australia and South America and Africa, at outrageous prices. Everyone here seems rich.

I laugh. "At home, I knew what was going on, and if I had something to talk about, I called somebody and talked to them. Here"—it is my turn to shrug—"I am not quite sure what will happen, what things mean, and I don't have anyone to talk to about it." I glance at him, to see how he takes it.

He looks thoughtful.

It's time to leave, I stand. "I am sure you are tired," I say politely.

"Oh, no," he says, equally as polite.

We go through the ritual of leaving. I realize I am taller than he is, although not by much. This is important to me in some secret way.

"Saturday," he says, "perhaps you would like some extra tutoring? Not suggesting that you aren't picking it up fast," he adds, smiling.

"I'd like that," I say.

"Of course, the class is most important," he says, "but it never hurts to have a little left-handed help."

Left-handed. My heart starts to hammer. It is all code, he is testing me. Or perhaps it's an accident, he just used the phrase, unaware that it can have any other meaning. Back home, straights are right-handed, we are left. Not really, of course, just slang.

"Thanks," I say, "I'm grateful, and I always appreciate a little left-handed help."

"Oh," he says, politely delighted, "I wasn't sure you would."

"More than you know," I say. "It's very lonely here for a *huaqiao*."

"I think a *huaqiao* like yourself should make very many friends quickly. You do not really have to go yet, do you?"

I am filled with terror and joy. "Well, perhaps if you are not too busy," I say. I am all desire, and I see he is as well. My knees are loosened, I feel as if I am seventeen again, waiting in the dark on Coney Island beach for someone to come along, while the smell of ash rolls off the burning harbor.

"Wait," he says, and does something swiftly with the room. The lights darken towards rose and then the sunset is inside the room, and the world is dark outside. Nanjing is lights that go on up the Yangtze River to the horizon; the river is marked by a curving road of lightlessness.

"I cannot believe this," I whisper.

"What can't you believe?" he asks, laughing softly.

"That you are here," I say, cliche, I know, but things become cliche because they express truths. And I cannot believe he is here.

We are waiting for something, I don't know what but we wait. I am shaking and aroused, he doesn't know what it is like to be alone in a foreign country. He doesn't know. And if he knew how badly I want him, would he want me at all?

"*Lai, lai,*" he says. Come here.

So for a few hours I can pretend that I'm not alone.

If to come is the *petit mort,* the little death—and it seems to me it is because everything is burned away for that brief, explosive time—then waking up in someone's bed is resurrection. It's only a little death and a correspondingly sordid resurrection. It is not life that falls on me so much as obligation. I have engineering at nine A.M. and I am in Haitao's bed. At the hour before dawn I'm rarely in love.

I sit up, Haitao stirs and opens his eyes. His hair is a mess and he is naked and ordinary, as am I.

"I must go," I tell him.

"*Weishemma*"? Why?

"I have engineering and I have to study."

He sits up, "Wait," he says, "I'll make tea."

Rituals, the same here as at home. You never let the coney go without making him breakfast, even though by that time you often can't stand the sight of each other. "*Bei-keqi,*" I murmur. Do not be polite.

He protests a little, but I dress and apologize for my rudeness in leaving so abruptly and asking him to understand. "I'll see you Saturday," I promise, not particularly wanting to at this moment, but knowing that by tonight I'll be thinking about nothing else. I press him gently back to the bed, and leave him going to sleep.

My eyes are thick, I'm slow. The hall is silent and dark and the lift opens with a sigh. I cross the empty arcade and stop to watch the sunrise. A sunrise is a special thing, I've lived north of the Arctic Circle, where night lasts for months. Then up to the suite where I shower and make coffee, and sit down to study my engineering.

Engineering is better that morning. I am beginning to follow what is going on, and I find I study better in the morning than I do at night. But once engineering is over, I think of Haitao. Will he want to see me again? I think of how many people I have wanted only once, maybe it was only the unexpectedness of the moment, the always incestuous discovery of our particular brotherhood, that interested him.

I'm so tired of being a colony of one.

Xiao Chen says, "Last night, out late."

I answer in Mandarin, "I was with my tutor."

"Studying?" he says, grinning.

I shake my head and smile. "No. I'm not that good a student."

He does not even begin to suspect, straight-forward Xiao Chen.

A couple of Xiao Chen's friends come over and we watch a vid. I work on my mathematics homework. I get a letter from Peter which begins, "You're in love? I'm so jealous I can't stand it. Tell me all about her, is she beautiful?" You never know when a transmission will be monitored. I write back extolling the charms of Haitao who I rename Hai-ming, Sea-jade.

Empty afternoon, empty evening. I am waiting, suspended, until Saturday evening.

I dress in my new clothes; calf-high boots, black jacket with swallow tails over red, and brushed gray tights like Haitao wore. Am I doing it wrong, I wonder? Have I chosen well? I could disappear on the street in a thousand similar outfits. Will he approve?

When he opens the door he is preoccupied. "Lai, lai," he says absently. Come in, come in. And he is not alone.

I despair at not having him to myself. I wonder if I have not been good enough. I am angry at him for doing this to us. I am curious about this other—one of us? And I am elated at the thought of meeting people.

"Hello," says the man on the couch, "You are Haitao's *hua-qiao.*"

"Hello, I'm called Zhang," I say, and we scrutinize each other. Haitao is not particularly handsome, in the face he is rather plain, but he has good hair and a good build and is so polished that the net effect is dazzling. This man is casually, even badly dressed. His hair is cut as if someone dropped a bowl on his head and cut whatever showed and he hasn't bothered to comb it. But he has a handsome face; something easy to miss. In my experience, no one is truly handsome or beautiful without working at it.

"I'm Liu Wen," he says, "have a seat. Haitao is suffering and we should not interrupt a master."

"Irony is the escape of the intellectual," Haitao murmurs.

"Escape is escape. And if I must be a bad element, I might as well allow myself the luxury of indulging as many categories as possible."

Bad elements. There used to be five categories of black elements; landlords, criminals, counter-revolutionaries, capitalists, and one other which I don't remember. We studied it in middle school in Political Theory, that was a long time ago for me. Capitalists have been rehabilitated. I don't remember where intellectuals originally came in, perhaps counter-revolutionaries, but bent as we are, we are criminals. That has not changed in all the years since the revolution.

"Let's do something," Liu Wen says.

"It's early," Haitao answers, still preoccupied with the view out the window.

"Then let's go get something to eat."

Haitao shrugs. And so we go out into the evening and catch a bus. Liu Wen is in charge and Haitao doesn't ask where we are going. So I don't either. I notice at an intersection that we're on Jiankang Lu but I couldn't retrace my steps. Liu Wen gets up and we swing off the bus and saunter into a restaurant. It's beautifully finished. My first restaurant in Nanjing. The floors are inlaid wood and one entire wall looks like red lacquer, finished in so many coats that it seems as if you could put your hand into it like water.

Liu Wen orders duck and four other dishes and beer. I apologize and explain that I can't drink beer. They bring tea, and eventually duck with creamy white skin and red tender flesh. "It's a specialty," Liu Wen says. It is tasty. I chase it with my chopsticks, and wash down monkeybrain mushrooms with my tea.

Liu Wen turns his attention on me. How do I like China? What is it like in New York? How did I get here? He is fascinated when he learns that I worked north of the Arctic Circle, on Baffin Island. He worked in Australia for awhile, he explains, in Melbourne. "Australia will be the next major economic power," he says, "now that they have the technology to use the Outback." He says "Outa-baka."

It is a strange meal. The food is good, but it is disturbing to watch Liu Wen animated while Haitao sits and broods, playing with his duck. I don't know the rules here.

"Did you go to Canada"—Liu Wen says *Jia-na-da*—"because of political problems?"

"No," I say. "I went because it paid a lot and I only stayed for six months." I feel like he is amusing himself with me, *hauqiao* from backward country. "Did you go to Australia for political reasons?"

Haitao laughs. "No," Liu Wen says, "I went because I had heard Australian men are very big." He grins. "And all that yellow hair. We didn't have a Cleansing Winds."

"Not in this century," Haitao says, to no one in particular. He is looking away from us, off across the restaurant. Is he defending me?

"The Ten-Years Disaster, the Cultural Revolution, was different. That was because Mao Zedong went senile," Liu Wen says, equally casual. "Cleansing Winds, that was because the American Socialist States had to make the ideological adjustment to the modern world. China didn't have to join a technologically advanced society, computers weren't invented until the twenty-first century." He leans towards me. "That is Australia's problem, they haven't really made the economic adjustment, their economy is still exploitive. When they do, the cultural adjustment is going to set them back. They'll have to have an ideological revolution."

You are full of shit, I think, nodding. Cleansing Winds was a civil war between Carson's conservatives who felt that the economy had to be controlled the way China's was the first fifty years, and the Red Party who felt that people had to change ideologically, to think as if they were good socialists. But it wasn't really an ideological struggle, it was just power. It is always just power. But I'm not going to contradict Liu Wen.

I have the feeling that he would like me to contradict, that he would like to see if he can make me look foolish in argument. When I just nod he seems disappointed. Maybe he is no more pleased to share Haitao with me than I am with him. Maybe I am just paranoid.

Liu Wen pays, they give him the debit statement and he doesn't even glance at it. Out on the street it is night. "Still too early to do anything," he says. At home I would suggest we go watch the kite races but here I don't know what anyone does. Liu Wen is attractive, fascinating, but he seems interested in me only as conversation. That is all right, it is better than being alone. I think. I'm uneasy and uncertain. Wait, let things happen, I tell myself, live in this moment, there is nothing but enjoyment in this moment.

We take a bus across town to Linggu Park and walk. "They used to close the park," Liu Wen says, "but now everything is monitored."

It is a tacit way to say "be careful." Liu Wen seems to catch Haitao's silence. The evening is cool. We walk up a road until we come to a building surrounded by a moat crossed by three bridges. We stop and I try to figure out the reason we are here. The building is small, square, white, with a graceful blue tile roof with upcurving ends in the tradition of Chinese architecture. It's a nice little building, but what is the point?

"The tomb of your honorable namesake," Liu Wen says to me, grinning.

"Zhong Shan?" I ask, stupidly. He nods. Sun Yat-sen is buried here. Well, imagine.

I glance at Liu Wen, he has a funny smile on his face. Haitao leans on the balustrade at the edge of the moat and looks down at the sluggish orange carp motionless near the light set under the bridge.

I don't know what to say so I say nothing. I am not even sure if they are making fun of me.

"Well," Liu Wen says to no one in particular, "let's go play."

Haitao straightens up and shoves his hands in his sleeves. We walk back and catch a bus.

We ride all the way back across town, out of the dark park into wide streets, then through the bright heart of Nanjing, back out into the dark edge of the city. The bus is only three segments when we get on, goes down to two, picks up two more in the center of town, loses them (people transfer from segment to segment but we just sit) and finally goes down to one segment before we get off. The air smells different down here. All of China smells different, I noticed a dusty, old-clothes smell when I got here, but I don't smell that anymore. Here is a damp smell. Liu Wen remarks we are close to the river.

Around us are godowns. We walk past loading docks and parked flat-skids for moving goods off trucks. I can't imagine why we would be here. Liu Wen stops at a metal door and hisses at me, "Don't give your real name," and opens the door on a badly lit stairwell. Up we go as I try to understand what he meant. At the top of the stairs another door, waiting behind Haitao I can't see what it's like when Liu Wen opens the door, only hear sudden music, people murmuring. I can't hear what he's saying, only that he is talking to someone at the door.

"Don't worry," Haitao whispers, "he is a member." Then he follows Liu Wen to the door and this time I hear the doorman say, *"Shi shei?"* Who are you?

"Li," he says, the most common surname in China.

"Shemma Li?" Which Li?

"Li Haibao."

I smile. "Haibao" means "seal." I have seen seals with their cat's heads and sad eyes in the waters off Baffin Island, and Haitao, in his sleek way, has picked a name that flatters him.

"Shi shei?" the doorman asks me, he is wearing a white mask with holes for eyes and a slit for a mouth.

"Ma," I answer.

"Shemma Ma?"

"Guai-zi," I answer. Ghost or demon.

Haitao glances over his shoulder at me and smiles. I smile back. We are inside.

The place is big, after all, this is a godown, even if it's not being used for storage. The light comes from floor level or just above our heads and the ceiling disappears in darkness. Looking up I almost think I see stars, which is of course an illusion. The lighting is all gold, our faces and hands are gold. There is a bar and some small tables, and then there are larger, square tables, with people standing around them. Gold light comes up from the tables.

"Want a drink?" Liu Wen asks.

I shake my head.

"Are you buying?" Haitao asks. "Mao-tai then."

Liu Wen shakes his head and laughs. I remember my mother buying mao-tai for her future boss when she was giving gifts to change jobs. A bottle cost more than she made in two weeks, and that was twenty years ago.

In China, a secretary makes more in a week than I make in almost a month at home as a construction tech.

I wonder if I am dressed right. Looking around I see a few

people dressed as I am, and a few dressed in long formals, tails almost sweeping the floor at their heels as they stand at the tables. Some are dressed like Liu Wen, with complete disregard for appropriateness. What is this place, a gambling hall?

There are no women. I look around, surprised. There are *no* women. Haitao is watching me, smiling a little.

"In New York, do you have places like this?"

"I don't know," I say, "I don't know what this place is."

"*Jiaqiu,*" he says.

I don't understand. In Chinese, one word can have many different meanings, "jia" can mean "family" or "home" or it can mean "beautiful" or "welcome." "Qiu" can mean "prisoner" or "ball." I try sorting through meanings and nothing makes sense. Mandarin is a hell of a language in a lot of ways.

"Which 'jia'?" I ask and he sketches the character on his hand.

"*Jiagong de jia,*" he explains, which doesn't translate into English. "Jiagong" means to be caught in a surprise attack by one's enemies and closed in, almost squished between.

"The *jia* of *jiazi?*" I ask. "Jiazi" means clothespin, which in Chinese is called a "press-pin."

"*Dui,*" he says. Right.

"*Lanqiu de qiu?*" I ask. "Qiu" meaning "ball" as in basketball? "press-ball" or "squeeze-ball?" What the hell is "squeeze-ball?"

He nods.

"I don't think we have that," I say.

"You'll like it," he assures me.

I am not so certain. But Haitao brightens up, he actually looks at Liu Wen when Liu Wen hands him a tiny glass containing mao-tai.

"Let's play," Liu Wen says.

We find a table with only three men around it. They don't glance up. The tabletop is featureless, a golden glow illuminating our faces like heat from a fire. Liu Wen picks up a contact and grins at me with gold teeth before jacking in. The three men shift slightly as if someone had stepped up beside them. Liu Wen seems engrossed in the glow. Haitao jacks in and the four—Liu Wen included—absently shift again.

I study the glow for clues.

Whatever is happening, it's not visible. I jack in.

The table is still there, but I have an overlay, I am in a circle with five others. It's a little like contact when making a call, that instant before sound cuts in; I don't see them but they are there. I try to see them and I can—five men around a glowing table—but then I almost lose the sense of contact.

I am a boundary, I am part of the golden glow. And there are balls in the glow; a golden ball (almost invisible), two silver balls, a black lacquer ball and a red lacquer ball. I find the red lacquer ball attractive. I reach out to touch it, it is not so different from working power tools, and it gently squiggles away from my touch.

I sense a slight hiss of disgust from my right, and I am shocked into actually seeing the man. He is tall, dressed in a high-collared cutaway coat and he has hair that brushes his collar (hair almost as long as mine, is he *huaqiao?*). He is staring into the table, oblivious to me.

Liu Wen stirs. "It is his first time," he says.

I am sliding back into the field and so I feel the acquiescence. I watch this time.

Haitao is after one of the silver balls. He attempts to cup around it, so that equally repulsed it will have no place to go and be held, but one of the strangers (not the long hair) hits it with a touch and it shoots towards my end of the table.

Haitao makes a start to stop it, a wild unfocused motion that suggests that I shouldn't want it too close, so I hit it rather like hitting a ping pong ball, back towards Liu Wen who deflects it, pool cue style, right into the stranger beside him.

We are suddenly dropped out of contact and Liu Wen says, "My point," and the stranger, "my loss."

Liu Wen smiles at me, "Good ball." Which in English is more like saying, "Good save."

We fall back into the golden ocean and the balls are distributed in the center. Silver are top and bottom, red and black revolving slowly around the golden in the center.

Liu Wen taps the red ball toward the silver and both rebound towards where no one is sitting. Haitao reaches out and slings the red towards himself and although the long-haired man and Liu Wen try to tap the ball it touches Haitao and we drop out of contact again.

"My point," Haitao says, smiling. No one takes a loss.

"Excuse me," I say politely, "but the silver should not touch one, the red should?"

The long-haired man nods. "The gold, the black and the red are friendly, the silver are not. Anyone who causes an opponent to take a silver gets a point, and the opponent loses a point."

"You can never start the gold in motion on the first play," Haitao adds, "and you can't touch the golden ball until it is already moving, although you can hit it with another ball."

I nod.

We are back in the gold. Haitao clicks the black into the silver and we play them around the table. I play cautiously, trying only to deflect, never attempting to catch, and trying always to send the silver to the center, particularly after someone sends the silver at Liu Wen and before it has even begun to cross the space between them he reverses it right back into them.

Finally by accident I send the silver into the golden ball. It has been in play a few times before but I have never even touched it. The long-hair reaches for it and one of the other strangers taps it away. Someone else jacks into our table as the golden ball is gliding past me and I feel everybody shift. It startles me and without thinking I reach out like a jai lai player and sling the ball my way.

When it hits there is an explosion of feeling. For a moment I am the golden ball and the golden ball is me and I am jolted with pleasure. It is orgasmic and threatens to unlock my knees but before I can even react it washes through me and we drop out of contact. I blink and everybody grins at me. I look at them.

Then I remember. "My point."

"Five points for a gold," Liu Wen says.

Back into the light, where I find my sensitivity is heightened. Now when the red or black balls come near I feel a tickle of sensation, with the golden ball it is even more definite. The silver balls seem colder. I become more aggressive in my play and catch the red ball twice. The explosion is less dramatic than the golden ball, and I remember to say, "My point," each time.

Only once am I hit with the silver ball, and it drains me, takes away the sensitivity, and I have the sense that what I have lost has gone into my opponent. Hungrily I play harder until I almost take the silver ball again, managing by sheer luck to deflect it into one of the strangers. He has been playing a long time, and I am jolted again by the power of what drains off of him.

"My point," I say.

"My loss," he says. Our eyes meet and he looks hungrily at me, and we drop into the light.

I am more careful, made aware by my near miss, and manage to catch the black lacquer ball once. It is like the red lacquer. I catch the red lacquer.

We drop out of contact.

"My point," I say.

"Time is up," Liu Wen says. "Nine points, you almost made it."

Time is up? "How long have we been playing?" I ask.

"Two hours," Liu Wen says. "That's how much we paid for. If I had realized you had nine points I'd have fed you the tenth, just so you could see what it was like."

"Like the golden ball?" I ask, staring into the gold of the table.

He shakes his head. "Different."

Better, I think.

I look up from the gold. Already the others are back in contact, only Haitao, Liu Wen and I are out. Somehow I keep expecting to drop back in, but instead, they take off their contacts and I take off mine. My bare wrist feels cold in the air.

I look at them, Haitao looks tense. Liu Wen looks like he always does. I am aware of perspiration on my neck, under my hair. I am even more aware of my aching testicles, and that I am tight against the seam of my pants. I feel as if I have been cock-teased for a couple of hours, which is precisely what has happened. But it doesn't seem as if we have been playing for two hours.

I lick my lips.

"He did pretty well," Haitao says.

"Beginner's luck," Liu Wen says.

I realize that Liu Wen paid for me. "Thank you for the game," I say.

"I love the way you talk," Haitao says softly.

"How do I talk?" I ask.

"Your accent, the formal way you say things."

"Do I have much accent?" I ask.

"It's charming, exotic, and yet you sound so refined."

I thought my Mandarin was pretty good. I resolve to work on my accent.

Liu Wen shakes his head, smiling. "I'll see you two later," he says and heads back towards another table. I follow him with wistful eyes, wishing to be back in the golden glow, although I ache.

"He's handsome," Haitao says.

"He could be," I answer, "if he would bother."

"Come with me?" Haitao asks. *Lai gen wo ma?*

Of course I will go with him. We walk through the godown to the back, where there is a narrow iron stair, and up above the lights he opens a door on a room like a coffin, a little more than

a meter high, the same wide. It is only then that I realize why he
has taken me here, that there is not another game at the end, or
at least, only the old game.

I laugh, although I am so aroused there will be damn little joy.

He stoops and enters, and sitting on the mat says, softly, *"Lai
lai lai."* Come, come, come. I stoop and follow him, kneeling in
front of him, aware of my boots on the mat. I lean awkwardly
forward, resting my hand on the mat next to his thigh, and we
kiss. I tug gently at his pants and he raises his hips for me to slide
them down. If there is a way to do this without a sense of interrup-
tion I have never found it. But then I kneel reverently and pay
homage.

And later, once, he asks me, "Why 'ghost'?"

"Waiguai," I say, foreign-devil or foreign-ghost. It's the old
slang term for a foreigner. Not very flattering. Like westerners say
Slope-head.

"You aren't a *waiguai*," he says, "you're *hauqiao.*" Not a
foreign ghost, but an overseas Chinese.

That is what it says on my identification. I was certain my IDEX
would be *waiguoren* but it says *huaqiao*. The flimsie they gave me
indicated that my genetic mother may have been Philippine Chinese (the combination of my mother's Hispanic genes and my
father's Chinese, I suppose). Haitao doesn't know that my mother
is Hispanic-American. I do not mention it.

"You look tired," the doctor says in Mandarin.

I am, I did not get much sleep the night before. It is Monday
and I met Haitao for dinner last night—late because he had
something he had to do before he saw me. I was jealous but did
not ask.

I am here for an examination, just to make sure that my new
kidneys are working.

"You are the first patient I have ever had who is the result of cosmetic gene-splicing," she says. "It's illegal here except for authorized disorders."

It is now at home as well. Except for things like Taysachs, Downs, Herodata's Schizophrenia. She has accessed my deep records, I wonder if she will change my IDEX, but she doesn't seem to think of it. I am jittery and nervous.

The doctor is astonishing. Gone is the perfect, concerned woman I remember from when I was sick. She says the correct things, like "You look tired," but she says them with an air of detachment. I don't answer her and it doesn't seem to matter. She explains things, tells me how my kidneys grew, how the old ones are beginning to atrophy. She holds me off with her words. "If you experience any depression or anxiety these days you are welcome to come and talk with a counselor."

I nod unhappily. She is jacked in to my medical records. What does she find in my medical records that makes her think that I need counseling? Something from Baffin Island? Or perhaps my constructed genetic make-up is flawed and I am prone to system imbalances? She certainly does not want to counsel me. Why did I think her so wonderful?

"Are you eating right?" she asks, and does not wait for an answer. "Still avoid things like beer and alcohol and not too much protein yet." She stands. I stand.

"Thank you Dr. Cui," I say.

It must be the unit that they used to keep me quiet. It must have encouraged me to trust my doctor, to assume that everything was all right.

All my life, or at least since I was five and got my jacks implanted, I have jacked in; in school, at work, to call a friend, to find out how much credit was on my account. But those are operations where the system is passive, where I draw on the information. In the West, active systems, systems that feed back into the human nervous system, are illegal. There are exceptions; the big kites that the pros fly, for example; they feed flight infor-

mation back to the flier, but those are licensed. I've never been
to the doctor and been jacked into an active system.

Jianqiu, pressball, is an active system, too. I know it is illegal,
that's why one doesn't use one's real name, although if the system
records a trace they can identify our individual nervous system
patterns. Still, that takes a lot of work, I suppose they'd almost
have to know who we were first.

Active systems are illegal, as everyone knows, because they can
cause injury. And because they are addicting. I wonder if *Jianqiu*
causes any sort of degeneration of my already taxed nervous
system. There are certainly ways in which it is taxing. But I have
no idea if I will ever play again. I'd certainly like to.

Is that the definition of addicting? If so, duck is addicting
because I'd also like to try Nanjing duck again.

On Tuesday I have my engineering tutorial again. I cross the
busy arcade and take the lift. I don't know if we are going to
bother with engineering.

"Lai, lai," Haitao says absently, opening the door. He is not
looking at me, and the flat is rose. He gestures and the lights come
up. So I suppose we are going to work. We sit down and he sighs,
sits for a moment as if too listless to bother before leaning forward
to look through the book.

It is quite a performance. But I'm not Liu Wen to make fun
of it.

"We don't have to work this evening," I say, "I can go back,
we can work another time."

"No," he says, "it doesn't matter." He pages through my book.

"No, truly," I say. "I'm doing better. It makes more sense these
days." This is the truth, although I have some questions I'd like
to ask.

He smiles. "You are always so polite," he says, "are all American *huaqiao* so polite as you?"

"Old-fashioned, maybe," I say, and begin to get up.

He puts his hand on my arm. "Don't pay any attention to me, Liu Wen doesn't."

"Liu Wen knows you better than I do," I say.

To my astonishment his eyes fill with tears and he looks away. Then he stands up and walks to the window. He stands with his back to me and I wait, confused and alarmed. What did I say?

He doesn't say anything for awhile and I have time to feel uncomfortable. What should I do? I don't know what to do so I sit and look at my engineering book, and then back at Haitao. I don't hear any crying. His shirt is as bright as yellow lacquer and the nape of his neck is pale between his hair and the collar.

"What's wrong?" I finally ask.

"A friend of mine is going to be arrested," he says.

Liu Wen? No it can't be. I wait.

He clasps his hands behind his back. "He is a teacher," he says. "They are arresting him on a morals charge, but it's more complicated than that."

I think, it always is. And I am relieved it isn't Liu Wen.

"I feel sorry for him," Haitao says, "of course. They'll send him to Xinjiang Province, to do Reform Through Labor. Do you know, if you misbehave in a labor camp, one of the punishments is to wire your thumbs together? They draw the wire very tight. It cuts off the blood. You have to eat rice out of a bowl like a dog, without using your hands. And then gangrene sets in and they cut your thumbs off. Or maybe you die."

What's to say? At home they used to send people to the corridor out west, convict labor. Now, sometimes they send them to Mars. Convict labor. Chinese citizens do not usually have much interest in going to the moon or Mars.

"I think we are a disease in society," Haitao says. "Bad cells. I think something has gone wrong with us."

"In my country there's a bird that lays its eggs in other birds' nests," I say. "The other birds don't know. They think this baby is their own. They raise it and feed it, in some ways it becomes almost a monster because it grows so large and demands so much. But eventually it simply leaves the nest, like any other bird. It's not a monster, it's really just another part of things. I think we're like those baby birds. We didn't ask for this, our parents didn't ask for this. No one is guilty, just maybe unlucky."

"So you think that we're accidents," Haitao says. He sounds sarcastic.

I shrug, even though he's not looking at me. That's what I think, and if he doesn't, that's okay.

"I'm afraid," he says. "If they interrogate my friend, they may arrest me."

I say delicately, "Perhaps you have a friend who can help you, someone who perhaps helped you transfer out of your teaching job. . . ."

"No," he says curtly.

It crosses my mind that if they arrest him and interrogate him, perhaps I will be arrested as well. But it seems too improbable to concern me.

He is still at the window, looking out with the city as a backdrop. This flat is like a theater for him, a shadow box for his own display. I get up and walk behind him, put my hand on his shoulder. He is trembling, like some small animal. I stroke his hair, he leans back against me and I wrap my arm around his waist. He turns his head so he is looking away from me and relaxes against me, his profile expressionless in the reflecting window. I tighten my grip, feeling his buttocks and back pressed against my stomach and groin, his fine skull under my fingers. Slowly the shaking subsides.

There's no doubt that his fear is real. But I cannot help but notice the flicker of the whites in the reflection of his eyes as he glances toward the window. He adjusts ever so slightly, improving the line, perfecting the pose.

"Don't worry, *haibao,*" I say, thinking how "seal" fits him, how sleek both he and seals are, "you are a perfect picture."

He laughs, shakily. "You see through me."

I don't really understand him at all, but I kiss his hair rather than answer, running my fingers across his chest. His pulse beats visibly in his temple.

"No," he says, chiding, "we must study engineering." His voice is playful and so I pay no attention, sliding my hand under the waist of his tights.

He sighs. "At least," he says softly, "we must darken the windows."

"Oh no," I say brightly, pulling my hand away, letting go, straightening his clothes like a mother with a toddler, "we must study engineering."

He growls at me, baring even, perfect little teeth like pearls.

I laugh, "First we study engineering and then we screw."

He gapes, astonished. "Did I hear you right? The namesake of Zhong Shan, vulgar?"

We do study engineering. I get my questions answered, draw out the session, teasing him, distracting him, pretending to be serious. It's a little like pressball, everything done by indirection. When I think his attention is wandering I press my thigh against his. I bring him a beer, brush fingers when I hand it to him, reach over and drink from his without asking while I watch him over the rim, and he watches me.

Finally I admit I have no more questions and kiss him. He grabs my hand and pulls me towards the bedroom, but I laugh and hang back, stopping him in the doorway where I press him against the frame, peal down his tights and go down on him there. He gasps, and laughs and swears at me, his hands wrapped rather painfully in my hair. Only after he comes do we make it to the bed.

Late, he dozes next to me and my arm is draped over his chest. I look into the darkness. It is about one. Peter is at work in New York, joking with Rebecca, the girl who does all the correspondence and filing. Peter would be astonished and proud of me, to know I have done so well with Haitao. To see me thinking about someone else in this way.

"A ministering angel," he would say, "a regular Florence Nightingale."

Peter, who so often did the same for me.

I am terribly homesick.

Haitao helps me with my engineering, a classmate, Wai Ling Zhung Fan, graciously helps me with my engineering. Even Xiao Chen, who knows nothing about engineering, uses my notes to ask me about my engineering. The midterm examination is very difficult, I work until the end of the hour and still do not get a real answer for question six. I walk out despondent, knowing that I missed at least three questions completely, and parts of many others. For days I will not stop at the Professor's office and look at the grades posted on a flimsie on the door. But the Professor's office is next to my Practical Applications class (my tool-handling class) so one day I simply go and look. And I have passed the engineering midterm with a score of 62 points out of 100 which on the grade curve is an 86%! I didn't know there would be a curve! I thought a 62 would be a failing grade!

Of course I go straight up to the arcade (the University is the base on which the four towers rest). I take the lift to his flat and then stand outside his door in an agony of apprehension. I have never come on Haitao unannounced. And each day it is problematical as to whether Haitao will be pleased to see me or too despondent to care. Some days he is all wit and languid charm. Some days he is silent and withdrawn. Always he knows I am coming.

I imagine him opening the door smiling. Open the door frowning. Someone else there.

So I go back to the lift, take it back down and call from the arcade. I jack in and think the numbers in careful Chinese—the system will understand English, and thinking out the call in Chinese is not second nature yet, but it's good practice to do everything in Chinese. Then there is a wait so long that I think he is gone. Perhaps in a meeting with his thesis Professor? Not that I have ever seen Haitao work on his thesis, but then I'm never there during the day.

"*Wai,*" he says, Chinese for Hey and the way everyone answers the phone. No vid, sound only.

"Venerable teacher," I say, "this is your undeserving student."

"Who?" he says, he sounds as if he has just woken up.

"Zhang," I say. "It's Zhang. Did I call at a bad time?"

"Zhang?" he says. "No, you didn't call at a bad time. What is it? Something wrong?"

"No, I just wanted to tell you I passed my engineering midterm. And say thank you for your help."

"Oh, you passed? Excellent." He is trying to sound interested, pleased, but the effort is apparent in his voice.

"An 86%," I say.

"An 86%?" he says, "so high? When did you find out? I thought you weren't going to check."

"I had to, better to know the worst than anticipate. I just wanted to tell you, I didn't want to disturb you. I'll see you tomorrow evening as usual?"

"Right, right." A pause. "Where are you now?"

"On the arcade," I say.

"Oh," he says, "are you busy?"

"Oh, sure," I say, "there are all these incredible men lined up waiting to spend the afternoon with an engineering genius."

He laughs and sounds a little more like himself. "Tell them to go away and come up. No wait, tell them to keep you entertained, buy you lunch or something, and give me thirty minutes. Everything is, ah, let me think of the Zhang way to say this," his voice changes, he speaks softly and mimics my American accent and northern pronunciation, "things are a bit untidy, and if you do not mind, I must inconvenience you a little, respectfully request you wait."

"*Ta ma-da,*" I say, Your mother. "Just get dressed and come down to the coffee bar. Go shopping with me. Show this poor confused foreigner what clothes to buy that will make him look less like he comes from a second-rate country."

"Mao Zedong and Lenin, I thought you'd never ask," he says and breaks the connection.

But it is twenty-five minutes before he shows up. I am sitting in the coffee bar nursing my coffee—or at least the sweetened syrup that passes for coffee in this country—when Haitao stops in the doorway. He scans the room, which is full of students. His gaze flickers past me a couple of times, although I wave. He is pale and lost; his hair looks as if he has run his fingers through it, his long yellow and green tunic doesn't match his tights. At last he sees me. He puts his head down and enters the crowd like a swimmer making a long dive.

"Do you want anything?" I ask him when he slides into the seat.

He shakes his head.

"What's wrong?" I ask.

"Nothing," he says. "Where do you want to go shopping?"

"I don't know, where do you go?"

"We don't want you to look too much like a fag," he says, off hand. "Why have you got your hair that way?"

My hair is tied back in a ponytail. I keep it shoulder length so there's not much tail. "I had my tool-handling class today, I like to keep it out of my eyes when I work."

"It looks nice," he says.

"It looks *huaqiao,*" I say. "I think maybe I should cut it."

"No, don't," he says. "Please don't."

The din makes it hard to carry on this conversation. Students call to each other in nasal, six-toned Nanjing dialect and shrill four-toned Mandarin. At home, my non-Chinese speaking friends say Chinese conversations often sound like arguments. I wonder how long it will be until I hear the liquid vowels of Spanish again. *"Yan Chun!"* the young man next to me shouts, *"Yan Chun! Zouba!"* Let's go. Across the floor, a tall young man with an open face, dressed as if he just came off the gym floor, turns and smiles. *"Shemma?"* What? The Mandarin word for a good time is *renao,* hot-noisy.

"Let's go," I say.

The arcade is busy, too. Haitao has his hands jammed in his tunic pockets, and moves with his head down.

I want to get out of this, to some place where it is quiet and private. Sometimes I take real pleasure in being with a person when there are all these straight people around and that person and I are just two people together. But right now Haitao and I aren't together, he is there and I am here and the physical space between us is not nearly so vast as the emotional distance. But I can't suggest we go to his flat, since he made a point of telling me it was a mess. I can't take him to my dorm because Xiao Chen might bring friends back from class and then we'd have no privacy and have to act straight.

So we walk down to the bus stop. "Have you heard any more about your friend?" I ask.

He shakes his head. "I talked to someone back home last night. He said my friend is still suspended from teaching, but nothing else. Everyone is still waiting."

"How did they find out about your friend?" I ask.

"It's complicated," he says.

Rebuffed, I say nothing.

The sun is hard on the street. Traffic is not heavy at midday, a street sweeper running off a power line raises and absorbs clouds of yellow dust. The window across the street is full of empty bird cages; in a square of sunlight, a white cat sleeps beneath them. It doesn't feel like home, the light is different or something. Maybe when I go back to New York I'll get a cat. Chinese people do not keep pets very much, it seems particularly Western to make an animal a member of the family.

"The District Superintendent of Education is a fag," Haitao says. "He hired my friend and me. He was arrested in a park. Then my friend was suspended. That's all anyone really knows."

The District Superintendent must be how Haitao got to study engineering. It must be a big scandal that someone in education is gay, someone so important, a big person.

"Do you think they'll be looking for you? The school hasn't suspended you."

"Not yet," Haitao says. Chinese never say no.

I see the bus, far up the street. Segmented buses look as if they are hinged in the middle, they bend a bit when they go around corners.

"I'm not feeling very well," Haitao says. "Maybe I'll go back and take a nap. You go on, celebrate your good mark." He smiles tiredly, "I forgot to say congratulations."

"Don't go back," I say. "You'll just sit by yourself, that's bad, I know."

"I'll take a nap," Haitao says.

"No you won't, you'll try to sleep but you won't. I promise, we'll only be gone an hour, you'll sleep better if you do something."

He shakes his head. The bus is coming.

"Haitao," I say, "I don't know how to dress, what to buy." I remember feeling the way he does. "If you won't come shopping with me, I want to go back to your flat with you."

The bus stops, the door hisses open.

He shakes his head again, but gets on. I palm the credit and pay for both of us. He slumps down into the seat and looks out the window.

I feel as if I shouldn't leave him alone, although I'm not sure if it's him that shouldn't be alone, or me. Surreptitiously I run the flat of my hand over his thigh. He glances over at me and smiles a little.

"You are one son of a bitch," he says.

"Have you talked to Liu Wen?" I asked.

"Not since the night the three of us went out."

"He is an unusual person," I say.

Haitao laughs dryly. "You have such a way of putting things. Yes. Liu Wen is unusual." He watches out the window for a moment. "Maybe I'll call him. Do you have an early class on Friday?"

"Yes."

"Then Saturday. Maybe we'll go play pressball, if he'll pay."

"Is he rich?"

"Sometimes. When he has a good week."

"What does he do?"

"Cui cui."

Hurry-hurry? Slang is the most difficult part of Mandarin for me. "What's that?"

"Sells himself."

My face must betray me. Haitao breaks out laughing. "You are right, it's good to come out with you, you cheer me up. You look as if I told you he murders little girls."

"Why does he dress that way if he, *cui cui?*"

"Because they like it. Talk softly."

"You say I always talk softly," I hiss, feeling the heat rise in my face. I glance around, the bus is nearly empty.

"Well, don't stop. Do you not want me to call him?"

I want very badly to play pressball, I want to get ten points. I've never been out with a man who goes for money. I mean, pick-ups, of course. When I was fifteen I used to go out to Coney Island and wait to get picked up, and when I was older, go to pick up, but not for money.

"What's wrong with it?" Haitao says.

"It spreads disease," I say.

He rolls his eyes. "I won't call him."

"No," I say, "call him."

"We are corrupting you," he says, then laughs. I, of course, do not find this funny.

New clothes. I have waited all week for Saturday night. Because Haitao likes it that way I have tied my hair back. My suit is black and in Haitao's words, "So ruthlessly conservative it's not. Everyone will think you're a vid artist or something."

Liu Wen, sitting on the couch and needing his hair brushed, as usual, approves. "Pretty," he says. "Need to make some money on the side?"

"No," I say curtly.

He grins at Haitao. Liu Wen is wearing a business suit coat that has seen better days, over gray tights that have been worn so often that they bag at the knees. Haitao is in white and looks, this evening, perfect. He is also in a good mood. A delightful mood. His hair is freshly trimmed, he smells ever so slightly of ocean and evergreen. He smiles when he sees me, gives me a beer which I shouldn't have but which I drink anyway.

We look as if we are going to three completely different places.

"You look like a bride," I tell Haitao.

Liu Wen laughs, "I told him he looks like a funeral."

"Funerals in the West are still in black," I say.

"And brides in the East wear red," Haitao says.

"The East is red," Liu Wen says, "and now that we've had our cultural exchange hour finish your beers because I'm hungry."

But we don't. Haitao doesn't want to leave yet, he wants to watch the sunset from his window. So we talk, about my engineering mark, about Liu Wen's week (in carefully vague terms). Liu Wen has apparently had a fair week, business-wise.

Outside the window it is the West which is red. The towers of the overcity, the new communes, rise above Nanjing. The sides that face west are red, and those between us and the horizon are black silhouettes. Red and black, the colors of good luck. While Liu Wen and I talk, I watch Haitao. He is engrossed in the window. The city goes blue-gray, and we sit in the half-light until it is almost dark, finally silent, as the lights come on in the city.

"I want to give you each something," Haitao says, "you have both been my friends through this difficult time."

Liu Wen looks amused. I'm taken a bit aback. To Liu Wen he gives a ring set with Australian opal. "It is not your style, I am aware," Haitao says, smiling, "but it is one of my favorites."

Liu Wen looks perplexed but tries it on. It fits his smallest finger.

To me Haitao gives a small gold box set with a tiger eye. "It's very old," he says, "Qing Dynasty, 1600s. Open it."

Inside it says *Guai-zi,* Ghost.

"A tiger eye always seemed a bit *guai-yi*"—strange, or unusual, same first character as ghost—"and so I thought of your assumed name," he says.

"Thank you," I say. Chinese people do not usually give gifts in this way, they normally leave the gift and you look at it after they are gone. I am uncomfortable and so is Liu Wen.

Haitao says, "Let's go."

The hall is painfully light, and Haitao's eyes are too bright. As if he was about to cry. But he moves quickly, excited. "Are we going to the new place?" he asks Liu Wen.

"If you want," Liu Wen says. "I don't care where we go."

"Somewhere where business is good," Haitao says, watching me and smiling. Liu Wen grins. I am still confused by the little ritual, I wonder if I should have had something. I search for something to say.

"Something I have wanted to ask," I say, hearing in my own voice the diffidence that Haitao teases me about.

Liu Wen cocks an eyebrow as if to say, Yes?

"The last time we went out, why did we go to the tomb of Zhong Shan?"

Liu Wen grins again. "Did you think we were trying to tell you something?"

"I didn't know," I answer.

"No reason," Haitao says. "Truly. We often go to the park, but usually we walk down the Avenue of Stone Animals. Just once we were there it seemed fitting to go by the tomb."

"Do you mind if I ask you something?" Liu Wen asks.

"Go ahead," I say.

"Why do you ask people to call you just 'Zhang'?"

"If your first name were 'Zedong' would you want people to call you that?"

Liu Wen shakes his head, "I understand why you don't use Zhong Shan. But to just call you Zhang sounds . . . well, rude. If you know what I mean. Don't you have a nickname?" I know what he means, it sounds too short. Chinese people like names to come in two syllables.

"Rafael," I say.

"Shemma?"

"Rafael."

"Ur-ah-fa—"

They both try it. Mandarin has a different "r" than the West, and they have difficulty ending with an "l." They keep wanting to end with a vowel, since Mandarin ends in a vowel, an "n" or an "ng."

"Ur-ah-fa-eh-la," Haitao manages.

I shake my head, "Rafaela is a woman's name."

"So, Zhang," Liu Wen says heartily, "how do you like it here in China?"

"We can't call you Xiao Zhang," Haitao says. Xiao Zhang would be the diminutive, "Young Zhang." It's like saying 'Billy' for 'Bill.'

" 'Lao Zhang,' " Liu Wen laughs. Elder Zhang.

"Must be the suit," I say.

We eat a leisurely dinner. Pork and bamboo shoots, french fries, Sichuan (spicy) cabbage. I drink two beers, I know I shouldn't but it's always hard for me to eat spicy food without *pijiu*. We get down to the warehouse district. I assume that we are going to the same club, but Liu Wen leads us to a heavy red door—was the last door red? I cannot remember. Up the stairs we go into a red and gold place, full of rooms with two or three tables in each and gilt sitting platforms along the walls. Some of the tables have men and women at them, which surprises me. We wander through a maze.

Liu Wen buys Haitao a mao-tai and I have a beer. Liu Wen says he'll be back. I gaze, mesmerized, at the gold light rising like mist off the tables.

"You have an unusual face," Haitao says.

I am not bad-looking, I know. Not truly handsome, the way Liu Wen would be if he chose to be. I fancy I hear wistfulness in Haitao's voice, little does he know how much I envy him, a Chinese citizen, worldly and polished.

"Do you know where in China your family was from?" Haitao asks.

"My gene scan said that my mother's family was apparently Philippine *huaqiao*, " I say. It didn't make any difference. Since I qualified by working on Baffin Island, I could still go to Nanjing University without having to qualify for a *huaqiao* seat. Competition for the *waiguoren* seats is fierce. Many candidates, few places.

If my genetic map is within tolerance, then I am Chinese, right? Physically, if not culturally. I mean, they are obviously not concerned with the information in my files, that my mother is not Chinese. The University has to know. Someone at the University, at least.

"You are more yourself tonight," I say.

He looks thoughtful. "Truly?"

"Have you heard any more about your friend?" I ask.

"Let's not talk about it," he says. He puts his hand on my arm, looking off across the room, and then shudders.

Idiot, I shouldn't have said anything. I search for other topics. "How did you meet Liu Wen?" I ask.

"Through friends," he says. "I don't really know Liu Wen very well. I like him though, he has been good for me." He smiles sadly, "So have you, ghost."

"Have you been here before?" I ask, trying to push him away from this mood.

He nods.

Liu Wen comes back and I am relieved to see him. If we play, Haitao will be distracted. "We're at a table in the back," he says. A young girl with a smooth white face and painted eyebrows comes to lead us to our table. I watch the swing of her narrow hips in her imperial Chinese gown embroidered with cranes and realize suddenly, she is not a woman.

Fascinated and more than a little amazed I cannot take my eyes off the boy. He gestures with exaggerated grace, catching hold of one sleeve and pointing with the other hand. He keeps his eyes cast down, glancing up at me only as I pass him. He doesn't smile and his eyes flicker down.

Am I aroused? No, only curious. There is nothing in cross-dressing I find stimulating.

But I watch him walk away, watch his hips swing, and look back to see Liu Wen grinning.

Into the golden glow. There are the five balls; one black lacquer, one red lacquer, two silver and in the center, a golden ball, almost invisible in the glow. Liu Wen flicks the silver ball directly at me and I barely manage to avoid taking it. I ricochet the red ball off the edge hoping it will come back towards me and Haitao hooks it in a long gliding curve and captures it and we drop out of contact. So fast.

"My point," Haitao says. He is all edge and excitement, and I think, this will be his night.

And it is. Even Liu Wen and I together can't stop him.

Every time we break contact Haitao is more exhilarated. His color is high, sweat beads along his upper lip and his wisps of hair lie wet at his temples in fine black curves like pen strokes. His hands rest lightly on the table edge, fingernails pink with perfect white half-moons. He doesn't move and yet like a cat, perfectly relaxed, he has the air of something on the edge of motion.

We break contact and Haitao says, "Seven," and I am clenching the table, my palms wet. He smiles, perfect white teeth, golden skin, white clothes and all wrapped in golden light. White and gold and electric. Liu Wen looks at him hungrily, and so do I.

Haitao looks down at the table, the light under his eyes carving his normal flat face into planes and high cheeks. His eyes are hooded. Liu Wen opens his mouth as if to say something—I know what he is going to say, to stop the game, and I want him to say it and I don't because I want the game to end but I don't want Liu Wen to get Haitao—and we drop back into contact.

I score four points and never once touch the golden ball. Liu Wen scores more often, but is hit with the silver too many times. He scores six points only by taking the gold ball. And immediately after that, Haitao, at seven points, reaches past where Liu Wen and I are playing with the black lacquer ball and effortlessly sets the red spinning into the gold. I reach reflexively for the golden ball, and Liu Wen sends the black careening to cut it off but I end up interfering with the black and it collides with the red and both skid off on tangents towards empty parts of the table. And Haitao effortlessly takes the golden ball.

We break contact. Haitao's head is thrown back, his eyes closed, his back slightly arched. His hands remain resting lightly on the edge of the table. He sighs, a shudder more like a sob, then opens his eyes and looks at us and smiles. "Ten points," he says.

Liu Wen starts to say something, clears his throat, "Do you want to keep playing, Zhang? I'm sure they can find a table for you." He isn't looking at me.

I should be good, I should disappear, as Liu Wen did the last time, but I wait, because it is Haitao's night. It is Haitao's choice. I swallow. He looks at Liu Wen, and then at me, and then back down at the table. I am reminded of the boy who led us here, and the way he didn't look at me. I think I have read something in Haitao's look, my heart begins to hammer. He will choose me. Choose me, Haitao.

The lights on the table flicker, and the lights above us dim, for a moment I see the bare bones of the building, normally hidden by a scrim of light and color, and this is an old, not very attractive place. The light comes back even brighter, distantly I hear the sound of glass shattering.

We look towards the sound, through the opening we see other people listening, and then I see someone yank off their contact.

"Turan soucha!" Liu Wen hisses, Police raid! He peels the contact off and flings it, it jerks at the end of the cord and swings. Liu Wen does not wait to see if we are coming, but goes into the room next to ours.

Haitao is motionless.

"Come on," I say. Liu Wen will know how to get out of here. Haitao looks at me.

I grab his hand and pull him into the next room, I think I see Liu Wen. People begin shouting and pushing past us towards the entrance, but I am counting on Liu Wen to know a back door. We are buffeted by two men and a woman running into us. I can't see Liu Wen, so I go in the direction I think he went. There is a service door, and I know I have found the exit, I open it.

A stairwell going up.

"Fuck," I say in English. Behind me the sound has changed. A woman screams. And some of the shouts have a different timber, the voice of authority. Reform Through Labor, or that old-fashioned penalty, a bullet in the back of my head. I panic and take the stairs, Haitao a weight I pull behind me. It's only one flight up to another door, a heavy industrial door, the kind they don't make much anymore. I try it and it opens and we are in a huge, dark space. Along one edge, far to our left I see a faint line of light.

The ceiling doesn't seal against the wall, that's the light from the club below us. I put one hand against the wall and start to jog to the right. This is the godown, the space could be huge, but there would have to be an office and from the office an entrance.

Haitao is breathing hard, sobbing for breath. "Zhong Shan," he whispers, "Zhong Shan—"

"Hush," I say in English and run hard into a pole, face and shoulder. The pain staggers me, brings tears to my eyes.

"Zhong Shan!" he says loudly.

"Xing xing," I say, it's okay. *Madre de Dios,* I think, Mother of God, help us. "Watch the pole," I say, and guide him around. Then go more slowly along the wall. I find a door, try it, it's locked. Of course. We keep on and get to a metal stair going up. "Careful," I say, *xiao xin,* in Chinese, small heart.

It seems to me that our feet are very loud on the stairs. We go up twelve steps, a door? A landing. Up twelve more steps. Around the landing. Up twelve more steps. I'm a construction tech and I've built a godown. I know I've fucked up; this is the stairs to the catwalks and the grid they use to hang the tackles to move heavy things. My cheek throbs. I have a grip on Haitao with my right hand, and hold on to the railing with my left.

The stairwell rings mutedly with our footsteps and we climb blind in the dark. At the back of the catwalk maybe there'll be another set of stairs to the loading bay. *Madre de Dios,* I pray in the language of my mother, who believed in Mao Zedong and Kierkegaard. We had a tortured Christ on a crucifix in the hall when we lived in Brooklyn. *Dios te salve, Maria, llena eres de gracia,* Hail Mary, full of grace. We are at the top, the landing is different. I feel the railing, find the catwalk. I can't do it in the dark, can't walk an industrial catwalk.

I follow the railing to the wall, nothing else, we are standing on a square platform with the wall behind us, the stairs to our right, the catwalk in front of us. The only thing to do is to go back down.

Below us there is a sudden surprisingly distant square of light. It is the door we came in. I sit down, pulling Haitao down against me, and a moment later lights flicker across the walls and ceiling, heavy search lights. I pull Haitao's head against my chest and he draws up against me. Perhaps we should make a break for it, run across the catwalks. At worst they will shoot us or we will misstep and we will fall and die. If they come to the stairs that is what we should do.

I can't do it. I can't move from this spot. If they climb the stairs they will find us here.

Their voices are distorted by space and distance. They will find us wrapped here in each other's arms and there will be no question of guilt or innocence. I don't really believe any of this. I have been picked up by a policeman once, when I was fifteen, for loitering, being out after curfew at Coney Island. He knew what I was there for, but just gave me a lecture and called my mother. And I was beaten up by nighthawks once in almost the same place where I was arrested. Both times I had the same sense of unreality.

I am rocking, rocking Haitao tight in my arms, but I can't stop myself.

The lights have stopped but I still hear voices. *"Sigue,"* I whisper, I can't think in Chinese, when I try to think of Chinese it comes out Spanish. Go on. Do it. Arrest us. Anything, just make it end.

They stop talking. I listen for the sound of their feet. I can't tell if I hear them or not, an empty godown is not a silent place. I can hear our breathing. I can hear my heart. I think I can hear Haitao's heart.

I listen to the words running through my head, *Padre Nuestro, que estas en los cielo, santificado sea tu nombre. Venga a nos tu reino.*

Hagase tu voluntad asi en la tierra como en el cielo. . . . Meaningless snatches of prayer. I think they are on the stairs, I can't exactly hear them, but I think I do. I count again. They are coming without lights. They wouldn't come without lights. I rock Haitao, he has my jacket clenched in his fists and he is hyperventilating. I can't hear over the sound of his breath.

Will Peter ever find out what happened to me? He will call Mama, and she'll tell him. She knows Peter is my friend. She may even suspect that there is more, she has never admitted that she knows what I am. She doesn't ask me about my life, I don't ask her about hers and every Christmas when I am home in New York I go and see her second husband and my half-brothers, and Craig came to stay with me when he was eleven and I still had a place. We went to the kite races.

They will tell her, will she tell Craig that his *huaqiao* half-brother is a fag?

It has been a long time.

Maybe they aren't coming.

But we wait for a long time.

Even when we know they aren't coming, we wait. Haitao begins to shake. "I want to die," he whispers, "I can't stand it. Stop it, please, make it stop."

I stroke his hair and rock him. I kiss his hair as if he were a little boy. "Hush," I whisper, "they're not coming." They may still be downstairs, we'll wait. "We're okay, nothing's going to happen to us here."

He shakes and shakes. I doze, and wake, and he is still trembling. My arms ache. My back aches. I shift, try to shift Haitao and he grabs hold of me. "Shhh, shhh. It's okay, here, lie this way. Shhh." I rub his back and his temples and soothe him as best I can. His face is wet. "I want to die," he whispers, "I'm so afraid."

But he stops shaking eventually, and we doze together. We stay there until dawn comes in through the dirty skylight.

*   *   *

I am so stiff I can barely move. In the night I have slid down
on my side and Haitao lies curled beside me. The light is not very
good, only enough to make out shapes. Haitao's white suit is a
little more visible.

"Haitao," I whisper.

He stirs.

"Now we should try to go," I say.

He sits up but doesn't look at me. I try to work the cramps out
of my back and arms, stand up and try to move about a bit. I am
chilled to the bone and my teeth start chattering. Haitao sits
woodenly.

"Come on," I say, "stand up." I reach down and take his upper
arm and he stands up.

The catwalk is too narrow for us to stand side by side. It's wider
than an I-beam, of course, but we are high above the floor and it
looks narrower. I take Haitao's wrist with my left hand and start
across it. I can see the control panel on the other side and a set
of stairs going down, but that side of the building is shadowed and
I can't see if there is a loading dock. There should be.

"Hold on to the railing," I say. Haitao does what he's told. I
wish he would think a little for himself, I am cold and I ache and
he's acting like a child. Damn it, I ought to leave him here, let
him find his own way out.

Anger is good. Anger is better than what Haitao is feeling, than
apathy or, what did Maggie Smallwood call it? *Perlerorneq*, the
awareness of the futility of it all. Despair. Underneath my anger
I am all too aware that I've been just as paralyzed as Haitao is
now.

There is something exhilarating about being the one who is
intrepid. I think, I have done it, I have saved us. We go step by
cautious step across the catwalk and I am exhausted and angry
and full of a hard, terrible joy. We have survived. Yes, it was luck

as much as anything else, but we made our own luck. The chain and tackle system dangles in lines and shadows all around us, the light slowly brightens above us. There is a purity of form and line; reality, hard lean reality is very beautiful.

We take the stairs down. I'm so tired my knees are shaking, but Haitao follows me without complaint. The door to the loading dock is bolted shut, but it isn't meant to be safe from the inside. And then we are outside and we walk away, not going around the front but climbing the fence in the morning half-light. I make a stirrup of my hands and boost Haitao up, then climb the chain link and drop, shaking with fatigue, on the other side. Haitao's white suit is streaked with rust like old blood, but we come out on a street two blocks away.

And then, it is all too normal. It is Sunday morning.

"It's okay," I say to Haitao. "We're okay."

He nods, listlessly.

"I'm never going to play pressball again," I say, grinning, but he doesn't respond.

I start watching for bus stop signs. "What is our bus?" I ask Haitao.

He doesn't act as if he heard.

"What number is our bus," I say. And when he doesn't answer, "Haitao!"

"Seventeen," he says. "A seventeen or a seventeen Special."

It is too easy, I find a stop for the seventeen and we stand, Haitao slumped against the wall with his eyes closed. The bus comes and the driver eyes Haitao's stained suit but nobody says anything. "Nanjing University," I say.

"Back," he says, "Up."

We climb up and go back and collapse into seats. Haitao nods. I stare out the window. Eventually his head comes down against my shoulder. The bus is warm and slowly the warmth creeps into me. I doze with my head against the glass, waking when we separate from the front, then again when we join another bus. I awake the third time when our segment peals off to go up, and I know we are close to the University so I wake Haitao. He is bleary-eyed.

We get off, the stop is familiar, and yet different. Just as the morning, which would usually be a beginning, is an ending to the night.

"I'll come up with you," I say to Haitao.

"It's okay," he says.

"No problem." I go up in the lift with him, and when we get to the flat, I send him in for a shower. "I just want to go to bed," he protests, but he has no fight in him. While he is in the shower I make tea and sweeten it. I check out the bruise on my face in the mirror in Haitao's bedroom—I have a blue knot and the side of my face aches. Tea and aspirin. I take my hair down.

Haitao comes out in his bathrobe and I feed him sweet tea and aspirin, and remembering Maggie Smallwood, talk to him softly. "It is a pretty morning," I say and, "you are warm now, and tired, and you'll sleep well. Finish your tea, the sugar will make you feel a little better, and then into a warm bed. We'll darken the windows, and I'll call this evening."

Then I make him drink all the rest of his tea and put him in bed. I dim the windows. I am so tired. I want to be clean like Haitao. But I sit for a moment and he says something for the first time since I asked him about the bus. "Don't go," he says.

"I'm here," I say, feeling a little foolish. "I'll stay, and I'll call you this evening."

He closes his eyes and I sit what seems like a long time, but which is really only five minutes by my watch. (I count the seconds. I decide to stay ten minutes, then seven, and then slide carefully off the bed at five.)

I dim the windows in the front of the apartment. It is easy, I've seen Haitao do it so many times, I just rest my fingertips against the glass and say "Dim," and when it is dark enough I take my fingers away. On the little table next to the door I see a letter signed with the red official chop of the University. I am tired and I almost leave it, but I pick it up.

"Comrade Yang:" it begins, they all begin with "Comrade." "This is to inform you that pending an official investigation from your home district, you are suspended from study—"

It is dated for Friday and it is open. Haitao has seen it, knew about it, but hasn't said anything. And Saturday night he was in a better mood than I have seen him in a long time. I think of his exhilaration at pressball. How he glowed gold and white.

I assume I have misunderstood the letter, read it again. My Chinese causes me to make mistakes, perhaps it is telling him he has been cleared? No, I go through the sentences carefully, my head beginning to throb from fatigue and strain. He is suspended, they are investigating him. Maybe he hasn't read it? But why would he print it out on Friday and then not read it?

I put the letter down and go, closing the door softly behind me. I am too tired to care now, I'll call him this evening and ask him. In the lift I put my hands in my pockets and find something in the right. The gold box with the tiger-eye lid that Haitao gave me the night before.

Xiao Chen is watching the news when I open the door.

"What happened to your face?" he asks.

"Very good party," I say, grinning. "Except that I walked into a door."

He shakes his head appreciably.

I shower and sleep. I awake a little before dinner, the sun is strong through the window and I am disoriented and still tired, but I know if I keep sleeping I won't sleep tonight. When I sit up all my joints crack like old sticks.

I wander out to the kitchen and flash heat some fried rice. Xiao Chen kids me about my dissolute life, tells me I've got mail. I figure it's Peter, I owe him a letter. Guilt makes me avoid printing the letter before I eat.

It's only one page—Peter's letters run to four or five pages and use every type of punctuation available.

Ghost,

Not to fret, I have sent this to you from the arcade, it is not on my system. This is just to say thank you. I have received my suspension notification and I cannot go through Reform Through Labor. I cannot face my family.

I wish to thank you for all you have done, I believe you will understand. From the first you have always understood, even when no one else did. Even your choice of names. I think perhaps I hoped that last night would show me I made the wrong decision, but when we were almost arrested I knew that I had been a fool to wait.

Think of me with kindness.

Haitao

"What is it?" Xiao Chen asks.

I don't know what to say, I am not sure what it is. He has run away, I think. Where will he go?

I call, there is no answer. The letter is dated today and the time on it is five-fifteen. It is a little after six, which is marked as the delivery time, meaning he sent it at five-fifteen on a forty-five minute delay. He can't have left this fast, unless he sent it on his way out.

I pull on my coveralls.

"What is wrong?" Xiao Chen asks.

"I don't know," I say, "I don't understand this message from my tutor."

On the arcade I pass where he would have sent the letter and catch the lift. When the lift opens the hall is full of people and there is a strong breeze. People are standing around chattering, their arms crossed, the way people stand around an accident.

There is a police tape blocking the hall right before Haitao's door and the breeze is coming through the door. It is more than a breeze, it is a strong wind. They have arrested him, I'm sure. The wind is like being up on the superstructure when a building is going up.

"What happened?" I ask two women standing there.

"The person in that apartment"—she points—"he broke his window and jumped out."

"Jumped out," I say, and then stupidly, "did he die?" We are over a hundred fifty meters above ground level standing in this urban cliff.

"Oh, yes," she says.

"He is my tutor," I say. And then add, "I am an engineering student."

"Why did he do it?" she asks.

"I don't know," I say.

We stand there for a minute and then I duck under the police tape. I should not, I should get on the lift and go back downstairs, but I have to see. The wind is strong in the doorway, it is coming from the great shattered starburst in the window. Police are picking through the pieces of glass or standing talking.

A man looks up at me, "Hey, what are you doing here! Don't cross the barrier!"

"He, h-he was my tutor," I stutter, "I am an engineering student."

"There is no tutoring today," the officer says.

On the floor, covered with crystals of glittering glass, are a pair of shoes, neatly folded white tights and white shirt. As if he had taken them off there, in front of his window.

"How did he break the window?" I ask. The windows are supposed to be shatterproof.

"He used a softening agent on it, then heated it with a hairdryer until it was brittle," the officer says. Then his expression softens. "Where are you from?"

"America," I say. "I'm American."

"Well, *tongxue,*" student, "there is nothing you can do here. You should go home.

"I can't go home," I say, "I have eighteen more months until I finish my classes."

He looks at me oddly. "No, no, I meant your dormitory."

A woman comes into the room, "He wiped his system," she says, "He made sure that we couldn't use the trace, either." Her feet crunch in broken glass.

I don't know what they are talking about. I back up. I duck under the police tape again, walk through the crowd with my head down. I am afraid. There are people in the lift. I look at the numbers and then at the floor.

In the arcade, I sit down for a moment on a bench, because I don't want to go back to my dormitory, and then I get up and make a call to New York. It is five-thirty in the morning in New York, Peter is not up.

"Rafael!" he says. "Hey! How are you doing!"

"My friend," I say, "You remember the one I wrote you about? My tutor."

"What happened?" he says.

"He killed himself," I say.

"How?" he says.

Why do we always have to know? What difference does it make? "He broke his window and jumped."

"Are you going to come home?" Peter asks.

Well, yes. I hope so. I don't want to die here. Then I think, he means right now.

"No," I say, "I have to finish school. I did well on my engineering examination."

We talk, I cannot say why so I say I don't know and talk around it. I think, it's good to talk, better than being alone, the money doesn't matter.

But all our words are empty.

Homework

(Alexi)

The inside of Martine's house is pretty, after two years of living here it still seems a luxury to live in this place. A lot of the homes on the Ridge are pretty. I never pictured life on Mars like this—I grew up in a frontier town on the edge of the corridor, my daddy was a scrap prospector, not a farmer but there were a lot of farmers and so I had an idea of what frontier farming was like. Some years they got crops, some years the People's Volunteers brought drinking water into town in trucks and when I was in senior middle school I used to go get water for my mother. We had two big fifty-liter plastic containers that we put in the back of an old three-wheel bike. I'd get them filled and then have to stand on the pedals to get the bike to go anywhere. I wanted to join the PV, but after I finished school and married Geri there were too many applicants. Then the party said that the drive to reduce carbon dioxide use was working. That the global temperature was falling, and it would be possible to resettle the corridor. So we went. A few years of hardship, and then, see, we'd be sitting on good, farmable land. When I left earth they were still talking about global temperatures falling, maybe a degree in fifty years. Three degrees, and they'll get back to temperature levels in the 1900's and it'll rain in Idaho, and across north central Africa and who knows, maybe it'll rain carp in Beijing, and flowers will bloom in the Antarctic but Geri still died and Theresa spent half of her childhood in resettlement camps.

The Ridge is hard work, Martine and I are up by five. I don't know if I've ever worked so hard in my life. But it's not like the corridor, where it didn't make any difference whether you worked or not, it all died. Martine and I put in another tunnel and goat yard to increase the goat herd, and now there are nineteen nannies and four of them are pregnant. And we added a room for Theresa. I didn't really want to do it, but I felt then as if it was really Martine's decision and if she wanted to take the risk, I was pretty well along for the ride. We're into negative credit, it'll take us a couple of years to pay the Commune back and if those goddamn goats get sick we'll spend the rest of our lives paying it back, but so far we're making our contributions. Martine's honey business is steady and I keep getting sidework doing re-programming. Even if the nannies all dropped dead tomorrow we'd probably get by. Give up beer and sell the strawberries instead of eating them, but get by.

Not that you ever really know how things will turn out. On the corridor, when things got bad, I got us by for awhile by scrap prospecting, like my daddy. Farming was a waste of time, anything we planted dried up if it ever made it out of the ground, so I used to take my little scooter and find what was left of some old road and go look for scrap. It never made much money, but at least it brought in something to buy food. Until the little scooter just gave up and I had to walk back the last twenty-five kilometers. If I had been farther away and had to walk I don't know how I'd have made it without water, but I was young enough then, I just walked home. Scared to death about how we'd make it without prospecting, but certain we'd make it somehow. When you're young it's always been all right before, you trust it will be all right this time.

But things are different here in the Commune. As long as there's the supply, the Commune has to make sure everybody has enough to eat, so we won't starve. And it looks as if Martine's expansion is going to pay off in the long run, as long as nothing major goes wrong. We complement each other, Martine and I. She's good with animals and I'm good with keeping things running smoothly.

We're good business partners, Martine and I. That's the one part of our lives we handle well.

Wednesday afternoon. I sit down and watch the tape of my class. I have a tutorial at five and I wanted to watch the tape last night, but I ended up working longer than I expected on reprogramming the tow-motor programs for the Commune.

I'm monitoring a class at Nanjing University, a systems class. I guess Nanjing is a very good school. I'd never have gotten near a university at home, and certainly never had a chance to do anything connected with a Chinese university, but some universities have this special, patriotic program to help the frontier effort so I get to audit the class. They get money from the party, and they get to pat themselves on the back and think of themselves as forwarding the party ideals.

This is the second rec I've watched and all that happened in the first class is that the prof belabored some obvious points about programming. Things are broken down into major points for easy memorization, the way the Chinese do everything. Four Modernizations. Three Revolutionary Ideals. Eight Legs Proof. The textbook is a little theoretical. The first class didn't have much to do with the book. I don't see how taking this course is going to help either me or the Commune, but the Ridge is footing the communications bill. Maybe I will learn enough to modify the Ridge controller system.

The translation is good. The prof is really speaking Chinese, of course. All I can say in Chinese are a few phrases I remember from senior middle school. *Ni hao. Ni hao ma? Wo hen hao, xiexie.* Hello, how are you? I'm fine, thank you. And I'm sure my tones stink.

The second class takes off at a gallop. I sit with the book on my lap, stopping the rec, reading the textbook until I have an idea what he's talking about, then letting him talk again. He whips through the first chapter in an hour, and starts on the second chapter and it actually gets kind of interesting, although I still can't see what good it's going to do me. The he assigns problems which I scribble down.

I took an advanced chemistry course in senior middle school. It was a correspondence thing, about five of us took it. My teacher had decided to "make a difference." We were going to pass entrance exams and go to university at Salt Lake. Anyway, the course had us do experiments where we'd have questions like:

> A sample of iron oxide was heated and treated with a stream of hydrogen gas, converting it completely to metallic iron. The original sample weighed 3.50 g and the resultant iron metal weighed 2.45 g. What is the empirical formula of the original compound?

It's like those jokes that start "A man, a woman and a duck cross Main Street," and go on for five minutes and at the end say, "and what was the name of the duck?"

Needless to say, that is the feeling that I have looking at the questions in front of me.

> A class 3 bundled reinforcement circuit with a
> 10^7 base can learn to recognize handwriting. It is

> run on three samples of different handwriting dis-
> played below. Using the word "cat," diagram two
> probable sensitivity patterns.

Right. The whole beginning of the question sets me up to think that I'm going to test for degree of error. I'm hell on degree of error. When I was learning to be a pilot and systems tech in the Army, we were always testing for degree of error, that tells you if the system is going to work or not. When I reprogram, I run a simulation and test for degree of error. Who cares which bundles are becoming sensitized?

I go back and read part of the chapter again. Maybe it's the fact that the text is translated from Chinese, but somehow I have trouble following the leap from the explanation to the examples of how to figure this stuff out.

Well, that's what I have a tutor for. I've got about an hour and a half until the appointment. Theresa calls and asks if she can stay at the creche and play with Linda and I tell her dinner is at six. Martine comes in from the goats.

"The CO_2 level's up in the new yard," she says.

Check the hardware. My area of expertise. "My tutorial's at five, I'll look at it after dinner. Theresa's at the creche with Linda. She'll be home at six."

So I kill time until almost five, then sit down and wait.

The screen beeps, but remains blank. There's a seven-and-a-half-minute delay, approximately. That's the amount of time it takes the carrier to flash the signal from one planet to the other. Somewhere in China my tutor has sat in front of a similar blank screen. So I introduce myself. "I'm Alexi Dormov," I say to the blank screen, feeling a little foolish. I tell her or him what I've done and explain my problem. Then I wait and kill time by paging through my book.

Seven minutes is a long time when you don't have much distraction. Then the image coalesces and I see a Chinese man making himself comfortable. He looks at a book in his lap and then at the screen. Actually, this is seven and a half minutes in his past. Right now he is receiving my signal, watching me recite.

"My name is Zhang," he says, "I'm in my second year here at Nanjing, studying systems engineering. I'm actually between my third and fourth year of study because I have a two-year certificate. I'm your tutor. My C-Mail Number is NJDX167, my personal suffix is 7994. Why don't you start by telling me what you've done and asking me any questions you might have. I'm going to let the screen record what you ask me so my answers will have, you know, maybe a better context. To fill time, I'll answer some of the questions most people have." He talks for about three minutes, I have elapsed time displayed on the screen, and then he looks at his book and notes.

He's speaking English—translation programs don't bother to lip synch. His English is very good and I wonder why someone studying systems at Nanjing University would have first studied English. Why is he my tutor? Do all students have to tutor someone? I feel as if I am staring. Will it look as if I am staring at him when he sees it seven and a half minutes from now?

I say that his procedure sounds fine. After a few minutes more I hear my questions, almost fifteen minutes after I asked them. He's looking at the screen and then his book. He has long hair, is that the fashion in China? He nods. "Turn to page, ah, twenty-six," he says. So I'll have a chance to get about four exchanges in an hour of tutorial. Well, maybe I can prep my classes ahead of time and be able to shoot him a whole stack of questions.

He explains sensitivity patterns, a lot of which I already know, then he makes up a problem and solves it step by step. I ask him to download any supplementary material he thinks would be helpful.

"Okay," he says, "Next session, give me a list of the references you have available, I mean, things like Qia's, ah," he pauses a moment, translating the title from Chinese to English I guess, *"Reference Guide to,* ah, *System Types."*

The session ends.

I shut the screen off, feeling more than a little unsatisfied with the whole arrangement. The Ridge is paying good credit for me to take an hour of carrier time. It's not like the class, that's a squirt, takes no time at all to receive the whole thing. I know there's a lot of space in the signal, that other things come in with it and get separated, but it doesn't seem worth what it costs.

Taking the class doesn't seem worth what it costs, even if the actual class doesn't cost anything. It's all theory. It's not practical. I don't see how it's going to help me with the Ridge's main problem. All of our system is over-extended, everything adapted to do more than it was designed to do, and we don't really have much back-up. It's a raw material problem, we just don't have enough hardware.

Theresa comes in and drops her bookbag on the floor in the living room. Martine dishes up dinner and asks me about my tutorial. I talk and watch her move around the kitchen. She is a tall woman, taller than I am by a finger's width, big-boned. Not pretty. She was an officer in the Army and that still shows in the way she holds herself. I review what I have done today, cleaned after the goats this morning and run the waste separator and distiller and spent the afternoon figuring out abstractions of systems engineering. Martine has worked all day, I know. And I have so much to do. I should be out in back, checking the garden, and she mentioned the CO_2 levels are off.

She clears the table. "The two of you can do your homework together," she says to Theresa and me.

"Have you got homework?" Theresa asks.

"A lot," I say.

Theresa giggles.

*   *   *

First thing Thursday morning, I check the CO_2 levels in the new yard. Eskimo, one of the old billies, plants his feet wide and shakes his head at me in challenge but the nannies all crowd around me. Theresa sometimes brings handouts and they've all become beggars. She's already fed them, that's her before-school chore. I break the litmus pack and stick the indicator on the wall, then I shovel goat manure for waste separation. Martine wants the goat yards as clean as the house, which I suppose is a good idea, but the goats aren't very cooperative.

The CO_2 levels are higher than usual. Not life-threatening to man or goat by any means, but unusual. I go back to the old goat yard and crack the second pack and stick the indicator on the wall. Lilith follows me around. She's one of the pregnant nannies. She's also my favorite, she's affectionate. I think Martine holds this against her, she said once that Lilith was easy. Nobody could ever accuse Martine of being easy. I pet Lilith, and shoo her out of my way and clean up.

The CO_2 levels in the old goat yard are high, too.

I put a sticker in the garden, oddly enough, O_2 levels are abnormally high. Of course, the plants are oxygenators but the system takes advantage of that. When Martine said there were problems in the new yard I suspected a leak, even a tiny leak can throw a regulator off. But in both goat yards and the garden?

The regulators are simple, like thermostats, really, and it seems an unreasonable coincidence that all three would go out at once. Which suggests that there's a problem with our controller. I put a sticker in the kitchen.

"What's that for?" Martine asks.

"All three of the yards are off," I say.

"Is it the programming?" she asks.

"The programming was fine until now," I say, keeping my voice normal. I did the programming to extend the system when we installed the yard. I handle the technical things, it's my half. Martine talks to the goats.

Martine looks at me, clear-eyed, direct. "Well, is it the system?" she asks.

"I don't know," I say. "I don't know what it is." If it's the system, we'll have to apply to the Commune for a new one. More negative credit. If they have one. If they don't we have to wait until some are allocated, and we're pulling away from the shipping window. Two years without a system. This holding couldn't go two years without a system, we'd have to close it and then start all over again in two years. Five minutes and I pull the sticker down and throw it in the paper box.

Martine is waiting, arms crossed.

"Too much O_2, like the garden. Maybe a leak is throwing everything off."

She opens a drawer and gets out a candle. I shut off the ventilation in the new yard and go out and spend the rest of the morning looking for leaks. Martine is good at finding leaks, she has an instinct, but even a newcomer like me can tell after a couple of hours that I'm not going to find anything. No drafts at any joints, the seams are all straight, no bubbles in the sealer. I turn the ventilation back on and turn it off in the old yard. After that I check the garden, find the cat sleeping on top of the ductwork, which tells us where she goes when we can't find her, but no leaks.

Martine comes out to the garden. "Find anything?" she asks.

"No," I say, "the joints all look fine. I'll check the programming and run some diagnostics."

"Do you think it might be the programming or do you think it's the system?"

I shrug, I don't know.

"Alexi," she says sharply, "we'll deal with it, whatever it is."

Martine and her iron will. Sometimes an iron will isn't enough.

I go back into the house and jack into the system and set up tests to run. When I jack out Martine is standing there. I'm sitting on the floor next to the panel so I have to look up at her. She's got Martine's intent look. If you don't know her you'd think she was frowning at you.

"The tests have to run," I explain. "It'll be awhile."

"I just came to tell you come eat some lunch." She puts her hand on my shoulder, and I cover it with mine. Uncharacteristic of Martine, that touch. I don't know whether to take it as comfort or an indication of the gravity of the situation.

So we eat lunch, and I go out and clean the filters in the garden. Martine comes out and opens the skylight. Light wind on the surface. Sand shushes softly, the sky is an unnatural cobalt and the sunlight is thin but hard, even with the ultraviolet filtered out. We work through the early afternoon. Martine's bees drone, working the garden with us. We're the only place with screen doors in the whole Ridge, but I like the bees. I like the screen doors, too. They're normal, like home on earth.

At three-thirty the one between the house and the garden slams and Theresa comes in with Linda.

"Hi, Little Heart," I say, and realize my mistake too late. She gives me a withering look. It is not appropriate to call an eight-year-old by what she refers to as her baby-name in front of her friends.

"Hello, Comrade Alexi," Linda says politely, "Hello, Comrade Martine."

"Dad, can we have lemonade?"

I glance at Martine, who nods. "Okay. Don't do anything with the system, I'm running tests."

"Okay."

Linda started coming over about a year ago and she and Theresa have become "best friends." At first I was afraid that the attraction was the fruit juice in the cooler, but I think that the truth is that there just aren't that many children. There are less than fifteen hundred people in Jerusalem Ridge.

At four I go inside. I can hear the girls talking in Theresa's bedroom—although I can't hear what they're saying. I jack in. My diagnostics indicate something is off. Maybe it really just needs reprogramming. I don't care if I screwed up the programming, I can handle that.

Martine has a council meeting so I flash soup and biscuits for dinner. Linda's mother comes by at a little before five, Linda is watching for the scooter and she and Theresa run down to the pull-off.

It is all so normal, so family. What if the problem isn't something I can solve with reprogramming? What if our system is shot?

Martine puts on her council meeting outfit, a blouse and slacks. We eat dinner and Theresa tells us about the report she has to write, on one of the leaders of the Second American Revolution. After dinner, she has to be reminded to feed the goats, she does it every evening, but she always has to be reminded. Martine keeps telling me that if I keep reminding her she'll never learn to think for herself. I keep reminding Martine that she's eight years old.

Martine takes our scooter, she has to talk with Aron Fahey about something first, so she leaves early. Theresa and I settle at the kitchen table to do our homework.

She doesn't know whether to do her report on Zhou Xiezhi or Christopher Brin. "Can I use the system now?"

"Go ahead," I say. She calls up an index and I help her pick out sources. Her reading scores are excellent, ahead of her age group. She's still behind in math but her teacher says not to worry, she's catching up. She reads the story of Zhou Xiezhi to me;

> Zhou Xiezhi was the son of doctors. When he was a boy, he went to his grandmother's farm. His grandmother had many animals, including a big, pink pig. Zhou Xiezhi liked the pig. Each day, Zhou Xiezhi talked to the pink pig. He fed the pig apples and called the pig "Old Man." The pig

would make happy noises, grunt, grunt, grunt, and Zhou Xiezhi would laugh and laugh.

On New Year's Day the family had a big dinner. They had chicken and beef. They had fish because in Chinese the word for "fish" sounds like the word that means "more food." There were dumplings and pork ribs. Zhou Xiezhi ran to wish the pink pig a Happy New Year.

But the pig was gone. Where was the pig? His grandmother told him, "The pig was part of New Year Dinner."

Zhou Xiezhi cried and cried. After that day he never ate meat again.

I remember the story of Zhou Xiezhi's soft heart, of course we studied it in primary school. When I got older I was disappointed to learn that the famous vegetarian from China who came to America to help the Soviet Revolution cold-bloodedly ordered that every third captive be put to death until the capitalist defenders of Gatlinburg surrendered.

Don't get me wrong, I realize that killing some sixty captives saved him from having to kill thousands of capitalists and lose thousands of his own soldiers, taking Gatlinburg, I just wonder at the mind that could calculate that way, balance human life against human life. No matter how anguished his diary entries.

Theresa writes her report about Zhou Xiezhi, the military genius from China who left his home forever to organize the People's Army of America, and died a martyr to the American revolution. I help her draw a timeline. At seven-thirty she watches half an hour on the vid, then at eight she gets her bath. In bed by eight-thirty, she's allowed to read until eight-sixty and then lights out.

I read through my textbook, looking for clues that will help me with the system. Martine gets home and goes to bed and I continue to work, trying to solve problems. When I give in it is after eleven. I sleep in the third bedroom, where I slept when we were first married, because I don't want to wake Martine up. It's good that I do, in the morning the bedclothes are twisted from tossing all night.

"I got your questions and your list of sources," my tutor says. "If you didn't get the sources I sent you, let me know." He glances at me, or at least at the screen. He has a funny look. "Thank you for the compliment on my English, but I'm from Brooklyn."

From Brooklyn? New York?

He clears his throat and begins answering my questions. Some he answers quickly. Some take him longer. I find the seven-and-a-half-minute delay frustrating.

"Comrade Zhang," I say about forty-five minutes into the hour, "This doesn't have anything directly to do with the class, but the biggest problem I face as a tech is that we keep having to use our systems to do things they weren't constructed to do, and to expand them to maximum capacity. If you can think of any information on how to increase the system's efficiency, I would be very grateful to see it."

He is looking through his textbook for a problem to use as an example. He finds one, says, "Turn to page sixty-seven." He reads a moment, smiles briefly at the screen, a quick, kind of apologetic thing. "Okay," he says, "for example." He tends to over-explain, since I can't tell him what I already know.

Fifteen minutes later I hear my voice asking my question. "Ah," he says, "I can't think of anything off-hand, but let me see what I can come up with."

End of session. From Brooklyn. American, I assume, unless there's a Brooklyn, Australia or England or something. But he sounds American.

He must be one smart son of a bitch.

*   *   *

We get our oxygen out of Mars' atmosphere and most of our energy is solar. New Arizona uses fission, but we don't really need it, having lots of unused surface space. Before I start reprogramming I decide to check the solar collectors and the CO_2 tanks. Ultraviolet radiation breaks some of the CO_2 down, but not enough. We use algae for the rest. Occasionally somebody cracks a tank and the algae gets loose, New Arizona screams about corrupting the martian environment. There isn't really much martian environment to corrupt, some indigenous pseudo-algae and lichens at the poles. Our algae gets irradiated out of existence anyway. But I try to get out and check the tank about every six months. Sandstorms are tough on everything.

We have an airlock between the house and the garden, set in the roof of the tunnel. It's tiny, big enough for a person to crouch in. I have to go down to Equipment in town and borrow an ARC, we don't have one and don't really need one. The suits don't fold, and it's a pain to get it bundled up enough to tie it on the back of the scooter. The Army would have fits if they ever saw it, it doesn't exactly fit safety specs. The couplings are old-fashioned gaskets and the whole suit is a mess, but when I get home I pressurize it and stand it out in the garden for an hour and if it has any leaks they're slow enough I'm not going to care.

The cat, Mintessa, is alternately fascinated and irritated. She haunts the garden while I fiddle with the suit. I polish it up, the last time I borrowed one the heating system was very efficient and besides smelling like every other poor soul who'd ever sweated inside it, it nearly roasted me. I scoot a boot across the pavement at her and she arches her back, goes sideways and hisses. Maybe Geoff Kern had it last, he's got three dogs. Or maybe she just doesn't like highly reflective surfaces.

The inside has the ethene reek of cleaning solvent. I stand a moment in the garden, modeling my underwear for the hostile cat, and then clamber into the thing, sealing the front and then boots and helmet and gloves. The pressure holds in the suit, the back-pack doesn't quite follow my back and the flat powerpack at the base flares into a fishtail that presses above my kidneys if I stand too straight.

I put the ladder under the little airlock, pull myself into it. I couldn't pull myself up so easily in earth gravity, but it's easy to lift myself in and crouch, close the door. I hope Martine doesn't move the ladder for some reason—she knows I'm doing this, she wouldn't move the ladder, just a moment's paranoia.

The little airlock has a pump that labors mightily to pull out some of the air mixture. It doesn't create much vacuum, but it's always a shame to waste mixture. Then the outer atmosphere vents in and I crank the outer door open, straighten up and brace against the wind. My facemask polarizes. I can't remember what season we're in. I squint at the sky, almost black through my darkened facemask, and it seems to me the sun is north. Of course, we're pretty far down in the southern hemisphere, the sun better be north. There's the crest of the ridge behind me, sunlight glinting off the curve of our skylights. The rest of the settlement is in the other side of the ridge. In front of me the land is full of dark chunks of rock in rusted soil.

I always thought of Mars as a desert and somehow expected it to look like home. Other than being dry, it doesn't. The soil color is wrong, for one thing, for another, the only erosion on Mars is wind erosion. For another, there are more rocks. I guess most of our soil comes from water and the action of plants and insects on rock. Pictures of some of the areas down at the pole show stuff that looks more like the baked ground of home, but a great deal of it is huge, cracked areas, like baked mud. Except the plates of cracked soil are meters across, and the cracks are bigger. Step-into bigger. Martian landscapes are exaggerated, simplified. Every school child has seen pictures of Olympus Mons; there's not a mountain on the whole of earth as pure or as huge as Olympus Mons. The crater is ninety klicks across.

Still, I like coming out once in awhile. There's no real distance in the ridge, no vista, no perspective. Everything feels inside. Most of the time I don't think about it, but when I get outside in the sunlight I always find myself stretching. Unfortunately when I stretch in the ARC the powerpack digs into my back, but it still feels good.

Walking on Mars is difficult. I've tried to make a kind of path to the tank but the stones are wobbly and there's no flat place to put my feet. I pick my way across, arms waving for balance, and check the filters.

They're full of sand, but they're built for that. I empty them but the next sandstorm will fill them. The big, black O_2 holding tank looks fine. I take the panel off. My fingers are cold. Just my luck, the last suit I had overheated, this one doesn't heat at all. The panel covering the instrument readouts is, of course, on the windward side. I turn my back into the wind, hoping the backpack will keep me a little warmer. It's only about ten centimeters thick at the dorsal ridge, not very protective, and even so the backs of my legs begin to get cold. Everything looks fine, all the quaintly old-fashioned L.E.D.s registering the way they should. There's no way to jack into the system out here, no external jack on the ARC anyway.

I pick my way back to the airlock and squat, pull the door closed over my head and crank it shut, feel the goosebumps on my arms and thighs while the pump tries to force most of the CO_2 out.

The ladder is still there, too. I swing down to it.

Martine is standing by the screen door with two trays of seedlings. She was supposed to be building a bee box, either she finished or she's taking a break. She waits while I pop the helmet. "How's the tank?"

"Fine," I say. "I emptied the filters. The heater doesn't work on this thing."

"I thought you were back in a hurry." She puts down the trays.

"Have you seen Min?" I ask.

"The cat? She's up on the ductwork, in a snit."

"She doesn't like the suit either," I say.

Bright words. I didn't expect to find anything wrong out there. Maybe it's not the system. Maybe I'll find the problem reprogramming.

"Are you going to check the programming this afternoon?" Martine asks.

"Not this afternoon," I say, "I've been fiddling with this thing for days, I've got to get caught up on some other things." I don't look at Martine. Martine gets right down to things and if it takes all night, it takes all night. But I'm not Martine.

The bed is too warm, I can't get comfortable. I'm aware I'm keeping Martine awake, I should go and sleep in the other room, but I'm not really awake or asleep, and if I get up she'll ask what I'm doing. I don't know if she prefers sleeping with me or not. I *think* that we have a decent sex life, I mean she's never said anything one way or another. Not that she should have to, of course. I mean that the *act* seems satisfying enough to her, and although she once made the comment that she had gotten accustomed to sleeping alone, I feel she prefers to have someone in bed with her now. I have tried to make her feel it was a good idea to marry me, that it benefited her as much as it did me. I am grateful, for myself and for Theresa.

Sometimes I feel as if I carry this marriage on my back. There were times I felt trapped by my first marriage, by Geri, and the obligation of a child in that situation, it's a normal enough feeling in any marriage and I'm certain that there are times Martine wonders why she ever took us on. But I have to believe that this marriage is what Martine wants.

I jerk awake, the alarm has gone off and for a moment I am thinking that it can't be morning and I can see the chron blinking 2:18 in blue numbers, and then I realize it's Martine's alarm signaling that the air mixture is off somewhere. A leak. Sometimes she'll have three in a month, sometimes we'll go three months without one.

I hear her get out of bed, listen to her move around the room, out into the main room. I won't be able to go back to sleep until she leaves, and I won't really sleep well until she's back, which tonight probably means I won't get much sleep because it usually takes a couple of hours.

I hear her come back, the light is on in the main room and I am trying to avoid it, digging my face in the crook of my arm. "Alexi?" she says.

"Hmm?" I say.

"The alarm is from our yards."

"What?" I say.

"The alarm." She speaks quietly, but doesn't whisper. "It's ours, the air mixture is off in our goat yards. It's pretty far off in the new yard, not as bad in the old."

I get out of bed, grab my pants and check the system. Our system shows a high CO_2 level in the old yard so I jack in to manually raise the O_2 levels but I can't manipulate the system. I'm doing everything I'm supposed to do and the relays feel frozen.

I jack out, run a clear, jack back in. I feel the tension that says I'm controlling the regulator and change it, but instead of changing it freezes up on me again. I know we're screwed. That's not programming, that's a glitch in the actual system.

Martine is waiting. "The system's frozen," I say. "It's not regulating the house or the yards." I shut it down, throwing everything on the little back-up manual system. Then I jack in and turn on the lights in the yards and the kitchen. "I don't know how high the CO_2 is out there, I don't know if the system was registering correctly or not."

"I'll test," Martine says.

"Put one up in the kitchen, too." I use the back-up system to start cycling CO_2 out of the yards, but it can take a couple of hours. I check the house temperature, we're running a little cold.

The O_2 levels in the kitchen are a little high. I wonder why the system would do better in the house than in the yards. I hear Martine calling me from the garden.

"Alexi, there's too much CO_2, the goats are groggy."

"It's okay in here, how's the garden?"

"It's all right." Martine frowns. "I can't put the goats in the garden."

They'd have a field day and we'd never see strawberries again. "Bring them in the kitchen," I say.

Martine looks at me as if I have lost my mind. "Nineteen goats in our kitchen?"

"What else are you going to do with them? It'll be a couple of hours before the air quality is all right in the yard."

I use furniture to block off the kitchen from the Main Room.

"What are you doing?" Theresa asks. She's standing in the hall, wearing her white nightgown, her hair sleep-tangled and her first under her chin the way she used to do when she was younger.

"The air mixture is bad in the goat yards," I say. "We're going to put the goats in the kitchen. Can you go out and help, hold the doors open? Go get your slippers."

Martine comes in, a goat under each arm. She drops them splay-legged on the floor, and one of the nannies, Carlotta, I think, folds to her knees with a plop. The goats close their slit-pupiled eyes. I climb over the furniture and follow her back to the new yard. The air smells stale, or is it just because I know? The goats lie around, most not bothering to move when we come in. Strange sight, all the quiescent goats, black and whites, whites, bearded.

I pick up a nanny and Einstein, who, groggy or not, manages to knock me in the chin tossing his head. Next trip back he is standing just in the door to the kitchen, shaking his head to warn me back.

"Theresa?" I call. She climbs over furniture. "Keep Einstein, baby."

She pulls the goat away from the door and sits down on the floor with him. Martine and I haul goats. They're not heavy, just not made for carrying. They're better for Martine, I pick them up and like as not they struggle.

Coming through the garden with my fourth armload of goat I hear hooves on the kitchen floor. Carlotta is on her feet. "Well, we're not going to have brain-damaged goats," Martine says, coming towards me on her way for her next armload of goat.

"How could you tell a difference?" I ask.

Nineteen goats fill Martine's kitchen. They revive awfully fast and clamber all over each other.

"Do you think we'll be able to put them back in the yard to milk them?" Martine asks.

"Yeah," I say, "in a couple of hours they should be all right. You two go on back to bed, I'll watch goats."

"Come on, Theresa," Martine says.

"Do I have to go to school tomorrow?" Theresa asks.

"Why not?" I ask.

"'Cause of all this," she says, exasperated. "I won't be rested."

"Life's tough," I say. "Go to bed now so you'll be rested."

"Dad," she says, "I need to help."

"Nothing to do. Go on."

She says good night rather sullenly and climbs over the furniture. I sit up on the counter.

"Dad!" I hear her call.

"What?"

"My light won't go on."

I hear Martine say, "You don't need a light to sleep."

"Go to sleep!" I call, reinforcement, I hope. The lights are on the system. Everything is on the system. Which reminds me that I have to increase the O_2 to the kitchen, nineteen goats are going to use a lot of air. I climb—rather awkwardly actually—over my furniture barricade and Martine comes back down the hall. "I want to increase O_2 in the house," I say. "Go on to sleep."

"I won't be able to go back to sleep now," she says.

"Well, go lie down, then," I say. Behind us something clunks and thumps at the barricade and Einstein is in the living room.

I start after the goat, who takes off down the hall, and Martine and I finally corner him in the bathroom.

"That furniture isn't going to stop him," Martine says. Einstein is a shaggy white goat, the kind that look like someone threw a stringy carpet over them.

"Any ideas?" I ask.

Martine thinks a moment and then closes the bathroom door. "Let him stew," she says, "there's nothing he can hurt in there."

His hooves clatter on the bathroom tile. It's dark in there. I hear a muted bleat. I don't think I've ever heard Einstein sound nervous. Maybe he'll have a nervous breakdown and never be right again. It's not that I don't like Einstein, exactly, it's just that he's always been a pain. As Martine says, he's smart.

"Did you lock Einstein in the bathroom?" Theresa calls from her bedroom.

"Yes," I answer, "do you need to go?"

"No," she says, to my relief.

"Go to sleep, Theresa."

I help Martine climb over the barricade, and shove the table more solidly against it. We wade through goat and perch side by side on the counter.

"Do you want a shirt?" Martine asks.

"Not bad enough to go get one," I answer. "You've seen me without a shirt before."

Martine touches her hair self-consciously, barely brushing it with her fingertips, then smooths it firmly.

"It looks all right," I say.

Startled, she drops her hand in her lap. Martine takes personal compliments badly. "Cleo!" she snaps at a goat pushing at the barricade. Cleo doesn't stop and Martine sighes but doesn't go after her.

Oh, I'm tired. And things are a mess. "We're almost out of indicator packs, aren't we?" I ask.

"I imagine," Martine says. "In the morning I'll pick some up, and tell Equipment that our system is down. Can you fix it?"

"No," I say.

"I didn't think so," Martine says and sighs again.

"What are we going to do?" I ask.

"Can you keep the air mixture good manually?"

I shrug. "After a fashion. I guess if I had to I could make some sort of automatic regulator. I don't know if I could do the house, the garden and both goat yards."

"Then we'll close off the new yard and sell some of the goats," Martine says. "We'll see if we can run one yard on manual, at least until we get a new system."

"It might have to wait until the next window," I say. The next window is over a year away.

"We could get one on the free market in New Arizona," she says.

"We don't have the credit," I say.

"We can borrow."

I don't say anything.

After a moment she takes my hand. "Alexi," she says, "this isn't the end of everything, we're not going to lose the place. We may have to give up beer and lemonade and sell strawberries and green beans for awhile."

"It's a lot of money," I say.

Irritated, she says, "You are the most paranoid man imaginable. You think this is debt, you wouldn't believe what I did to get this place started."

"Things don't always go right," I point out.

"And they don't always go wrong, either. And stop talking so quietly. You know, whenever you're upset about something it's as if you had to iron all the expression out of your voice."

"That's better than screaming and raving, isn't it?" I say. I do sound curiously flat, even to my ears. I don't feel flat.

"All right, Alexi," she agrees. Disappointment in her voice, in her body language. We're still holding hands, but I'm sure she doesn't realize it.

"I didn't ask you to marry me," I say, defending myself.

"Son of a bitch," she says, not particularly at me, it has the sound of a general expletive. I'm taken aback, Martine doesn't swear much.

"I should have known. Okay. You want a divorce, we'll divorce."

There it is, proof of how badly I've failed her, failed this whole thing. "I don't want a divorce," I say, "but I'm willing to do whatever you want." I never saw myself sitting on the counter in the kitchen, our feet disappearing into a sea of goats, holding Martine's hand while we discussed divorce. Cleo shoves at the barricade. "Damn it," I leap off the counter and haul the nanny away, shove Theresa-the-goat down. When I turn around, Martine is watching me, and she looks so sad, so, what is the word I am looking for? So devastated. Martine has great huge dark eyes, funny how I never thought of how big her eyes are until this moment, in her pale long face.

"Alexi," she says, forlornly, and to my great consternation she starts to cry.

You have to understand, Martine doesn't cry. At least not in my experience. Martine is iron. She's Army. Discipline. For a moment I don't have any idea what to do. So I wade back through goats and climb up onto the counter and put my arms around her.

"It's all right," I say, and other, soothing things, things you say when someone is crying.

"I know I'm old," she says, sniffling. "I know it wasn't fair, using the holding as a bribe. I thought, though, it would work out." Martine's strong, rather prominent nose gets red, and she looks older when she cries. Certainly not prettier.

"You're not old," I say.

"I'm forty-four," she says, "I'm ten years older than you—"

"Eight," I correct.

"Men like younger women."

"I never felt worthy of you," I say, deeply, from the bottom of my heart.

That makes her cry harder. "I don't want you to feel worthy," she says, "I want you to like me!" She pulls away and gets down among the sea of goats and shoves Lilith out of the way so she can open a drawer and pull out a dish towel.

"I do like you," I say, perplexed. "I like you, I even love you."

"But you're always worrying about pulling your own weight," she says. "You're always going to feel like this was my farm first, so you owe me. Everything is debt, debt, debt. You owe Theresa because her mother died. You owe me because of the holding. You owe the Commune because of the new yard so you take this class and try to figure out how to make it useful. Nobody gives a damn if you ever use this class or not, it's *politics*, Alexi. It looks good on the report to New Arizona!"

I don't know what to say. After a minute I say, "You make it sound as if it's a crime to be grateful."

"It's not being grateful," she says. "The flip side of grateful is resentment. You're not my slave, I don't want you to be my slave."

"Hold it," I say. Goats bleat. We are getting loud and Theresa is going to hear this. I grab her arm, "Come on," and haul her out into the garden. "You've exaggerated this all out of proportion. I'm not your slave, I don't feel like your slave, maybe I do worry about keeping up my end. But I never know what you think! You never tell me if you like the way things are or you don't like the way things are. I don't know how you feel about me. I don't know if you like being my wife. Hell, I don't even know if you like sex with me!"

"You don't have to talk so loud," Martine says.

"A minute ago you were complaining I didn't talk loud enough!"

Martine starts to laugh. It runs through my mind that she's hysterical, after all it's between two-thirty and three in the morning.

"What's wrong?" I say.

"It's funny," she says, laughing.

"What?"

"Here we are with a kitchen full of goats, having our first married argument."

"Is this our first argument?" I ask, trying to remember previous arguments.

"Our first real one," she says.

"We argue about Theresa, you're always telling me not to remind her to feed the goats."

"That's not an argument. I say it, you say she's eight years old and then we don't say any more." She grins at me, red-nosed from crying.

"If this is our first argument—" I say thoughtfully.

"And we've even brought up"—she drops her voice—"the 'D' word, so it qualifies."

"—then we must really be married. Like people who don't get married so one of them doesn't have to go to the South Pole."

"Which would normally mean that right now we should make up," she says, "except—"

"Yes?" I say.

"We have a kitchen full of goats, Mr. Dormov. But I do like," her voice quavers a bit, "sex with you."

"And I like sex with you. And I don't think you're old," I say. "Ms. Jansch." I put my arms around her and give her a hug. "How about if we go back into the kitchen and sit on the counter and smooch."

"As long as the goats don't start chewing on the furniture," she says.

Daoist Engineering

Zhang

The train rests heavily on track three, long, gleaming and white. White is the color of death in the East and dawn is the time of burial. My breath is white. The platform is lined with people waiting to get on the train. I have a soft-seat ticket and stand near the end of the platform in a cluster of people waiting for soft-seat and sleeper berths. By sheer foolish luck I am privileged, Engineer Zhang on his way to the site. I am not yet really an engineer, I have to co-op first, but the co-op company has paid for this.

My fellow passengers are business travelers—men dressed as I am in black suits with red shirts, the uniform of the *bailing jieceng de*, the white-collar class (so why, if they are called "white collar" do they wear red?), and *qingderen*, "green men," except that of course the army wears silver-gray trimmed in red. The businessmen hunch their shoulders a bit and read their flimsies, straddling their briefcases. The officers, there are three, stand in a small group, shoulders thrown back, oblivious to the weight of the early hour, talking quietly to one another.

I find a fax and pick up the day's news and carry it back so as to blend in. World news first, in America there is a drought in the corridor, families along the fringes are being evacuated. In related news, the world CO_2 level has fallen for the third straight year and science predicts that if the trend continues in fifty years we'll see more rain across northern Africa, Australia, the middle of China and western America. In Paris a structural failure caused a wall to collapse in an apartment complex and thirty-two people are missing, believed killed.

I turn the pages until I find an article on a commune in Hubei which is celebrating its one hundred fiftieth year of existence. Imagine that, a hundred and fifty years. Haitao couldn't even make it to thirty-five.

The doors sigh open. Further down the platform the people press forward trying to push on before all of the hard seats are taken. Above us huge smiling conductors hang in the air saying gently but firmly, "Do Not Push To Get On The Train." At soft seat, we wait in line, our seat numbers already guaranteed.

The air in the train smells new and unused. The seats are pale gray, the soft music is about the same color. The officers fit the decor. I find my seat which is next to a window, shove my bag in the overhead and hope they start soon. Trains serve coffee as well as tea and I'm looking forward to a cup. Finally I feel the sudden suspense as the mag-lev comes on, and then we begin to slide smoothly out of the station. Pale faces upturned watch us go. A dispenser hung off the ceiling comes down the aisle and I get my cup of coffee, peal off the top and wait for it to heat. I bow my head, wreathed in the aroma and somewhere deep in my head some primitive portion of my brain is momentarily lulled into believing I am home. For a breath I feel ease. Home.

Wuxi. The name means "tinless" and refers to tin mines exhausted over a thousand years ago. We cross the Grand Canal before we get to the train station. I am the only person in my car who gets off; the next stop is Suzhou and after that, Shanghai, the financial heart of China. The door sighs open and I swing my bag in front of me and step down. The air is full of mist and drizzle, thick with moisture even under the cover that protects the platform.

"Engineer Zhang?"

I turn, looking, and find a dark, neat little man. "Not yet," I answer smiling, "only Student Zhang."

He laughs politely. "I am Engineer Xi. I will see to it that you are called Engineer Zhang by the time you leave here."

We make the requisite small talk on the platform, did I have a good journey? Did I eat yet? Chinese do not often talk about the weather. Behind us the mag-lev shifts from inert to alive, although not watching closely I don't see the train rise bare centimeters above the track. It begins to slip soundlessly forward and I follow Engineer Xi back to and through the station.

Students in a university live transient and comparatively marginal existences. That is true the world over. A university is concerned with preparation for the future and there is an underlying philosophy that overcrowded living conditions and a lack of the comforts of the middle class is not only excused but somehow educational. In Brooklyn, students who lived at school were six to a room. At thirty-one I am not particularly interested in a marginal existence, feeling that perhaps I have paid my dues. But student life in Nanjing has not seemed very marginal, at the very least the amount of hot water is astonishing. I shower every day without regard for cost. The rooms are clean and pretty in their way. Comfortable. For a foreigner life in a Chinese university is a pleasure, full of unexpected amenities—for example, when I discovered therm containers. The idea that I pull the therm of coffee out of the cupboard, open it, and in a minute it's hot just amazes me. Sure I know all about the way the lining reacts with light to excite the water molecules. I'm just astounded that they would go to all that trouble.

It is only now, in Wuxi, that I discover that the definition of marginal is comparative. Which is to say that "marginal" means one thing in New York, and an entirely different thing in the Middle Kingdom. The first lesson is the car waiting for us.

"Engineer Zhang," Engineer Xi says, "this is Driver Shi."

Driver Shi nods at me and smiles. The car is a *Renminde-Hou,* a "People's Tiger." I've heard of Renmin cars. Engineer Xi opens the back door and I get in. The door closes and my ears feel the way they did on the flight over here, as if we have been completely isolated. It smells different than I expected, faintly sweet, lemony. The interior is uniform gray. I've been in a car before, three times, in fact. My mother hired a car to take me to the hospital when I broke my arm; my father hired a car to take us from the port to his father's place in California. (That car was red and had a slogan across the front panel where the instruments are. My father told me what it said: "Revolution is not a dinner party.") I rode in a car when Janvier got married just out of middle school; I was a member of the wedding. That car was also red. The cab that took us to the hospital was yellow, of course.

The feeling of movement in a car is stronger than it is on a train, acceleration pushes me firmly back in my seat, and when the car goes around corners the pull right or left is very sharp. The first time we turn I grab the door, and am embarrassed that Engineer Xi doesn't, but he pretends not to notice.

The next surprise is the office complex of Wuxi Engineering Technologies. Red lacquer roof tiles swoop in graceful waves down the hill. The buildings themselves are black matte. Engineer Xi describes how the building fuses traditional Chinese architectural details—the many connected buildings and the roofs with the upturned eaves—with more modern architectural technology. The black matte walls actually absorb enough light and sound radiation to provide the energy needed to run the complex. Driver Shi glances back. "Do you know why the eaves go up?" he asks. "Demon slides. Demons can only travel in straight lines, so when a demon came down from the sky it would hit the roof and be shunted along to the eave and whip off the end back into the sky."

"So we are well protected at Wuxi Engineering," Engineer Xi deadpans and we all laugh.

Inside everything is red and black. Black oriental rugs that look like silk with huge red medallions in the centers, red lacquer walls. The young man at reception is dressed in red and black, of course, but here the effect is even more conservative, as if the young man is actually a part of the decor.

The wonders multiply, maddening and exhausting. Here no one jacks in, instead, Engineer Xi explains, the system will be attuned to me and I will be, in a sense, permanently jacked in. I can call on information anytime I want. Included, he says, is a syntax and vocabulary in Mandarin, should I ever need it. Although, he adds politely, I speak very well.

I am shown my cubicle and desk, beautiful shining black lacquer with red lacquer fixtures. I am taken to the systems department where I am attuned to the system. All I do is jack in and a technician instructs the system to attune and it does. I jack out and query the time. 10:52. The information pops up. Always before I could only access information when I was jacked in, it gave me a sense that I knew what I thought and what the system told me, but now, how do I know what is system and what is Zhang?

We eat in the cadres' dining room. There is a cafeteria for workers, although I am assured that the food comes from the same kitchen. There are cold plates on our table which no one eats; sliced, spiced tofu, pickles, kimchee and peanuts. We are offered beer, I decline after Engineer Xi does. The chopsticks are cloisonne, the plates china. We have cloth napkins. Lunch is white fish cooked with ginger and scallions and tender vegetables.

I have the feeling that they will discover who I am, that I'm just some *huaqiao* student masquerading in my suit. Everyone else has short hair. I promise myself that I will keep my ponytail.

I'm jacked into the system. Is it monitoring me? Surely I'm not focusing, it can't follow the random pattern of normal thought. A system would be overwhelmed trying to process unfocused thought, wouldn't it?

I don't even know if it's a stupid question. I am without perspective. I have always been told that we manipulate the system, but what's to keep the system from manipulating us? Symbionts. Soon, perhaps it will be impossible to tell where human ends and machines begin.

Engineer Xi has to work, so someone else shows me to my desk, introduces me to the Engineer with whom I will apprentice, a tall woman named Woo Eubong, a Korean. We are about the same age. "Good," she says, "I'm tired of dealing with adolescents."

"You train them that young?" I ask.

"Twenty-one. Not really adolescents, but not adults yet either."

I don't know how to take her, I suspect I will miss her humor, irony doesn't translate. She'll think I'm dreadfully serious. Maybe the system will flag irony for me?

I live in an apartment so beautiful I am certain I will never live in anything like it again. It is three rooms with a tiny courtyard of raked stones and twisted rocks in back. The rooms are a little bigger than the front room of my apartment in Brooklyn, but what is so amazing is the finish. The bed is an alcove hung with white gauze curtains, the alcove and one wall (hiding a closet) is completely faced in wood with lacework carving at the corners. The black and red carpets are in every room except the kitchen, which is red and white tile. The couch has two little footstools of wood, purely decorative. The walls are hung with calligraphy. Over a black lacquer desk (very like the one at work) hangs a scroll with the characters spelling out "Inaction" followed by a verse from the Dao De Ching.

"I'm sorry it's so corporate," Woo Eubong said before leaving

the night before. "It's a bit impersonal, but you're only here for
fifteen weeks. And it's better than the guesthouse."

I'm not sure I ever want to leave.

I go to work in the morning through the clean, twisting maze
of the Wuxi complex, walking through passages with carved
wooden handrails and climbing immaculate stone steps. People
sympathize with me for having to spend so much time here. Woo
Eubong tells me I have to come to her place for dinner some
Saturday, just to get away from work. Hard to explain that I like
it here just fine.

In the morning, from eight to noon, I do donkey work. I check
figures, run things through the system, review jobs. Engineers
hate that sort of paperwork. Mostly it's routine, although once in
a while there's something unusual, a novel solution to a problem.
It's a good way to learn a lot about engineering. Building plans
in front of me on flimsies, the system presents the entire building
to me, supplements my own capacity and allows me to hold the
entire building in my head and go over it. Although the work is
routine, it takes me a morning to do five jobs, I have to call on
the system to explain techniques to me. Woo Eubong tells me not
to worry, in twelve weeks I'll find myself reviewing thirty or forty
jobs in a morning, finish two or three complete buildings a day.

"It's the only way to really learn," she says. "You just have to
get the experience of knowing so many jobs. Now you can run
through the construction jobs as fast as anyone, it's the systems,
the electrical, the utilities, the aesthetics that slow you down."

Particularly the systems and the aesthetics.

In the afternoon, I am Woo's student.

Woo is an organic engineer. That doesn't mean she works with
growing things, it means that she plans work so that it makes
organic sense. It seems to me that she doesn't plan at all. Daoist
engineering. I refer to it that way once, and she says, "Right,"
without blinking. Irony doesn't translate.

Each daoist engineer learns from working one on one with a

teacher, as I will learn from Woo Eubong. There are only a handful of daoist engineers in North America. It's not a specialty that is in much demand at home, mostly because we do not make the kinds of buildings that call for the subtlety of daoist engineering. They are very subtle buildings. Complex as bodies, with systems for nervous systems and circulation and musculature. For homework she gives me the task of studying the Wuxi Engineering Technologies Complex.

So at night I sit with flimsies in front of me, studying energy distribution and environmental monitoring. Normally because of air-flow, room size, room adjacency, exposure and window size, different rooms have different temperatures. The system for Wuxi Complex monitors temperature and humidity. But for an organic system, temperature is relative. My hands and feet are cooler than my head and chest. If I am sitting, I will find the room colder than if I am up and moving around. And different people respond to temperature in different ways, some are perpetually cold, some aren't. We are sensitive to light as well; a well-lit place feels subjectively warmer than a dark place, and radiant heat from a window may heat one small area differently than another. Many buildings adjust room temperatures. The Wuxi Complex system also monitors the people jacked into it. People tell the system they are cold or warm and it adjusts. People, in fact, become nerve endings for the system. And the rooms are ingeniously structured so as to transfer heat from windows to darker areas, to increase the amount of outside light that comes in. It is part of the reason that the place is such a maze. Again and again I study a room and think, "Isn't *that* clever."

The number of ingenious little details in this Complex stagger the imagination. It is not only that the particular details are so good, but that they dovetail. The way a room is shaped to create heat transfer also allows for efficient use of space, creates offices that have some privacy without requiring that they be walled off, allows enough ambient noise for human comfort and privacy but not so much that noise becomes an irritant. I request the system alter a detail, see what would happen if a window were put in somewhere else, only to find that the result, while bringing in more light, reduces the effectiveness of energy absorption, or affects ventilation. It's as if this building were the result of biological evolution.

During the afternoon I draw paper houses. I sit, attuned, and imagine very simple buildings.

"Don't plan the building, let the system do that," Woo Eubong says. "You just let go, let your mind drift and do what it wants."

At first I don't even produce buildings, for two days I produce scribbles. Then one day I produce a very shaky-looking pyramid sort of thing. I believe it is an accident, but Woo nods. "A pyramid is a very efficient shape, using the minimum number of surfaces. The only thing with fewer sides is a circle."

"Engineer Woo," I say, "I can detail a building a hundred times better than this."

"Certainly. But could you detail the Complex?"

"I'm not an architectural and engineering team," I say.

"Wuxi Engineering Complex wasn't detailed by a team, it was detailed by one woman, using, of course, feedback from the departments that would be using the building."

I gape.

"Exactly," she says, smiling. "A team would not have constructed the building as a unit, but as a series of connected, but compromised and adjusted, ideas."

"It can't be done. It had to have taken years."

"It did take over two years, but it can be done. I can't do it, there aren't many people who have the ability to do work on that grand a scale."

"But all those little details," I say.

She stops for a moment. As I said, she is a tall woman with a square face. She stands out among the company people, not for her height, but because she is different. Many of the engineers have this air about them. They are more casual—today she is in black coveralls—and they tend to work different hours. Sometimes they come in late, sometimes do a lot of work at home. When I came I thought there were two classes; cadres and workers. But the cadres sometime refer to organic engineers as talent.

"An example," she says. "Stand up."

I stand up, a little nervous.

"Walk to Hai-hong's desk."

I walk over to Hai-hong's desk, Hai-hong glances up at me expectantly, her look saying, "What do you need?"

"Woo Eubong is making an example," I say.

Hai-hong nods and looks back down at her work. I walk back to Woo Eubong. "Yes?" I ask.

"When you passed your desk, you changed direction. How many degrees? How many steps did you take? How many meters to Hai-hong's desk?"

I shrug. "I don't know."

"You didn't calculate?" she asks. "You didn't analyze the situation and determine the best possible method to get to Hai-hong's desk?"

"No," I say, smiling a little, "I just walked over."

"But you had to figure the best way to walk. In fact, standing in front of me, your muscles are constantly adjusting to keep you upright, correct? Muscles in your legs and feet adjusting constantly to make sure you don't balance too far one way or another?"

"Well, yes," I say, "if you want to think of it that way."

"But you don't think to stand, or walk, or dance. Gymnasts don't calculate trajectories." She is smiling, too.

"I understand," I say.

"Good, I want you to make buildings the same way that you walk to Hai-hong's desk, thinking about the product, not the process."

"You are going to try to make me a mental gymnast," I say.

She shakes her head. "No, Li Jian-fen, who built this Complex, she was a gymnast. You, I am teaching to walk."

I work using a tutorial. It's a feedback system, when I start to think analytically the system cuts out. I sit down and try to imagine a space. I try to determine the qualities I want in the space. I try to imagine a sense of this space. I imagine white walls, realize that I have no idea of the roof and consciously start to sort through possible roofs to go with the concept I have—

System cuts out. Flimsie prints and I have a tangle of schematics. If I look I can sort of identify four walls. The timer indicates that I was in the correct mode for twenty-two seconds. About average.

Woo Eubong glances over my shoulder. "You are a stubborn man," she says.

I shrug, not knowing what she refers to.

"You aren't using the system, you're staying in your own head. You have the manipulative skills but not the storage capacity."

I still don't know exactly what she's talking about.

She sighs. "Words don't really explain what you should be doing, you just have to do it, then you'll know. *Dao kedao, feichang dao.*" The first line of the *Dao De Ching*, roughly translated, means that "The way that can be spoken is not the way."

She doesn't look like the kind of person who would spout Daoism, philosophy out of the *Dao De Ching*. She has a short ruff of hair and looks like an athlete. A swimmer maybe, long straight lines.

"Maybe I can't learn to be an organic engineer," I say.

"Maybe," she says, surprising me, I expected (hoped) that she would say, "No, no, no, you'll learn, don't worry."

"Do you have a lot of failures?"

"I've only trained two others, one of them learned it, one didn't."

"Both of them were young?"

She nods. "And correspondingly more flexible than us elders. I really wonder if we shouldn't teach this to ten year olds." She smiles and I realize she is joking. "Truly, you cannot teach it to ten year olds, because in order to do it, you have to have experience with buildings, have to have buildings in your memory."

"When you do this, aren't you really an architect?"

"Yes," she says.

"I imagine architects do not really care for the idea."

She shakes her head. "No, there are also organic architects. They come at the problems from a different direction, but basically they do the same thing. But I tend to sacrifice aesthetics for engineering, architects tend to sacrifice engineering for aesthetics."

"Can I see some of the work of architects?" I ask.

"Of course," she says. She looks into the middle distance, her eyes drifting left as people's eyes tend to do when they are querying the system. "I had them print out in your apartment," she says.

"So I don't get any time off."

"Ah," she laughs, "you are clever."

Clever in Mandarin means almost the same thing as sly. I grin and try to look wicked. Then I make more scribbles.

I do not confess to her how frustrating this whole process is. I am here by a fluke. The University charts our actual performance against our expected performance. Once I had a tutor, and that helped my grades. Then my tutor died and, oddly enough, that helped my grades. I worked very hard. Everything else seemed sour but in the second semester I had a systems course and found something fascinating. I learned to tie systems into all my other courses. My projects were systems related. And I was tapped for a co-op job at Wuxi Engineering Technologies, where

I would be working with systems, because Engineer Xi, who reviews applicants for co-op positions, read one of my projects.

It wasn't until the list was posted and people started to congratulate me that I even understood I had been awarded something, that for maybe the first time in my life, I have been succeeding at something. And now, I am failing. And wasting an opportunity for someone who could have learned this.

It is worst at night, sitting in that beautiful apartment, making scribbles, going over flimsies. I get cold, although when I access the system it tells me that the temperature in my room is in fact higher than normal. I wear a ridiculous sweater, one with leather ties, from New York. All I want to do is sleep, but I go back over the Wuxi Complex. How did Li Jian-fen learn to do what she does? On my black desk sits a smooth stone carved into a walrus. It was a Christmas gift from Maggie Smallwood the year I spent on Baffin Island. I thought that what I learned in Baffin Island tempered me. Haitao thought we were damaged. I thought we were simply different. Maybe he was right. Then again maybe I am just too old.

I imagine a space, a clean clear white space like light through ice (clarity and sadness and the round-eyed faces of the seals in Lancaster Sound, but this is unfocused, as is the memory of Haitao's white clothes neatly folded by the broken window). I try to hold that, but everything seems formless. All right, everything is formless, I let it drift, thinking, the building will form. A room unfolds, but it's hard to hold it, hard to concentrate without concentrating. The system has the capacity to hold it for me, just as it holds a building I am studying, but usually I am conscious of the system when I work with it. I am not even aware I have reached into the system's capacity, tapped the system's space.

For an instant I have vertigo, and then a complete lack of perspective. A multiplicity of options, substances to use for walls, shapes in my mind flowing and shifting like ice. Everything becomes mutable, nothing stable, there are no boundaries. I did not know the perimeters of my own mind because I never had any

sense that there was any more than my mind but there is a sense
of my thoughts fleeing out and out and expanding and I feel as
if I am diffusing—

Forty-seven seconds. My heart is pounding. The scribble is
complex, beautiful, abstract and inhuman. It has nothing to do
with building, it has nothing to do with me. I am having a panic
attack, my heart is racing, racing. I want to get up, get away, but
I don't want to go out. I get up, go into the bedroom, lean on the
chairback and take deep breaths, hoping I will calm down.

Deep breath. Hold a second, let it out. Deep breath, hold a
second, let it out. I want to talk to someone. I don't want to be
alone. My heart won't slow down.

Anxiety attack. What do I know about an anxiety attack? That
it is unfocused fear. I sure as hell don't know what I'm afraid of,
although I know what started this.

I call Peter, my hands are shaking as I make coffee and wait
for the system to put me through. What time is it? The system
tells me it is 22:41.

Peter is at work, it's morning in New York. I can't go home for
another six months. I close my eyes and try a relaxation exercise
(my thoughts skittering like dry leaves). First, visualize a calm
quiet place. But the place I imagine is the nightlandscape of
Borden Station. The long inhumanly white sweep to Lancaster
Sound, a black line of open water, and then the deep sky paling
slightly at the horizon.

Go to bed. I leave my cup of coffee and crawl into bed behind
the white gauzy curtains. It is a bed big enough for two. I leave
the lights on, instruct the system to turn them off when I go to
sleep and turn them on again if I wake up. I lie there awhile,
listening to my heart pound, which makes me nervous, which
means that my heart rate doesn't slow (charming little feedback
loop) until finally I guess I wear myself out, and eventually the
fear subsides. I close my eyes and painstakingly imagine Peter's
living room, his couch. I remember where everything is in rela-

tionship to me sleeping on his couch. I am sleeping on his couch.
I am thinking about Peter and Engineer Xi. It is morning, and
time to put on my red and black and go to work.

I feel normal, a bit tired but in the morning the room is only
wearing in its insistence that I am not back home. I take my latest
scribble to Woo Eubong.

She spreads it out on her desk. "It's interesting," she says.
"What is it?"

"It's forty-seven seconds in the system," I say.

"Well, that's something. It's a little like calligraphy," she says.

"Tutorial art," I suggest.

"A little flat," she says. "Too Western. Maybe that's the problem, a Western mindset."

I do not know if she is joking or not. "Right," I say.

I review jobs, but I am slow because I keep losing concentration. I keep thinking about Chinese calligraphy. Calligraphy emphasizes line, the variation of width and blackness in the stroke,
flow. There's a lot of talk about the rhythm of the character. For
example, when I write the English word "talk" I don't cross the
"t" until I finish the "k." A character is supposed to be a kind
of circular movement. I tend, when I finish the "k" in "talk" to
drag my pen so there's a faint line from the "k" to the crossbar
of the "t." In calligraphy the faint line is supposed to be implied.
It can actually be there, a brush of ink, but whether it is or isn't,
there must be a sense of the artist's brush moving in that connected, circular pattern.

I keep thinking about all of this when I am supposed to be
checking jobs. Thinking about how calligraphy might be connected with imagining buildings.

Frankly, I don't see any connection at all.

On my fourth Saturday in Wuxi, I go to dinner at Woo Eubong's flat. It's a pretty place, less perfect than the apartment I'm

staying in, but more like a home. Woo Eubong has two daughters—official policy is one child, but it's not really so difficult to get permission for a second.

I have spent a few hours in Wuxi, shopping, and finally paid a small fortune for a Wuxi teapot. Made of brown clay, the spout and handle are very realistic-looking branches. Mine was made in the second half of the twentieth century, the really valuable ones were made before the Liberation, in feudal China. But it's still an antique. It's tiny and comes with four cups that look as if they actually only hold about a quarter of a cup each. The shopkeeper explains that the teapots used to be stuffed with leaves and the tea brewed was very strong. The four little cups sat in a tray and were filled by being splashed first with tea and then with hot water. The tea, he says, never had a chance to get cold. He wraps them, folding the paper so that he doesn't have to use any adhesive.

It's tiny, if she doesn't like it, at least I made the gesture. And she can put it in a drawer, I'll never know.

I take the bus to the complex where she lives, way out on the edge of town. The buildings are three and four stories tall, and give the impression of careless irregularity, of flow. Tiled roofs jut, balconies look out, roofs are finished as gardens with round moon gates. I look with a more practiced eye. This building was designed by an organic engineer or architect. Woo Eubong?

The gate checks me, opens and I follow my directions back three buildings and then left to the second walkway. There is an archway, as the directions promise, and next to the archway, a child's three-wheel gleams as red as the roof tiles.

I climb a ramp, there is a lift, and ask for the second floor. It is so clean, so polished. They must pay to keep it so clean. Woo Eubong's door is blue and before I knock it is opened by a child—maybe four years old? She is sucking on a purple ice lolly and does not speak, only looks up at me.

"Hello," I say.

She regards me seriously and then runs back into the flat, leaving me at the door. She is wearing blue coveralls and yellow shoes.

An older girl with long pigtails peers around the corner. "Mama!" she hollers, "he's here!" She smiles at me, showing missing teeth, and disappears.

A man comes around the corner, tall and fair-skinned. "Engineer Zhang?" he says, "I'm Zhang Chunqing, Eubong's husband. Come in."

The flat smells of food cooking, and from somewhere I hear Woo Eubong saying, "I know he's here, I'll be right out. Go talk to him."

Zhang Chunqing calls, "Girls? Come out here?" He takes my jacket, the girls skid around the corner on the hardwood floor like puppies. "These two worthless daughters are Xiu-ping and Xiu-lin."

The girls giggle madly and take off back for the kitchen.

He sighs, "You will find we are not a very formal household, I'm afraid."

I find it is very hard not to feel at home here. Woo Eubong comes in bringing finger dumplings and sliced vegetables and Zhang Chunqing gets beer. The girls want to watch the vid and are told they can't do it in the front room. They disappear into their bedroom but reappear every fifteen minutes or so to get some snacks and regard me owlishly before breaking into giggles and dashing off to the bedroom. Zhang Chunqing tells me that the older girl, Xiu-ping, is going to a special school where she learns piano and Japanese and we fall into a discussion of the best way to learn a language. Woo Eubong quizzes me on how I learned Mandarin. Chunqing is a biology teacher at a middle school for students who are preparing for university work.

The room is pretty, but there is a pair of small red shoes by the doors that lead to the balcony. A stack of papers sits on one end of a shelf that displays pottery (perhaps my teapot was a good choice). It is not as beautiful as my apartment, but I like it. And the beer works on me and I begin to relax a little. It is hard to completely relax, I am always watching my behavior, trying to be Chinese. There is a *huaqiao* saying that when you step foot in China you become Chinese. Maybe it is true if you are first generation, maybe it would be true for San-xiang's child, Foreman Qian's grandchild, but it is not true for me. Maybe I am more my mother's son than I ever knew.

But I like Woo Eubong a great deal and her husband is easy to talk to. Dinner is delightful, thousand-year-old eggs, sweet and sour pork and spiced cabbage with anise, a chicken roasted with its head tucked under its wing, fresh sliced tomatoes with a dusting of white sugar, candied yams. The girls have to be told to pick up their rice bowls when they eat, they want to leave the bowls on the table, stick chopsticks in them and carefully try to get the rice in their mouth without spilling anything. Woo Eubong is a little embarrassed, but I am relieved to be treated to real life. Everything at Wuxi has seemed to consist of glossy surfaces, effortless perfection, with me as the only flawed example of the other life I knew. It is nice to see that children are still children.

After dinner we talk some more, and I find myself admitting that I am frustrated.

"You try too hard," Woo Eubong says. "You have this feeling that what you are trying to do is very difficult, but it isn't. Once you find a way in, it will not be difficult at all."

A way in. A way in where?

Monday at Wuxi Engineering Technologies. I spend the morning reviewing jobs. I am starting to pick up speed, this, my third week. I eat lunch with Woo Eubong in the cadres' dining room (five pink prawns on the side of my plate like five shingles, slices of green kiwi fruit from Australia, cooked cucumber and tomato).

"Today," she says, "you're not going to scribble. Today you are going to design doors."

"Why is that?" I ask.

"I am trying something different."

Ah. Okay. So that afternoon I sit and design doors. Imagine a door, the system draws it. A wooden door. A metal door. A garage door. A great Chinese double gate, each side set with eighty-one brass studs. A moon gate, the opening a round zero. Then back to wooden doors. Without windows, with insets, with carvings, with a window, with square panes, with panes like a fan. I take a stack to Woo Eubong. She nods.

"Keep working," she says.

"Doors?" I say.

"Doors," she says.

So I do doors with transoms. Doors with security systems. Doors that fold, that retract, that slide. Doors within doors. When I run out I do doors of varying widths. Doors of varying finishes. A stone door. I start to indicate a little bit of entryway but Woo Eubong, leaning over my shoulder says, "No, just the doors."

Glass doors. Stained glass doors. Revolving doors. Doors for openings with arches, with triangles. Doors in doorways with lintels. I rack my brains for variations of doors. I do doors that open up. Doors that swing, slatted doors, bamboo doors, half doors. My desk is covered in doors. People passing stop and look, shake their heads. By four-thirty I think I have done every kind of door known to man. But Woo Eubong keeps me making doors until five.

I walk back to my apartment, noticing the doors I pass.

There are a lot that I hadn't thought of. Hell, when I get back to the apartment I find that I hadn't even done my closet door. So that night, I do a few more doors, and when I pull out my schematic of Wuxi Complex, I run through all the doors in the place.

Li Jian-fen was incredible with doors.

I begin to realize the importance of doors. They set the tone for the building, they are the second interaction between building and person, the first being the sight of the building. I think about the black doors of the main entrance to Wuxi Complex. They are opaque, lusterless matte. It is not just the efficiency of energy absorption, it is also the effect they have when one enters. They are like walls, they protect.

China is obsessed with walls. The university is walled, every factory, every school, every office complex or hotel is surrounded by a wall. And so doors are very important because they represent vulnerability but also opportunity, which is a great metaphor for every endeavor.

Excited, the next morning I am ready to tell Woo Eubong all about my understanding of doors. I see why she has had me study doors. But she is planning and I don't get a chance to talk with her. She has a luncheon so I eat lunch with a couple of people in the department and when I get back from lunch there is a message from her in the system.

Do floors.

And so I do floors. And the next day steps (a long, difficult afternoon). Thursday I do windows, which is a pleasure after steps. And Friday I do lighting. Saturday, usually my half day, there is a message in the system for me. More lighting. Monday, more lighting. Tuesday, oh bliss, I do sinks.

I learn to dread the afternoons again. There's no more failure, no more twenty-seven-second scribbles, but it's so tedious. Still, I find myself looking at lighting, at sinks, at stairs. The Wuxi Complex isn't enough, I use the schematics from the organic architects and observe what they did with doors, with windows, with stairs. I never really thought much about landings or mezzanines. Li Jian-fen used a lot of mezzanine areas at Wuxi Complex, but her use of stairs isn't particularly inventive.

Still, by three-thirty, there I sit at my desk, haunted, trying to invent another sink and hoping that Woo Eubong won't come by and see me sitting there not doing anything. She never says anything, but she notices.

I do walls and ceilings. I have learned a lot by the time I do walls and ceilings, I have more ideas. But I do them faster and then there I sit. It is work a child could do. It is meaningless, a catalogue. Has she decided I cannot do the real engineering? Except for the one assignment in lighting, after three more weeks I haven't done anything even remotely resembling engineering. I wonder, does Woo Eubong keep count of the number I do? Does the system report the amount of time I sit motionless?

One Saturday night I sit down again and try to scribble. Four walls, light through ice, and then I think, what kind of windows? I remember doing all those windows and try to remember if there were any that I liked and—

Sixteen seconds. Worse than when I first started.

After that I don't try again.

When I have been there nine weeks, Woo Eubong comes to me one day and tells me that I am needed on a project. They are building a complex (in the conventional way, no daoist engineering this time) and are involved in a competitive bid. So for four days I work with other engineers doing real engineering work. We discuss ideas, have the system construct analogs, modify and change them. By the time I join the team, they have already been working for over a week, and on Saturday night, at nine, we submit our rough plan for the competitive bid and then go into Wuxi and have a drink.

I feel as if I am one of these people, I have been working with them ten to twelve hours a day for four days and they accept me as a colleague. I realize, sipping my beer, that I am a colleague. I am an engineer. When I go back to New York, no matter what else, I will be an engineer, I will have my degree in Construction Engineering from Nanjing University, and I will be something of an expert in the use of systems. Not to mention particularly inventive with doors.

It is a comfort. Almost enough to make me forget the last sixteen-second scribble.

After the project I settle into days of reviewing jobs and creating variations on whatever themes Woo Eubong assigns me. Ten weeks, eleven weeks. The Wuxi Complex begins to matter less and less to me. It is late May. I will be in New York on July first.

I pick out my final project. I must do a final project for Nanjing University based on my co-op experience. I chose to expand on the systems work I did with the project team. It is interesting, mildly diverting. But it is hard to care. My credit balance is blooming, my apartment is beautiful, but all I want to do is go home. I will eat fried chicken and biscuits, pasta smothered in cheese (cheese is not eaten very much in China). Peter has promised to make me lasagna my first week home. Rice and beans my second week home, although I make better rice and beans than Peter.

Woo Eubong shows me the specs for her projects. A housing complex, an office building. A beach house.

A beach house sounds nice. I ask her about it. It will be on the island of Hainandao. Hainandao was one of the original special economic zones like Hong Kong, Shenzhen and Taiwan. It is still a free-market zone, a place of virulent capitalism, meant to fuel the socialist system. The beach house is for one of the old mercantile families of Hainandao, built by the clan corporation.

She points out the setting. No specs, she says. "The only reason they didn't give it to an architect is that Comrade Gao, the big man of Wuxi Engineering, is friends with Comrade Wang. Comrade Gao wants a number of designs. Engineer Li Jian-fen is submitting one."

"And you," I say.

She looks down.

"Humble administrators build gardens, too," I say, referring to

the *Zhuozheng,* the Humble Administrator's garden, one of the
famous gardens of Suzhou.

She glances up at me but doesn't answer and I wonder if I've
offended her.

"You should try," she says.

"I can't compete with organic engineering," I say.

"Okay, then see what you can do with heating and cooling,"
she says. It is an infuriating answer. Why did she suggest that I
try? Does she feel that I might be able to create an adequate
building? She doesn't ever much comment on how I fulfill her
assignments, I never know if I've met with her approval or not.

I fiddle with heating and cooling systems. Convection. Conduc-
tion. Old-fashioned systems. Expensive systems. Efficient systems. This is a big area, I suspect I will do heating and cooling
systems for awhile.

Hainandao. The name means South Sea Island. The first character, "hai" means "sea." It is the same as the "hai" in Haitao.
Sea-wave. I think about heating and cooling systems. (On Hainandao they would only need a cooling system. There's a lot of
sunlight.) I try to imagine a beach house in Hainandao, lots of
wood. Maybe paper screens, like they use in Japan.

I scribble more heating and cooling systems. And eventually I
stop thinking about Hainandao. And I do not think about Haitao's
white clothes folded neatly by the shattered starburst of the window.

That evening I spend a long time making dinner, trying to
concoct rice and beans from the local ingredients. The result is
pretty close, although not what my mother would make. Not even
what I would make under normal circumstances. I leave it on
cycle; flash, stand, flash, stand. My mother cooks on a stove, but
I have only a flash wok and an oven, it is hard to slow cook
something.

Then while it is cooking I sit down and tap the system. I am
not going to scribble anything, I just want to try to imagine a

beach house. And so I try. I try to imagine something that looks as insubstantial as paper, maybe sliding walls.

Twenty-three seconds.

Disgusted, I get up and go back to the beans and rice. But there's nothing to do but wait. I try the beach house again.

Twenty-eight seconds.

Back to the rice and beans. And then again, the beach house.

Nineteen seconds.

Woo Eubong taps in for twenty, thirty minutes at a time. She sits at the desk for three hours, working, answering questions, dropping back into her work. I have even tried to mimic her posture. I am so frustrated I could hit something. I force myself into the chair and decide I will keep doing it until I manage. I imagine the beach house.

Contact breaks.

I imagine the beach house.

Contact breaks.

I tap in.

Contact breaks.

The flimsies pile up by the printer and finally I override the system and tell it not to print unless I tell it to.

And finally, I give up, get up, put away my beans and rice uneaten and go to bed. I am not, am not, will never be, a daoist engineer.

I wake up. Some burden has been lifted. I have discovered that I am not capable, and now I no longer have to try. Or even if I am capable, it doesn't matter. Tonight I will come back, eat rice and beans, and work on my project for the University.

I work well this day. Woo Eubong told me that by the time I left I'd be able to review thirty, forty jobs a day, and she is correct. I have learned a great deal about engineering and however strange her teaching methods may be, I am grateful. Even for all those days of doing heating and cooling systems.

At the end of the day I am feeling pleased with myself. It doesn't bother me when Woo Eubong says, "You have homework."

I wait. I'd prefer to work on my project, but I have three weeks to do that and it is almost finished already.

"I want you to scribble again, the way you did when you first came."

"How many?" I ask.

"Three," she says.

Okay. I'll have time to work on my project. "Good," I say. If I finish my project I can do some shopping, buy things to send home.

So I go home, take out my beans and rice and sit down to scribble. I'll do my three, eat, and then work on my project. Above my desk the scroll reads "Inaction."

I can say for the first time that I really don't care. I am thinking a little that when I finish I can do some work on my project, but my mind is empty. I am not trying to succeed.

I tap in, remember to tell the system to produce a flimsie. I do not think of anything for a moment, I have to think of something to scribble. The beach house is as good as anything else. All white, but this time it isn't paper I think of, but ice. I think again of Borden Station. I invision a huge expanse of window. It's not very Chinese, more like the glass and steel tradition of New York. Something long and low, and I know how it should flow. A great room, a kitchen divided by very little wall, slightly higher than the long great room with its window looking over the ocean—

And I reach. For a moment there is no perspective and I am on the edge of panic, but instead I give in, I let myself be swallowed by the emptiness and instead I expand, the system becomes my own memory. I fall through. I feel my mind's boundaries, I know how little I can think about at one time, and then those boundaries become unimaginably huge and I am myself, myself, but able to think and have the thing I think in my mind without holding it, without concentrating, because I am using the system to concentrate for me. The system is there for me, a part of me. To modify the house I only have to think it and it is so, it hangs there. I am outside it, seeing the long portion of the house that is the kitchen and great room, off the kitchen the steps down to the beach (and at the landing, there I use my paper screen, although I have to come up with some substitute for paper that has the lucent qualities but is not so fragile). The bedrooms are beyond the kitchen, higher to take advantage of the uneven terrain (also in memory) and I think that this Western building needs a tile roof. Blue Chinese tile. Soften the variation in the roof height and the roof becomes a wave.

I stop, and look around the room. The printer sighs and there is the flimsie. I pick it up. The things I have designed (little more than a shell, not real finish yet) are all there. Fourteen minutes.

I begin to shake. What if I can't do it again? I close my eyes, tap in, look for the beach house, expand—

It is there.

I drop out and look at the flimsie I am holding. I feel limited, I miss the system. I close my eyes, expand—

And even sitting there, the shell of my beach house just hanging there, I can feel that I am crying. Because I have done it, I have done it.

I feel whole, and now it is time to go home.

⊬

Three Fragrances

San-xiang

It is a terrible thing to go to work with a new face. I finger my new jawline and chin. Do I wear make-up? Is it right to try to look prettier? But now that I have a nice face, isn't it right that I try to do something with it? To not wear make-up, isn't that saying that I think I don't need it?

Everyone at Cuo knows that I have a new face. All those cards, "San-xiang! A sweet girl! May your new face match your heart!" I mean I should have had my face fixed a long time ago. I would have if my father hadn't spent my face money trying to make *quanxi*, connections, so that we could get back to China. As if there was any chance when America went crazy during the Great Cleansing Winds campaign. If we had been in China we would have been safe from that, too. China is too old, too well established to have indulged in anything like the Great Cleansing Winds.

When I look in the mirror I think of all those weeks while the virus told my bone cells to divide. I was so frightened. They told me everything that would happen, but I would be awake at night and I would think, what if it doesn't stop? Long lines of jaw grew down from my ears like curving ridges, and my teeth ached and shifted like old stones in a mountain. I would imagine my jaw grown long and heavy until my head resembled a long-faced baboon, a praying mantis. And then they injected another virus, carrying its cargo of RNA-string materials, its molecules to tell my bone cells to turn off, and it all stopped.

I think it is a beautiful face. Really, Mama says I am pretty now. I am normal, she says, not a vid star, but when I look in the mirror I can't believe it is there. My eyes are bigger—not *waiguoren* big, of course, but bigger. I have such a nice oval chin. This won't be the first time I've been out, Mama and I have gone shopping and people are so different. Sometimes they aren't as nice; it's wonderful, no pity.

At Cuo, everyone will stare at me. And even though I know I'm not ugly any more I'm afraid to have them all look at me. They'll be thinking about my old face and comparing it to my new one. I don't want to be the old San-xiang anymore. Poor, ugly San-xiang who had no jaw and little squinty eyes and who looked like she was congenitally stupid. This is it, my chance. I'm going to change my life. I'm going to look for a new job, have new friends, be a new person.

I'm going to put on make-up. When I get a new job no one will ever know that I was ugly and I'll wear make-up there, so I might as well start now. Practice, so when I change jobs, I'll be accustomed to my new face, and no one will ever suspect that I once looked ugly and stupid. I put on new clothes, I have a new haircut to match the shape of my new face. My temples are shaved back and my bangs fall like a horse's forelock. Very how can, as they say.

The world is new.

All day long people have been saying to me, "How beautiful." "Come out for a drink," Celia says. "Come celebrate, we won't stay late."

So after work we all troop to The In-Between, the place where everybody goes after work to get a drink and I order a beer. Celia and Carol get those neon-looking drinks with sprays of those plastic fibers with glowing ends sticking out of them. I only see them in drinks, where do bars get them? Tim and Qing Yang get *baijiu,* man-type drinks, no-nonsense drinks. I only drink beer. I didn't even used to like beer but I learned to like it.

"Such a good Chinese girl," Tim says, teasing, "sipping your beer."

"*Baijiu* makes me dizzy," I say and he and Qing Yang laugh although it's the truth. They laugh at a lot of things I say and at first it makes me nervous, but then I think that they're just being nice. They act as if I am clever. They laugh when I say that I have to call my mother and tell her I'll be late.

"Mama," I say in Mandarin, "Tonight I will be late. I'm at a bar with some people from work."

"*Hao, hao,*" she says, nodding complacently. Looking at her double chin I think with surprise, I am prettier than my mother.

"*Qing ni gaosu baba,*" I say. Please tell papa.

"*Meishi,*" she says, "*ni gen nide pengyou, wanba.*" Don't worry, have a good time with your friends.

It's a funny thing to say, Chinese words in an English way. She does not seem to care at all that I am sitting in a bar. I go back to my seat. There is the bar, then the space for the bartenders, then a counter with rows of bottles and rising above the bottles is a pretty Chinese woman in a business suit.

She looks a little nervous, but she is still having a good time. You can tell.

Qing Yang asks me to The In-Between on Thursday. I have my political study meeting but I say yes. Then I call Gu and tell him that I can't make it, I have to work late.

Qing Yang is an ABC. I would like him to ask me out. He is

not too handsome, he has a round bald spot, like a monk, only small. He is not as handsome as Zhang, another ABC I went out with a couple of times. Zhang is the only other person I have ever dated and he only went out with me because he worked for my father and my father asked him to. I wonder what he would think if he saw me?

Qing Yang is nice. Handsome men are usually not very nice, they usually can't be bothered. So we go to The In-Between and I have a beer. I don't know what to say to him. At first we smile a lot and things are very uncomfortable, but then we get talking about his job and he starts telling me about all the people he meets and the people he tries to sell systems to. I never really knew what Qing Yang did. I suppose I thought that people who needed systems came to Cuo, I never realized that some people in Cuo actually sold them. Which is pretty naive of me, I realize.

Qing Yang sounds like he's a pretty good salesman, all his stories are about how he found some trick that would make the person who bought the system like him, like the woman who didn't like ABC and didn't like Qing Yang, of course, until she found out that he grew up in West Virginia, just like she did. "We were neighbors then, you see?" he says. "It's that personal identification, you have to draw the client in to you."

I'm sure I could never do it, I mean, what if he hadn't been from West Virginia? I've never even been to West Virginia.

Qing Yang goes to the bathroom and I look at my watch. It's an hour after work. I don't know when I should go home, actually I'm getting hungry. He comes back. "Want to get something to eat?"

"Okay," I say.

We go to an Indian restaurant on Seventh Avenue. The sign says that it's been there over one hundred years. "Have you ever had Indian food?" Qing Yang asks.

"Is it like Thai?" I ask.

"Sort of." Inside is old-fashioned brick walls and tables with silver and white linen tablecloths. It doesn't seem very Indian. It's one of those antiquey places that has two glasses and three forks at every place; it doesn't look like there would be enough space on the table to put our dinner. Qing Yang orders for me, something called tandoori chicken. It's chicken baked with a yogurt covering, but it doesn't seem very yogurty. It's all right. I tell him it's very good. The bread is called poori, it puffs up like a pillow. We use it to scoop up red and green spicy sauces from a server in the middle of the table. I really like the bread.

I have a beer with my dinner, too. It's an Indian beer called Golden Eagle, but it just tastes like beer to me. Beer is beer is beer. I can't tell much difference.

After the restaurant he takes me to this place he knows where we can listen to music, "Just for an hour or so." At the place they are pattern dancing. Qing Yang tries to get me to dance, but I don't know any patterns. Finally he shows me a simple one. It's only twelve steps, well really fourteen if you count the curtsey/bow at the end and then he kisses my hand. When I curtsey, the tails of my suit brush the ground. If I start to go wrong, Qing Yang kind of pulls my hand to show me the correct way. "I'll teach you the quad," he promises. "What those people are doing."

The man holds the woman's hand in the air, she is wearing a ring that sparkles blue and white. They take two steps together, and make this kind of slithery glide, then a turn so that somehow she ends up in front of him, then he puts his hands on her hips and they lean sideways, bending away from each other like graceful trees, like tall courting birds. It seems to be very complicated, there's more after that. I don't think I could ever learn it. But it's so pretty. Pattern-dancing music just seems to ripple along, at first I can't really tell the beat in it, but after a bit I realize it's very easy.

At nine Qing Yang says he'll be right back, and then he'll walk me to the subway station. I wait by the bar.

"Excuse me, what time is it?"

I don't realize that the man is talking to me until he repeats himself. "Excuse me, miss? Do you have the time?"

"Oh," I say, flustered. I look at my watch, although I just did. "It's a little after nine."

He is a *waiguoren*. He smiles at me and I smile back. He has light brown hair, very thick, that he wears in a queue. He reminds me a little of Zhang, the ABC I dated. He is wearing a burgundy sweater with a little cape, not a suit like he came from work.

"Your boyfriend?" he asks, gesturing towards the bathroom.

"No," I say, "just a friend." How casual it sounds. I like the sound of it. Qing Yang could be my boyfriend, but he is not, he is just a friend.

"What's your name?"

"Qian San-xiang," I say.

"San-xiang," he says, "that's a pretty name. What's it mean?"

"It means 'Three Fragrances'."

"My name's Bobby." He shrugs. "Unfortunately, it doesn't mean anything."

I giggle, he's funny.

"Are you from around here? I've never seen you here before." He has very nice, big eyes. Like a puppy. He isn't comparing my new face to my old face.

"No," I say, "I work for Cuo, down on Water Street. I live in Brooklyn." Just then I see Qing Yang coming back from the bathroom and I wonder if I'm supposed to be talking to Bobby if I'm with Qing Yang. But Bobby just smiles and turns back around, understanding. Just goes to show that all handsome guys aren't jerks.

I can feel my new life opening, like one of those paper pills you put in water that opens out into flowers.

At work I have a letter from Aron Fahey. Aron Fahey is a martian settler, I contacted him because of an interview I saw in

Xin Gongshe, a political theory magazine I subscribe to. The
interview was about commune management and he was talking
about political infrastructure in his commune. My political study
group hopes eventually to establish an urban commune, and he
had some interesting things to say about a community's politics
versus a larger society's politics, and he also talked about the
difference between a small commune's politics and a larger commune's politics. His commune has over two hundred families, our
commune might have only sixteen or so, so I wrote him a letter.

I get letters through the Cuo System Mailbox, I couldn't really
afford the interplanetary rates on my own. I gave Aron my access,
so he can afford to answer me. His letters are really interesting,
it seems strange that I've never seen his face or heard his voice,
but I know all about him. I know about his wife and his daughter,
and about his farm. His life seems so straightforward, he knows
what he has dedicated his life to. If it wasn't on Mars, I'd probably
ask him if I could join his commune.

I save the letter until my mid-morning break, but I'm just
sitting down to enjoy it when Celia overrides my system shunt to
tell me I've got a personal call. I imagine it's Mama, calling to ask
me to stop and get something in the city on my way home. I'm
really surprised to see the guy from the bar, Bobby.

"Ah," he says, "it *is* you. I thought I remembered you saying
you worked for Cuo."

"Hi," I say, startled.

"I'm really sorry to bother you," he says, "is this a bad time?"

"No," I say, "I'm on break."

"Oh, good," he says. He smiles, really nice. "I felt really bad
about calling you at work, usually I never call anyone at work, you
know? But I didn't know any other way to get in touch with you.
You seemed so nice at the bar last night and I've just kept
thinking about you. I bet you don't even remember me? Hell, I'll
bet you get calls all the time."

I am blushing, I can feel how hot my face is, and I can't help laughing although it comes out all high-pitched and silly sounding. "Oh, no, I remember who you are. You were sitting at the bar. You asked me what my name meant."

" 'Three Fragrances,' right?"

"Right," I say.

He says that he's never seen me there before, although he adds that it isn't like he goes there all the time. I tell him it was my first time there.

"Hey, maybe I could meet you there? Buy you a drink? I'd really like a chance to get to know you. Although"—he looks downcast—"on a Friday night, you're probably busy."

I almost say that I am, I mean, I don't know him or anything, but I think about it. I can just have a drink and then go home. I don't have to stay. It would be nice to meet someone. And he doesn't know anybody that I know, and he only knows the new San-xiang. He thinks I'm the kind of girl who has dates all the time, and he's handsome. "No," I say, "I'm not busy tonight. I'd love to have a drink."

He brightens up. "Great! What's a good time? How about seven or so?"

I have a date. I'm going out with this guy. Just like any normal girl.

The rest of the day goes so slow. And then I have to do something until seven. I can't really go home, I would just get home and have to turn around and come right back. So I get something to eat, and then I go shopping. I want to be late, I want to get there about five minutes after seven so I don't have to be sitting there when he gets there, but I start walking over too soon, and I get there at almost ten minutes of. He's not there.

Seven. He's still not there. I wait by the door because I don't want to sit down until he comes. People keep looking at me. I know I look silly, standing there.

Finally at ten minutes after seven the door opens and it's him. He's frowning as if he's thinking about something but when he sees me he suddenly has this great big smile. He looks like a little boy when he smiles.

"I'm sorry I'm late," he says. "Have you been waiting long?"

"No," I say, "I just got here." I don't want him to feel bad.

He puts one hand in the small of my back and takes my arm and directs me towards the side where there are some tables. I get a whiff of his scent; the leather ties of his sweater and a curious smoky smell that is a mixture of his cologne and him. No one has ever touched me that way. It's a little scary, but Bobby does it so it must be very normal. How would I know, I haven't had many dates, and Zhang never touched me except to kiss me good-night.

We sit down and he says, "I feel like I know you."

I don't know what to say so I don't say anything.

"You know what I mean, don't you, don't you feel as if we know each other?"

"Yes," I say, because it's what he wants me to say.

"I'll bet you drink Chrysanthemums," he says.

"I do," I say, even though I don't and I feel a little uncomfortable.

"See," he says, "I know you."

He orders drinks. He is so handsome, and I feel so pretty, people must look at us and envy us.

Bobby asks me about my job and I tell him, although it's really very boring. He asks me if I'm from China and then why am I living here? A Chrysanthemum is a bright, clear fuchsia with one of those light sprays in it. It tastes sweet, but a little hot, like cinnamon. It's good. While I am telling him how my father caused us to come here and about how old-fashioned my father is and how my cousins in China think my father is terribly feudal, he buys me another. At first I think he is just being polite, but he keeps asking me questions, how did it feel to leave my friends, did I feel out of place here? "You're like an aristocrat," he says, but he is serious, not trying to flatter me. "Your breeding shows, when you were young you were accustomed to finer things."

I never thought of myself as aristocratic. It's true that Mama and I buy some things from China, and Mama keeps the apartment looking like China. Not shabby, the way people do here, but finished, with a system that changes the wall color and dims the windows. We have all our old furniture from China, not like the new furniture in China that ties into your system so you can change the color to match your decor, but still much better than anything you can find here.

"Someday I will go back," I say, although until this moment I didn't really think I would. But saying it I realize it is true, I must go back. I don't know how I will do it, but I am a citizen. "This job at Cuo, it's just for now. I'm going to change my job."

"Good for you," he says. "So you live with your parents?"

Just the way he says it, the way it sounds, makes me wish I didn't. Here I sit, drinking a Chrysanthemum, wearing my suit from China, with this handsome man. I should not live with my parents. I cannot say I live with my parents, he'll think I'm a child. "No," I say, "I have an apartment."

He is surprised. His eyes grow wider, respectful. "Really. Alone?"

"It is only for awhile," I say, "a group of my friends and I plan eventually to establish a commune out in Brooklyn, down by Brighton Beach or Coney Island." I look casually down at my drink. It is true, the part about my friends, although I have often wondered if we will really ever do anything except talk. Surely everybody must feel that way when they start something as difficult as establishing a commune.

Then it occurs to me that some people disapprove of landlords. Perhaps he is disappointed in me. I add quickly, "I don't really condone the landlord system. It is just that the only other alternative is living out in Pennsylvania or West Virginia. And it is only temporary."

He nods, looking thoughtful.

I want to ask him if he condones landlords, but what can he say after I have said that I have an apartment?

"Where do you live?" I ask.

"New Jersey," he says, "but right now I am staying with friends. San-xiang"—he pauses and smiles—"I love to say your name, it is such a pretty name, so old-fashioned. San-xiang. I've been invited to a party later tonight, would you like to go with me?"

"I'd love to," I say, feeling worldly.

I feel funny when we get to the party. It's in a very small apartment that doesn't have much furniture. Not even a bed. Then I realize that the couch thing on the floor is a futon. The apartment is painted white; floor, ceiling, walls, pipes, even the bricks that make up a kitchen wall. But the paint is old and has black scuff marks in places.

Everybody knows Bobby. Nobody is wearing a suit. Some of the people at the party might be from the University, although it is hard to tell. There is no place to sit. Some of the girls are very strange-looking and one of the boys is wearing a dhoti. I think dhotis look funny, very pre-industrial revolution. Why would anyone want to look pre-industrial revolution?

The music is weird, too. All that harmonic tonal stuff and complicated percussion. We walk towards the second room. A girl is saying, ". . . people as musical instruments, rather than the homocentric view that people are foreground and instruments background—hi Bobby."

"Hi Cara," he says, and keeps walking. He leaves me in the middle of the second room and says he'll be right back. I don't know what to do, so I try to stand out of the way and look like I'm expecting him right back. I don't know what I'm supposed to be doing. Some people are walking around but most people are standing in groups, talking. I hear snatches of conversation:

". . . so I told him, 'Empathy is a measure of emotional maturity. . . .'"

". . . Debra, how can, how truly can. Where did you . . ."

". . . it's all a matter of continuous consciousness, reassembled, I would not know I was not he, but that consciousness would have been interrupted and a new consciousness, identical, would replace it, and so it would be a death. . . ."

". . . simulating length to time when it flies by before it can even be recognized, if that makes any sense. . . ."

I feel very stupid. What if somebody talks to me?

I see Bobby coming back and smile at him. "Tomas isn't here," he says, "they said he's not here yet. He's a friend of mine. Here, I couldn't find much to drink so I brought you a Grenade." He hands me a white container, then shakes his and opens it. I shake mine and open it. I take a taste, it burns. "Wait," he says, "I need to talk to someone—"

I'm alone again. I shouldn't have come. At least I have my Grenade. I hope that Bobby doesn't want to stay long, maybe—I check my watch, it's nine-thirty—in an hour I'll leave. An hour is enough time. Besides, the Chrysanthemums have made me tired.

I've drunk half of my Grenade before Bobby comes back. "Come on," he says, "there are some people I want you to meet."

So we go back towards the room that is not the kitchen. All this white, it's like a funeral. In the back room they have the lights way down and people are sitting on the floor. I am wearing my good suit—even if it is an old San-xiang suit it's still good—but when Bobby sits down I carefully sit down, too. Bobby says "San-xiang, this is Dana, Carlos," and he names four other names but it's hard to keep them all straight. Everybody smiles at me. I am wearing a good red suit and sitting on a dirty white floor. I smile back. They are all wearing tights. Dana is maybe forty and she hasn't had her metabolism monitored in a long time because she's overweight. She has large, soft haunches, but she's not dirty and she smiles at me.

I listen to people talk, they are all talking about people I don't know. I want to look at my watch but it would seem rude. I drink my Grenade. It's milky white and tastes like bitter almonds. Or maybe bitter vanilla. Everything white, except the scuff marks on the walls. In the dim light the scuff marks almost look like characters. I find *ren*, people, and *xiao*, small. Bobby puts his arm around me.

It feels strange, but nice. His arm is heavy, in a good way. I can feel his fingers on my collar bone. Nobody notices. Maybe they assume that I am Bobby's new girlfriend. Maybe I am.

Bobby's girlfriend. *Bobby de nupengyou.* I try to find the characters for girlfriend in the scuff marks; I find *nu*, girl, and the second character in friend, *you*. My head feels funny, too many Chrysanthemums and Grenades.

"Come on, baby," Bobby says all of the sudden, "let's get some air."

He pulls me to my feet and I look around, everybody is looking at us in a bemused sort of way.

Bobby smiles at me and brushes me off, straightens my suit. I feel wobbly. Not drunk exactly, but definitely wobbly. "My head feels funny," I say, my voice sounding very small.

"Come on," he says. "No more Grenades for you."

I laugh, it sounds silly, no more Grenades for me. "Blew me up," I say.

Bobby laughs, he sounds really pleased. "Yes, darlin' it sure did. Come on."

We leave the party, the middle and first room are very bright. "Blew me up," I whisper, glad to have said something clever, something that made Bobby laugh. I'm as clever as all these people. I could be Bobby's girlfriend if he wanted me to. Bobby has his arm around my waist and I lean against him. It is very nice and it is not my fault because I'm wobbly. I don't mean anything by it, I'm just wobbly.

We go down the lift and out on the street. The subway rumbles up through the grates and the trucks that make night deliveries in Manhattan growl by. A party in Manhattan. Well, it wasn't my fault that I didn't know anybody. When I am Bobby's girlfriend I'll know more people and then I'll have a good time. Bobby says we should walk and we do, left foot, right foot, both marching in step. I remember a Chinese marching song and I want to sing it but then I decide that I shouldn't because drunks sing.

We turn a corner and there is a doorway. We stop in the doorway and Bobby says, "San-xiang, listen to me. Take a deep breath of this."

He takes a piece of paper, but it is really two pieces of paper stuck together. He pulls them apart under my nose and I take a deep breath—

Sweet cold smell, like taking a fast drink of cold milk, hurts my head, bigger and whiter and bigger and whiter, I clutch my forehead and grit my teeth and it doesn't stop and then all of the sudden it's like a balloon that has been getting bigger and bigger and ready to explode, someone lets the air out and it gets small real fast and is gone.

Bobby is looking at me. "Better baby?"

I nod. I feel better, even if I do have a little bit of a headache. I don't feel wobbly. "What's that?" I ask.

"It's an icepick," he says, which doesn't tell me anything. He crumples the paper up and throws it in the corner of the doorway. I hold my temples, watching him, but he doesn't pay any attention to me. He takes out another icepick and peels it apart with a rip, takes a breath and tosses it in the corner. I want to see if it gives him a headache but it doesn't seem to. "Come on," he says. "Do you like to dance?"

"I don't know how," I say. "Look, I really ought to get home, I mean, I'm really kind of tired, you know, I worked all day."

He takes hold of my arms. "I really meant to show you a good time tonight, but I haven't really, and I feel really bad. Let me take you to this place I know, and then if you want to go home, I won't say a thing. I won't call you again, I won't ever bother you."

"That wasn't what I meant at all," I say. His face is so wonderful, everything is so clear, it's like I can see in the dark. His smell, the smoky cologne smell, is fresh and intoxicating. "That wasn't what I meant." I don't want him to never call me.

He leans forward and gives me a kiss. The kiss makes me kind of uncomfortable, he puts his tongue in my mouth and I keep thinking that I haven't brushed my teeth. But he wraps his arms around me and pulls me against him and I can feel his silky sweater and smell the leather ties. He squeezes me real hard, and lifts me up a little bit so my feet are off the ground. I don't know what to do. It feels very good, I want him to hug me harder. I don't really want him to kiss me, but I want him to hug me and hug me.

"San-xiang," he says, "I love your name. Three Fragrances. Come with me now, okay?"

"Okay," I whisper.

But first he has to go back to the party to meet the Tomas person. He takes me to a restaurant and buys me a cup of tea. "You don't have to go back, I'll be back as soon as I can. Okay sweetheart?" He gives me his little-boy smile, "That's the perfect thing to call you, 'sweetheart.' Like a sweet fragrance. Wait right here for me, sweetheart. Promise you won't go anywhere?"

"I promise," I say.

He is gone for thirty-five minutes while I have three cups of tea and read a newspaper. This isn't what I expected at all. This isn't like a date with Zhang, he picked me up, we went to the kite races, then we had something to eat and went home. We didn't do all this running around. Of course, Bobby has all these friends. My headache goes away but then I feel tired. It's only ten-thirty but it feels as if it's later. In the bathroom I look in the mirror. My face is still there, but I don't care. I try to think of how nice it looks, but it's like a dress I have worn all day, it is just there.

In the restaurant they are playing sweet old people versions of popular songs. A cup of tea is expensive, and the sandwiches and samosas are as much as a dinner in Brooklyn. Each place is laid, as if they are expecting two hundred people to come in during the middle of the night, and each table has its canister of chopsticks.

Bobby comes back and whisks me out of the restaurant into the night. I am sleepy again. I'll go to whatever this place is he wants to take me to and then I'll go home, and I don't care if he ever calls me again. Up and down, up and down, all evening, and now I'm tired.

"Here," Bobby pulls out another of those pieces of paper.

I shake my head.

"It'll make you feel better," Bobby says.

"They give me a headache."

"Don't breathe quite so deep," he says.

So I don't and it still gives me a headache, but not as bad, the coldness rising into my head and white little sparkles in my eyes and then everything clear. Bobby is looking at me, not smiling, and I don't know what that means. "Come on," he says.

We get on the nearly empty subway and ride, swaying and nodding, for two stops, then get off. Bobby's face is green-white under the old lights of the station, his burgundy sweater is the brown-red of bloodstains. While traveling he does not look at me. He is angry at me. Maybe he is tired, too. I hope he is tired, although I'm not anymore. I can't keep a train of thought in my head, many thoughts just skitter around, my head is a cricket cage.

He will be angry when he finds out that I don't know how to dance. The new San-xiang should know how to dance, but I just

don't. I can't help it, I don't. When he gets mad, then I'll go home.
In the subway station there are mosaics of beavers in the tiles. I
wonder if beavers used to live in New York City.

We walk and I try to piece together an outline of the evening.
The bar, the party, waiting in the restaurant, riding in the subway.
When Mama says tomorrow, "What did you do?", what will I
answer?

"Do you like to swim?" Bobby asks.

"Yeah," I say. I haven't been swimming in a long time, but I
used to go to the health club when I was a teenager. When I was
six we went to Hainandao, in China. It is an island, like Hawaii,
only bigger. We stayed in a huge hotel and went down to the
beach. I remember the big hotel. I remember getting lost on the
beach. I remember there were steps into the blue pool, the first
step and the second step were fine, the third step was pretty deep
and everything after that was over my head.

We go through dark glass doors into something like the lobby
of a hotel. Bobby smiles at the girl behind the counter. "Hey
sweetheart," he says and for a moment I think he is talking to me,
but then I realize he is talking to the girl, who smiles back at him.
He pays her money in cash and she has to have somebody come
out and take it and put it in an envelope with a lock. I don't know
many people who use cash. I wonder why Bobby has it. Whatever
we are going to do is very expensive, I wonder how Bobby can
afford it.

Then we go through another glass door and I smell pool chemicals. I look at Bobby but he isn't looking at me. He has his arm
through my arm but he is looking at some windows up above us.

This must be something illegal, but I don't know what it is.
Maybe gambling? It is a little scary, but exciting. Ginny, my
friend from my political study group, has gambled. She told me
about it, the dealers with no sleeves so you can be sure they're
not cheating, the men in suits who are managers and who carry
guns, the cards and tiles. You would have to have real money to

gamble, because the gambling place wouldn't want a record of debits and credits on your account, unless you were in Monaco, where it is still legal. And if you gambled in Monaco, your boss at your job could find out.

"Is this a gambling place?" I ask.

"No," Bobby says, "it's a bath house."

"What's a bath house?" I ask.

Bobby laughs, the sound bounces off the tile. "This." He points towards a pink door. "Go on and get a suit and get changed, I'll meet you on the other side."

He lets go of my arm and turns. He walks through a blue door, waving to me. I don't know what to do. Maybe I should go home. But he spent a lot of money on me. So I go through the pink door. On the other side, everything is pink. The floor is pink carpeting, the walls are pink, there is a girl in a pink bathing suit. "Do you need a suit?" she asks, smiling.

She lets me choose which color I want, I pick white. Then she shows me how to open the packet. "Put it on quick," she says, "before it sets."

Through another door. There is a locker room, with pink tile and pink lockers. I sit on a pink bench and read the instructions on the suit packet. It's from China. I peel it open, and peel out the suit. I step into the leg holes, pull it up. It's soft, like gelatin and I tear it pulling on it, but I close the tear with my fingers and it seals together. Using the pictures on the back of the instructions I pull it and stretch it until it has straps and it isn't too tight. By the time I have gotten it pretty much the way I want, and torn off the bits that I don't like, it is getting tougher. The back isn't quite even, but I hope that it looks okay. I brush my hair and freshen my makeup, then I go back to the girl in the pink room.

"Everything okay?" she asks, smiling.

"I think so," I say.

"Well, just go on through the locker room and out to the lounge. Do you want a robe?"

"Yes please."

She hands me a white robe with angel sleeves, the kind that could fit anyone, and I put that on and go out looking for Bobby.

He is standing in the lounge, holding a drink. His bathing suit is black and very tight. Bobby looks pretty nice in a black bathing suit, except that he has a little bit of a belly. But I can see him, I can see *it* kind of next to his leg, his suit is that tight. I look up, glad that he didn't see me looking. There are other people in the lounge. Most of the women are young and a few of them are very pretty. One girl, a Eurasian, has a spray of what looks like stars in her hair. They are so pretty. I have seen them in Mama's Chinese magazines, but I have never seen anyone wear one. I wish I had one, but where would I wear it? Out with Bobby?

Some of the men are our age, some are older. A lot are very handsome, but some aren't and they look foolish in their bathing suits. Why are men never worried about how they look when they are with a woman who is pretty?

Through an archway by the bar is the pool, and I can see a few people swimming, their heads sleek above the water, but Bobby takes my arm and walks me over to the bar. He orders me another Chrysanthemum without asking me and I take it even though I really don't want it, then we go the other way, away from the pool. "You look nice," he says, "let me see your suit."

I take off my robe although I would really prefer to keep it on.

"What are you wearing that thing for?" he asks, "you're too pretty to hide under a sheet. San-xiang," he says, kind of singing my name, "Saaan-xi-aaang." He says "Xiang" like a *waiguoren*, "she-ung" but it still sounds nice.

I want to put it back on but I don't.

We sit down at a little table and there are jacks. The room is dark, each table has a light above it. Bobby jacks in, so I do too, and there's a show. It's a comedian, but she uses all sorts of swear words, English and Chinese, and says all sorts of things that should be censored. I am embarrassed at first, and I'm afraid to laugh, because I don't want Bobby to think I am the kind of girl who likes this kind of talk, but Bobby is laughing, and some of the things are really funny, so I start laughing a little, too.

Bobby takes my hand and kind of keeps rubbing my wrist with his thumb, back and forth. At first it's okay, but after awhile, he keeps rubbing back and forth in the same place and it doesn't feel so good. But the show is fun. I don't drink very much of my drink, but Bobby drinks his.

Then we go swimming. It is so strange to be swimming in the middle of the night. We swim in one pool for awhile, and dive off the diving board. Then we go to another pool. The room is darker, and there is a light that reflects across the water, like the moon, Bobby says.

He holds my wrist as we walk down the steps into the water. I can see him, his skin is so white, and I can see my suit. There are other people here, I can hear them and barely see them. The water is warm, much warmer than the pool where it is light. I can smell plants, and there is a cricket. It must be a recording, but I can hear him, sawing away. A cricket is good luck. Maybe even if it's a recording.

The water is up to my chest, and Bobby pulls me against him, hugs me. I don't know what to do, he is not wearing very much and I can feel his skin and I can feel him kind of against my leg, even though he is wearing a suit, but I don't want to pull away. "San-xiang," he says in my ear and he strokes my back. I don't do anything, I don't pull away and I don't move my hands. I just stand with my arms around him and hope that he stops. There are other people in the pool, they must be doing the same thing.

He kisses me. I don't know what to do, so I kiss him back. If I don't kiss him, he'll think I don't like him at all. After this I'll go home and I'll never see him again, so it doesn't matter. Nothing else is going to happen.

He kisses me and kind of bends his knees—I have to, too—

until just our heads are above water. He pulls away, I'm relieved, but then he starts to touch my breast and I pull away.

He doesn't do anything for a moment, then he says, "Okay." I can't really see his expression, so I don't know if he's angry or not, he just says, "okay."

Then we go back to the other pool and swim some more.

We don't swim very long, and then he asks me if I'm ready to go. He doesn't act angry. I say that I'm ready. It must be late. I go back into the pink locker room and take off my suit. There's a canister with a sign above it that says "Discard Suits." I drop my suit in the clear liquid in the canister, mine is the only suit in there, and right away I see why because it starts to dissolve. By the time I am dressed, the liquid in the canister is clear.

"Good night, dear," the pink girl says.

"Did you like it?" Bobby says as we are leaving.

"Yeah," I say, "I did. I've never been any place like that."

"I told you that you'd like it." He keeps looking around him, all full of energy, I realize he has used another icepick. "Hey, why don't you come back to my place, have a drink or a cup of tea or something. The place where I'm staying isn't far from here."

"I really can't, Bobby," I say, "it's late, I've got to get home." I almost say that my mother will be wondering where I am but I remember I told him that I have my own apartment.

"Just for a little while," he says, "you don't work on Saturday, do you? Or we could go to your place, except mine's closer."

"It's really late," I say.

He just keeps walking, doesn't look at me.

"I mean, I worked all day," I say, trying to make excuse.

"Fine," he says, angry. "I spend all this money on you, and you just go home."

I feel terrible. It's true that he spent all that money, but he didn't seem to care.

"All I ask," he says, "is that you stop and have a cup of tea, a goddamn cup of tea."

I look at the ground, watch our feet.

"I know I'm not Chinese, not like your boyfriend," he says, nasty-sounding, "and I realize you're doing a *waiguoren* a real favor, gracing me with your presence, but I just thought you weren't like that. I thought you were nice, San-xiang."

"That's not true," I whisper, "he's not my boyfriend. I wasn't being like that. I like you, you're nice, I don't care if you're a *waiguoren.*"

"Well, just come and have a cup of tea," he says, suddenly pleading.

"Okay," I say. I won't stay long. "Just a few minutes."

"That's okay," he says, his voice normal again.

It's twelve-thirty. In an hour I'll be home. I tell myself that, in an hour I'll be home.

We walk and my heels click. We don't take the subway. My hair is wet, but it's not too cold, and I'm not cold. I'm tired, but I don't want Bobby to know because I'm afraid he'll give me another icepick and I don't want that.

The place where he is staying doesn't even have an elevator. We have to go up stairs. It's on the third floor and my legs are tired. I have that tired feeling you get after you've been swimming, my knees are all trembly and I'm a little hungry but mostly I'm just tired.

He unlocks three locks. The flat smells musty. He switches on the light and it's just two tiny rooms, one room really, because there's not even a door, just like an archway between the two. The bed is in the back half and it's not made, the apartment is full of man smell. Like a man's laundry.

"Sit on the couch," he says, "I'll make some tea."

I sit down. I'm so sleepy. Mama is going to be worried. The kitchen is really tiny, like the bathroom. I can see into the bathroom and the floor is dirty. It's worse than Zhang's apartment. I remember when I stayed at Zhang's apartment I had hoped that we would become lovers. Not that I was sure I wanted to have sex with him, but I thought that after I did I would learn to want to. And then I could leave home and live with Zhang and maybe we would fall in love. Except I was so ugly he never really liked me.

I wonder if he would like me now. It doesn't matter, right now I don't want to be anyone's lover. I want to be home in my own bed. I glance at my watch. It's almost one. I'll be home by two.

Bobby comes back in with the tea. He makes me nervous, but there's no reason. I'm just going to have a cup of tea and then go home, we talked about that.

He hands me the tea and sits down on the couch next to me. "You are really beautiful," he says.

I don't know what to say. "Thank you," I say.

"Really," he says. "Like a princess. A goddamn Chinese princess. Looking at you makes me want to touch you. When I saw you in that bar last night I just had to touch you."

I sip my tea. Maybe if I don't say anything he'll stop. But he doesn't, he keeps talking. "When I saw you all cool and golden in that white suit, I thought you were an ice princess, but I knew you were just looking for a man to melt you, all creamy golden." He touches my cheek and I start. His voice is soft, but it doesn't sound gentle. "My very own ice princess. You don't know a thing, do you sweetheart? San-xiang. Three Fragrances."

He touches my breast and I pull away. "Don't," I say.

"Three Fragrances," he repeats, like I haven't said anything, and uses one finger like he was drawing a line down my arm.

I start talking, too fast, but it's like I can't help it. "Bobby, I really have to go, it's late and I'm sure you're really tired. I mean, I'm sure you're really busy, and I have to go, I really have to go, my mama will be waiting up and she'll be wondering where I am because I never stay out this late—" I scoot over away from his finger as I am talking and I put the cup down on an end table with a clatter. "She's not accustomed to me going out and she'll worry because I'm on the subway so late and you never know what will happen on the subway this late"—and he grabs my arm and pulls me towards him and I hear myself whispering, "Bobby, don't, Bobby, don't, Bobby, don't," and he kisses me and sticks his tongue way in my mouth. He kisses me a long time, holding me tightly by one arm with his other hand touching my breasts and pinching them so they hurt and he kisses me and kisses me and he finally stops, I try to get up, and he pulls me back, and then I try real hard to get up and he lets me and then pushes me hard so I stumble back against the bed and sit on it, except he still has my arm and he tries to make me lie down on the bed and I say, "I won't, I won't, I WON'T," and then I scream except while I am screaming he slaps me real hard and I bite my tongue and I stop because of the hurt and he says, "Don't make a sound, sweetheart."

Everything in my head stops then, because I know I am going to die. So I let him kiss me, even though my tongue is bleeding a little bit and it hurts. I lie still while he touches my breasts and then he raises my skirt and makes me lift up so he can take off my panties. I feel the cold air on me and while he stands up and takes off his pants I hear this noise, kind of like a puppy or something whining, going "unnn, unnn," like it's hurt. It's me, I'm making this strange noise. But it doesn't matter. And then he climbs on top of me with his thing with its bald head sticking up and shoves it into me. It hurts, it hurts, and I start to cry.

When it is over I am afraid to move, but he doesn't pay any attention to me. He gets up without his pants and his thing is just hanging now, all shriveled, and he goes into the bathroom. Then I hear the shower.

I put my feet in my shoes and grab my purse and run, leaving my underwear. I run down the steps. I keep expecting him to come after me, to hear the sound of the door. I run down the street to the empty subway and I stand on the platform begging the train to come in, because I am afraid that he'll come down the steps. So I cry, and the train doesn't come, and the train doesn't come, but neither does he, and then finally there is a train and I am on it. I am sitting on the train with no underwear. I hurt.

People get on, and get off, and I am afraid of all of them. None of them look at me because I am crying. Then I have to change trains at Atlantic and I have to stop there. I have this terrible smell, I can smell it. And I am not wearing underwear. There are three people on the platform, two of them are men, and I am afraid one of them will touch me, because he will know, because of the smell. But my train comes.

It is two-fifteen when I get home and Mama and Baba are asleep. I keep hoping Mama will hear me, but she doesn't. She doesn't come to the door, she just sleeps. So I close my door and I take off my clothes and then I run to the shower and wash myself off. But the dirt doesn't come off. I climb into my clean nightgown, into my clean bed, but there is still the smell, like a man, like a man's dirty laundry. And I cry and cry until I go to sleep and no one ever comes.

I keep meaning to look for a new job, but I never see exactly what I am looking for in the paper. I do apply for a transfer at Cuo, but it turns out that a lot of people want that job so I don't get it. I never tell anybody about Bobby. Celia asks me how my date went and I say it was boring.

On Friday he calls. I am sitting there working. I'm really not thinking about him, sometimes I do, but when he calls I'm really not thinking about him at all. I don't expect his face. When I see it I don't know what to do.

He smiles and says, "Hi, are you busy?" His hair is down and with it down he looks kind of, well, cheap. I just stare at him for a minute.

"San-xiang?" he says.

I cut him off. Then I shunt my calls to Celia. As an excuse I go to the bathroom. I sit there and feel sick but after awhile I feel okay. If nobody knows it's as if it didn't happen.

So I go back to work. I expect Celia to tell me that he called back, but she doesn't. But he can call at any time. It occurs to me that he could come and see me at work. He knows where I work. Or he could be waiting in the subway when I get off.

I watch for him in the subway. Once I think I see him when I am shopping. I wish I could have my old face back to wear on the subways. But we can never go back.

Rafael

(Zhang)

"I'm sorry, the only housing we have available is in upstate Pennsylvania." The clerk looks over my yellow tunic and gray tights, my Chinese boots. "Where are you staying now, comrade?"

"I am staying with a friend in the city," I say.

"Well"—the young man leans forward and lowers his voice—"if I were you that's where I'd stay. We've been getting a lot of complaints about the buildings."

I nod. "Put them up too fast?"

"Overextended the water table. The water pressure is so low that only the first five stories get water."

"How many stories are there?"

He pulls out a brochure, white buildings off in the middle distance, trees. "Nine," he says, showing me the brochure.

"What do you do for water if you're on the ninth floor?"

"There are taps in the yard. You take a bucket downstairs and fill it up." He shakes his head. "It's crazy."

"Ah," I say, nodding. "Can I have this?"

262

"Sure," he says, handing me the brochure.

Back in New York. All I wanted was to get home and here I am, standing in line in the housing office so I can be offered a flat without running water. I turned down job offers in Wuxi for this. This is my second office this morning, I've already waited an hour and fifteen minutes to see an Employment Counselor at the Bureau of Employment, only to be told that since I was specialized labor I needed to make an appointment with the Office of Occupational Resources. And now I've waited in line for twenty-five mintues to be told the only thing available is a frigging flat in Pennsylvania without running water. I wonder if the architect that designed this office designed Pennsylvania housing. It's institutional green and needs painting. The floor is concrete, once painted green. Behind the counter hangs a fly strip, curled into a helix by age.

There had to be flies in China, I think, climbing a narrow stairway surfaced in black, industrial no-slip material, I just never noticed them. (Right, flies in the Wuxi Complex. A fly in Wuxi would have realized its hubris and died of embarrassment.) Every public stairwell in New York seems to be surfaced in that squishy no-slip stuff. I don't use it when I design because disposing of it cleanly is difficult and besides, it's ugly. New York has gotten around the disposal problem by never disposing of it. It's nearly indestructible, but going into the subway it's worn to holes. The holes provide slippery spots and heel catches, which contradicts the only reason for using it, that is, to provide a non-slip surface.

New York, in fact, the States seems to suffer from a serious lack of follow-through. I understand that maintenance is expensive, but what about the apartments out in Pennsylvania? When they found there was insufficient water pressure, why did they keep building? (Because where else are they going to put people.)

The subway station smells, a familiar, reassuring stink. Home again, home again. People talk all around me, their voices rise and fall, get to the end of the sentence and sing a bit, falling to say this is the end, rising to ask a question. Not like Mandarin, the staccato clatter of tones. I lean against the door, under the sign that says "Do not lean against doors" in English, Spanish and Chinese. Like the warnings in Chinese stations not to push, some things are meant to be ignored.

A woman sits under one of the signs that tell you where to call for information about resettlement on Mars, she is reading a textbook on med tech. She's very serious. She wears a waitress uniform, all day she flash heats cheap food. I imagine her on fire in her class, going into work the next day and watching the elaborate physics of the bodies around her, the balancing act of a woman leaning down to get something off a shelf, her whole body flexing and relaxing in symphony. The waitress amazed, her whole world expanding outward, suddenly complex and fascinating.

I know she's studying to be a med tech, a job not really different from flash heating food in terms of intellectual stimulation. She's doing it so she can get her certificate and get out of her free market job, get real benefits. The train stops at De Kalb, she gets out and crosses the platform to wait for the M train. The Mystery train we used to call it when we were kids, because we didn't know anything about the places it went.

I get out too, and upstairs to cross to the Atlantic station, connected by tunnel to De Kalb. At Atlantic Avenue someone says, "Zhong Shan?"

It's a young woman I don't recognize, an ABC, I think. Short hair in the style that all the girls in New York seem to be wearing, shaved high at the temples and glossily varnished everywhere else.

"You don't know me, do you," she says. "It's San-xiang. Qian San-xiang."

For a moment I can't place her, the face doesn't go with anyone and then I remember San-xiang. Ugly little San-xiang. She has had her face fixed. She looks normal.

"San-xiang," I say, "you're very pretty! How are you?"

"Okay," she says. "How are you?"

"All right. What are you doing, still working at Cuo?" I remember the place where she worked, that's good.

She nods, "For now. I'll be leaving in March."

"Transferring?" I ask.

"No," she says, "I'm going to Mars. I'm going to join a commune called *Jingshen.*" She says it flatly, without excitement, watching my reaction.

"*Shentong de shen?*" I ask. Which meaning of *jingshen?* It can mean "essence" or "profound" or a host of other things.

"Vigor," she says, which sounds like a Cleansing Winds name.

"I remember you were always interested in communes," I say lamely, wondering why anyone would go to Mars, wondering if she has any idea what it will be like. Of course, she has moved before, when she was a girl and her family came from China, but surely she doesn't realize how wrenching it will be to exile herself from home.

"You look like you are doing well," she says.

"I've been studying in China, I've only been back a week."

She asks the usual questions, where in China, what did I study. She's changed, she seems older. She is older, it's been four years since I saw San-xiang, she must be, what, twenty-six?

"Let's go get coffee," I suggest.

She hesitates a moment then shrugs. "All right."

We find a place to get coffee on the concourse between the Atlantic and Pacific stops. It's a depressing little place that, like most places in the subway, never sees sunlight. We sit down at metal tables with pressed simulated wood grain. "How is your father?" I ask.

She smiles. "About the same. Still believes he has the right to run everybody's life."

We don't talk about the last time we saw each other, when her father came to collect her at my apartment, but we do talk a little about kite racing. The conversation lags.

"Why are you going to Mars?" I ask.

"I've been corresponding with someone there for years," she says. "I admire the philosophy of the commune, it is a good compromise between the ideal and the practical. I think it would be a good thing to start over in a place where people pay attention to what is important."

It's a set speech, she must say this a lot. "So you'll go alone?"

"Yes," she says, a little defiantly, "they'll be my community."

"What does your family think?" I am sure Foreman Qian has not taken this quietly.

"They're adjusting to the idea," she says, evasively.

The conversation sputters again, we both sip our drinks. We were strangers when we met, strangers when we parted, we are strangers now.

"What are you doing," she asks, "now that you are back from China?"

"I don't know. Waiting until I get my life in order. I have to go to the Office of Occupational Resources and see about getting a job."

"Here in New York?" she says.

"Oh yeah." I say. "I found out in China, I'm really a New Yorker." I laugh. "Even if it is a dump."

She doesn't say anything to that and I remember again that San-xiang is Chinese. I don't think of her that way, she's been here so long. If she could, would she go back to China? I wonder if she'd find it foreign, she's been here for longer than she lived there.

I try to think of something to say, the only thing I can think of is to tell her how nice she looks, and I'm not sure whether I should say that or not.

"I'm sure you're very busy," San-xiang says.

"Oh," I say, "not so busy, but I know you're working and you don't have much free time."

Politely we dance through the formulas of ending, of parting. We walk back to the platform and say things like, "It was really good to see you again."

The trains, of course, don't come and we are left hanging there gracelessly.

"You know," San-xiang says suddenly, "I'm sorry about the way it worked out, but I'm glad we went out together."

"I enjoyed your company," I say.

"Was it because of my face?" she asks.

"Was what because of your face?" I say, knowing I don't want to hear her question.

"That you couldn't really like me?"

I could say that I did like her, but that isn't what she means. I look up, the board says her train is coming in. I want to explain, but I don't know how she will react, if she'll be disgusted. It is hard to break silence, it's a habit not to.

"Was it because you're only part Chinese?" she asks.

Her train slams into the station, cushions to a stop. "Good luck on Mars," I say, as people push around us. I am unable to think of how to answer her, of what to say. She has pretty eyes, now, turned up at me, asking, what is so wrong with her that I wouldn't do the dance, the dance that men and women are supposed to do? She starts to duck her head, to get on the train.

I touch her arm, "San-xiang," I say, "it didn't have anything to do with you."

Her face is closed. It sounds like everything else I have said to her, a polite lie to escape feelings. The doors will close any time now. "San-xiang, I'm gay," I say, and gently push her on.

She stops in the door and looks back at me, looking in my face, while her mouth shapes the word. She doesn't understand right away. Then as the doors close I see a look of wonder as she begins to realize. The train starts up, accelerates away. I hope that in this moment she feels some sort of absolution, some understanding that it was not her lack.

I am relieved that I didn't have to see if that look of wonder was followed by disgust. And now, I tell myself, it doesn't matter anyway.

I get back to Peter's flat and there's a call. I barely catch it, slap the console. I am looking at the reason that I have to find another place to live.

"Hello," says the reason, "is Peter there?"

I glance at the clock. "He's running a little late, probably stopped for something," I say.

"Tell him Cinnabar called," he says.

"Sure," I say and he cuts the connection. So now I know his name. Peter is involved, a fact he keeps secret from me. It is hard to come back and find that Peter is in love. I've been gone on and off for four years, and I had thought, maybe, when I came back, that Peter and I could try again, that we've matured and now maybe it will work. But I never said anything to him, and he never said anything to me. It probably wouldn't have worked for all of the same reasons it didn't before. And now we're good friends.

This Cinnabar, he seems, well, short. I don't know how to explain how someone looks short on a monitor, but he does. I think he's a flier. Peter always had a thing about fliers. He's not very good-looking, I'm a lot better looking than he is. He seems nice. If he seemed like a son of a bitch it would be different. (Different from what, Zhang?)

I've hardly been home a week, and my life is so complicated already. Peter's flat is so small; tiny kitchen, main room, bedroom. I'm sleeping on the couch, which isn't very comfortable (I wake up some mornings without having the slightest idea where I am). I should stay here, save my little bit of money left over from my Wuxi salary, wait until I get a job placement, but I don't know

how long I can stand living here. I have to get out. I can't stand
Peter pretending I don't complicate his life, I can't stand any of
this.

"Hey, Rafael." Peter is at the door, balancing the canvas bag
he uses for groceries. "Did you clean the flat?"

"And painted."

He looks around. "And you matched the old color exactly,
down to the smudges."

"Hey," I call as he disappears into the kitchen, "I'm an *engineer.*"

"Pijiu?" He tosses me a beer. "There, shook it for you."

"Cinnabar called," I say.

He comes back around the door again. "Oh yeah?" Not knowing what to say or how to act. Even though it's July, he's wearing
the yellow jacket I sent him from China, shining with silk thread,
embroidered with long-life medallions and stylized phoenix. Everybody wears jackets all the time. Fashion.

"No message, just tell you he called." I flick on the vid. "I went
down to the housing office today, the nearest available housing is
upstate Pennsylvania. And it doesn't have running water. I got a
prospectus for you." Now I have to think of an excuse for an
errand so I can get out of here and Peter can call this flier person.

I develop the habit of walking the boardwalk. The air smells
salty these days. It doesn't have that burnt smell anymore, the
project to clean up the harbor must be working. Reassuring to
know that something is working. But I miss the smell, for me it's
exciting. Sexual. Not that I'm cruising these days. Hell, even if
I wanted to, where would I take them, back to Peter's couch? And
I'm too old to climb under the boardwalk and let some kid do me
in the sand.

I remember kneeling in the sand, shivering, with the light
coming down between the cracks in the boardwalk. Going to

school in the day, pretending to be like everybody else, feeling like I had some secret knowledge, some understanding of the real world that the people I went to school with didn't have. Gooseflesh and the smell of ash. Some chickenhawk with his fingers locked in my hair.

I walk every night from eight until almost nine, regular as clockwork. The first couple of nights it's all right, but Friday night it's altogether too hot, and the boardwalk is crowded with people. Couples, girls in cheap flashy clothes, bright flimsy things. The young girls are shaving high up the backs of their necks, up even with their earlobes, and just leaving a tail of braided hair hang down.

"Ever had a hot dog?"

I'm leaning up against the railing, watching the kids go by. He's older than most of the kids, but only by a few years.

"Si," I say, *"Yo habito aqui."* I live here.

For a moment he looks confused. He looks Hispanic, but that doesn't mean he speaks Spanish. That will teach me to try and be clever.

Then he grins. *"Donde?"*

"Coney Island," I say.

He shakes his head. "For a moment I didn't realize what you were saying, you know, I just didn't expect you to speak Spanish. Chinese clothes and all."

"I grew up on Utica Avenue," I say. He's handsome. Dresses cheap, short matador jacket (no shirt) and tights. He has a tattoo of a tear at the corner of his left eye, it hangs on the edge of a sharp cheekbone. He's darker than I am. "So you were going to poison a foreign guest with a local hot dog."

He shrugs. "I just thought, here's this foreigner, all by himself on the boardwalk. Somebody ought to give him a taste of the ethnic cuisine."

We walk a bit. He struts, gestures as he talks. The boys seem spaced along the walk at regular intervals. They lean against posts and watch us. Coneys. The couples become static, white noise. The salient features of the landscape are the boys, and this amazing young man walking with me who talks about growing up out here on the edge, in the part of Brooklyn some people call Bangladesh.

"See," he explains, "there's always going to be a group of people who aren't ideologically sound. There's always going to be a bad element fringe. So the party doesn't mess with Bangladesh. We're a safety valve surrounding Coney Island. So out here we can be free."

"What about all the communes being established?" I ask. The girls dress in bright colors, the coneys dress dark. A coney in dark pants, dark sleeveless shirt watches us from the corner of his eye. He rests one muscled arm on a post.

"They won't stay," he says, airily. "Out here it never really changes. They pretend to clean it up, but they just pick up a few deviants and everybody else hides and two hours later the meat market is back in business."

Hot night for a meat market. I've seen it change. Used to be there wasn't anything out here, no couples, no hot dogs, just boarded-up stands, the coneys and the chickenhawks and the squatters. The squatters are mostly gone and the whole place is now free marketeers and the people who want housing in the city bad enough to stick it out. They clean up the two-hundred-year-old buildings, then make the neighborhood domestic.

He's so fresh and young. Is he waiting for me to make a move? I would if I could. "I have to get back," I say, regretfully.

"Good talking to you," he says.

"I come out here and walk pretty often," I say. "What's your name?"

"Invierno," he says. In Spanish that means winter. What kind of name is Invierno? Obviously not his real name. Not giving one's real name or number is a time-honored tradition out here on the boardwalk.

"I'm Rafael," I say. "Like the angel."

He grins and makes the sign of benediction, standing at the top of the steps.

When I glance back a second time he has already turned and stalks back down the boardwalk, prowling.

Back at Peter's building two women are carting boxes out the front door and piling them on the sidewalk. They watch me, flat, hostile faces. Their belongings make the usual pitiful pile on the sidewalk. I step over blue-green pillows like the kind Peter has tossed on the floor, palm the door.

The hallway and the elevator are hot and airless, in China even the hallways were kept cool. I wonder how much money it would cost to keep the halls heated and cooled. There are old ducts, at one time the halls of this building were temperature controlled. In an old building like this it would help the tenants keep their own costs a little lower.

"Hey," I say, "someone is moving out of the building."

Peter is flicking through vid programs. "Who was it?"

"Two girls. No one I know." Peter must be as frustrated as I am. I leave coneys on the boardwalk, he talks to his flier. "Maybe I could rent their place."

"Don't rent, save your money until you get a job," Peter says.

"You need your own place back," I say.

"You're no problem, and you pay half the rent."

"How's what's his name, the flier." I say pointedly. How's your love life? I've got this roommate and he's driving me crazy.

Peter glances up at me, back at the vid. "Cinnabar's just a friend. He's not a flier, he's retired." He sits stiff and defensive. I shouldn't have said it.

"I need a place of my own," I say and sit down next to him.

"You don't get a job," he says, "you'll start borrowing money from me. Pretty soon they'll kick both of us out."

"Hey," I say, "I'll rent for a few months and then we'll move to Pennsylvania together."

Then I get him a beer and rub his shoulders.

"A regular Florence Nightingale," he says.
The room has ghosts.

So I become a tenant. I move to the fifth floor, griping about
having to take the psychopathic elevator to the top of the building.
Moving is not difficult; as Peter remarks, for a man with a truly
astounding wardrobe, I seem painfully short of possessions. (Not
that my wardrobe is really much, it's just Chinese.) The flat is two
rooms, not counting the tiny kitchen and bathroom, both about
the same size.

I live in a dump. "The floor has to go," I say. Someone painted
the walls aqua, the floor is blue-green slip, it's like living under
water on a bad film set. Cheap. But this building was built before
the second depression, when they built to last, and underneath
that garbage is a solid floor, underneath the walls is good solid
wood frame. I wonder what would happen if I knocked the wall
out between the two big rooms. The little front room, which is
supposed to be the main room, has no window. The back room
is barely big enough for a bed. Together they would make one
decent room.

But it's my own. Once moved in I decide I have to take my life
in hand. I've been home for two weeks and haven't done anything
but sleep on Peter's couch and walk the boardwalk.

The morning after I move in I put on my black suit and go to
the Office of Occupational Resources.

The office has carpeting, something that marks it as a step up
on the scale of bureaucracy, but why is it all so ugly? This office
is dirty green; gray-green carpeting (the kind that doesn't show
dirt, wear or aesthetic value) pond-scum green halfway up the wall
and scuffed white the rest of the way. I meet a middle-aged
woman, dressed in a boxy beige suit with tails that come precisely
to the backs of her knees.

"Comrade Zhang?" she says, "I'm Cecily Hester. I'm the counselor who will be assigned to your placement."

I have a counselor assigned to me. I am not certain how to feel about this. "Counselor," I say, politely.

She indicates a seat, not at the desk but at the flyspecked window that looks out on the street, and sits down beside me. "Tell me, just exactly what does an organic engineer do? Are you a medical engineer?"

So I launch into a description of my training.

"We'll have to start looking around to see who could use your particular skills," she says, thoughtfully. I suspect she still isn't sure just what I do.

"What kind of people do you usually place?" I ask.

"Doctors and highly technical people like yourself." She gets up. "I'll need to get some information on the system." I follow her over and we sit, she behind the desk.

"How long does it take to place someone?" I ask.

"That depends on what they do. A few months. Do you have a preference as to what part of the country you'd work in?"

"New York City," I say.

"East Coast," she says, entering the information, "Northeast."

"I'd really like to stay in New York."

"Engineer," she says, "you have a very specialized skill. Hopefully I'll be able to find a firm in the city that is interested in you, but it's not very likely."

"Do you mean I won't be able to get a job?" I ask. "They offered me work in China." Marx and Mao Zedong but I sound desperate.

"You'll be able to get a job," she says. "Off the top of my head, I can think of two places that will probably be interested in you. One is in California, one is in Arizona."

"The corridor," I say. Baffin Island, only permanently.

"They have a beautiful compound," she says.

She asks me to repeat my education, enters it all. I give her a rec with my resume and final project, my beach house, on it.

I sense dislocation ahead. Moving. I feel so tired, life was a hell of a lot easier when I was just a job engineer, another dumb construction tech.

What the hell am I going to do? All that time, Baffin Island, Nanjing. All that, so I can work in the corridor? "Ah, if this is going to take a few months, can you help me get some sort of short-term work, maybe as a construction tech? The only housing available is in Pennsylvania, and they told me it doesn't have running water, so I'm living in a commune out in Coney Island and I have to help with the building maintenance."

"I'm sure you don't need to be a construction tech," she says, sounding a little as if I were a research scientist who just offered to be a janitor. "Let me think about it and I'll call you."

The ride out to Coney Island takes forever.

All this time on my hands. When I finished the job on Baffin Island and passed my exams, I waited ten months to go to China, but I worked construction jobs for all but the last month. I don't remember time hanging on me during that month. Since then I have been in China, always struggling to catch up, struggling with language, with taking three years' worth of courses in two regular school years and a summer.

China falls into two neat halves in my memory—not chronologically, the first "half" is really only about three, four months, the last "half" the better part of two years. But there is Haitao, and then there is the time after Haitao, the white time. That's the way I think of it, I don't know why. Or rather, I know some of the reasons why, but they don't seem sufficient to describe the feeling.

The white time is crowded with activity. I have never studied so intently as I did in the year after Haitao died, I don't suppose I ever will again. For a year I was this amazing creature, the envy of my classmates, Zhang, the *huaqiao* who destroys grade curves. I read the assignments, did supplemental readings. I got tutoring assignments because I discovered having to explain systems analysis to some martian made it clearer in my own head (especially because Alexi had an agenda of his own, he asked questions that made me think about systems in different ways than the textbooks did).

I did it the way you'll play solitaire for an afternoon, because the alternative was being alone with myself.

The apartment is depressing. All that green. I try to read, but I start thinking about what I could do with it. On a job once, we used this sandstone flooring. The flat isn't very big, the flooring wasn't outrageously expensive and it would be better than blue-green slip. I wonder what the subflooring is like.

I shut off the climate control, open the door and put my new bed and boxes out in the hall and tear up a corner of the flooring. Underneath the flooring is hundred-year-old thinsulation and under that was chipboard. Imagine having so much wood you can use it as trash building material.

"What are you doing?" Someone says from the doorway. It's Yoni, one of the two people who chair the co-op's managing committee.

"I'm going to replace the floor," I say.

"You should have cleared it with the committee first," he says.

"I'll pay for it," I say.

"That's not the point. What if you get halfway through and stop. The co-op would have to replace the rest of it. You're damaging the building." He strokes his walrus moustache.

"I'll put some money in an *zhuazhu* account until I get it finished," I say.

"A what?" he asks.

"*Zhuazhu.*" I say. I'm not exactly sure how to translate. "An account to hold money. A holding account. I'll put the cost of replacing the floor in a bank account in the co-op's name. When I'm finished, you can give it back. It's what they do in China. Look at this, you know what's underneath this floor? Chipboard."

"What's chipboard?" he asks.

"Pressed wood chips. Look at it."

He comes and crouches next to me. "Hey," he says, "it's kind of pretty. Do you think that's under most of the floors?"

I shrug. "Depends on how the place was put together, if this flat was remodeled. I'd say they have it next door, it looks like these two flats used to be one. See how it goes under the wall?"

"Vanni might like this stuff on her floor," Yoni says.

"You have to seal it." He wants to know why and I explain how wood is soft and damages. Then I explain about sealers.

He goes next door and gets Vanni, my neighbor. It's noon but Vanni is a bartender and at first she's not at all thrilled about being woken up to look at her neighbor's floor. She's come by a couple of times to see what I was doing, she's a little dark thing, not more than twenty-five.

She crouches down sleepily. "There's *that* under the blue stuff?"

"Hard to tell," I say, "but probably. These old buildings are like archeology, they come in layers."

"Hey Yoni," she says, grinning, "do you think there's another layer under that garbage I've got for plumbing? Some sort of decent pipes? Maybe copper?"

"Most archeology is done on garbage dumps, isn't it?" Yoni asks.

"You mean under the garbage is more garbage. Rafael," she says, "want to come rip up my floor? I can't pay much."

"If I don't get a job soon I'll rip it up and if you've got chipboard I'll seal it."

I don't seal the chipboard on my floor. I knock out the dividing wall and repair the wallboard at the break, paint the walls white and then lay pale sandstone squares from somewhere out in the corridor. The whole job takes six days, mostly because I don't have much in the way of tools. I rent a cutter for four hours for the wall, and buy a little hand cutter to trim stone, but other than that the whole thing is pretty much done by hand. Once in awhile I find myself looking for shapes of states in the insulation and stone. Divining my future. Some people read tea leaves, I read building materials. The stone is a bitch to haul in, but when I'm finished the place is light and clean-looking. Next job will be making the window bigger.

For a few minutes I feel pleased with myself. I haven't felt adrift all day, and sitting in this apartment I now have a place where I can escape the oppressive shabbiness of everything.

But hell, there's not a lot to do. Watch my little vid. I have a kitchen table and two chairs, and a bed. Nothing to do but think about the interview and all the questions I should have asked. Why did I even bother to redo the place? I'm not going to live here. I've done it all for a stranger, who will probably hate it because there's no bedroom. Time to get out, otherwise I'm going to brood myself into catatonia.

I wander downstairs to see if Peter is in. To talk, to tell him about the interview.

"Zhang," Peter says when he opens the door, surprised. He doesn't usually call me that. "Come in. How's the place?"

"Bu-cuo." Not bad. "Mostly finished, you should come up and see it sometime when I have beer in the cooler. You busy?"

"No, a friend just stopped by." He gestures to come in.

It's the one who calls. He is short, short and tiny. Stringy. Definitely a flier. "Hi," I say, "I'm Zhang, or Rafael."

"I met you once a couple of years ago," he says, "Cinnabar Chavez." He stands and offers his hand. "You and Peter were at Commemorative."

"I remember," I lie. There were a lot of nights at Commemorative, a lot of fliers. But this time I connect, maybe it's the last name. I guess the reason I didn't connect before was that I had it in my head that he died. Obviously not.

"Pijiu?" Peter says, elaborately casual.

"Sure," I say. It occurs to me that I'm not going to talk to Peter about what to do with my life. At least not tonight. "So you are Peter's secret," I say.

Peter pops out of the kitchen, looking irritated. Somehow this delights me, makes me feel wicked. Peter ducks back in the kitchen.

"I've heard a lot about you," Cinnabar says. "You and Peter have been friends a long time. Which do you prefer, Zhang or Rafael?"

"Which does Peter call me?"

"Mostly Rafael."

"Rafael is fine. Peter's a good guy," I say, "a good friend. The best."

"I can see that," Cinnabar says softly.

From the kitchen Peter calls, "What is this, my eulogy?"

"Except, of course," I add, "he thinks he's everybody's mother."

This strikes some cord in Cinnabar, he starts laughing. Peter comes out of the kitchen scarlet with embarrassment, silently hands me my beer, and glares at Cinnabar when he gives him his.

"Don't look at me!" Cinnabar protests. "I didn't make him say it! I didn't say a word!"

I am in trouble. This job thing, I have too much time to think about it.

I read and watch the vid. In the evening I walk on the board-walk, sometimes late at night go back out and on Friday night I even end up underneath the boardwalk with a kid who looks seventeen but says he's twenty. We're at a stretch where the stands are boarded up for the night and there aren't as many couples, but still, above my head there are the click-click-click of heels. The act is fast and depressing, sordid without being thrilling.

I remember being a coney. Hawks seemed old.

White time. Baffin Island time. Two weeks of my life slide by. A couple of evenings I go downstairs and talk to Peter and Cinnabar. Cinnabar is having a party, I agree to go to make Peter happy. Instead, the Friday of Cinnabar's party becomes a landmark, a navigation point, something happening. It's like a white out, where the wind is blowing the snow sideways, and the windows of the observation station might as well have been painted white. We came back from Halsey Station in one, using instruments to navigate. I got so disoriented I had trouble standing up when we got inside, I'd lost all sense of right and left, up and down.

Then Cecily Hester from the Office of Occupational Resources calls. "I have lots of news," she says. She is excited. "Western Technologies in California. They're offering ninety-two hundred, but I think that's low. It's only to get you to come and talk to them anyway. And I think I've got you something to tide you over."

"In California?" I say stupidly. Ninety-two hundred? I made eleven hundred a year as a construction tech. Thirty-two in my year of "hazardous duty" on Baffin Island. My father lives somewhere in California.

"Right, Western Technologies. But the place that's really going to be interested in you is New Mexico-Texas. That's where you're going to get the real offers. They're both multinationals, with headquarters in the free economic zone in Hainandao. That's why they can afford to offer the salaries. Of course, when your salary is paid by a free market corporation, you're taxed. I imagine you've never been taxed. It's a lot of money, thirty, forty percent, but that's still a very good salary." Comrade Cecily Hester smiles at me. "I've learned a great deal about organic engineers in the last three days, Engineer Zhang. There aren't very many of you outside of China. It's nice to see that you came back."

The braindrain to China. All the brightest and best go there. How funny that she lumps me in with molecular biologists who go to China to do grad work and never return.

"Also," she says, "Brooklyn College would like to have you teach an engineering course. They were very excited when I told them you were in the city." She looks thoughtful. "It's a pity they don't pay much, that would allow you to stay in the city. But they're not going to be able to come anywhere near sixty."

So much money. "Thank you," I say,

Cinnabar's party. I'm not sure I'm in a party mood. I'd really like to talk to Peter about this New Mexico-Texas thing, but I probably won't get much chance. I have a bad feeling about this party.

I decide to wear the black suit Haitao said was so conservative it wasn't. I wonder if Liu Wen still plays *jiaqiu*. I never found out if he was arrested or if he escaped that night when the club was raided. If he did escape, I don't know if he ever found out that Haitao was dead. What would they think of Liu Wen at Cinnabar's party? Would they understand how decadent it was to be beautiful and appear to throw it all away?

I take the train down to Brooklyn Heights where Cinnabar lives. Peter is helping to host so he's been there all day. I carry beer, my contribution.

Cinnabar lives in an old building, it was probably once a single family residence, now apartments. Cinnabar has the top two floors. The hallway is cluttered with kite frames, a bicycle, a couple of chairs turned on their sides. He's a consultant for one of the companies that supplies kite frames. The door is open. Cinnabar's place is pretty big, rather dark and cool. I haven't been to many places the size of this, Cinnabar Chavez obviously does pretty well, but I've been to a lot of places that looked much the same, if smaller.

It's an old building, built strong and decaying slowly. Inside seems shabby and cheap. It's not, not by New York standards, I know. (I think of the Wuxi Complex, beautiful red tile roofs.) On one wall is a short vid loop. It's a flier hooking into a kite harness, talking to a kid on his crew. The flier isn't Cinnabar, although he's Hispanic. After a moment I realize the kid is, a young Cinnabar. There's no sound, just this flier jacking in, a real short clip of him taking off in an old-looking kite with bright blue and violet silk. Then a clip of another flier, probably Cinnabar, touching down in a kite with red silk. Then repeat.

There's music, that tinkly, percussion stuff for pattern dancing. I take my beer into the kitchen and stuff it into a cold box already full of beer and wine. Nobody's dancing yet. I see Peter talking to a couple of people and say hello. I go back and get a beer so I have something to do with myself until I fit into the party. I see Cinnabar talking to another flier, a woman with long crinkly hair, a red jacket and hips like a twelve year old. I don't recognize many fliers, I know some of their silk colors and that's all, and I haven't been to a race since before China.

Cinnabar doesn't seem to have much furniture. Makes a great space for parties.

I drink my beer and say hello to a couple of people I know from Peter's building. I end up talking to Robert, who doesn't know anybody here either. "You're in the building? How come I haven't seen you at the meetings?"

"I've only been there a couple of weeks."

We make small talk. It's eight-thirty, I figure I can sneak out at eleven, maybe ten-thirty.

I glance around and to my astonishment make eye contact with the guy from the boardwalk, Invierno.

"It's the angel!" he says and saunters over.

"Hey," I say, delighted. "Are you a friend of Cinnabar's?"

He is, well not exactly, he's a friend of a friend. "I almost didn't come tonight," he says.

"I'm glad you came."

He knows a lot of people at the party. "The woman talking to Cinnabar? That's Gargoyle, the flier. Only her name's really Angel. And that guy over there? That's Previn Tabat, the guy on the news."

He tells me that the flier in the vid is Cinnabar's elder brother, dead in a flying accident. He flirts with me. He flirts with Robert. He has large dark eyes and very long eyelashes. He's dressed in his matador's outfit again.

"I haven't seen you on the boardwalk," I say.

"I don't get out too much." He shrugs. "I work at a bank, I work weird hours in Routing." Something about keeping track of credit.

Robert drifts off while we stand talking. Invierno's such a kid, full of himself, aggressive, almost obnoxious. But I keep finding him funny.

"Dance with me," he says. People have started dancing.

"I don't know how," I say, amused.

"I don't believe you."

"It's true," I protest, laughing. "I really don't know how."

"I'll teach you a pattern," he promises, and taking me by the wrist, pulls me to the center of the room where we are most noticeable, and teaches me a pattern, a simple one. We dance and I think he'll get tired of me, but he doesn't. He changes pattern dancing into something baroque, to go with his Spanish clothes. He invests the steps with a stiffness, machismo. He holds my hand high and when he looks at me, he has veiled his eyes under those lashes. He looks like a willful boy who is sensitive to slights. And the more I laugh, the more he warms under the attention.

So, of course, late in the party I take him home. We slip down the steps to the subway and sit on the train, casually uninterested in each other, my left knee touching his right, while an old man sleeps across from us and a girl in a waitress' uniform knits next to us.

I take him into my room, out of the dark hall where the lights go off the moment you open your door, and he says, "This is where you live?"

I imagine it's too bare for him, I don't even have a comfortable chair. "I haven't been here long."

Then he surprises me. "This is really nice," he says softly, enviously. "Is this the way they do things in China?"

"No," I say, "in China you'd program lights and wall colors. And there'd be more furniture."

He nods, touches the walls with the tips of his fingers. "It's white. Doesn't white mean death?"

"It also means life. It depends on whether you're Eastern or Western."

"What are you?" he asks.

I shrug. "A little of both."

He stands there, looking at me. Waits for me. I am the older man, I make the first move. That is a shock, too. I've always been the pick-up, or we were both young and there was no older/ younger, like with Peter. But now we are in my place and I have Invierno.

So I take him to bed.

I sleep and wake, turn carefully on the bed not to bother him, sleep again, coming half awake to shift. He shifts against me a couple of times, often only a moment after I do. We didn't sleep until four or five. The light through the one window is bright by mid-morning. He has a lovely shoulder, hairless, the color of tea. Broad flat shoulder bone like an ax.

Used to be I'd be lying here wishing he would leave. Young men leave, don't even sleep, they grab their tights, stand in the bedroom like one-legged storks, getting dressed. Once I'd have shifted around until he woke up, then I'd offer him breakfast. I'll be thirty-one in four months. I'm tired but I like him here, sleeping on his stomach, his face turned away from me.

He told me the tear tattoo was a prison thing a hundred years ago. Fashion now. After the liberation, gay men doing reform through labor had the tattoo. A totem. A sign. A signal. I don't touch him, he'd wake up.

Someone knocks on the door and Invierno sits straight up.

"Just a minute!" I call.

"Shit," Invierno says, rubbing his face. "What time is it?"

"Around ten-thirty." I drag on the pants to my suit—lying on the floor next to the bed—and push my hair out of my face, open the door just wide enough to see out. It's Vanni, my next door neighbor. She's fresh, brown face turned up, big eyes, wild black hair caught back.

"Oh," she says, "were you asleep?"

I slip out in the airless hall, the heat is hard, makes me feel as if I can't breathe. "What are you doing up so early on a Saturday morning?" Vanni works late hours, I hear her come in at two, three in the morning.

She's embarrassed. "I was just up, I was wondering about if you could help me strip my floor this weekend. I didn't mean to wake you."

"Sure, I'll help you strip it." I say, "I'm so bored I don't know what to do with myself. Look, I've got company, are you going to be home later this morning?"

"Oh God," she says, covers her mouth, "Oh Rafael, I'm really sorry. I'll be home."

I smile at her, "Okay, I'll see you later." I guess I should be irritated, but I'm pleased. I like the idea of having neighbors.

Invierno is still sitting on the bed, bare feet on the floor. "I didn't know it was so late," he says.

"Are you late for work?"

"No, but I've got to do some stuff first." He grabs his matador pants. In the bathroom my reflection is a revelation, haggard face,

hair stringing all over the place. I splash water on my face, drag
a brush through my hair and tie it back.

While he's in the bathroom I make coffee. He downs a cup,
refuses my offer of breakfast. I tell him to call me if he's free, give
him my number. He stuffs it in the pocket of his jacket without
looking at it or me. The morning after. But he smiles at me in the
hallway.

Smiles are like tears. Totems. Signs. Signals.

In the white time, you cling to signals.

I become a teacher.

It's laughable, in a way. The way I become a teacher is simply
to have someone say "You're a teacher." A *professor* no less.

Brooklyn College is an old school with a long and illustrious
tradition. They say that even before the liberation, anyone who
had a college diploma could go to Brooklyn College and that it was
free. There's a statue of Christopher Brin in front of Martyr's Hall
and a plaque explaining that and that Brin was a graduate of
Brooklyn College. I don't exactly understand the logistics of all
this. If anyone who wanted to could go to school, how did they
keep from having classes of two hundred or two thousand students?

My preparation for teaching my course, a course titled "Engi-
neering-Systems Applications" is an interview with Dean Eng.
Dean Eng asks me my teaching experience and the only thing I
can think of is tutoring. I tell her I tutored a martian settler and
she asks me if I could possibly get him to enroll in my class here.
He could audit for free.

I use the terminal in her office to send Alexi Dormov a telex.

Her major piece of advice is to wait until class has started and
then walk in without looking at the class, walk straight to the
blackboard and write my name. Then announce my name, the

class name and call numbers and say that anyone who needs to add the class to their schedule should see me afterwards.

I assume this is some method of intimidating students with professorial manner.

"Not at all," she explains, smiling in a kind of motherly way, "it's a method of reducing stage fright. This way, when you turn around and look at all those faces you'll have something to say."

She is absolutely correct. There are fifteen people officially registered for my course, but when I turn around after writing "Zhang Zhong Shan" on the board there are easily thirty people in the classroom. I've never talked in front of so many people in my life and the minute I start with my lecture they're going to know that I'm a fraud. I make my announcement about which class this is and nobody moves. Thirty faces, almost half of them ABC, all looking at me, most of them Invierno's age. My knees are shaking. I stand behind the desk.

I glance back at the board behind me. The class before mine is a required politics class, someone has diagrammed the classic Marxist historical progression on the board: Primitive Society to Feudalism, Feudalism to Industrial Revolution to Capitalism to Proletariat Revolution to Socialism to Communism. All sorts of irrelevant things run through my mind. My first year in China, my roommate, Xiao Chen, was a Scientific History major. I can remember helping him study for exams. I can still remember the three major advancements in pure science in the twentieth century: Relativity, Quantum Physics and Chaos Studies.

"I know you are all going to be disappointed," I say, "but this is an engineering course, not a politics course."

Some of them smile politely.

"There is a member of the class who is present but several minutes behind us," I say. "We will have a martian auditing the class by monitor, so please speak up loudly so Alexi can hear your contributions to class." My voice sounds very shaky. They cannot possibly believe I am a teacher. But they all sit very expectantly.

When I start to talk, they all start their transcribers, highlighters ready.

When I wrote it, my opening lecture seemed brilliant. I don't really want to teach anything today, I just wanted to get my feet wet and entertain them a little. Looking at my notes I realize I'm going to bore them all bonkers. I talk about how we think of using systems, and how we assume that we jack into the machine.

"Stimulation of your nervous system from an artificial system is illegal," I say. "Why?"

There is silence. *Madre de Dios,* what do I do if no one answers the question? Then one young man raises his hand and I call on him gratefully.

"Because it's addicting," he says.

"How many of you have ever been to see a kite race?" I ask. It sounds like one of those teacher-questions (I am amazed at how much I sound like a teacher). Most of them raise their hands. "Well, a flier experiences the kite as a kind of second body," I say. "The fliers feel the kites sail as if they were the flier's wings, and if the kite develops a structural problem then the flier feels it as an ache. Something has got to be stimulating the flier's nervous system," I say. They glaze over. Did you know you can see boredom? I have other examples, the medical stuff in China, for one, but I decide to just finish up on fliers and forget other examples. I tell them about the system at Wuxi, where people didn't jack in. Some of them look interested but nobody uses their highlighters. "In the future we might all be cyborgs linked into systems. In that future, we would all be organic engineers." This sounds like a teacher lecture. Amazing how you don't have to have any training to sound like every dull teacher you ever had in middle school.

I explain about organic engineers. I expected the lecture to take an hour, but I find it's only taken twenty-five minutes. I tack on a little about the relationship of science to society, about how social thought always lags behind scientific change. Mostly because of thinking about Xiao Chen. Then I realize I need an example.

What's an example of how social thought lags behind scientific change? I mean, it's a cliche, but other than talking even more about how everyone is afraid of feedback but how it is the way things will go in the future, I really can't think of anything. Religion. But everybody knows about religion, and it's not relevant to them.

"Take for example the diagram behind me on the board. Does anyone recognize it?"

They all look at me, blank. Of course they all recognize it. But it's politics. Nobody in their right mind is going to volunteer anything about politics. Keep your head down, don't get into trouble. Nervousness makes me a tyrant, I point at one young woman. "Tell me what it means."

She looks around, hoping for escape. Normally I'd feel sympathy for her but now I am only concerned with how to fill another fifteen minutes.

"Ah, it's Marx's analysis—"

Her voice is so soft I can barely hear her. "Sweetheart," I say, trying to put her at ease, "you've got to talk loud enough to be heard on Mars."

Louder she says, "It's a Marxist diagram of historical progression."

"Right. Now, what the diagram says is that primitive society eventually organizes into feudal society. Usually as a result of farming. That society eventually allows a few landlords—whether you call them lords or landholders or whatever—to accrue enough capital to invest in something other than farming. That capital forms the base for an industrial revolution, which paves the way for capitalist society. Capitalism exploits workers the way feudalism exploits serfs. But capitalism is an unstable system, with its boom and bust cycles, its violent corrections, and eventually there is a proletariat revolution and a socialist system is established. So far so good?"

I expect them to be bored out of their minds, they've been chanting this relationship since junior middle school, but they are rigid with attention, the glaze of boredom is gone. Apparently there is some novelty in having an engineering teacher lecture them on politics.

"Okay," I say, "when did China move from primitive to feudal?"

"The Emperor Qin," someone says dutifully.

"From feudal to capitalist?"

There is a moment of silence. Finally an ABC raises his hand.

"Laoshi," he says formally, Teacher, "Mao Zedong changed the diagram. The revolution in China was a peasant revolution, not a proletariat revolution."

"Wrong," I say. The young man's eyes get large. *"Lenin* changed the diagram. Other than that you are perfectly correct." I sound like Comrade Wei, my calculus teacher in middle school. Marx and Lenin, I hated that man.

There is a nervous laugh. I find it very exciting to have their attention. "Can you name me an example of a country that did have a proletariat revolution?"

A young woman pops out without raising her hand, "We did."

"Right. In the early twenty-first century the national debt and the trade deficit of the old United States precipitated the second depression. In effect, the country went bankrupt, and as a result, so did the economy of every first-world nation at the time except for Japan, which managed to keep from total bankruptcy but lost most of its markets, and for Canada and Australia, which created the Canadian-Australian alliance, a holding measure to preserve their own systems which survives until this day. The Soviet Union also went into bankruptcy because it was deeply invested in the U.S. bond market, whatever that was"—they all laugh, we've all been taught that the U.S.S.R. was deeply hurt in the economic collapse because of their involvement in the U.S. bond market, but I'll be damned if I ever met anyone who really knew what that meant. "And what did China do?"

"Went back to a soft currency system," someone volunteers.

"What is soft currency?" I ask.

Silence.

The boy who called me *laoshi* has his nerve back. "Ah, it is an economic system which does not tie its own currency into the world market."

"Meaning?" I ask.

"Meaning"—he takes a breath—"that a Chinese yuan inside the borders of China had value—that it bought things—but that outside the Chinese border it was just a piece of paper."

"Ah," I say. Then I tell the truth. "You're the first person ever to explain that to me. Unless I slept through it in middle school, which is possible." Honest laughter this time.

I continue. "The U.S. could no longer provide social services, keep schools open, hospitals, banks. Eventually, the Communist Party organized well enough under Christopher Brin to take over portions of New York City and attempted to provide basic social services. We will skip over the struggles of the early party, which was, as everyone knows, given a major shot in the arm by the help of the Chinese who had managed to get their economic shit together."

Grins in the room.

"Along comes the Second Civil War, led by Brin until he was killed in Atlanta and after that by Darwin Iacomo and Zhou Xiezhi and the United States becomes a socialist country. So there we have it, capitalism to proletariat revolution to socialism. Now," I ask, "where is the American feudal period?"

Actually, it was a Canadian who first asked me that, Karin, happily poking holes in my education. The class has the same answer I do, which is to say that they have no idea.

"Well," I say, enjoying myself immensely and not giving Karin any credit, "unless you count slavery, which was regional, there was no feudal period. And the only American primitive period was the Native Americans, and their economic history is discontinuous from ours."

A young woman who hasn't spoken thus far raises her hand. "Our feudalism was in Europe," she says.

I nod. "Okay," I say, "I'll give you that."

Up until now everything I've said has been fine. I stop. I don't really have the nerve to go on. I look up, there are students in every seat, and there are two people leaning on windowsills. They are all waiting, waiting for me to make my point. "But now, all of this so far has been very fine from a political point of view. But from a scientific point of view it is clearly a very Newtonian way of thinking."

They all watch me. I don't know what they are thinking.

"Newtonian," I say, "From Newton. The guy with the apple." Marx and Mao Zedong, I am the last person anyone would ever expect to be standing here lecturing on science and politics. Maybe I can just explain why it's Newtonian and stop there, that doesn't seem too dangerous.

"Newton thought of the universe as like a giant clock. He said that the universe was rather like a mechanism, wound up and set in motion by God and therefore moving in grand patterns, much like planetary orbits. The nineteenth and twentieth century were mostly involved with trying to figure out Newton's patterns and describe them all.

"Marx attempted to reduce society to its component forces. For Newton, the forces that described the universe were basically gravity, motion and inertia. Marx's major forces were economic. He thought that an analysis of economic relationships would explain the movement of history. And when he had analyzed these relationships he could extrapolate to predict the way society would move in the future." I tap on the board. "This is his analysis."

Some nods. I notice the flicker of highlighters. "I would appreciate it if you didn't take this down," I say softly. "You will not be tested on any of this."

The young man who calls me *laoshi* grins and leans back.

"Marx assumed that either things were predictable or they were random. Things are either predictable or random, aren't they?" It is a trick question, these are engineering students. Engineering tends to work with things we can solve. Things we can solve are usually predictable. "What are the two kinds of predictable equations?" After I ask it I realize they may not know.

A young man, "Linear or periodic."

"Right. Linear. If I drop this book you can calculate the speed of the book as it falls. Correct? Linear or periodic?"

"Linear," he says.

I tap the blackboard behind me. "Linear or periodic?"

"It's not an equation," says the woman who said our feudal period was in Europe.

"Ah, but it looks like a graph, would the equation be linear or periodic?"

"Linear," a couple of people say. Obviously. It's a line, from primitive to the communist utopia.

"Give me an example of periodic?"

The *laoshi* young man. "The seasons."

"Right, spring, summer, fall, winter, spring, summer, fall, winter. Capitalism assumed that an economy cycles in a boom and bust cycle. Expansion, adjustment, expansion, adjustment. After all, economics is not unpredictable, is it? The law of supply and demand holds true, reduce the supply and demand will force prices higher. A system that's predictable isn't random.

"So which was right, Marx with his linear view of history, or capitalism with its cyclical view? Obviously not capitalism, because history didn't repeat. We did progress from primitive society to feudalism, to capitalism. Unless the cycle is just longer than we realize and we are all going to drop back to primitive and start the climb all over again."

"But a periodic equation is a loop," the feudalism woman says, "it has to repeat exactly."

"We're using mathematics as metaphors," I explain. "Science filters into the general public as metaphors that describe our world, our history. For Marx, there were only two possibilities, that history was either predictable or it was random. If it was random, then it should have behaved in a random fashion, but Newton had described the universe as governed by natural laws. Marx's genius was in determining that social history was also governed by recognizable factors. He set out to systematically define those factors—the basic ones economic—and then, once he thought he had, he did for society what Newton's system did for planetary motion, he predicted the future."

I should stop. But it would sound ridiculous if I stopped. And there's something exciting about standing up here, thinking all this, saying all this.

"That is what you have been taught, and that's the prevailing social view. It's basically a Newtonian view. Since Newton we've had a number of major revolutions in the way we think the universe works, three of them in the twentieth century. The first was relativity, the second was quantum mechanics, the third was chaos. What is chaos?"

Laoshi says, "The study of complex, non-linear systems."

"Good. What's the butterfly effect?"

"Laoshi, pardon me?"

"Any of you interested in physics?" I ask. "Can someone describe 'sensitive dependence on initial conditions'?"

The young woman who said American feudalism occurred in Europe says, "Sensitive dependence on initial conditions refers to the way small factors affect non-linear systems." The definition is textbook, the voice is Brooklyn. She and the ABC, I like them.

"Right," I say. "The most classic example is weather, which is not random—for example thunderstorms occur at the leading edge of low pressure systems. But weather is not cyclic, if it rained on August the ninth last year that doesn't tell you what it will do this year. The mean average temperature for this year is not the mean average temperature for last year, nor this century for last century. In fact, the climate of the earth has changed radically, through ice ages and warm periods, and no one has ever been able to identify a pattern that repeats itself.

"If I am trying to predict weather, I can feed huge quantities of information into a system; temperature and wind direction and humidity for places all over the globe, the effect of the earth's rotation, land masses, mountain elevations, oceans, and get a fairly reasonable representation of weather. But if I change one temperature in one location by one-tenth of a degree, pretty soon my model's weather will start to diverge from actual weather conditions. In a few months, the system and the real world won't resemble each other at all. Weather shows sensitive dependence on initial conditions. It is so sensitive to variables that the movement of air by a butterfly's wings in New York eventually has an effect on dust storms in Beijing."

Stop now, the conclusion is obvious. I pause. But they are waiting, thirty people willing me to finish. And I want to, I am proud of my theory, I don't want to be careful this one time.

"History is also a complex system. It is not-random, but it is non-linear. Marx's predictions were based on the assumption that history is a linear system, and using those assumptions he predicted the future. But if weather is a complex system, it seems reasonable to assume that history is also a complex system. History is sensitive dependent on initial conditions. You cannot predict the future."

There is a sigh in the classroom. I have said what everybody knows but no one says. It is in the room, hanging.

Marx was wrong.

"For class on Thursday please read the first chapter and prepare problems two, six and seven," I say. "I know we haven't discussed how to do the problems, but I want to see how you tackle engineering problems using systems. That's it, I'll see you Thursday if I'm still a teacher."

They sit for a moment. I check the time, it is a little over an hour. I am wringing wet under my black suit, exhilarated, more than a little scared. Suddenly they all start getting up and six or seven people are standing around my desk asking to be admitted to the class.

Apparently nobody says anything, because come Thursday, I am still teaching. Nobody that is except Alexi Dormov, who leaves me his usual list of questions and a note. "If you keep this up, you're going to end up here. Hope you like goats."

Comrade Cecily Hester from the Office of Occupational Resources calls me. I can see her excitement. "I've been reviewing the responses I'm getting, I think you had better come talk to my supervisor," she says. "I think you're rather out of my league. Congratulations. How about today?" she says.

Today is fine. Around ten.

I get dressed in my Chinese suit and go downtown where I meet with Comrade Cecily Hester's superior, Comrade Huang. Comrade Huang is ABC. As one goes further up in any hierarchy, one meets more and more ethnically Chinese. We discuss what kinds of things the companies will offer me, what should be important to me. Comrade Huang talks about the difference between paid salary and the value of benefits. "When you enter a big multinational," he says, "you are entering a community. You should be aware of the kinds of environments the managerial philosophies create."

Whatever that means.

"If I decide on a company, can there be a three-month trial?" I ask. "Can we set something up so that either I can get out of the company or they can let me go if I'm not comfortable or right for their environment?" He says it's possible.

Comrade Huang calls two corporations, Western Technologies and New Mexico-Texas Systems and talks to them while I wait in a shabby green waiting room with dusty slipcovers on government issue chairs.

"Engineer Zhang," he says when he comes out to get me, "would you possibly be able to fly out to Arizona for an interview Friday?"

No, I am thinking, I'm not ready. "I have a class to teach," I say.

"I understand that is Tuesday and Thursday, this would be only Friday and Saturday."

There is nothing to say, no defense.

I fly to Albuquerque to meet representatives of New Mexico-Texas Light Industrials. I am met at the airport by a driver and a representative. Ms. Ngyuen is as brown as my mother and despite her Asian name looks Chicano. She has a short bob of hair, conservative, and wears a tan short-sleeved shirt and pants; like a geologist or an archeologist. Albuquerque is in the Western Corridor, water is a constant problem, and Ms. Ngyuen and I talk water all the way to the headquarters.

I expect something dramatic like Wuxi Technologies, perhaps an oasis of green in the middle of this rocky landscape. We come to a chainlink fence and drive parallel to it for miles. Beyond the chainlink is nothing, the landscape is the same on either side. We stop at a guardhouse, turn in and go through a gate. The sign says "New Mexico-Texas Light Industrials" but it's very small.

It is ten in the morning and light sears the landscape. I keep hoping for the oasis, but we drive for fifteen minutes and see nothing but rock and brush. The brush looks dead; Ms. Ngyuen informs me that it comes alive in the spring. Like Baffin Island, I imagine, the living things live their whole lives in that narrow time when conditions are favorable, and all the rest of the time they wait.

Eventually, far ahead I see a complex of buildings. They are low, the same color as the land, a kind of bleached brown. When we get closer I see they're surrounded by gravel. Well, why waste water on grass? It's untended, nothing like the raked garden of stones at my flat in Wuxi. The site is a cluster of half a dozen buildings. But the size is deceiving, buildings I assumed were a story high are actually three stories. We drive under one right into the garage.

When Ms. Ngyuen opens the door the heat is not nearly so bad as I expected, although of course we are in the shade. We take an elevator up three stories.

Inside, the floor is polished and painted concrete, the walls are adobe, it looks a little pinched. The offices are drab, the only color comes from calendars. The staff wears khaki; crisp brown and tan, short sleeves. I'm not sure if it is exactly a uniform, because even in one office it's sometimes coveralls, sometimes shirts and pants or skirts. Some people wear white blouses. A few glance up as we walk by, the rest seem engrossed in their work. We come through a double door into what must be the executive offices and things look better. Our footsteps are muffled by sand-colored carpet, wooden desks have Native American pottery on them, plants are growing out of Native American baskets. Prettier, but Wuxi it's not.

I meet Vice President Wang. He is from the main office in Hainandao, here for five years. He is a small, neat man with a short brush of hair. His office is all sand-colored, with huge windows that look out at miles of scrub. In his khaki he gives an impression of military correctness. He leans forward, smiling, and shakes my hand. "Engineer Zhang," he says, his voice forceful and full of energy, "we are pleased you could come." His English is accented but good.

We have tea and discuss my journey, and then the water shortage. Finally he gestures towards a tube on his desk, the kind for storing plans and large flimsies. "My engineers have been looking at your project from Nanjing University. It is very impressive.

You designed this using the techniques of organic engineering?"

My beach house. I explain that it was an assignment during my internship. (Woo Eubong's design was the one eventually accepted; mine, I tell myself, was not to the taste of the owner.) Vice President Wang explains that New Mexico-Texas has an organic engineer. "I don't suppose you have much need for a man who can design beach houses," I say.

"We don't need too many beach houses, although we have one in Hainandao, and plan to have one in San Antonio." Vice President Wang smiles. "There are other things you can do, I am sure."

"What would you need?"

"How about if I have you speak with our engineer after lunch, she can explain."

We break for lunch, which is red snapper Veracruz and icy cold Mexican beer. The cafeteria is sand-colored, with soft accents of mint and melon. Very institutional. The windows look out on scrub. The noon landscape is blasted white with sunlight.

After lunch I meet Mang Li-zi, the organic engineer, trained in Shanghai. Her office is also carpeted, but her desk and tables are metal. She is finishing the second year of a five-year rotation from Hainandao. She is Chinese and her first words to me are, *"Ni shuo poutonghua ma?"* Do you speak Mandarin?

"Shuo," I say, Yes.

"Good," she says in Chinese. "It's easier that way. Do you need augmentation?"

"No," I say, "I think I can understand. You speak very clearly." Actually she has a heavy Shanghai accent, the kind that changes "Shanghai" into "Sanghai."

She is the first person I have seen who is not in khaki, she wears a pale green tunic over yellow pants, soft spring colors. She is pretty, has an oval face with a rosebud mouth and small nose. Very polished, very Shanghai, which is, after all, the fashion capital of the East. She sighs. "It's not like China," she says. "But

the system is good, we're connected with Hainandao, it's as good
a system as you'll find here in the West."

"What kind of work do you do?"

"Mostly I run the Engineering Department, administration.
Once in awhile I modify plans, or do some design work. It's all
right. Not what I expected, I'm looking forward to getting back
to Hainandao. I still keep my hand in, though. In the evening I
do some systems work, for recreation. Let me show you some."

The system is conventional, not like Wuxi where I didn't have
to use a contact. We jack in and she shows me some designs she's
done. Two, which she tells me have already been accepted, are for
office complexes. She talks about using available materials. It's
obvious that the office complexes will be used here, not in China
or Japan. She's at work on an industrial complex right now. She
takes me through it using the system and flimsies. She has an
interesting touch, very Chinese but very different from Woo Eubong. Woo Eubong's pieces are subtle, sometimes with bits of
fancy technology. Many of Li-zi's pieces are less complicated.
They have the virtue of appearing gracefully simple but not cheap.

"You did these for New Mexico-Texas?" I say. They don't look
like desert designs, I wonder where else the company has offices.

"Yes," she says, as if admitting something. "I've gotten
bonuses for both works."

They're nice, but I don't think particularly worth bonuses. Of
course, I have to remind myself, she did this on her own time. Do
they expect her to design office complexes for them? It seems to
me they ought to have her do it on their time. "Do they come to
you and tell you they need the plans, or do you ask them for the
work?" What I am really trying to discover is if New Mexico-
Texas will expect me to give them all of my free time.

"No, they have to be posted, let me show you." She uses an
outside access and shows me a list of competitive bids. There are
listings and specs for hundreds of jobs all across the nation, from
hundreds of corporations. It's some kind of national posting. She

keys an index and pages through screens of proposal requirements. None of the jobs listed today are projects for New Mexico-
Texas.

"What do you do," I ask, "watch until New Mexico-Texas posts
a job?" Seems foolish to me, why couldn't they just offer it to her?

"No." She frowns at me. "You don't understand. New Mexico-
Texas didn't post these. They're office complexes for other companies, not for New Mexico-Texas. The first one is for Intek, the
second is for Senkai's Western Division. I find a posting that looks
interesting to me, and I submit a bid in New Mexico-Texas's name.
It's a way to keep my hand in."

"What about the fees? How do they pay you if you submit the
bid as New Mexico-Texas?"

"Well, the company gets the fee, then they give me a bonus."

It takes me a moment to figure out. She is looking up postings,
designing complexes on her own time, and New Mexico-Texas gets
the fees. "But you do all the work," I say.

"I use the company's system," she says. "I work for New
Mexico-Texas. I'm not a company. If I sell a project, good, I get
a bonus. If I don't"—she shrugged—"it doesn't matter. They still
pay my salary. And I get all the benefits, medical, housing, all of
it. If I was on my own, I'd have to take care of all of that."

I nod. I understand. But it bothers me. "So most of the organic
engineering you do, you do at night or on weekends?"

She shakes her head. "Mostly I run the department. There's
not enough time to do it all."

"Do you teach?" I ask, thinking of Woo Eubong.

"No," she says, looking at the readout hanging in the air in
front of us, the clean, spare lines of her office complex. Without
looking at me she says, "It is not like China. Why didn't you stay
in China?"

"I wanted to come home," I say.

That evening, over dinner, Vice President Wang explains salary and living arrangements. He tells me that I would work with

Mang Li-zi until she goes back to Hainandao, after which I would be Senior Engineer. It is, he points out, only three years until I would be Senior Engineer. "I understand you were offered a job with Wuxi," he says. "May I ask why you didn't take it?"

"I was grateful for the opportunity, but I did not feel comfortable. Comrade Huang is fond of saying that a placement is like a marriage." I know better than to say to this man that I didn't want to live in China.

"If you were interested in the position, when would you be available?" he asks.

"I am teaching a class at Brooklyn College," I say. "I would not be able to come until the class finishes."

That's fine. "You look very Chinese," he says casually.

I know he has access to my records. "Gene splicing," I say. And add in Chinese, "It does not matter if the cat is black or white, as long as it catches mice." An old political saying.

Vice President Wang laughs appreciatively. The dinner is a spicy southwestern dish; chicken in molé with a salad of avocados, tomatoes and onions. As there was at lunch there is icy Mexican beer. Outside the window the sun sets. The landscape glows brilliant and beautiful red, then lavender, and as we sit talking over coffee and a sweet chocolate dessert, it grows black. We are reflected in the glass of the window. Someone who didn't know better would look at us and say that I, in my Chinese suit, was the one with citizenship and he, in his khaki, the ABC.

"You are not married, Engineer. Anyone special in your life?"

Just a fag I met on the boardwalk in the part of New York City they call Bangladesh. I don't know if he'll ever call me again. "No," I say, "I think I've been moving around so much I haven't had much chance."

He nods. "This might strike you as a difficult place to meet someone but you'll be surprised. We have a number of single women on staff." He smiles. "I think that you are already a topic of discussion, an eligible bachelor. Someone like yourself should have no trouble making friends."

I am shown a comfortable room in the guesthouse. There is a big double bed, carpeting on the floor, fantastically colored prints of the southwestern landscape. All very nice.

(I wake up alone in the middle of the night, disoriented, and it takes me a moment to settle myself, to think, "The door is THAT way, the window THIS way, the bathroom in the direction of my feet.")

We discuss salary and living conditions in the morning. The salary they have offered is extraordinarily high, one hundred and three hundred. There would be a tax rate of forty percent, they will take care of all taxes. After taxes my salary would be in the area of sixty-two hundred. Plus they would provide housing, and I would have unlimited system time.

I tell them I think the offer is very generous. I will give it very serious consideration and I will be in touch with them through the Office of Employment Resources. I am very polite, I thank Vice President Wang in Mandarin. I hear my own voice, my old-fashioned phrasing, my northern pronunciation. Haitao always found it so amusing.

Vice President Wang seems impressed, maybe pleased.

I am, in fact, terrified. I cannot live that way, I can't live in a compound in the middle of the desert, surrounded by chainlink. Like Baffin Island, except for the rest of my life.

I have to think. What do I want?

I want to keep teaching. None of my subsequent lectures have been as exciting as the first, but I like the work. I don't want to end up in a corporate compound. So I must make some money.

While I am thinking, I use the number Mang Li-zi showed me to access the job posting. There are well over a hundred of them. I go through them, stopping to look something up when it strikes my fancy. I get a call while I'm in the middle of the proposal specs for an office complex and I just switch over audio.

"This is Zhang," I say, trying to decide if this complex is too big.

"Pardon me? I was given this number for Rafael?"

It is Invierno. I flick over to vid. "That's me."

"Rafael," he says. "Rafael Zhang. Or Zhang Rafael, which?"

I laugh, "Neither. Either Rafael Luis, or Zhang Zhong Shan."

"Okay." He looks cautious. "Which is your real name?"

"Both, my mother is Hispanic and my father is ABC. I use Zhang when I work, but a lot of my friends call me Rafael."

He bats his long eyelashes while he considers this.

"Hey, a man with a name like 'Winter' doesn't have a lot of space to complain. What are you doing?"

"Nothing much," he says. "My first name is Jeremy. Invierno's my last name, but I like it better."

"Let's go to the kite races," I say.

He ignores that. "That's why you speak Spanish?" he says.

"Street Spanish. Nothing they would understand in Bogotá."

"You sure as hell don't look Spanish." He is frowning.

"I'll tell you all about it at the kite races."

"One more thing," he says. "Where the hell have you been?"

"What," I say, "you left your wallet over here or something?"

He gets visibly flustered. "No, it's just a friend of mine had a party last night and I thought you'd like to go. Look, I was just asking." The matador look is back, pouty and sensitive to slights.

"I was in Arizona interviewing for a job."

"Arizona," he says, aghast. "What the fuck do you want to go to Arizona for?"

"I don't."

"Then why did you go," he says, reasonably.

"Who made you my mother?" I ask, laughing. He makes me laugh, Invierno, and as usual, he doesn't really take offense. So we go to the kite races, and Invierno comes home with me since it's Friday and he doesn't have to work on Saturday.

He rolls over in the morning and I'm staring at the ceiling, thinking of Mang Li-zi. Thinking of myself stuck out in Arizona.

He pillows his chin on his arms. "You sure as hell don't look like much fun."

"I'm worried," I say.

"Oh," he says.

After a long bit of silence he says resignedly, "What are you worried about?"

"I just had a job offer to make about sixty a year, but I have to live in a compound in Arizona and be an administrator, and incidently they'd really like me to marry someone within the company." I climb across him and pad into the kitchen to start coffee.

"Sixty a year?" His voice follows me to the kitchen, he is astounded. "I thought you were a teacher!"

"I'm an engineer," I say.

I hear him shift on the bed. "Are you going to take it?"

"No."

"How can you turn down that much money?"

"Because if I live there I'll go crazy. I'd have to be a monk, those people live in each other's hip pockets."

"I can see how that would be a problem," Invierno says. "Couldn't you just work there a couple of years? You know, save it all or something?"

"No," I say.

"Why not? That's what I'd do."

"Because I just couldn't do it." I'm irritated.

"Okay," he says. I bring him coffee. "Why do you always wear your hair in a tail?" he asks, sitting up, "I like it down."

"Because I was in love with a guy one time and he told me he liked it back."

Invierno sips his coffee, considering. "Do you still see him?"

"No," I say. "He's dead. He jumped out a window, one of those big complexes in China." I put my coffee down on the floor and rub my eyes. It's too complicated, too early in the morning to get into this with a twenty-two year old.

"Hey," he says, "Rafael, I'm sorry." He sits up and rests his cheek against my back, a pleasant scratchy feeling. "I just asked you because I wanted to change the subject."

"Don't worry about it," I say. Invierno doesn't ask any more questions (although he's dying to) but he does stay for breakfast, which is very sweet of him. "I'll call you," he promises in the hallway. "I will, I'll really call you."

I'm suddenly invested with tragedy. The poet, Byron, once told a friend of his that he wished he had consumption. The friend— who had consumption—was appalled and wanted to know why. Because the women would think he was so interesting, Byron told him. Probably preening.

I'm not at all displeased to think that I have become interesting to Invierno.

I go back to the postings, thinking of Mang Li-zi. It would be better if I did some laundry, but I'm too lazy to go down to the basement. There is a proposal for an office complex, not very big. I print out the information and suddenly decide I should do something so I go down to the library and buy time on the system.

It's not a very good system, too many users. Sometimes you have to wait for it to do something. And it's expensive to use for long periods of time. I don't have that much money any more. It's exasperating to think of something and have to wait for it to happen, knowing that I'm being charged for the time I wait. But it's the only system I have access to.

It's interesting, building this little office complex. It's crazy to try to build on a public system, but I have the advantage of knowing there aren't many organic engineers in this country. I can probably do a better job than the usual team.

I could start my own business. I wouldn't have to make that much, if I kept teaching that would just about pay my rent.

I spend about five hours Saturday and another three on Sunday working on a little office complex. The fee wouldn't be very much, I'm hoping not many companies would take the time to do it.

Monday Mr. Huang from the Bureau of Resources calls and tells me that Sung of Wisconsin wants me to come out to meet them.

"They have already said they cannot match New Mexico-Texas," he says, "you might as well not go."

My first inclination is to agree, for one thing I want to work on my design. Of course, Sung's system is going to be a lot better than the library's, if I could just get a few hours on it I could get a lot done.

"I'd like to hear what they have to say. I'm not certain I would be comfortable in the corridor," I say, hearing in my voice the softness that Haitao mistook for courtesy. Duplicity. I whisper when I have something to hide, to protect. In China I was protecting myself from mistake, from derision, eventually from exposure. Now I am merely lying. I am hoping for something from Sung. "I could fly out Tuesday afternoon, after my class, come back on Wednesday."

I fly out to Eau Clair, Wisconsin. It is a pretty place, green and full of flowers. I am met by a polite young man and a driver and driven to the corporate headquarters where I spend the day talking in the same soft voice to the Executive Officer, Comrade Cui. Sung does not have an organic engineer. It's more comfortable than New Mexico, not so severe, there are more people around. But both of them are strange to someone like myself, an urban person, and it's overseeing the engineering department. What makes them think my degree has anything to do with administration?

I am fed trout and creamed potatoes. The windows of the executive dining room look out on a green meadow.

Comrade Cui, the Executive Officer, is a woman with a firm handshake. She is ABC. She does not make any comment about my Hispanic mother, but does say something about my being single. The room in the guesthouse is blue.

And in it I have access to Sung's system. I do not get much sleep, and at a little after four, I dump my work back into the file I use in the library system. I'm surprised when I look up and the room is blue, I've been in a red and cream office complex.

Then the trip back home. I sleep in my seat, and leave the airport in a fog. But there is too much to do and not enough money or time.

The project swallows my life. I have to do material estimates. At Wuxi I could have asked the system for some information, and had a clerk do the calling on the rest. But now I must call supply places and ask them, "How much a ton?" "How much a square meter?" I calculate by hand because I cannot afford wasting expensive system time on calculations and I can do them in the evening when the library is closed. Some of the answers I get force me to change my ideas. Back to the system.

I assign my class a project: design a room that they couldn't design without using a system. My ABC comes to me and asks if he can design a sound system instead. "It's my senior thesis," he explains. I tell him to do it.

I run out of money.

Completely. I don't even have the money for coffee and rice. And I'm not finished. I need to get the proposal submitted in four days and I am out of money. So I call Peter.

"What's up," he says.

"I have a problem," I say.

Eyebrows quirk. "What's wrong?"

"I'm trying to start my own business. Doing organic engineering."

"Oh?" Peter says, his voice neutral. "What happened to the idea of getting a job?"

"I've gone on two interviews," I explain, "one in New Mexico, one in Wisconsin. I don't want to leave New York. I like teaching, I like my flat, I like having friends. I'm sick of starting over again, even in this country. Lenin and Mao Zedong, Peter, do you know what it's like to be alone in a country where being bent can earn you a bullet in the back of your head? I want friends, I want some sort of community!"

"Okay," Peter says gently. "Why don't you come downstairs and talk. Or I'll come up."

"I'll come down," I say. Then I smile for him. "I'm out of beer."

He grins. "Okay, China Mountain."

Peter makes me a loan. And two hours later, Cinnabar Chavez calls and says, "I talked to Peter. Listen, how about a partner? You have this specialty, this engineering thing, and I have a little money."

And after that, the only thing left is the work.

I dump my submission at deadline, six P.M. Friday night, and leave the library. Down the steps, past the lions and into Manhattan. I think about going for a drink, but I don't feel right spending Cinnabar's money that way. So I call Cinnabar and tell him we've submitted our first project.

"What do you think?" he asks.

"I think it's positively inspired, but who knows what they'll think." I shrug. "Actually I'm sick of it. But it's done. Did I ever show you my beach house?"

He says Peter's on his way over for dinner, why don't I come, but I'm tired and I beg off.

Then I call Invierno.

It takes awhile for him to answer.

"Hi," I say, "It's Rafael."

"Hi," he says, disdainful.

"I got your messages, I've been meaning to call you back but I've been caught up with something."

"That's all right," he says. "I'm kind of in a hurry."

"Look, I'm sorry I haven't called you for awhile, I've been trying to get a business started."

He's contemptuous. "Well, good luck." He reaches for the cut-off.

"Hey," I say, "wait. Are you busy tonight?"

"Yeah," he says, "as a matter of fact, I am."

"Yeah," I say. "I guess you're not sitting around waiting for the phone to ring."

He purses his lips. "I, ah, I'm not busy tomorrow night," he says finally.

"Great. What do you want to do? I'm broke."

He is incredulous. "You call me for the first time in two weeks and ask me what I'm doing and have the nerve to tell me you're broke?"

"That's right," I say. "But I'm real fun to be with. Why don't you take me to the kite races?"

He laughs. And then we talk some, he asks me about my business and I tell him a little.

"So you won't have to go to Arizona," he says. "What's that noise?"

"It's a train. I'm calling from the subway. I've been working on something for two weeks and I just finished it, so I called you right away."

"Oh yeah?" The idea tickles him, that I called him right away.

"Yeah, I just submitted the damn thing, not fifteen minutes ago. I haven't eaten dinner yet."

"Rafael," he says, "did you eat lunch?" I must be attracted to motherly types. I pretend to consider. "I probably did," I say. Of course I ate lunch, I had a sandwich.

"Listen," he says, "I was going to go to this party, but it's no big deal. How about if I pick up some noodles or something and come by your place."

"Okay," I say, "I'd like that."

I catch the train and go home. The old D train all the way out to Coney Island, under ground (except for the bridge) to Prospect Park and then up into the evening light. It's the second of November. In Baffin Island the days are almost gone. In Nanjing it's six in the morning. I don't have a dime, but I feel curiously light.

If this project sells, the fee will allow us to put a down payment on a system. A small system, but that will be better than going to the library. And I can talk to someone at the City University. If I take on a student intern in return for teaching that student organic engineering, I'll have someone to do some of the donkey work. Eventually we're going to need a clerk. And Cinnabar said we'll have to file papers and get permits for the new company. Daoist Engineering. That's what I want to call it.

I wonder if I could hire someone from the building? Years ago I allowed Qian San-xiang to drag me to a political study meeting and I remember someone, maybe San-xiang, saying that a community needs a shared purpose. Well, in addition to doing office complexes, Daoist Engineering could do the kind of thing that I did for my flat, and for Vanna. Some people would be interested in making their flat prettier.

"Una luz brillara en tu camina." Used to be subway advertisements for the church that said that. During the Great Cleansing Winds religion was dangerous, but about five years ago they lifted the restrictions on religion. For awhile every time I got on the train I'd see one of those ads. *"Una luz brillara en tu camina. Descubre lo que te has perdido."* A brilliant light in your path. Discover what you have lost.

The light angles across Brooklyn, red now. It comes through the train windows. Sunset used to depress me. But I learned in Baffin Island, you've just got to remember the light, keep it inside you, and wait. The sun comes back every morning.

Afterword

There seems to be a tradition in books that use Mandarin of explaining which version of Chinese romanization the author is using. If you need an explanation, here it is.

Mandarin is, of course, a tonal language that uses characters, and it does so for a very good reason. Mandarin spelled alphabetically (or romanized) contains insufficient information to be clear to the reader. A simple example is that, for the sound "jiu," there are twenty common meanings—including "old," "alcohol" or "wine," "nine," "uncle" (or more specifically, "mother's brother"), and "vulture," written with twenty different characters. When the word is spelled out using an alphabet, there is only context to determine its meaning.

There are a multitude of systems to transcribe Chinese characters into alphabetical forms. Probably the most familiar is the Wade-Giles. (Examples of Chinese rendered in Wade-Giles are "Mao Tse Tung," "Chungking," and "Peking.") There is also the Yale system, and a system used in Taiwan. I, personally, am most familiar with the version used in the People's Republic of China, usually called Pinyin Romanization. (In Pinyin, "Mao Zedong," "Chongqing," and "Beijing.") I have used Pinyin for two reasons: First, because it is the conceit of this novel that the People's Republic of China has become the dominant world power, and second, and if I am to be honest, the more pressing reason, it is the system I studied under both in the U.S. and in China.

—Maureen F. McHugh